Praise for Karen Brooks

'Historian and novelist Brooks shows her research and imaginative chops in a luscious and astonishingly affecting chronicle of family scandal, political unrest, and redemptive hope in 1660s London.'
—*Publishers Weekly* on *The Chocolate Maker's Wife*

'Brooks masterfully deploys surprising plot twists, deftly pacing the opening of closets to reveal hidden diaries and family skeletons ... A charming and smart historical novel from a master storyteller.'
—*Kirkus Reviews* on *The Chocolate Maker's Wife*

'*The Darkest Shore* is meticulously researched, taking a real historical event, and [Karen Brooks'] academic experience and merging it with exceptional storytelling. The characters are complex and compelling ... a powerful novel, at times brutal, but always enthralling, *The Darkest Shore* is a major achievement for Karen Brooks.'
—*Better Reading*

'Karen Brooks has handled such a dark history with care and empathy ... I can't recommend this one highly enough, it's a brilliant read.'
—*Theresa Smith Writes* on *The Darkest Shore*

'a compelling, fascinating, and disturbing historical fiction novel ... Beautifully written, with authentic characterisation and vivid description ... a captivating, even if sometimes confronting, read.'
—*Book'd Out* on *The Darkest Shore*

'a completely absorbing historical novel'
—*Other Dreams Other Lives* on *The Darkest Shore*

*K*aren Brooks is the author of thirteen books, an academic of more than twenty years' experience, a newspaper columnist and social commentator, and has appeared regularly on national TV and radio. Before turning to academia, she was an army officer for five years, and prior to that dabbled in acting.

She lives in Hobart, Tasmania, in a beautiful stone house with its own marvellous history. When she's not writing, she's helping her husband Stephen in his brewery and distillery, Captain Bligh's, or cooking for family and friends, travelling, cuddling and walking her dogs, stroking her cats, or curled up with a great book and dreaming of more stories.

Also by Karen Brooks

Fiction

The Brewer's Tale
The Locksmith's Daughter
The Chocolate Maker's Wife
The Good Wife of Bath

The Curse of the Bond Riders trilogy:

Tallow
Votive
Illumination

Young Adult Fantasy

It's Time, Cassandra Klein
The Gaze of the Gorgon
The Book of Night
The Kurs of Atlantis
Rifts Through Quentaris

Non-fiction

Consuming Innocence

The
DARKEST
SHORE

KAREN
BROOKS

FICTION
HQ

First Published 2020
Second Australian Paperback Edition 2021
ISBN 9781867207993

THE DARKEST SHORE
© 2020 by Karen Brooks
Australian Copyright 2020
New Zealand Copyright 2020

Published by
HQ Fiction
An imprint of Harlequin Enterprises (Australia) Pty Limited (ABN 47 001 180 918),
a subsidiary of HarperCollins Publishers Australia Pty Limited (ABN 36 009 913 517)
Level 19, 201 Elizabeth St
SYDNEY NSW 2000
AUSTRALIA

* and TM (apart from those relating to FSC®) are trademarks of Harlequin Enterprises (Australia) Pty Limited or its corporate affiliates. Trademarks indicated with * are registered in Australia, New Zealand and in other countries.

A catalogue record for this book is available from the National Library of Australia
www.librariesaustralia.nla.gov.au

Printed and bound in Australia by McPherson's Printing Group

To all the wonderfully 'wicked' women in my life, especially Kerry Doyle, Caragh Brooks, Sara Warneke and Selwa Anthony.
To the good men who love their women wicked, particularly Stephen Brooks, Peter Goddard, Hugh Swingler, Jim McKay and Adam Brooks. And a special thanks to Mr Nick (Mark Nicholson), and Bill Lark, two more good men, for giving me the gift of a story.

CONTENTS

CONTENTS

EXPLANATORY NOTE

*I*n this novel, married women — many of whom are fishwives — don't always carry their husbands' names. This wasn't peculiar to those in the fish-trade, but appears to have occurred in small towns and villages in Scotland where generations of the same family or others with the same name lived. To distinguish, for example, one Mrs Morag Bruce from another, she might keep her maiden name and thus remain Morag Nichols even though she is wed to Duncan Bruce. So it was with some of the women in this book — real and fictional. The real Janet (Nettie) Horseburgh was married to Thom White, Beatrix Laing to William Brown, and the fictional Sorcha McIntyre to Andy Watson, and so on.

Likewise, some characters bear the same surname, but aren't necessarily related. I have mostly kept these out of respect for history and the real people involved in these events. As a consequence, there's both a William Brown (Beatrix's husband) and Thomas Brown, an old fisherman, but they aren't kin. However, when it came to the Cooks, I added an 'e' to the end of the advocate's name to distinguish him from Bailie Cook, who appears much earlier. Hopefully this alleviates any confusion. Please also note that the character Nicolas Lawson — based on a real individual — is a woman. In the Lowlands in the 1700s and 1800s, the name Nicolas (or Nicholas) was not uncommon for a girl.

In no other place in Scotland were witches hunted with such fervour as in Pittenweem.

— Raymond Lamont-Brown, in John Donald, *Discovering Fife*

PART ONE

December 1703 to August 1704

My Lord, I reckon myself very much honoured by your Lordship's letter, desiring me to write to you an account of that horrible murder committed in Pittenweem. I doubt not, but by this time, your Lordship has seen the gentleman's letter to his friend thereanent [concerning the matter]; I refer you to it, the author thereof being so well informed, and ingenous, that I'll assure you, there is nothing in it but what is generally talked and believed to be true.

— *An Answer of a Letter From a Gentleman of Fife*, 1705

ONE

Freends 'gree best separate.
(Relatives agree best when they don't live too near each other.)

𝒫erched atop a patient cob on the western braes of Pittenweem, Sorcha McIntyre wasn't prepared for what the familiar expanse of water — or the brackish smell of brine, fish and seaweed and the sweet chanting that carried on the wind — did to her senses. It was as if the combination whipped her heart from her breast and cast it adrift upon the pounding waves.

She inhaled deeply, and it took her a moment to register the serious regard of the man who'd ridden beside her all day. Ignoring his scrutiny, Sorcha pressed a hand to her ribs and raised her eyes to the louring sky, where hulking grey clouds were pushed along by icy, sea-bitten gusts.

'That be Pittenweem,' she said, indicating the small township spread out before them. 'Home.' The word was both reassuring and bitter.

The man made a gruff noise of acknowledgement. He would wait until she was ready to draw their journey to a close; a journey that had begun that morning, but in reality had started months ago.

Waves that matched the oorlich palette of the sky thundered against the crescent-shaped shore and its stone-walled harbour, sending curtains of wash over the ruined pier, drenching the men who scrambled along it in their hob-nailed boots. As she'd suspected, not even the lure of Hogmanay kept them from work.

Errant beams of afternoon sunlight pierced the thick canopy of clouds, spears of defiance that cast a holy light upon the scene. Sorcha could almost believe that God Himself was welcoming her back.

Just as the thought rose, the sunlight was doused as if it was a figment of her overwrought imagination.

Maybe the Almighty wasn't welcoming her after all, but sending her a warning. God knew, she'd left the town of St Andrew's with enough of those ringing in her ears.

'I never want to see you again, you hear? Don't ever come back.'

It wasn't the first time those words had been said to Sorcha, only now they had been uttered by her sister, the last remaining member of her family, they hurt worse than any threats or insults delivered by a self-righteous clergyman.

Sorcha shivered and pulled her shawl tighter. There was no doubt it was a dreich day for a dreich homecoming — Hogmanay or not. She just prayed the rest of the village would not be as work-minded as the fishermen and their families. She was relying on folk being preoccupied with the date and consequent merrymaking to reach her house unseen; to give her time at least to prepare a story.

Beyond the natural harbour and the dilapidated man-made one lay the silvery-grey expanse of the Firth of Forth, heaving and shifting, a restless lucent mass. Midway crouched the Isle of May with its weary lighthouse and never-ending whirlpool of seabirds swooping and gliding above the seething waters. Closer to Pittenweem lay Beacon Rock. From a distance, Sorcha's practised eye could identify to which village, and even which owner, the boats dotting the sea belonged. The mast of each flew the flag of either the Weem or Anster, along with the sigil of the owner's family. Sails snapped as the wind filled them and the boats raced the weather back to shore; rising behind them loomed a wall of rain so thick, it threatened to swallow all before it. No wonder there was so much activity; the storm was about to break. It was bustle Sorcha knew as well as the scars that bit her fingers. She curled them now, her gloves protecting the ridges cut by years of baiting lines, furrowed by fish-hooks and sharp shells.

Her eyes dropped to the canting wreck heaving in the harbour waters, entombed, depending on the tide, by rock, sea and sand. How many years had the *Sophia* rested there? Too good to dismantle and repurpose its wood and iron, and too expensive to recondition, like the rotting pier beside it, it awaited funds that clearly had still not manifested. War and famine had long ago destroyed Pittenweem's fortunes and it would take more than one of the Reverend Patrick Cowper's much-touted miracles for them to recover.

A scattering of moored boats, recently returned, surrounded the wreck. Men in their brooks — heavy cotton pants worn over their trousers — crawled over the decks. Shouts of frustration and warning issued from weathered faces. Baskets of fish were raised to eager arms and run to the harbourfront to await sorting. From the way they were being carried, it was evident the whitefish were shy for this time of year. She'd hoped the poor drave, as the fishing season was known, that had struck the town before she left had ended. Clearly not. It explained why the ships that called Pittenweem port, the *Mary* and the *George*, were not to be seen. Neither was her father's large boat... nae, *her* boat, the *Mistral*. The crew were taking their chances up north in Stornaway. She sent a swift prayer to the sea gods to keep the men dry and safe and make the terrible risks they took worth it. Though Sorcha could not reconcile how a good catch and the coin that followed ever compensated for a life.

Scrawny children ran hither and thither betwixt rocks, sand and waterfront, their caps and scarves blown off by a malicious squall, the young ones too intent on helping their elders to pay heed to lost clothing. One cap tumbled along the dock, sending a coven of gulls screeching into the air.

Directly to her left, clustered in an arc around the harbour like watchful sentinels, were the fishermen's houses. Not even the whitewashed exteriors and pantile roofs could quite disguise the dirt and mud, the cracks and holes, the havoc the contrary seas and passionate tempests wreaked upon the walls and windows. Just like the harbour, no one could afford to repair their dwellings, not when every last penny was spent feeding hungry mouths. Funny, she'd never noticed before how mean the place looked. Dark smoke coughed from chimneys, a couple of shutters swung loose. Fishing nets, ropes and an assortment of hooks, cogs, lines and empty creels grew like an untamed hedgerow by each peeling door. It was as if by going away for a time she was able to see her home through the eyes of a stranger. But no incomer would feel as she did as she drank in the sight, the people, the odours, the sounds. Memories unfurled. As sharp as the white walls, as blood-red as the tiles upon the roofs, as shrill as the cries of the terns; they were stark reminders of what she'd left behind.

To what she'd returned.

It was only then that she noticed a pair of fishwives, their creels strapped to their backs, heads and shoulders, colourful neepyins tied tightly over their hair. Their sleeves were rolled despite the cold, and their skirts tucked up beneath their aprons, exposing dark boots as they wove their way among the men, never once getting in the way, and passed the women crouched on their crowded stoops, bent over lines, mending them for the following day. The fishwives moved swiftly towards West Harbour, turning on occasion to check the advance of the storm. Depositing their empty creels, they reached into the full ones awaiting their attention. Taking up positions before the assembled trestle tables, their knives flashed as they began to gut and then salt the catch, moving from table to basket to salt bucket and back again. It was a dance Sorcha could do in her sleep and had filled her dreams of late.

Recognising the women, she longed to cry out, draw their eyes towards her, only she'd also attract the attention of others whose welcome was less certain. Still, she longed to see her friends again. They were more than friends. They were akin to sisters. God knew, her only blood one was now lost to her.

Wasn't that what the fishwives were? Sisters of the sea. 'Twas the sea and its siren call and the men to whom they cleaved that made sisters of all the fishwives, regardless of who their mothers were, where they hailed from, and whether their husbands, fathers or brothers were alive or dead.

Once a fishwife, always a fishwife. Sorcha was both blessed and cursed, doomed to live by the very element that had claimed those she loved.

Seeing Pittenweem again, seeing its people and breathing the very same air, brought everything back. She could flee to her estranged sister or the ends of the earth, try to put the past behind her, and it wouldn't alter a thing. The sea wasn't only in her blood. It defined her past and present.

But that did nothing to assuage the guilt that was only ever a breath away, infecting the bliss and pain of remembrance and reawakening senses she'd repressed for months.

Now she had another crime to add to her tally: her sister Dagny had cast her out. Before she could prevent it, Sorcha's eyes welled and a sob escaped her throat.

Aware of her chaperone's discomfort, the snickering of his horse as he shifted in the saddle, she pretended it was the wind making her eyes water and forced herself to cough. Using the kinder memories that came with the raised voices and tangy scents to give her strength, she managed to control the sadness, the terrible shame. After all, she couldn't go back — in time or to St Andrew's. She must go forward, forget what had been and gone, face the present and create a different future. A fresh start. Fitting it should happen on the eve of a new year.

She turned to the man on his mount beside her.

'I thank you kindly for your troubles, Mr McDonald. I can find my own way from here. I'll not be needing your —' She'd been about to say company, but the man had scarce said a word the entire way and it wasn't as if he'd chosen to come with her. He'd been ordered to travel to the coast — not so much to see her home safe, but ensure she never came back. '… protection any more.'

Mr McDonald grunted and tugged his cap. A gust tried to lift the plaid from his shoulders, but the brooch bearing the insignia of his laird kept it in place. 'I told Master Kennocht I'd see you to your door, lassie, and that's what I'll do.'

With a heavy sigh, Sorcha dismounted and began to untie her belongings from the saddle.

'Nae, Mr McDonald, that you won't do.' She pulled a lock of hair from her mouth and tucked the escaped tendril into her scarf before the wind could snatch it away again. 'While I appreciate the sentiment behind your insistence, I cannot accept your offer.' She took a deep breath. She'd nothing left to lose. Not any more. 'I've no doubt the reasons for my homecoming will follow me whether I wish them to or not. Even so, I would rather be on my own to greet them when they do and introduce them to those I call kith and kin my way.'

Mr McDonald's thick grey eyebrows beetled. He opened his mouth to say something, but Sorcha, closing the distance between them, continued before he could.

'Forgive my bluntness, but the last thing I need is for an unfamiliar man to ride through there —' she indicated the harbourfront with a push of her chin, 'past those I've known my entire life, whether you promised my brother-in-law and his wife, or not. You'll be doing me no favours and the protection you offer will have been for naught once the gossips start their clecking and finger-pointing, do you understand?'

Mr McDonald peered down at the harbour, then back at Sorcha, his eyes becoming mere slits. Rain began to fall; light, fast drops that beat a tattoo upon the grass and rocks.

Sorcha raised her face to the heavens briefly, blinking.

'Very well, lassie. But I'm not leaving here until I'm assured you're safe past the harbour. Mistress Dagny tells me your house lies on the eastern side of town.'

Surprised she could hear her sister's name without anger, Sorcha nodded. 'Aye, in Marygate, up past the kirk.' She faced the town. 'You can see the spire of the Tolbooth over there.' She pointed towards a tall tower that rose above the buildings. Abutting the kirk, the Tolbooth served as both gaol and council chambers.

There were shouts from the harbour. The wall of rain had swallowed the Isle of May and was moving swiftly. The sky darkened; the wind became stronger. As one, the nagging birds wheeled away from the storm front, heading west.

There was no time to waste. Heaving her burlap over her shoulder, Sorcha took the reins of her mount and reached up to grip the old man's wrist. It was thin but strong.

'I thank you for escorting me back, Mr McDonald. If the storm should catch you, there is a place in Anster Wester where you can bide. It's not too far from here. Look for an inn with the sign of a corbie on the left-hand side of Dreel Burn.'

Mr McDonald looked embarrassed. 'It was nae bother, lass.' He patted her hand and then took the reins she proffered, clearing his throat.

With a fleeting smile, Sorcha gave the horse that had borne her one last caress and, with a wave, began to descend the path winding down the cliffs. Before she'd taken a dozen steps, Mr McDonald hailed her.

'I ken what happened back at the estate weren't your fault. Despite what some did blether.'

Sorcha stopped and turned slowly in shock.

Mr McDonald continued. 'Remember: *freends 'gree best separate.*'

Relatives agree best when they don't live too near each other. Aye, well, that summed up the relationship betwixt her and Dagny. They'd always been better apart.

Not yet finished, Mr McDonald walked the horses to the very edge of the braes. 'I might be an auld man, but I'm not blind. I can see what's before my own eyes even if some in your family choose to remain ignorant, if you ken what I'm saying.'

She did. His kindness almost undid her.

The drops grew heavier. Sorcha nodded and found her voice. 'I thank you, Mr McDonald. I thank you from the bottom of my heart.'

Without another word, she concentrated on her descent, aware of Mr McDonald's eyes on her back. She was grateful that none of the figures growing more distinct as she approached had registered her presence... yet. They were too busy. She had a little time yet to prepare a tale.

God dammit. Her excuses.

The skies opened and in moments the harbour and even the path down to it disappeared in a thick veil. Sorcha didn't mind. It was a game she'd oft played, hide and seek in the rain and attendant fog, so she walked the steep path with confidence. A confidence that, whenever she thought of facing the Pittenweem folk melted faster than the clumps of snow clinging to the grass.

After all, how would the town react when they learned that Sorcha McIntyre, the woman some called husband-killer and baby-murderer, the woman once praised as a boon to her family but ultimately cursed, had returned?

At that moment, a fork of lightning split the sky, throwing the tower of the distant kirk into stark relief, as if God's house and His heavenly bolt were the only things standing between her and long-delayed justice.

Justice that, if some had their way, would now be meted out.

TWO

I'll give you the dreel.
(You are just about to get into real trouble.)

*I*t wasn't so much Hogmanay preparations but the pouring rain that provided the miracle for which Sorcha had prayed. The fishwives had finished sorting and, before she'd even reached the path along the harbourfront, had disappeared up the wynds, taking the catch with them. The men secured the boats and, along with their women-folk and children who had gathered the nets, escaped indoors. The few souls remaining outside were too intent on completing their tasks or raising a dram to the new year to notice a young woman scurrying along the shore or slipping on the cobbles of the High Street. Those who did, with one exception, failed to give her a second look.

The Tolbooth and kirk at the top of the road emerged briefly out of the sheeting rain and mist, landmarks that melded the sacred and profane. Sorcha kept her head down, neatly avoiding those also heading for shelter and, when she reached the looming edifice of the kirk, chose not to think about the man who occupied its hallowed halls or those under his blessed thumb, but turned left into Kirkgate. Passing the walled cemetery, her thoughts leapt the crumbling barrier to roam the gravestones that bore her family's name. She would pay her respects soon; truth told, sooner than she'd thought she'd be able.

About to enter Marygate, the street where she'd lived another life, she thought she heard footsteps before they were replaced by the faint ring of a horse's clopping hooves. Spinning around and wiping her face, she saw the street was empty. There were the vague shapes of the buildings hunched on the corner, candlelight wavering in the windows. The heavy shower, swirling fog and encroaching evening had turned the world into one of shifting shadows and outlandish sounds. Still, the noise echoed around her and she wondered briefly who in Pittenweem had a horse abroad in this weather. She thought of Mr McDonald, who because of her was left with no choice, and hoped he — and the horses — managed to find the inn of the corbie.

Striding past her neighbours' houses, she slowed as she approached her destination, her chest tightening. As she'd intended to be absent from the Weem until at least late spring, she'd leased her cottage to her friend, the fishwife Nettie Horseburgh. Though married, Nettie had always been independent and let it be known even before wedlock that she wasn't inclined to share a roof with her husband. Understanding if he wished to call Nettie Horseburgh wife he had to accept her condition that they live apart, Thomas White agreed. The arrangement drew the opprobrium of many in the village, in particular that of the minister, Patrick Cowper, but Nettie and Thom hadn't cared. Their love transcended a roof and walls, or so they said. If Nettie was most content living on her own, then Thom was happy to accommodate her. When Sorcha made the decision to accept Dagny's summons to go to St Andrew's and help with the bairns while her sister awaited the birth of a new one, she'd offered her cottage to Nettie — a decision that drew harsh criticism from the reverend, who reproved Sorcha publicly, accusing *her* of undermining the sacred bonds of marriage, even though Nettie and Mr White had lived separately for years.

'Just because you've lost a husband,' he'd said outside the kirk after service one Sunday, his tone cold and unapologetic, 'you think it's all right to divide a man and his wife? That's not your decision to make.'

Sorcha had met his gaze, ignoring the whispers of the others assembled outside. 'You're right, reverend. It's not. It's Nettie and Thom's,' she'd said calmly, even though her heart was somersaulting.

Fixing a tight smile, he'd shaken his head. 'We'd all be better off if the likes of you never came back.'

'Nae, reverend,' Sorcha had said, tilting towards him and lowering her voice. 'Confess. *You* would.' Pretending a composure she didn't feel, she'd walked away, aware of the dark mutters and the reverend's poisonous glare following her.

As she'd suspected, Nettie had jumped at the offer. But how would she feel now Sorcha was back and months earlier than she'd intended? Sorcha couldn't very well ask her to remain, could she? God, but she could do with a friendly face to wake up to.

She paused outside her house and stood at the foot of the stairs that led to the loft where nets, creels and her da's fishing equipment was kept, and stared at the harled walls and pitted front door. Apart from a stack of books in the window, nothing seemed to have changed. She shouldn't be surprised after only six months, but she was. Especially when she felt so transformed.

As she hesitated, she allowed recollections to fill her head. She could hear the roar of the ocean, a chorus accompanying her memories. Or was it a dirge? When she was a child seated at her father's feet in the loft, her brothers and sister arrayed around him while he carved a piece of wood or mended lines, her mother downstairs alone with her knitting, she'd thought the ocean sounded like the world breathing.

Her father would cup his hand around his ear to alert his listeners to the constant rumble, then launch into one of his stories about the sea and the seamen who rode its waves. They were as endless as the ocean. Holding a piece of rope, he'd demonstrate how certain knots could call or calm the wind, or a special whistle tame it; how words such as 'rabbit', 'pig' and even 'salt' were forbidden on a boat and that if they were uttered, cold iron must be touched immediately to counter the damage. If one saw a man of the cloth on the way to the harbour, he must not sail, and so on. The rites and superstitions of the fisherfolk were woven into many of his stories.

Sorcha wasn't very old before she understood her father's purpose with these tales filled equally with warnings and promise. He was preparing his children for a fisher's life, one dependent on unpredictable weather, the mercurial ocean, fish, wood, iron, sails, nets, oars, lines, creels and each other. 'Us fisherfolk stick together,' was a phrase he'd repeat over and over until, like the prayers said in kirk, it stuck like pitch to the mind.

Whenever he launched into one of his stories, her mor would turn away, a sorrowful expression on her face. She no more wanted her children to give their life to the sea than she wanted to remain in Pittenweem; but as Sorcha oft heard her father say, they'd no choice. Rather than getting angry with his wife or being hurt by her aversion to his home, he would kiss her head, explaining to his children that their mother couldn't be expected to understand local customs, being an incomer from Bergen and the daughter of a Kontor merchant — a man with his feet firmly planted on the ground. However, if his children were to survive, to be one with the Weem folk, he'd say, they needed not only to learn the tales and the rites they described, but to accept them as well.

What he never revealed, and Sorcha only learned later, was the price he paid for marrying her mor.

It was expected that fishermen would eventually take one of the local fishwives as a bride. Called 'wives' whether they were single or not, these were lasses born and bred to the sea, the daughters or widows of fishermen, and raised to their ways. In marrying an incomer, a foreigner who knew nothing of a fisherman's lot, let alone Pittenweem, Charlie McIntyre had done the unforgivable: spurned the customs of his village and the families he'd been raised among. But it was his wife who paid the price for what became known as his Norwegian folly — the beautiful, wide-eyed Astrid Grimmsdatter.

'You wait, Charlie McIntyre,' grumbled those who either hadn't profited from the journey that brought Astrid to Pittenweem, or had eligible daughters they felt had been spurned. 'Bad luck will find you, mark my words. Just pray it doesn't find us too.'

They were right. Bad luck found them all and there were many who could never forget or forgive Charlie for his wife, her strangeness, and the sorrow that wreathed her like an eternal evendoon.

There were many who couldn't forgive Sorcha either, and not merely because she was Charlie's daughter.

Sorcha's throat grew tight, her heart a weight anchoring her to the spot. Despising her self-pity, blaming the flood of remembrances, tiredness and her aching head, she willed herself to enter the cottage, noting with a half-hearted air that while the rain had all but ceased, the day had gone to bed. Night had begun to draw its cloak, casting deep shadows over the road and houses.

Again, she heard the remote ring of hooves. Closer this time was the distinct tread of boots.

Turning first towards the old Lady Chapel, then glancing up Lady Wynd before looking back to town, she tipped her head to listen. There was the steady drip of water, the growl of the ocean, a shriek of laughter, and even faint strains of music, but no footsteps. Had she imagined the sound? Was her mind playing tricks?

Nae, 'twas not.

From the direction of the High Street, moving unsteadily past the graveyard wall, three men were strolling up Marygate. They walked close together, halted, then started again. She could just discern their outline through the tendrils of floating mist. Who might these men be? Considering the tavern lay behind them, she wavered. It would be rude not to greet them, especially since it was Hogmanay. But there was something about the way they leaned into each other and, when they saw her, began whispering, that made her stomach lurch.

'Evening, lass,' one called, increasing his pace and dragging the others with him. The voice was deep, unfamiliar. English.

The men, who were sodden from the rain, stopped a few feet away, leaving the entrance to Lady Wynd on their left between them, and studied her brazenly. They weren't neighbours; they weren't even incomers in the usual sense, though they were that too. These were soldiers. Too late, she realised her mistake; she should have gone inside.

'I don't remember seeing you before,' said the tallest of them finally, one hand resting on his hip, his other arm slung around his companion's shoulders. He nudged his mate, and nodded towards Sorcha appreciatively. 'And I don't think I'd forget if I did.'

The men chuckled darkly.

Sorcha's throat grew dry. Before she'd left to go to Dagny's, a number of soldiers had been quartered throughout the town, either awaiting transport to the battlefields of Flanders or stationed to protect the coast from potential invasion. They were an undisciplined mob, a mix of English and Scotsmen drawn from around the country and mostly sympathetic to the Crown. There'd been trouble. Terrible trouble. A woman had been raped.

As she measured the distance to her neighbour's house, calculating if she could turn and dart down Abbey Wall Road in time, she understood her choices were few. The men might be drunk, but she was weary and, in her heavy boots, unable to run fast. Not even reaching her door meant safety, not with three armed men able to force their way in. She glanced at the knives attached to the belts at their waists.

Instead, she opted for friendliness, to disarm them with a smile — not too welcoming, but showing no fear either. 'Evening, lads,' she said with false brightness. 'Happy Hogmanay to you. I can see you've been celebrating. I guess it's time I go to my family — they'll be waiting for me.' She nodded towards the door of her cottage and pulled her burlap further onto her shoulder.

'Who's your family?' asked the shorter of the Scottish soldiers, reaching out to delay her. She didn't recognise the face but the accent was local. 'That be the McIntyre place. I heard the woman who lived there leased the cottage to the Horseburgh woman. You're not her, by chance, are you?' He leaned forward to peer at her face, blinking.

Not wanting to reveal who she was, she danced around the outstretched hand and straight into the clasp of another.

Fingers tightened on her wrist. Determined not to cry out, she forced another smile. 'Please, let me go. I don't want any trouble.'

'Please,' said the Englishman, imitating her burr perfectly, 'let me go. I don't want any trouble.'

The men laughed loudly.

'Not so fast, lass. We just want to talk,' said the local soldier. Sorcha tried to place him. He must be from over Anster way.

Before she could wrench free, the men closed around her. The odour of ale and whisky combined with peat smoke and oysters was overpowering. Their clothes were wet and bore the stench of their bodies — unwashed and stale. Their faces shone under the burgeoning moonlight peeping through the clouds.

'What about?' asked Sorcha more bravely than she felt.

'I ken who you are,' said the local man suddenly. 'You be Sorcha McIntyre.' He elbowed his friend in the ribs. 'Andy Watson's widow.'

Sorcha shut her eyes briefly. Damn the man.

'Andy Watson?' The other soldier scratched his head. 'Weren't he the one who drowned because his wife didn't carry him to the boat?'

'Aye, that's the one,' said the local. He jerked his chin towards Sorcha. 'And she be the wife —'

Sorcha could barely move, the men were pressed so tightly against her.

'So, you're the bitch what killed Andy...' said the soldier, his breath hot in her ear. 'I think you need to be taught a lesson...'

'Gentlemen,' said the Englishman from behind her, his mouth against her hair. 'You're missing the point. This woman is a widow, you say? It's not a lesson she needs...'

Sorcha felt a rush of gratitude. Perhaps this man could yet talk sense into the others.

'It's a man.'

Her blood turned to ice.

'Och,' chuckled the local. 'What she needs is three...'

With a swiftness that belied his state, the man grabbed her face between his hands and pressed his moist lips against hers. One of the men restrained her arms, pushing himself against her. The kiss deepened as the local groaned and his slimy tongue dredged her unwilling mouth. Her burlap was dragged from her shoulder, her shawl with it. Hands began to roam over her body, grasping, squeezing. She strained against them, tried to cry out, pull away. Their breath was loud, heavy, rancid.

They began to force her away from the house, towards the cemetery gate, holding her upright, half-carrying her into the darkness. Before they reached the wall, she leaned into the man kissing her, surprising him. Pretending to enjoy his mouth upon hers, she drew his lower lip between her own then bit down hard. Throwing her head back, she pulled a chunk of flesh with it.

There was a yowl of pain, followed by a hot gush of blood. Then, she was free. She spat the piece of lip out as the man staggered away in shock, forcing the others to break their hold.

'The fucking bitch bit me,' he cried, blood pumping from his ravaged mouth. 'She fuckin' bit me.'

Sorcha grinned, swiping the back of her hand across her lips, uncaring that her face was smeared with his blood. 'Aye, and I'll do it again if you come near me, you fucking bastard.'

Down by the kirk, a dog howled. A curtain shifted in a nearby window, but no one came to her aid.

The mood altered.

'You can't bite us all, lass —' The Englishman lunged.

Sorcha tried to move, but he was too fast. He seized her dress. Sorcha let out a scream, before it was cut off as she was struck across the face.

'Maybe she can't,' shouted a welcome voice. 'But we can.'

Pouring through the doorway of Sorcha's house, silhouetted against the sudden light, were three women brandishing gutting knives and a broom. It was her friends Nettie Horseburgh, Beatrix Laing and Nicolas Lawson.

They ran towards the men, weapons raised, their faces grim. Sorcha was thrust away as if she were a hot coal.

Before Sorcha could call out a warning, the man with the torn lip raised a dirk. The wicked blade glinted in the dim light. The other men drew theirs. One pulled a gun from his breeks.

Sorcha ran to join the women, turning to face the men. There was nothing but the slash of a blade separating them.

'How about you put those away, lasses,' said the Englishman calmly, nodding towards their knives. He gave a bold wink. 'And we take this party inside.' Quick as a gull snatching a fish, he disarmed Nettie and levelled his weapon at her breast. Beatrix and Nicolas raised their own knives higher.

There was a loud cough. The men froze. The women twisted to see where it came from.

'I don't remember sanctioning a party, Private Donall,' said a deep, deadly voice.

Emerging slowly out of the shadows of Lady Wynd came a man on horseback. He carried a sword, which he deftly spun. Behind him rode another, older man. Sorcha hadn't been imagining the horse's hooves after all. But how they had ridden down the wynd without making a sound until now was a feat worthy of a phantasm.

'Captain Ross,' said the one called Private Donall, sheathing his knife and standing to attention. 'I didn't see you, sir. Nor you, Sergeant Thatcher.'

The soldiers quickly put distance between themselves and the women, replacing their dirks, the gun disappearing. The man with the torn mouth tried to staunch the blood with his sleeve and hide the damage.

'That much is apparent,' said Captain Ross. 'But since we *are* here, I'm ordering you to return to your quarters. Once you get there, I want you all to think on an appropriate way to celebrate Hogmanay — one that doesn't involve unwilling women.'

'Unwilling?' squawked the man with the torn lip. 'They were willing to start with, sir.'

'I can see that by the blood bubbling from your mouth, Private Dyson.'

Dyson? Sorcha tried to place the name. Surely that wasn't young Jamie Dyson from Anster Wester?

'In my experience,' said Captain Ross, 'and no doubt the good sergeant's here, willing women don't oft express their consent in such a manner.' He paused.

Sergeant Thatcher nodded grimly. 'Nor in mine,' he growled.

'I want you to think long and hard about the type of celebration I'm going to insist you enjoy.' Before the men could exchange even a puzzled look, the captain continued. 'Here's your choice, lads. You can either spend the next two days in the stocks or, if you'd rather, aboard a frigate bound for Flanders. What do you say to that?'

The men stared at him in disbelief. 'But... sir, you said we'd be celebrating.'

'Aye. I did. You'll either be celebrating the cold here in Fife or celebrating the same in the Low Countries. Take your pick.'

Sorcha couldn't help it, she laughed. Nettie and the others did as well. The men's shoulders sagged.

Captain Ross cast an amused look towards the women. 'Would you call that fair, lasses?'

'I would, captain,' said Sorcha, enjoying the men's discomfort. Jamie Dyson shot her a poisonous look. Here she was, home five minutes, and already she'd added another enemy to her tally.

'And me,' chorused her friends.

Captain Ross quietly gave orders to his sergeant. His blade gleamed in the light from the doorway, a reminder that he would enforce his orders if he had to. Sorcha thought he looked rather grand astride his silvery steed, high above them, wreaking vengeance upon these drunken sots who would call themselves soldiers. He was like a character from a tale. Only, he wasn't. He was as real as the blood upon her lips and cheeks.

She swiftly found a kerchief and began to clean her face, her mouth. She longed for a dram to rinse out the taste of Jamie Dyson.

At the sergeant's prompting, the men lined up in single file and, when he barked a command, began to run down the street. He followed on horseback.

Their equipment jangled as they jogged, their hats bounced until Private Donall staggered towards the graveyard wall. Leaning against it with one hand, he loudly lost the contents of his stomach. The sergeant waved for him to continue, and the man straightened, spat and stumbled after his friends, who hadn't stopped to help him.

Once they had rounded the corner, the captain sheathed his sword and drew off his hat, allowing Sorcha to see his face for the first time. It was a hard face, a worn one framed by black hair; large, deep-set eyes took in everything around him, including her. Self-conscious suddenly, Sorcha put a hand to her head. She'd lost her scarf in the tussle, her hair had come unbound. She tried to gather it in her fingers, twist it into a semblance of a bun.

'You have my apologies for the behaviour of my men,' said the captain, watching Sorcha's efforts. 'The sergeant and I saw them following you up the High Street and guessed they were up to no good.' He sighed. 'Rest assured, you'll not be bothered by the likes of them again. As for the others stationed hereabouts… While they ken not to touch the local lasses, it's the incomers I cannot always protect — as much as I try.'

'Sorcha be no incomer,' said Beatrix, a wide grin revealing her missing teeth. 'She's a born and bred Weem lass like the rest of us.'

'That be her place,' said Nicolas, pointing to the open door behind them.

'Is that so?' asked the captain, studying Sorcha with interest before examining the house. 'Why have I not seen you before?' He gave a half bow over the horse's withers. It was a surprisingly elegant effort.

Laughter issued from a nearby house. A pipe began to play, followed by voices raised in song. Underpinning it all, the ocean breathed.

Sorcha looked around her. The encroaching night was cold, the street bleak, despite the singing, the candlelight, the roiling mist. All she could recall was the feel of the men's bodies pressed against hers, the taste of blood in her mouth. She'd foolishly hoped for a different kind of welcome; a different kind of Hogmanay. Perhaps this was what she deserved. But that didn't mean the others did.

Suddenly, the events of the day, the reason for her leave-taking and early homecoming and the threat and fear that greeted her on her very own doorstep became too much. Men became too much, even this gallant who not only showed such courtesy, but looked to their safety.

'Thank you for what you did, sir. But if you don't mind, it's growing late and I would like to get inside before the new year passes.' *And have a wee drink with my friends.*

Before he could protest, Sorcha gave the captain a nod of dismissal and ushered the women, who added their thanks to hers, back towards the cottage and through the open door.

She was about to close it, when the captain put his boot between the door and the jamb. His fingers curled over hers where they rested. He'd dismounted both quickly and quietly and moved with a speed that unnerved her. Taller than she expected, she was forced to tip her head to see his face. Up close and by the mellow light of the fire, it didn't seem as hard, but rather one shaped by experience and, if his twinkling eyes were any guide, humour and kindness as well. God damn if her heart didn't flutter and heat that had nothing to do with the growing warmth at her back flooded her cheeks. Had she learned nothing?

'I said,' Sorcha looked pointedly at his boot obstructing the door and then at his hand covering hers, 'I want to get inside.'

The captain removed his fingers slowly. 'Aye, and I heard you. But I thought you might also like to have these.' He heaved her burlap and shawl into her arms.

Before she could thank him, he strode to his horse and threw his leg over its back. Tipping his hat to Sorcha one last time, he disappeared down the street, swallowed by the mist as if he were one of the fae folk and had never really been.

THREE

She's a toon's crack.
(Everyone's speaking about her.)

The only sounds Sorcha could hear were the wind rattling the windows and the crackle of the fire. Wriggling her stockinged feet before the flames, she rested her head against the back of her da's old armchair and looked fondly at Nettie curled in her mor's. Initially, she'd worried that returning home would reawaken the ghosts of those who used to live there, those she'd tried so hard over the years to make peace with, but once indoors and surrounded by friends, she realised sadness hadn't leached into the walls, nor had death left its pungent scent. At least, not while she had a cleckin' o' women to distract her.

Once the captain departed, Sorcha and her friends had fallen into each other's arms, talking over the top of one another as drams of whisky were poured, downed and poured again. Only then did the women, who'd entered through the back door and barged straight through the house when they understood Sorcha was being threatened, set about making the cottage warmer and shedding more light on their doings. As Nettie prepared food, Beatrix shovelled more peat onto the fire while Nicolas lit extra candles, placing them where they'd illuminate the cosy room best.

'Go, lass,' said Nettie, waving a knife in Sorcha's direction. 'We'll take care of this. Put your things away. Get settled.' She nodded towards her burlap. 'That is, unless you're planning on leaving us again soon?' There was a note of apprehension in the question.

Sorcha shook her head. 'I might be back earlier than anticipated, but I'm here to stay.'

With a look of relief, Nettie returned to cutting the smoked fish.

Sorcha carried her burlap and a candle into the rooms beyond, stroking the worn furniture as she passed — the rough table, the unsteady stools — pressing her cheek against the tattered but clean curtains, picking up and replacing a book, an ornament.

In the main bedroom Nettie's belongings were arranged neatly upon the dresser. Sorcha sat on the bed she once shared with her husband Andy, the same bed that had belonged to her mor and da. Dropping the burlap at her feet, she brought a pillow to her nose and inhaled deeply. Convinced it no longer smelled of Andy or her parents, as she used to believe, but bore the cherished fragrance of Nettie, she replaced it carefully, smoothing it out. Lying back on the covers, she folded her arms behind her head and studied the ceiling. Little light found its way into this part of the house come nightfall, but she could still remember the shapes the damp had imprinted above her. When she was a wee bairn, she'd climb into bed when her mor was sad or ill and try to identify them. Years later, Andy had indulged her by playing the game too, and together they'd discovered seals, urchins, the sail of a boat, a mangy cat and even, one time after a few drinks, the face of an old woman.

'A witch,' Andy had chuckled.

'Nae, a wise woman,' she'd countered.

It was a game she once imagined she'd play with her own child.

A sudden sorrow threatened to engulf her and she sat up and found a shawl she hadn't realised she'd left behind draped on the end of the bed. Marvelling it was still where she'd evidently left it, she wrapped it around her shoulders. Hanging on the opposite wall was a mirror, still covered with a swathe of fabric from when Andy died. There hadn't even been time to remove it before wee Davan's soul was also taken.

God bless Nettie, she'd kept it there. Perhaps now she could, should, take it down. After all, it had been almost two years.

She rose and drew the cloth away slowly. Her shadowy reflection stared back at her in the spotted glass. The light from the main room behind her made her hair glint, threads of fire that formed a halo about her head. Waiting until her eyes adjusted, she could see her face was fuller than she remembered; her mouth looked wider as well. Her eyes were great dark pools, their vibrant colour surrendered to the gloom. Touching her cheek, she ran a finger down her face, pushing into the soft flesh, watching the way it resumed its former shape. Would she?

In returning home, what was she doing but revisiting herself as she used to be? Before... before everything changed and so had she. Nae. She would never return to the way she was. How could she? She was no longer a daughter. How could one be, without parents? Nor did she have any siblings — none that wanted to acknowledge her, or even could. She was not a wife or mother either. Her heart shrank painfully. She was defined by loss: an orphan, a widow, a grieving mother.

Leaning closer, she examined her face in detail, plucked her lip to check for blood stains, stared hard until the blue-green of her eyes became apparent. Beatrix had always said how much she resembled her mor. Unable to see it when she was younger, now, apart from her bronze hair, she had to admit she did look like her mother. This is what age, loss and guilt do to a child: turn them into younger versions of their unhappy parents.

The chatter of her friends rose and fell in the background and she released a deep breath and stared at the woman in the glass once more before her eyes studied the room around her, reversed and sub-dued into a palette of greys and browns. It was important to focus on the life that had blossomed within these walls, not the sorrow. That wasn't the way of things here. Everyone she knew had lost someone to the sea — husbands, fathers, brothers, lovers, sons. Nettie had lost a beloved brother; Beatrix so many: sons, brothers, a father. Nicolas had never met her father, the North Sea claiming him before she was born. Some had given even more. It was an expectation that when you took from the sea, there were dues to be paid. Some paid more than others, but somehow, between them, the balance was maintained. You buried your loved ones if you could, mourned for a period, and life went on. To talk about them, dwell upon their absence, wasn't fair; it only reminded everyone what they'd lost. Sorcha wouldn't do that. Not any more. The period for grieving had passed.

Even before she'd reached the braes of Pittenweem, she'd made a pact with herself that it was time to put all her dead behind her, including the bitter memories her mor and her marriage to Andy conjured. It was time to live once more. She'd known that being back in the house would stir memories of them and her da and brothers as well, but what she hadn't anticipated was that they would still have the capacity to hurt her so much. Though not enough to do what young Anna Warren up in South Loan had done when her husband Hamish drowned, filling her pockets with bullets and chuckie-stanes and walking into the Forth in the dark. Then there was Agnes Black; after her three sons died on a voyage to Stornaway, she threw herself off the braes. Her broken body was found washed up on the shore. Sorcha would never cause her friends that kind of pain. Not if she could help it. That wasn't to say she hadn't been tempted, especially after Davan died. Her throat caught and her hand covered her stomach.

Before he'd taken a breath, the Lord took him away. And now not even her sister wanted to be with her.

It was just Sorcha. Alone. Again.

And Robbie. She hadn't given up on her older brother even if Dagny had. The last she'd heard he was a prisoner of war and, until she was informed otherwise, as far as she was concerned he was alive. No matter how long his absence, she'd care for their house, make it a home for him to return to as well.

There was a loud cackle followed by a joyous shriek from the outer room.

A smile spread across her face and into her heart. As long as she was a fishwife, she wasn't really alone.

Sorcha threw the cloth that had covered the mirror on the bed and went back to the others. Grateful for their blatter, as well as the care

Nettie had taken of the house while she'd been gone, she slowly began to relax as they ate, talked and drank.

Settled into her da's chair, Sorcha watched the women as she sipped whisky, relishing the taste, enjoying the slow build of warmth from the fireplace.

'How'd you know I was back?' she asked finally to no one in particular.

Nicolas sank into the chair opposite. 'Nettie said she saw you up on the braes. We didn't believe her at first, but she was all doolally and insisted we come and see for ourselves.'

'Will you listen to them?' said Nettie, hands on hips. 'You'd think I was half-mad Mona the way they're carrying on. Should be ashamed of themselves; they didn't count on me recognising my best friend.' She laid out some bannocks on a griddle, passing it over to Beatrix who put them over the fire. 'Would you believe, I had to bribe them to come up here with me?' She held up the bottle of whisky to show what she'd used to persuade them.

Sorcha burst out laughing.

Beatrix chuckled. 'It's well known I'd do pretty much anything for a dram. Including take on a group of drunken soldiers — and at my age!' Leaning back on her heels, she stretched out her bony arm, holding up her wooden drinking cup, the quaich, by the handle for a refill.

Nicolas swooped on it, holding it steady while Nettie topped it up.

'Just as well we came by, hey?' said Nicolas, passing the cup back to Beatrix. 'Those men meant business.'

'I'll give young Jamie business next time I see him,' said Beatrix, shaking her head and frowning. 'The lad deserves a thrashing, and if the captain doesn't do it, I'll be happy to oblige.'

Nicolas lifted her dram. 'I'll drink to that.'

'Wait!' cried Nettie and, depositing a plate filled with cheese, pieces of smoked fish and some chunks of mutton on a stool between them, knelt beside Sorcha, one hand on her knee, the other holding her quaich aloft. 'I want to propose a toast.' The women raised their cups expectantly. 'Now, I ken you weren't due home yet,' said Nettie, one brow raised, which Sorcha understood meant there'd be questions aplenty. 'But I'm glad to have you back.'

'We're all glad,' added Nicolas, and Beatrix nodded vigorously in agreement.

'Here's to Sorcha,' said Nettie. They knocked their cups together and tossed back the contents.

Sorcha looked at the women. Nettie's mother had been one of the very few to try and befriend her mor, which had brought Nettie into her sphere. Despite the dozen years between them, Nettie had been her friend for as long as she could remember — nay, not just a friend. Over time, Nettie had become the older sister Dagny had never been and Sorcha had always wanted. Not even Nettie's marriage to Thom and the birth of their daughter Rebecca had changed that. There wasn't much they didn't know about each other and hadn't shared. Likewise old Beatrix, a wool-spinner married to William Brown, a fine tailor, had been a great friend of her da's mother. When Grandma McIntyre died, Beatrix had stepped in and been like a mother and grandma to all the McIntyres, even though she had her own daughter and granddaughter to think about. Astrid had rejected her efforts, but it didn't stop Beatrix. Then there was Nicolas. An incomer from nearby Crail, she was married to Alexander Young, a farmer who leased a small block of land between the Weem and Anster. Raised to be a fishwife, whenever Alexander was called away to help with harvesting on his laird's land, Nicolas would come and stay in the Weem and resume the work she knew best. A bit older than Sorcha, she'd been a boon to her when Andy died, not to mention everything afterwards.

Perhaps seeing where Sorcha's thoughts were taking her, Nettie refilled their drinks, and raised her quaich again. 'To old friends and new beginnings.'

'To old friends and new beginnings,' the women said in unison, almost shyly, touching the lips of their cups and drinking solemnly. Smiles were exchanged that filled the eyes and made Sorcha's soul melt.

God, she'd missed these women.

'Welcome home, Sorcha,' whispered Nettie, her eyes brimming with those unasked questions before she rested her cheek briefly on Sorcha's knee. Sorcha stroked her hair.

'It's good to be back. Better than I hoped.'

'And better than those soldiers intended,' added Nicolas.

'I hope they're enjoying *their* celebrations,' said Beatrix drolly.

'I'll drink to that too,' said Nicolas, and with shrieks of laughter they all toasted the men.

As the evening wore on, they barely ceased talking, determined to fill Sorcha in on what had been happening in her absence. There'd been two marriages, a few births and deaths, and a couple of drownings at sea — the Morrison lad and a man from Anster Easter. Hesitant at first to tell her, it was only when Sorcha insisted that they revealed the sad tidings. Three families had left Pittenweem to try and improve their fortunes in Edinburgh and another had arrived from St Monan's. Though, as Nicolas noted wryly, how that family expected to fare better in the Weem than a neighbouring village a mere walk away, she couldn't fathom. The catch had, overall, been poor, even for the ships that had left the Forth and sailed north. Not even the salt pan was as productive as it had once been. If it wasn't for another coal mine opening nearby and a maltster setting up operations, there'd be more families relying on the parish for sustenance. As it was, men were being lured away from fishing to other occupations, including soldiering. Things were fairly dire.

Talk of soldiers turned the conversation to war and the men who'd taken up arms for the Queen, including the trio who'd accosted them earlier. Sorcha began to think of her brother Robbie again, praying that, against all odds, he was alive. Though how he could be after so many years locked up in a prison in a foreign land, she knew not. Best not to dwell on him either.

The conversation shifted to the recruits billeted in town, the women reassuring Sorcha they weren't all like Privates Donall and Dyson or the sneering Englishman.

Finally, Sorcha was able to raise the question she'd been longing to ask. 'Tell me about that dragoon, Captain... What was his name again?' she asked, fooling no one.

'Bonnie?' teased Nettie with a leery grin.

'Was he? I barely noticed.' Sorcha laughed. 'Aye, him. Why's he riding about town with a drawn sword? And who's the burly sergeant? I confess, they made me start when they first appeared. I wasn't sure whether they'd come to help us or the soldiers.'

'The captain's sworn to protect us poor Weem women.' Nettie swooned in her chair.

'Aye, and the fine sergeant too,' added Beatrix with a salty wink.

'From what?' asked Sorcha. If Weem women need protecting then more had changed since she'd left than she first thought.

'From their men,' said Nettie dryly.

'Not *their* men, exactly,' countered Nicolas. 'Captain Ross replaced the former captain, remember him? Captain Douglas? Under whose command a woman was raped. His sergeant was transferred too and Captain Ross and Sergeant Thatcher came in their place.'

Sorcha sat up. 'I remember the rape. Captain Douglas said his men had nothing to do with it.'

'Aye. Only their bloody pintles. Poor Lizzie Johnson. She wasn't believed; not at first,' said Nettie. 'Didn't help that Reverend Cowper put it about that any woman fraternising with the soldiers deserved what she got.'

Sorcha shook her head in disgust. 'Lizzie Johnson comes from a good family.'

'Not as far as Cowper's concerned,' said Beatrix. 'They're Jacobites, remember?'

'Aren't we all,' sniggered Nettie.

'Anyways,' Beatrix frowned at the interruption, 'Lizzie was stepping out with a soldier so Cowper said she brought it upon herself. Didn't matter the man who ravished her was not the same as the one who was sweet on her.'

Nettie pulled a face. 'You know I've no time for the reverend and while I don't want to defend him, there were some who thought he said that to prevent fights breaking out between the fishermen and the soldiers. The Johnsons and the McMannings were fit to murder and God knows what would have happened had they set upon the soldiers. Cowper's words, blaming poor Lizzie, made them think twice.'

'Wasn't Cowper made them think twice,' said Beatrix. 'Was Captain Ross. He be a good man... for an incomer.'

'Aye,' agreed Nicolas. 'For an incomer.'

'To incomers,' said Nettie, raising her cup again. They drank another toast.

Reaching for the bottle of whisky and first topping up her friends' drinks, Sorcha added the last of it to her own. This captain had done the nigh-on impossible — earned the admiration, if not gratitude, of not just Nettie and her friends but the close-knit villagers. Something that had all but eluded her mor. Sorrow threatened to swamp her.

'Och, you've naught to worry about when it comes to Captain Aidan Ross,' said Nettie, misunderstanding where her friend's thoughts had taken her and nudging the others. They giggled. 'He's doing a much better job of keeping his men in order than his predecessor or those soldiers tonight indicate.'

'Well, he did stop them,' said Beatrix. 'Him and the sergeant.'

'According to the reverend,' said Nettie, 'the captain doesn't exercise enough authority. At least, not in the way Cowper thinks he should.' She rolled her eyes.

'Cowper only moans because he believes his flock is straying,' said Beatrix, flapping her hand. 'It's not up to the captain to force parishioners to attend kirk on Sundays. It's hardly his fault if some of the men like to share a drink with the soldiers instead of listening to Cowper blast fire and brimstone upon them. I know what I'd choose if I could afford the fine.'

They raised their cups in agreement, all except Sorcha, who was deep in thought. As an officer, Captain Ross might know something of the war. He may even know about the fate of any prisoners...

Talk wandered to what was going on within their own families, then they dared to wonder what the new year would bring. Nettie declared if Sorcha's unexpected return was anything to go by, the year 1704 would be a good one. But only a first-footer would reveal the truth.

An old custom, and not confined to Pittenweem, it was believed the first person to step over the threshold of a household after midnight on Hogmanay was an omen of the year to come.

If nothing else, discussing first-footers was a signal for the women to return to their families. They wanted to be home to witness who stumbled through their doorways after the clock struck twelve. With hugs, kisses and promises to meet down by the harbour early on the morrow, Beatrix and Nicolas left.

Finally, Sorcha and Nettie were alone.

'You sure you don't want to see the new year in with Thom?' asked Sorcha, secretly hoping her friend remained. 'I'll understand if you do. Now I'm back, there's no need for you to stay.'

'What would I want to see him for?' Nettie gave a careless flick of her wrist. 'I can see him any day. You, I'm not so sure about.' She smiled warmly to take the sting out of her words. 'That is, if you don't mind having me here.'

Sorcha smiled. 'Mind? I would have insisted if I didn't think it was wrong to usurp your husband.'

Nettie laughed and then her eyes took on a dreamy, faraway look. 'Thom understands. Once he heard you'd returned, he went over to Anster to celebrate with Rebecca and her lad, Jimmy.' She gave a slow, secret smile. 'Anyhow, I want to know why you've come back so soon. Far as I recall, you were to stay away till May.'

'Aye, well, that's true. But things change.'

Nettie drew her chair closer. 'That they do. But why did you change *your* mind? Not that I'm complaining. I couldn't be happier. But I ken something bad has happened to bring you home early, and at this time of year. So, tell me, lass. What ails you?'

FOUR

Ye wee lummer!
(Comment on a woman's wild and immoral behaviour.)

*I*t was a relief to finally tell someone she trusted why she'd come home. Nettie listened intently, her drink nestled in her palm as if it were a baby bird, her eyes locked on Sorcha as she spoke.

'I should have seen what was happening,' sighed Sorcha. 'I don't know whether I turned a blind eye deliberately because I was flattered by Kennocht's attention, even though he was Dagny's husband, or because I never thought my brother-in-law, the father of six bonnie bairns, would consider me in such a light.' She shrugged. 'Either way, I should've known. All those long talks after Dagny and the bairns were abed, the times he took me to help with the lambing, the trips to St Andrew's for stores, and even once to Edinburgh. But they weren't to spare Dagny, as he claimed, but so he might have me to himself. That's not vanity speaking either. That's what he told me, plain and simple.' She paused. 'That was before he kissed me.'

Nettie's eyes widened before she waved a hand dismissively. 'Och,' she exclaimed. 'He wouldn't be the first to steal a kiss from a bonnie lass, and he won't be the last — be she kin or no.'

'That's not the issue,' said Sorcha hesitantly.

Nettie arched a brow, her hazel eyes piercing. 'What was the problem, then?'

Aware her cheeks were hot, her body moreso and not just from the fire, Sorcha released a long, tired sigh. It was time to confess. 'I kissed him back.'

Nettie buried a smile and rearranged her skirt. 'When you say, "kissed him back", what exactly do you mean?'

Sorcha gave a dry laugh. 'What do you think I mean? Instead of pushing him away as a decent person would have done, I drew my body into his and felt yearning rise up in me like the sun on a hot summer's day. If he hadn't groaned when he did, reminding me of who I was a-kissing and where we were, I don't want to think what would have happened.' Sorcha reached for the whisky and frowned as a few meagre drops splashed into her cup.

Praying Nettie wasn't still regarding her with those all-knowing eyes, she rose to fetch another drink. Her hand found a flagon of ale, but she delayed returning to her chair, trying to dissemble. She wasn't being entirely honest — neither with Nettie nor herself. A part of her *had* known it was Kennocht she was kissing and didn't care. It was as if the devil had taken over her body, whispering to her that Dagny didn't deserve him. Her sister didn't give a tinker's cuss about her family, about Sorcha, having left her to fend for herself in the Weem even after their da, mor and brother died. She didn't believe Robbie was alive and had no compunction about sharing this view with Sorcha — or anybody else who'd listen — regardless of the pain it caused her sister. Why should Sorcha be concerned about her feelings? Dagny was a cold one anyway. Why, she hadn't come home when their mor died, nor when Andy or Davan passed. Didn't matter she was with another bairn. Nary a note or message, she'd left Sorcha to wallow in the grief she wasn't supposed to show.

But it was more than that.

Deep down, Sorcha worried that she'd kissed Kennocht back out of spite, to pay Dagny back for the way she'd treated her while they were growing up. Resenting Sorcha from the moment she was born, she'd been a cruel older sister, determined to make Sorcha's life as miserable as she felt her own to be. It didn't help that their mother never intervened in their bickering or, when she did, more often took Dagny's side. Loathing the ways of the fisher folk, hating that her name marked her as an incomer like her mor in ways Sorcha's did not, Dagny had done all she could to maintain the divisions she imagined between herself and her younger sister until they were real. The more Sorcha learned about being a fishwife, the more Dagny rejected their ways; the closer Sorcha became to their da and their older brother Erik, the more Dagny withdrew until the distance between them was an unbridgeable chasm. When Dagny finally did what she had threatened to do for years and left the Weem, accepting the hand of a lad who worked on a laird's estate outside St Andrew's, the greatest emotion Sorcha felt was relief.

In the course of infrequent letters, written more out of a sense of duty than desire, over time Sorcha had begun to recast their relationship in a kinder light, remembering the moments when they'd behaved like normal sisters, not jealous enemies. She was even able to forgive Dagny's absence from their mor's burial, accepting her excuse that it was too hard to leave her children. That was why, after Andy and Davan died, when Dagny's plea to help with the bairns when the new one was due arrived, Sorcha accepted. She wanted to believe her sister when she wrote that not only would Sorcha's presence be a boon with a newborn, growing bairns and household tasks to manage, but it would be a chance for her to heal a sorrowful heart, put behind her the deaths of her husband and son and for the sisters to start afresh as well. For all Sorcha was frustrated by Dagny and failed to understand her, she loved her. She really did.

Nettie had warned her about going; so had other friends, especially wise old Janet Cornfoot. They knew Dagny and the spite that ran in her veins; how it boiled in Sorcha's presence. But caught up in the romance of a reconciliation and a desire to help while mending the rent in their relationship, and to see if leaving the Weem would allow her to repair herself, Sorcha went.

Turned out Nettie and Janet were right and Dagny's overtures of sisterly affection were short-lived. Not that Sorcha could blame her sister, after the way she had behaved with Kennocht.

She resumed her seat, filled with shame and regret at what she'd done, and refilled Nettie's quaich.

'As it was, I told Kennocht never to come near me again or I would tell Dagny what he was up to.'

Nettie grunted. 'And what did he say?'

Sorcha took a swig, coughing as it bit the back of her throat. 'First of all, he tried to persuade me with words. You know — how he'd always fancied me, said we'd be good together if it wasn't for his wife and bairns (as if they were ill-fitting clothes he'd discard). How he knew I wanted him — the daft beast! I put him straight and told him I no more wanted him than I did the horse in the next stall who, I might add, was paying us a mite more attention than a mere animal should.'

Nettie chuckled. 'That would have hurt his pride. Especially if it were a stallion you were comparing him to. No man's tossel can compete with a stallion's.'

Sorcha snorted. 'Maybe that was the mistake I made. 'Twas indeed a stallion.' Her laughter ceased as quickly as it began. 'Anyhow, he did something I didn't expect.'

Nettie waited.

'He told Dagny.'

This time it was Nettie's turn to choke. 'He did *what*?'

Sorcha reached over and thumped Nettie's back a few times. 'Aye. He told my sister that I'd come upon him in the stables and begged him to take me. That I'd thrown myself at him like a moggy on heat. He said I claimed I'd been too long without a man.'

'And she believed the arse?'

'Of course she did. She feels and looks like a milch cow with babes hanging off her nugs and her body heavy, never mind she's always wanted to believe the worst of me. Kennocht told me she's too tired or waspish for bedding.'

'What a prick.'

'Aye, he had one of those. He may not have been a stallion, but it was a decent size all the same,' said Sorcha. They burst into gales of laughter.

When it subsided and they replenished their half-drunk cups, Nettie shook her head. 'And so 'twas Dagny sent you on your way.'

Sorcha took a deep shuddering breath. 'And told me never to come back. That the devil could take me and I was as dead to her as our mor and da. As our Erik and Robbie.' Sorcha paused for a beat. 'She said a great deal more than that as well.' She chewed her lip a few times. 'Something tells me it's what she intended to happen all along. Not her husband, but sending me away. For good.'

Nettie reached over and took Sorcha's hand, squeezing it hard. 'I for one am beyond happy you're home, lass. It's not been the same without you.'

Sorcha pulled a face. 'From the welcome I received and what I've no doubt Reverend Cowper will say when he hears I'm back, never mind if he learns the why of it, it appears things are exactly the same.'

She thought of the soldiers, their violence, their need. What was it one of them had said about Andy? *Weren't he the one who drowned because his wife didn't carry him to the boat?*

Seems that was how she was to be remembered — as the widow responsible for her husband's death.

Not surprising, really, since it was the reverend who first accused her. When he did, she could scarce believe what she was hearing. It was the way of the fishwives to carry their husbands to their boats when they were fishing inshore so they didn't board with wet boots and legs and thus fall sick, but Sorcha hadn't carried Andy on his last trip. He'd stridden through the waves to the craft himself. Having lost her last three bairns early in pregnancy, neither she nor Andy wanted to risk the one that now quickened in her belly. It had been Andy's decision and Sorcha was grateful for it.

She could still see him wading through the water, climbing on board, shouting he was fine. The other men had shaken their heads, regarding her with disapproval and touching whatever iron was to hand in an effort to counter any bad luck. Some of the fishwives had too. Only Nettie, Nicolas and Janet had stood by her that day, arms draped over her shoulders as they watched the boat carrying her husband row out of the harbour and into the Forth, where its sails would be raised.

As often happened during spring, the weather turned. One moment it was sunshine and clear skies. The next, a storm erupted. A rogue wave capsized the boat, taking with it not just Andy, but young James Crawford as well. The Crawfords held Sorcha responsible for their son's death and had not spoken to her since.

Sorcha rested her elbow on the arm of the chair and cupped her chin, staring at the fire.

'When he blamed you for Andy's death, hen, I thought I'd be the one to commit murder. Me and auld Janet.'

Sorcha gave a wistful smile.

'Reverend Cowper said if I'd carried Andy to the boat like other Weem fishwives do their men, he wouldn't have gone under —'

'Nae, lass,' said Nettie with a weary sigh. 'His clothes would have copped a drookin' in the storm. It had naught to do with whether you lugged him out there or not. Cowper just wanted you to bear the guilt and we both ken why that was.'

Mesmerised by the golden tongues of flame, it was a while before Sorcha spoke again. Then she whispered, 'Well, whatever his intention, it worked. He also said it was because Andy drowned that Davan died. God was punishing me for my negligence, for disregarding the laws of the sea. He took my son so I would learn to be obedient.'

Nettie made a noise of disgust and stood up, picking up the poker and jabbing at the fire. Sorcha wondered if, like her, she was imagining the peat was Cowper. Throwing the poker against the hearth, Nettie turned, hands on hips. 'Many a man walks to his own craft, even if he has a woman to bear him. As for Davan, he died as some poor wee bairns do, because the angels summoned him back to their side. His death wasn't your fault either, Sorcha. God wouldn't be so cruel, despite what Cowper says. Anyone who thinks otherwise is wicked.'

'That's what he called me, you know — a wicked woman.'

Nettie gave a broad smile. 'That's what he calls all us fishwives. We're all wicked women to him.'

Not just to him, thought Sorcha. An image of the soldiers, Private Donall and Jamie Dyson, calling her a bitch arose before a picture of the captain astride his horse set it aside.

'Enough about the reverend,' said Sorcha, sitting up. 'Tell me more about this Captain Ross, Nettie. Who is he? Where does he hail from? He doesn't sound like he's from these parts.'

'Ah,' said Nettie, sinking back into her chair. 'There be a man for you.'

Sorcha's chest tightened before she understood Nettie was talking in general terms. 'I hear tell he's a Skye lad. Since he's been here, he's stopped the soldiers in the village from running amok the way they used to.'

'I was thinking he's either a good man or very good at appearing to be one.'

Nettie cast her a sly look. 'Maybe you'll just have to find out for yourself.' She nodded towards the door. 'We can still hope he's your first-footer. You know what they say, if a handsome dark stranger is the first-foot come Hogmanay, then you'll have good fortune for the whole year. There's not many more handsome or dark than Captain Bonnie.'

Sorcha shrugged. 'I hadn't noticed.'

Nettie gave a bark of laughter. 'Aye, and I be blind as well.'

'Mind you,' continued Sorcha, ignoring her, 'I could do with some good luck.' About to outline what she'd do with it, there was a loud noise outside. She stared at Nettie. 'What was that?'

Before Nettie could reply, the door flew open, bringing an icy gust of wind and a bedraggled, terrified young woman.

Sorcha and Nettie leapt to their feet.

It was the seamstress Isobel Adam, a poor lass who lived with her father on the eastern shore and made a meagre living making shirts and doing mending for the fishermen. Pretty, with a small upturned nose, pale freckled skin, and a mane of golden hair, she was much sought after by the lads.

'Dear God, lassie,' cried Nettie. 'What's happened? What are you doing in this part of town?'

Sorcha wrapped an arm around the girl's thin waist and grabbed her shaking hands, propelling her into the room. 'Are you hurt?'

Nettie closed the door, but not before she'd taken a good hard look outside.

Sorcha pushed Isobel gently into her da's chair and crouched at her feet. Looking over at Nettie, she raised a brow and mouthed the word 'Soldiers?' Nettie shrugged, poured another ale and knelt next to Sorcha.

Taking Isobel's fingers in her own warm ones, Sorcha was astonished how cold they were. She brushed a lock of hair from Isobel's face and stroked her cheek.

Still trembling, Isobel could barely lift the ale to her mouth. Nettie undid her own shawl and threw it around Isobel's shoulders, rubbing her arms, trying to restore warmth.

As the heat returned to her body, Isobel looked around and her eyes alighted on Sorcha. 'Bless me darned tights. The rumours are true. You're back.'

Sorcha tucked the girl's skirts around her. ''Tis me. But what are you doing wandering down Marygate so late? It's not safe.'

Isobel's eyes darted to the door. 'Nae. It ain't.'

Sorcha rose then and drew the bolt across. 'Was it soldiers?'

'It wasn't them.'

'When you're ready, tell us what afeared you,' said Nettie.

Isobel took a long drink, wiped the back of her hand across her mouth, and began.

She'd been visiting the widowed fisherman Alexander McGregor. He lived on the crest of Lady's Wynd and had asked Isobel to stitch some shirts for him, promising extra money and a dram or two if she could come on Hogmanay.

Nettie gave Sorcha a pointed look. No doubt McGregor hoped for more than some mended clothes.

'When I got there,' continued Isobel, unaware of the exchange between the women, 'there was no answer. It was dark and there was a plout o' rain. I didn't want to get wet again, so I opened the door and let myself in. Mr McGregor was sound asleep. But I could see what needed doing, so I drew a chair up by the fire and began to sew.' She gulped and glanced towards the door again.

'It's all right, Isobel, I latched it. What happened after that?' asked Sorcha.

Isobel shrugged. 'I must've lost track of time. I might've dozed off myself. You see, I helped myself to the promised dram.' She gave an apologetic smile. Sorcha squeezed her leg. 'When I woke up, I noticed that Mr McGregor was stirring. I put down the shirts and went to greet him. He opened his eyes, sat up, and pointed at me. Before I could say anything, he began screaming that the devil had come into his home. It gave me a terrible fright, but no more than I did him. I tried to calm him, but when I stepped closer, he grabbed me by the throat —' Her hands fluttered at her neck. Sorcha saw there were red marks on her skin.

'I was afraid for my life and began to scream. I said, "Nae, Mr McGregor, 'tis me, 'tis me, Isobel Adam." I pointed to the work I'd done, but he couldn't see me even though his eyes were open. 'Twas like he was bewitched or a spirit or something had a hold of him —'

'The spirit of whisky would be my guess,' said Nettie. Sorcha swallowed a grin.

'I managed to get away from him, but he chased me about the room. I reached the door and ran as if the hounds of hell were on my heels. Then I remembered that your house was at the bottom of the hill. I knew Nettie was living here. I prayed someone would be home and thank the good Lord you were.'

Sorcha gave the lass a hug, then found a bannock and some cheese to feed her. She looked half-starved as well as frightened.

'What about McGregor's neighbours? Didn't they come to your aid when you screamed?' asked Nettie indignantly.

Taking the offered bannock and cheese, between mouthfuls Isobel explained. 'Och, aye, but they didn't come in. They just laughed and said it was auld drunk McGregor seeing things again.'

Sorcha shared a look of disgust with Nettie.

'They were probably right. McGregor's too fond of the whisky and anything else he can pour down his throat. He likely meant you no real harm.'

Isobel gave a tremulous smile. 'I ken that now, but when he had me by the neck and was screaming about demons, I thought I was done for.'

Sorcha patted the girl's knee. 'It's over, Isobel. You can stay here with us tonight. I'll not have you walking back through town, not this late.' She thought of Captain Ross and his sword. Where was he when they needed him? He would have put McGregor straight. If only he'd walked through her door at midnight, she'd send him straight up Lady's Wynd to deal with McGregor. Him and his sergeant. She glanced at the door, then at Isobel.

'Isobel,' she asked. 'Why didn't McGregor's neighbours come in and help you? Why'd they stay outside?'

'I suppose it was because the clocks had struck midnight and they didn't want to be a first-footer...' A hand flew to cover her mouth and she leapt to her feet, sending bits of bannock and cheese tumbling to the floor.

Nettie stood slowly, staring in horror at Isobel; Sorcha was looking at Nettie and Isobel was glancing from one to the other muttering, 'I'm sorry, I'm sorry.'

They'd been so wrapped up in remembering, they hadn't heard the bells toll the midnight hour.

Sorcha glanced over to the clock standing on the mantel. Like the mirror, it was covered with a cloth. Time had eluded them.

While a dark-haired male first-footer brought good luck to a household for the new year, a fair-haired woman brought ill-fortune down upon all who dwelled beneath its roof. Sorcha could see disaster and doom writ upon Isobel's features. And upon Nettie's, as she understood the bad omen Isobel represented.

It would not do.

'Sit down, the pair of you,' she said, emphasising her order with her hands. 'It's all superstitious nonsense. First or last foot, it doesn't matter. Stop apologising, Isobel, you've nothing to be sorry about. Put what happened with Mr McGregor behind you, and, like his neighbours, laugh it off. It means nothing and will be forgotten by dawn.

Instead, let's have one last drink to celebrate the new year. You're safe, and that's all that counts. Praise God, we all are.'

Before they could argue, she poured them an ale each and, as they sat in silence either drinking or staring gloomily into their quaichs, she glanced at the covered clock and wondered whether the cold in her bones was because the fire had guttered or if, despite her assurances, it was a premonition of what Isobel's status as a first-footer might mean for her.

Mean for them all.

FIVE

Keep a stoot he'rt tae a stay brae.
(Don't lose heart when faced with a steep slope.)

*I*t was still dark when Sorcha woke in her old bed on the first day of the new year. It was hard to believe that only yesterday she'd been in a little room in her sister's cottage on Laird Browning's estate, dreaming of Pittenweem.

She lay still and listened to the wind howling outside, slapping sheets of rain against the windows and roof. If she concentrated, she could hear her neighbours stirring; the clash of a kettle as it struck the hearth, the squawk of chickens being disturbed, the wail of a babe. The last noise plucked at her heart and she released a soundless sigh.

Beside her, curled into a ball and fast asleep, was Nettie. In the bedroom beyond, Isobel Adam slept. At least, Sorcha hoped she did. The poor thing had taken a while to settle last night. The ale they'd given her and the many reassurances — not only about McGregor, but about being their first-footer — seemed to have done the trick.

Faint but ever-present was the refrain of the ocean. It was calling to her. She shut her eyes and allowed its beguiling song to fill her. God, how she'd missed it.

Nettie stirred, straightening slightly before her knees retreated back towards her chest. She slept like a child, Sorcha thought, envying her. As if she'd not a care in the world, though she knew that wasn't the case. Nettie just buried her worries, as all the fishwives did.

Sorcha supposed she'd have to rise soon, tend the fire, seek out something to break their fast before they headed down to the harbour and a reunion she both longed for and dreaded lest it not meet her expectations — expectations stoked by having Beatrix, Nicolas and Nettie with her last night.

Funny how the fear of being treated as an incomer, as her mor had been, never deserted her. It was only as she grew older and was embraced by the fishwives that she understood her mor had brought her isolation upon herself. Recognising it wasn't simply the Weem folk rejecting her mother, but Astrid herself spurning their attempts to make her one of them, she also understood why Dagny behaved the way she did, why she refused to show an interest in fishing or the tasks the women were expected to master. She was merely imitating their mother. Their poor unhappy mor, who loved their father but never ceased to regret leaving Norway and coming to Scotland, especially once she understood her fisher-husband would leave her for months at a time. Not even her children compensated for his absences, or for what she'd left behind. It didn't matter what they said or did, or how some of the community went out of their way to include her, she refused all overtures and as a consequence earned little but the mutual suspicion and resentment of the Weem women, and many of the men, too. Astrid tried to share this attitude with her daughters, hoping to make them cleave to her, but only Dagny did so. Thank God I did not, thought Sorcha, feeling a rush of first guilt, before it was overcome by a swell of sentiment for the woman beside her.

Sorcha remained where she was, enjoying the warmth and the comfort of having a body next to hers, and reflected on the whispered conversation she and Nettie had shared until well after midnight when they'd finally come to bed. With her face only inches from hers on the pillow, Nettie had asked, 'So, are you all right, hen?'

'Me?' said Sorcha, propping herself up on an elbow and facing her friend, glad the night wasn't to end just yet. 'Of course. Isobel just gave me a fright, that's all. As for what I told you about Dagny and Kennocht, well.' She shrugged. 'What can I do?'

'That's not what I mean.'

Sorcha tried to keep her expression neutral. She'd known what Nettie meant and hoped to deflect her. It hadn't worked.

'You look well,' said Nettie. 'Better than you have for a long time.' She picked up one of Sorcha's long, tawny tresses and twined it around her finger, tugging gently. 'You've roses in your cheeks and your dress doesn't hang off you any more. Seems the countryside agreed with you, even if you didn't agree with it.' She grinned, releasing the strand. 'But I'm not referring to Isobel or your sister and her swither of a man, and you know it. I want to ken how you really feel. In here.' She pressed her hand against Sorcha's heart.

Sorcha curled her hand over Nettie's.

'You won't want to hear this, but you've suffered more than most the last few years — what with your parents, Erik, Robbie going missing and then Andy and the wee bairn being taken.' Nettie gazed into her eyes with such empathy, it took Sorcha's breath away. 'While most will be glad to have you back, there's some will seek to disturb any peace you may have found.' She nodded towards the front door. They both knew to whom she referred.

When Reverend Cowper dared to use the death of her Davan as a warning for all Pittenweem folk who strayed from God's path — as if Sorcha had deliberately done so and brought the consequences upon herself — she couldn't, wouldn't stand for it. No one, not even a man of God, had any right to use her dead son as a lesson — even a godly one, whether it was meant for her alone or not. Anyhow, she knew what Cowper was up to. Had he not told her the day he came to the house after her son died? Others might not have heard what he whispered to her, but she'd never forget. His words were seared in her mind.

Looking for all the world like he was offering comfort, his breath was hot and sour on her face. 'This is God's punishment, Sorcha McIntyre, for failing to do your duty. Like all the fishwives, you be an ungodly woman, one who doesn't ken her place.'

She'd looked long and hard into his pale face with its one sharp and one bleary eye and did the worst thing she could have done: she laughed. Sorcha knew what really drove his rage towards her and it was naught to do with her beliefs or anyone else's. It was because she'd seen what he attempted to do to her mother after her da died. He'd tried to force himself upon Astrid and would have succeeded had Sorcha not discovered what he was about and beaten him hard on the back and shoulders until he drew away and threatened to tell everyone if he so much as glanced at her mor again. She'd only ever told Nettie what had happened, but he didn't know that and foolishly thought if he could control her, quash her spirit, shame and discredit her, his dirty secret would be safe. He wasn't the paragon of virtue he pretended to be but a flawed man with salacious wants.

As she laughed at him, fury had twisted his features and she felt sure he'd been about to strike her, but Nettie had appeared and he'd quickly assumed his other face before walking away.

Unable to lie still any longer, memories prodding her like a hot poker, she quietly rose, pulled the covers back over Nettie and went to the outer room to stoke the fire.

Staring into the smoke and the burning centre of gold as the peat sparked and crackled, she thought back on her family — her brothers, her mor, Dagny, but mostly her father.

She settled back into the armchair that she still considered his and ran her palms along the arms, allowing the action to conjure thoughts of him. Her father was a rare man and not just because he wed outside the Weem. As the owner of a fishing boat, it was unusual for him to also crew. Most owners paid others to do the dangerous work — a pittance at that, the men would grumble. Not her da. Ever since the wars against France and Holland in his father's time had reduced the population of men in Pittenweem to a mere few hundred, never mind the losses sustained during the civil war when entire crews were killed, leaving fishing boats devoid of anyone to work them, he'd known how important it was to keep the fleet going. The days when a dozen vessels would leave the harbour sailing to different parts of Scotland and the northern isles of Europe were long gone, but as far as Charlie

McIntyre was concerned, that didn't give him permission to wait safe at home while others risked their lives. Loved by his men but not the town council — two of the bailies owned the town's remaining ships and were shamed by his courage — when he and his son Erik drowned at sea, there were those who attributed it to the bad luck his incomer wife brought him. The other boat owners took it as a sign to keep their feet dry.

By then, famine, the scourge of the countryside, had swept the coast. It was as if the sea was in sympathy with the land and as the staple crops that sustained the locals died in the ground, so too the sea failed to offer its rich harvest.

Unable to feed what was left of the family — Dagny having long since wed and left — Sorcha's remaining brother, Robbie, knowing how much his mother feared him going to sea, leased their father's boat to a man in Anster Easter and joined the army. Shipped to France, where England had joined her Dutch allies to fight the French, he had written as often as he was able.

When news came that Robbie had been taken prisoner and was most likely dead, her mother completely unravelled. Ignoring her youngest daughter, she took to her bed and never rose again.

The once crowded house was finally empty of all but one: Sorcha. It felt wrong; like a sin she couldn't help committing. Perhaps that was why she married Andrew Watson. She'd been desperate to refill the empty rooms, the vast chamber her heart had become, to replace the bodies and blether she so missed. There was also a part of her anxious not to be excluded, afraid that if she waited too long and remained alone, she'd be regarded as an outcast like her mother. No one could shun her if she wed a Watson, one of the oldest families in the Kingdom of Fife.

She reached for Andrew's pipe, which still rested upon the mantle, and twirled it in her fingers. Funny, she hadn't really thought about him for a long time. A fisherman contracted to a Crail merchant's boat, to her he'd been just another Pittenweem lad, frantic for work, hungry. Set in his ways, a man who bided no deviation from routine, he was like a barnacle that fixed itself to a rock and nothing, not even a gale, could move it. He attached himself to Sorcha whether she wanted him to or not.

Had she ever loved Andy? Not in the way she used to imagine she might love a man, the way a woman would a selkie lover, abandoning kith, kin and her human life for one beneath the waves, a complete and utter sacrifice. Nor was it, she was honest enough to admit, the way he wanted her to love him. Rather, she'd cared about him and loved the way he made her feel. Safe. Not alone. A real part of the Weem. To folk's way of thinking, if a Watson thought her good enough to wed and bed, then perhaps the bad luck her incomer mor had brought hadn't been passed on to her.

Perhaps with her mor's death, they'd whisper, it was over.

They'd been wrong...

As she shook herself out of her reverie, she was surprised to find that morning had broken. Dim light streamed through the windows, illuminating the furniture, the remnants of last night's festivities. The downpour had all but ceased.

A noise made Sorcha turn around, but not before she'd replaced the pipe and dried her eyes with her sleeve.

'You let me sleep when you should have been tossing me out of bed, hen!' exclaimed Nettie, dressed and madly trying to tame her sable hair by tying it under a neepyin. 'Come on, we promised we'd meet the lasses down by the harbour.'

Isobel appeared, rubbing her eyes. 'But it's New Year's Day. The men wouldn't have taken the boats out today, would they?' She yawned and stretched.

'What sort of mad question is that?' asked Nettie.

'One that someone who sews and spins for a living asks,' said Sorcha. 'If there's fish a-biting, then aye, they'll be out. But how about you, lass? Did you sleep all right?'

'I did. Thank you, Sorcha, thanks to both of you.' Isobel rolled her shoulders. 'It's almost as if what happened with Mr McGregor was just a bad dream.'

'That's the way to think about it,' said Sorcha.

'If you really want to show your thanks,' said Nettie, staring in dismay at the unwashed quaichs and the platter where crumbs of cheese and some half-eaten bannocks hardened, 'you can clean up and maybe find something left to bring down to us later.'

About to protest that Isobel could leave it, Sorcha was pushed towards the bedroom. 'Get dressed,' Nettie hissed, throwing clothes at her. She returned to the kitchen. 'If you could do that for us, Isobel, then we'll consider the debt paid.'

Sorcha smiled as she put on her clothes and arranged her hair. Nettie had always been direct.

Within minutes, Sorcha and Nettie were ready to leave. Isobel promised to bring vittles to them as soon as she could.

At the front door Sorcha took a deep breath, releasing it in a stream of white. As they headed down Marygate, Nettie looped her arm through Sorcha's, humming. It was easy to believe she'd never left, Sorcha thought as they strode down the road, dodging puddles and being careful not to slip on the ice that clung to the compacted dirt and stones.

Raising her chin, she studied the cottages as they passed. The houses might be old and worn, harled in grey and brown with more mould growing than the front doors had paint, but they were familiar. She could see the village gossip busy wiping frost from a pane. Mrs Porter dropped her cloth and pressed her face against the glass before disappearing. Sorcha heard her calling out to someone in the house. News of her return hadn't reached everyone, then.

Banks of dirty snow lay against the graveyard wall, resistant to the earlier rains. On the other side of the road a grey-muzzled dog sat outside a front door and raised his head to look at them, considering if they were worth a bark. It was Crabby, so-named because as a pup he was forever chasing crabs along the sand. That was, until one pinched his nose in its claws. Sorcha always used to save some fish for him. The door opened as they passed and a woman waved.

Sorcha waved back. Nettie called out, 'Good morning to you, Mrs Fraser. Happy New Year.'

'And to you, Nettie, and Sorcha. Good to see you again, lass.'

'You too, Mrs Fraser,' said Sorcha. 'I'll be sure to bring some fish for Crabby.'

Moira Fraser smiled and with another wave, shooed the dog inside and shut the door.

Feeling more positive and with a skip in her step, Sorcha urged Nettie to go faster. Lost in her thoughts, as they turned into Cove Wynd she failed to see a dark-robed figure come out of the Tolbooth until they almost collided.

'Watch where you're going,' a voice snapped.

It was Reverend Patrick Cowper. Sorcha stopped in her tracks, forcing Nettie to a halt as well.

The reverend's eyes widened and his mouth thinned. 'So, the rumours are true. It be yourself, Sorcha McIntyre. I thought you were gone till at least summer.'

Caught by surprise, Sorcha felt anger flare at the reverend's tone and her old spirit returned. 'And a happy New Year to you too, reverend.' Her heart beat worse than a drum and heat travelled up her neck. 'Seems I couldn't keep away.'

Nettie released her hold on Sorcha and stepped forward until she was but inches from the minister. They were of a height. 'Aye, reverend,' she said. 'Sorcha's back; praise be to God.' She paused, daring him to say otherwise.

A few people wandering up Cove Wynd from the water slowed to hear the exchange. Still more approached from where they'd been loitering on the High Street and gathered in a large circle, whispering. Among them were bailies Robert Cook and Robert Vernour, members of the town council and Cowper's friends. Cook started and his pale eyes narrowed as he spied Sorcha. He nudged Bailie Vernour in the ribs, bending to whisper in one of the man's rather prominent ears. Before he'd even finished, Vernour turned to leer at her, scratching his receding chin.

A small figure with a large basket over her arm pushed her way through the assembled crowd, shouldering aside whoever stood in her way. It was Janet Cornfoot. Her reputation for a sharp tongue and sharper elbows caused many to give her a wide berth.

'There you be, Sorcha. You too, Nettie,' she called. Ignoring the reverend, Janet barged past and, standing on tiptoe, embraced them both, smiling. When she did, her face transformed, folding into a maze of lines that criss-crossed her cheeks, somehow managing to emphasise the brightness of her mischievous eyes. Sorcha remembered the first time she met her. She'd been a wee lass, no more than four, and Janet had shouted at her for daring to steal an oyster set aside for bait. Instead of doing what most bairns (and grown-ups) did when confronted by an angry Janet Cornfoot, Sorcha had giggled, bit the oyster in half and offered the rest to the woman. 'I'm not stealing,' she'd said. 'I'm sharing.' Janet's eyes had narrowed and then she'd burst out laughing. From that day forward, she became one of Sorcha's, and by extension her family's, staunchest allies.

'Happy New Year,' said Janet warmly. 'Was waiting down by the harbour, wondering where you both had got to and now I know. You were just reacquainting yourself with the good minister.' She acknowledged him briefly.

Reverend Cowper folded his arms and frowned. 'Mrs McIntyre has no need to reacquaint herself with me or anyone in this town, Mrs Cornfoot.' He paused and his eyes travelled over all who stood there. 'We all know a brazen besom when we see one.'

There were gasps. One or two of the women shook their heads. Others lowered their chins. A couple of the men smirked, but no one dared correct him.

Sorcha gave an internal sigh. This is what she feared. 'I hope the year will be a blessed one for you, reverend; for you all,' she added, incorporating everyone. She took a step towards Cowper. 'I'd hoped it being a new year, we'd make a fresh start.'

The reverend's smile widened, as if a prelude to sharing a pleasantry. 'You ken how we can make a fresh start, Sorcha McIntyre, and it has naught to do with a new year.'

Sorcha understood: surrender herself to a man and marry again. Like so many, the reverend couldn't bear to see an independent woman, especially a widow with property. It was an observation he oft shared with his parishioners, even if they didn't all agree. From the looks on the faces of those standing about, many more did than before. The very idea made Sorcha's heart sink, at the same time making her more determined than ever to resist him... Nae, not resist, to prove him wrong.

There was nothing to fear from an independent woman, only a broken one — especially one who'd pieced herself back together.

Satisfied he'd made his point, and pleased Sorcha didn't argue, the reverend raised his voice, addressing the growing assembly. 'Happy New Year to one and all,' he said. The greeting was returned. 'Blessed be those who follow the ways of the Lord, who understand what it is to be a righteous man or woman. They do dwell in His light always.' He lowered his arms and faced Sorcha. 'Make sure you are righteous, Sorcha McIntyre, and that you understand your place. I tell you this as a warning because He and I will be watching and the moment you step from His path, I'll be there to set you aright... After all, we can't afford to lose any more good men... or bairns.'

Sorcha bit her tongue and forced herself to appear impassive as a storm raged in her chest.

Upon receiving no visible reaction, the reverend tore his eyes from her and regarded Nettie and Janet. 'That goes for both of you, too.'

Without another word, he swept past them towards the High Street. With some muttering and backward glances, the bailies and a few others followed.

Janet Cornfoot made a sign at his back with her fingers. 'What an auld clash-bag.'

'Don't let him or any of his followers see you doing that,' said Nettie sharply, slapping Janet's hands.

'Och, he be a whillywha. Nothing to worry about.'

'I'm not so sure,' said Nettie quietly.

Sorcha looked at her friends, then the reverend. 'Me either.'

Once he was out of sight, a few folk came forward to welcome Sorcha home and ask after Dagny. For all that Sorcha was touched by their words, it was obvious they feared to show her friendship before the reverend. She may have been gone for months, but the man held great sway in the village.

He also held a grudge.

Sensing her thoughts, Nettie gave her a nudge. 'Come along. We've fish to gut.' She dragged her away, Janet trotting by their side.

It was only as they passed the kirk that Sorcha saw someone else who'd been watching and listening from the opposite side of the wynd.

Captain Ross lifted his hat and gave her a half bow. As their eyes locked, she saw something in them that both disturbed her and made her mind gallop. Black as coal, within his gaze was a mixture of anger and defiance. Whether directed towards her or the reverend's words, she wasn't sure. But her heart pulsed in the most peculiar way. She lowered her head, hoping he didn't see the colour that filled her cheeks. When she raised a hand to return his courtesy and wish him a happy New Year, he'd gone.

She wanted to ask Nettie if she'd seen him, but the question was soon forgotten as they reached the East Shore. She halted where the wynd met the water. The Firth of Forth opened before her, the heaving seas and jagged coastline running as far as the eye could see. To the east, she could make out the colourful houses of Anster and its long harbour wall. To the west, the land cut away up to St Monan's, the steeple of its church rising above the braes. Out on the silver expanse, waves tossed the few clinker boats. She could see nets and lines cast, the men constantly moving shapes upon the decks. The wind was strong and icy, sharp fingers prodding and poking her face, making her eyes water and her breathing sharp. It caught her skirt, tried to tear the neepyin from her head. Shutting her eyes, Sorcha immersed herself in the moment, resting her head briefly on Nettie's shoulder, unaware of the whimsical smile Nettie and Janet shared. They understood how she felt.

It was only after they'd walked a distance, chins tucked into chests against the wind, that Sorcha heard voices. Coming towards them through the fine veil of sea spray was a group of fishwives.

Upon sighting Sorcha, the women let out a scream that made the dog on the harbour wall leap to his feet and release a volley of barks. The children playing with a hoop darted for the protection of their mothers and the men sitting on their stoops smoking pipes jumped up before shaking their heads in jovial disapproval.

'Sorcha!' the women shouted.

'If it ain't young McIntyre herself!'

'Come to speir the guts oot o' us again, chick? Drive us to distraction with questions like ye did as a wee one?'

'Where've you been? There be fish to sort, lass!'

Sorcha's heart soared. There was Jean Durkie, Lillie Wallace, Therese Larnarch, and again, Nicolas Lawson, all of whom she'd worked alongside since she was a bairn. With them was Beatrix, who so often left her spinning to come and gossip at the seafront. These were the women who had stood by her as they had each other through so many deaths and the grief that followed. The women who, like Nettie and Janet, had pleaded with her not to go when Dagny begged her to.

How she wished she'd listened.

Only now they were here, she was able to forget Dagny's cruel words, the soldiers of last night, even the reverend, and relish this very morning. With a shining face she turned to Nettie, who gave her a shove.

Uncaring how she appeared, Sorcha lifted her skirts and with wild, happy whoops ran as if she were a bairn and not a fishwife or a widow, tears streaming down her cheeks. Catapulting herself forwards, she was caught and folded into strong arms, before being twirled about and showered with laughter and kisses.

A slight distance away, two men watched the reunion with very different reactions. From the bottom of Cove Wynd, Captain Ross saw how Sorcha was greeted and was unable to prevent the smile that split his face.

In the shadows further away, at the corner of Water Wynd, the reverend witnessed how the women careened around, unconcerned by the spectacle they created, their ungodly shrieks echoing as if they were witches in some devil-spawned coven.

And standing in the centre, whipping them into a frenzy that had no place on the streets of his quiet village, was none other than Sorcha McIntyre.

SIX

Speirin' makes ye wyce.
(You'll never know if you don't ask.)

Just over a week later, Sorcha was wearily wandering back from Ninian Fields. She'd sold the last of the fish in her creel to Mrs Oliver at the farmhouse, and stayed to enjoy a dram with the lonely widow. Before she went away to St Andrew's, she'd surrendered her usual customers to Nettie, Nicolas, and the others. Though Nettie had offered to return them, Sorcha refused, content to roam the countryside seeking folk to buy her fish. But it also meant she had to walk further to find them. It hadn't been as hard as she feared. Before long there'd be some people in town willing to buy from her as well. Till then, she'd make do; after all, she was in the enviable position of having the monies from the *Mistral* to tide her over.

As her boots crunched through the thin covering of snow, she passed a herd of cows studiously indifferent to the honking geese in their midst. Like her, they were enjoying the weak afternoon sun. There would be rain again tonight, she thought, glancing at the sky, noting how the low-slung bank of clouds on the horizon were becoming darker and more menacing. Likely there'd be the thick fog of a

hoar as well. Quickening her step, she avoided a puddle, glad she'd
left her skirt tucked into her waistband so it didn't trail in the slunks.

If you didn't count the cows or the geese or even the sweet-faced
sheep chewing on a patch of grass they'd managed to uncover, there
was not a soul in sight. All she could see was the lapper of filthy snow
pushed to the sides of the well-trodden track punctuated by deep ruts
where carts had rumbled. Amid the fields, skeletal trees wrestled with
the sky. Occasionally she'd see a cottage peeking above the scrappy
hedgerows and dilapidated fences, coughing smoke and reminding
her that folk weren't that far away. Further ahead, the vast expanse of
water glimmered. She began to think of what she might prepare for
dinner, or whether Nettie had made a start. Thoughts of her friend
lifted her spirits. Deciding Sorcha needed her more than her husband
did, Nettie had told Thom she was remaining with Sorcha for the
foreseeable future. Grateful for her presence, Sorcha had worried what
Thom might think until he appeared at her door just the other day.
He'd wrapped his arms around Nettie, beaming while he kissed his
wife soundly on the mouth, and gave them his blessing. After all, it
wasn't uncommon for Nettie to live parts of the year in Anster, staying with her married daughter and keeping an eye on her house there
which she leased out, only staying the odd night with Thom in the
Weem. As the reverend would oft ask, what sort of wife lived apart
from her husband? It wasn't natural. Mind you, it didn't take much
to earn the reverend's disapproval, especially if you were a fishwife.
Grimacing, she pushed thoughts of the reverend aside and focussed
on her friends instead.

Welcomed warmly her first day back, Sorcha had been carried to the
harbour on a current of goodwill. She recalled how they'd all talked over
the top of each other, keen to share their news, eager to hear hers. It was
easy to forget there were those who weren't as happy to see her, blaming
her as they did for Andy's death and James Crawford's. They watched
her the way one might a stalking cat, to see which way it would pounce.

Much to her relief, by the third day Sorcha was again part of the
regular grind. The routine was a great comfort, the way her hands

didn't need to be coached and her mind could dwell on other things while she worked. Able to shuck off most of the guilt about her sister and Kennocht and push away the renewed pain of losing Davan by sorting and gutting the catch and working the creels, she was paying her dues, making peace with herself and with her dead. With the sea that both gave and took so much.

Lost in her reverie, it took Sorcha a moment to register that a horse and rider had come up behind her. She spun around and was astonished to see Captain Ross.

'You have an uncanny way of sneaking up on folk,' she said, immediately regretting her tone.

'I did hail you, Mrs McIntyre,' said the captain apologetically, walking the horse forward till it was level with her and touching his hat. 'I'm sorry. Wasn't my intention to scare you.'

Sorcha looked up at him. It appeared he'd been on a long ride. Not only was the mare splattered with mud, but his breeches and boots were as well. His riding cape had received a soaking then dried. His dark hair had mostly escaped the ribbon at his nape and his black eyes, despite appearing tired, managed a twinkle. Seeing it, Sorcha felt guilty.

'Nae,' she said quickly. 'It's me who should be sorry. I was unforgivably rude. I was all dwamish and you startled me.' She brushed his leg lightly with her fingers, aware of the firmness beneath the smooth fabric, then withdrew her hand swiftly, aware the gesture could be misread.

His eyes darkened. 'Considering we're both so full of apologies, would you allow me to escort you back home so at the least we've time to offer them properly?'

Sorcha laughed. As much as she enjoyed being alone, some company would be nice. 'That would be most gracious of you, sir. But only if you promise not to say sorry again.'

The captain grinned. 'Only if I can extract the same promise from you.'

'Done,' said Sorcha.

He dismounted and offered to take the creel strapped across her shoulders, but Sorcha refused. She'd not carried one for so long, it was reassuring to wear it again.

They walked in peace a while. In the distance, shouts came from the men labouring in the fields. A donkey brayed nearby. She could hear the captain's breathing, smell the musky odour of his clothes, of him. It was pleasant. More than pleasant. It made her think of rolling seas, the earthy scent of peat smoking.

'That's a fine ride you have there, Captain Ross,' said Sorcha finally, flashing an admiring glance at his horse. 'What's her name?'

'Liath,' said the captain, patting her neck. The horse shuddered in pleasure.

Sorcha nodded appreciatively. Well, what else would you call a grey horse, but grey?

'Not very imaginative, is it?' dimpled the captain. 'I should have called her spirit or ghost, or something with an uncanny ring.'

'I think Liath suits her fine, doesn't it, girl?' said Sorcha, leaning across to stroke the horse's withers.

They fell into comfortable silence once more.

All too soon for Sorcha's liking, the walls of the town loomed, the red rooftops of the nearest cottages peeping above them. Built on the rise, these houses had views of the entire Forth. Sorcha inwardly sighed. She'd so much she wanted to ask the captain — about himself, about soldiering, and here was her chance. The way to get people to reveal aspects of themselves was to offer the same. What did she do? Waste the opportunity.

As if reading her thoughts, the captain spoke. 'Do you mind if I ask you something, Mrs McIntyre?'

Sorcha gave a flourish of her hand. 'Be my guest.'

'Why did you leave town? Seems to me when folk do, they rarely come back. But you did.'

Throwing caution to the wind, Sorcha began to talk, telling him about Dagny's invitation, which led to her explaining about her mother, father and brothers as well. She even told him about Andy. Of Davan and the reason she left Dagny's she made no mention. When she'd finished, they'd breached the walls and reached the corner of Charles and James Streets. The captain had been a good listener. It was only as they nodded greetings to Mr Walker coming out of his cottage, an axe across his shoulders, his dog bounding at his heels, that the captain commented.

'I'm sorry for your losses, Mrs McIntyre.' He shook his head. 'Such inadequate words, but I don't ken what else to say.' The captain cleared his throat. 'I'd heard why you left, truth be told. There's not much you don't glean in the Weem.' His mouth curved in a smile that could have been mistaken for a grimace, but disappeared before she could tell. 'But I wanted to hear it from you. The fishing life is a hard one, but it seems to me you've had it harder than most.'

How curious, thought Sorcha, that was what Nettie said too. A wave of self-pity rose and she felt ashamed of herself for it. There had been enough of that over the years to fill a harbour's worth of creels and, anyway, wasn't she alive? Aye, she'd no father, mother, brothers any more, no husband or son, and even her sister was dead to her — well, she was to Dagny. But didn't that mean she owed it to each and every one of those no longer here to live?

Unaware she'd said this last bit out loud, it wasn't until the captain stopped and stared at her, that she understood she had. Red-faced, she found her feet very interesting. 'That must make me sound so selfish,' she said quietly.

'Selfish?' scoffed the captain. Catching her unawares, he took her chin gently in his hand. His fingers were rough, well-used. A shiver of pleasure ran over Sorcha and she prayed he hadn't felt it. Her cheeks began to burn and it was all she could do to resist pulling away. 'I would have said sensible, myself,' he said softly. The last of the light burned in the stygian depths of his eyes, mesmerising her. With eyes that black, how could you ever tell what he was really thinking? 'You're right, lass.' His fingers fell away. 'We owe it to the dead to live.'

Sorcha's stomach flipped. 'You've lost people too?'

They began walking again, Liath's hooves resounding on the road. Candlelight flickered in windows as they passed, folk appearing out of the tight alleys and wynds, raising hats, brushing past them, offering a good evening. Most carried baskets or sacks, some bottles of ale; a few pushed barrows. All looked eager for home and a warm fire. From inside the cottages came the rattle of pots, raised voices, someone singing.

Waiting until they were alone, the captain answered. 'Aye. My brother and two uncles. They died in battle. Then there was...' He swallowed and gave a slight shake of his head. 'Was a long time ago.'

Sorcha felt the pain of his words. Of what he omitted. She wondered who else he'd lost but didn't feel she had the right to ask. 'I'm so sorry.'

'Me too. Their bodies are buried over there, on foreign soil.' He jerked his head towards the Forth.

An image of Robbie laughing, his golden curls batting his cheeks as he baited a line flew into her head. 'Are you sure they're dead?'

The captain frowned. 'I'm sure. But why do you ask?'

'When I told you about my brothers... it's not the whole story.' She felt him studying her. 'Robbie, the one who's two years older than me, he went to fight with the Duke of Marlborough's men in Flanders, then Kaiserswerth. First, we were told the Bavarians had taken him prisoner, then it was the French. We never really knew — mor, Dagny and I. After my mother died, I never heard anything. Now, I doubt I ever will.'

Captain Ross gave her an inscrutable look. 'Marlborough, eh? I fought under him once as well. A good soldier, fierce.'

Sorcha didn't reply. Fierce or not made no difference to her.

'If your brother fought at Kaiserswerth, he could well have been taken by the French. Many were. An exchange was done.'

Sorcha looked at him hopefully. 'You know something about it?'

'Not really. But I know someone who might. I can make enquiries if you like. Find out what I can from my superiors in Edinburgh.'

Sorcha's heart filled and she resisted the urge to throw her arms around him. Instead, she took a deep breath and tried not to get her hopes up. She gave him her warmest smile. 'Captain... To learn anything of Robbie's fate... well, it would be... it would be...'

'Living.'

'Aye,' she smiled, grateful he understood. 'It would be living.'

'Consider it done, then.' He held her eyes for a beat then kept walking. 'You ken,' he said, after they'd gone a few more paces, 'there's those who believe Marlborough's really a Jacobite.'

Sorcha gave a little snort. 'I heard that the man changes his cloth to suit his fortunes.'

The captain chuckled. 'Just as well, as they change often.'

It was well known that the duke had served under five different monarchs, shifting from being a staunch supporter of the Stuart scions to William of Orange and back again. Under the current queen, Anne, old King James's daughter, he'd made his name and fame, leading her armies across the continent the last few years. Not that the duke's fine reputation had protected either the captain's family or hers.

'Sometimes,' said the captain, 'changing so as to blend in, so you don't arouse suspicion, is the only way a man can truly work for what he believes in. What he knows is right.'

Before she could ask what he meant by that — and wondering, fleetingly, if Captain Ross was alluding to himself, and what that might signify — they stopped again. Sorcha was astonished to see they were outside her house. Was he someone worthy of her trust? Or was he simply suggesting that he too, like most of the Weem, and despite fighting in the Queen's army, was a Jacobite? Why did it even matter to her?

Annoyed that she was so curious about this incomer, while at the same time acknowledging she wanted her interest sated, she noticed the glimmer had all but gone and the sky was a shifting mass of dark, bruised clouds. It began to spitter; a fine rain that rested upon their clothes and hair.

Sorcha unstrapped her creel and placed it at her feet. 'Thank you for bringing me home, captain.'

'It's been my pleasure, Mrs McIntyre,' he said and reached for her hand, but instead of kissing it (for which she was grateful, as she knew her fingers smelled of fish), he bowed over it.

She dropped a little curtsey and opened the door to reveal Nettie kneeling before the fire burning in the hearth. Scrambling to her feet, Nettie went to take the creel, but when she caught sight of the captain, she retreated into the shadows behind the door.

Suddenly self-conscious as she stared at the captain, wishing she had a nicer skirt, cleaner hands and face, that her hair wasn't so windblown around her neepyin, Sorcha wasn't sure what to say.

'If ever you need anything,' said the captain softly, 'anything at all, you've only to ask.' With a last touch of his hat, he spun on his heel and mounted his horse. He made a light clicking sound in his throat, and rode off down the cobbles.

Sorcha watched him from the doorway, oblivious to the rain that had begun to fall. 'Thank you,' she whispered, her heart pounding, her skin hot.

It wasn't until another voice whispered in her ear that she tore her eyes away. 'I ken what I'd ask for,' said Nettie, jerking her chin towards the captain's broad swaying back, nudging Sorcha in the ribs. 'And it's not something I can repeat out here…'

With a wicked laugh Nettie dragged her friend out of the wet and shut the door.

SEVEN

Ca' me what ye like but pinnae ca' me ower.
(Call me any names you like, but don't knock me over.)

Mid-winter arrived, announcing itself in bitter squalls, blashes of rain, roiling fogs and churning seas. Snow fell heavily, coating the cottages and the seafront. A crust of ice formed along the shore, a heaving barrier that sounded like an old man fighting for breath as it crackled and moaned. Out towards the Isle of May the waves were savage, their foam rising high above the rocky crags. The wheeling birds kept their distance. Still the fishermen would take their boats out most days, their wives or another willing female carrying them on their backs, wading through the floating ice to deposit them into the prancing craft. Once aboard, the men would tuck their flannel shirts, their serks, into their thick trousers before scrabbling into their gairnsey jerseys and donning long, thick coats. Some wore hand-knitted grauvits around their necks, tokens from loved ones that also kept them warm.

Each morning the fishwives would rise before dawn and walk to the harbour, creels laden with their tools strapped to their shoulders. The smell of salt, seaweed and the fresh crispness of freezing air and threatening snow was invigorating.

The fishwives were both loathed and loved. Unlike regular wives and other women, fishwives had a freedom the others could only dream about. Mainly single women and widows, those who were married surrendered their husbands to the boats and ships. Some only for the day, others for longer periods, often farewelling their men for weeks if not months. Left to their own devices, they were beholden only to themselves, the sea and its laws. Rumours and gossip surrounded all the women — from whose bed they were sharing to how recklessly they spent their hard-earned coin. Most of it was untrue and much of it vicious, but that didn't stop folk believing it.

Yet without the fishwives and the work they did, which fed the villagers and kept money in the council coffers, Pittenweem — and the villages beyond that also needed their services — would grind to a halt and all knew it. None more so than the fishwives themselves, who basked in the liberties they could take. Wilfully ignoring the social niceties governing the behaviour of women, refusing to be inhibited by the gossip and slander, they paraded about the streets in groups, chattering loudly, chuckling often, offering their opinions, back-chatting their betters, constantly telling the men what to do. The fishermen, understanding their worth, adored them and sought wives among them; the townsfolk mostly tolerated their presence, even if many lasses secretly longed to be one of them.

Yet to Reverend Patrick Cowper, the fishwives represented everything he disapproved of: loud, godless women, women either without men to control them, teach them how to behave and keep them tamed and quiet or refusing to accept their rightful ascendancy. That they were able to earn their keep and, in Nettie's and Sorcha's cases, had means and property besides, only added to their sins. They troubled him deeply, these wicked women. And now Sorcha McIntyre, the luminous-eyed beauty, was back among them.

Standing on the western braes, trying to disregard the freezing sleet piercing his exposed flesh, the reverend pulled his coat closer, screwed up his eyes and attempted to find her among the women and children working along the harbour. The smell of seaweed, fish and the decaying carcass of a seal that had washed up on the rocks below reached him.

He wondered how the women could bear working in such conditions — the stench, the cold, the wet. And then there was the endless cawing of the birds, their constant nagging as they hovered above or skipped along the ground as close as they dared in an effort to steal food.

He could see Janet White, the one they called Nettie Horseburgh, a woman who appeared respectable with her mariner husband, even if, unnatural woman that she was, she didn't dwell under the same roof as him. When Patrick first arrived in Pittenweem twelve years ago, his predecessor, Andrew Bruce, had warned him about the Horseburgh woman, saying she was nothing but trouble. Before Patrick's time, one of the former bailies, Alexander Griege, named her a witch over her refusal to concede seats in the kirk. What did the hizzie do? Brought a charge of slander against the man. Nothing ever came of what was said about her, except in the way that bad fame attends a person. Unafraid of men in power, she took them on regardless of the consequences.

Same with that auld crone, Janet Cornfoot. Now there was a contermashus woman if ever there was one. Known for threatening those who disagreed with her and working charms, most, including Patrick, gave her a wide berth. There she was, over by the harbour wall, clecking away to the Lawson lass — what was her name again? Nicolas? Aye, that was it. Wasn't enough being a fishwife, she also fancied herself a healer with her potions and lotions. Folk would go to her for medick instead of the local doctor. It wasn't right. None of those women were right, Patrick felt it in his bones.

It couldn't be a coincidence that all three carried the taint of witchcraft; nor, he was convinced, was it a coincidence they were friends with Sorcha McIntyre. Why even Mrs Lawson, though she was married to a farmer and worked the land during summer and the autumn harvest, still came to the foreshore most days to help with the drave. Raised to do the work, she declared it was in her blood; a calling she'd no choice but to answer. It was what they all said, these women of the sea. Coming from the countryside himself, the reverend couldn't understand it. Och, he enjoyed the sight of the ocean, the waves and birds that circled endlessly above. He even liked the seals that bobbed in the waters around the harbour. But to claim the sea was a part of you? A calling you couldn't ignore? It wasn't natural. Only God could call to a person and expect an answer. God and the Queen. To listen to anything or anyone else was blasphemy, heathen; bewitchment by any other name, surely. All the same, he ensured he at least gave the appearance of abiding by the laws of the sea and encouraged others to do the same. He feared if he didn't, he'd be treated as the incomer he was. Where would his authority be then? How could he hope to maintain order within the community, let alone among these women, if he didn't at the very least act as if he believed in the curious ways of the locals?

Just as he was about to make his way back to town, the reverend spied Sorcha. She hadn't been among those sorting and gutting but had accompanied a group of children collecting bait along the skerries for the next day's fishing. He watched as she appeared directly below him, walking across the sand, a wide basket pressed against her hip, leaning the opposite way to keep it in place. Her long hair blew in the wind, a mass of tangled curls that teased her swaying hips. The children not old enough to carry buckets danced about her, one walking backwards in front, holding up something to show her.

She could be the child's mother, someone's wife, only she wasn't. Stubborn, the woman refused to contemplate remarrying — even when a perfectly respectable suitor was found — going so far as to leave the village. Good riddance, he'd thought. One less wanton to worry about. But what does the lass do? Returns. Bolder and, he had to admit looking at her now, more tempting than ever. Now she was back, she posed an even greater threat to the village's peace of mind — to his, too — than when she first became widowed.

No matter what it took, he would bring Sorcha McIntyre to heel. Since she chose to remain, he would see her safely wed. If not to his eldest, then to someone he considered enlightened enough to take his advice on how to handle her. Only with a husband to answer to would she cease to disturb him; to pose a risk to his reputation — to the other menfolk, he corrected himself. Aye, that's what he must turn his attention to, he thought, as he took the path that ran along the top of the braes, descending towards the High Street. He would put his mind to how to tame Sorcha McIntyre. Her and the rest of the fishwives.

And if he couldn't fathom how to do it, he knew in his soul God would show him the way.

EIGHT

Garred dress is ill tae grow.
(Trying to force someone against her will is rarely successful.)

*B*eing able to resume her old work, including the running of her boat, meant Sorcha was busy. In consultation with the captain of the *Mistral*, Cameron McDougall, an experienced seaman from Anster whom she had hired to command the vessel, they decided to send it up to Inverness and then, if the seas allowed, on to Stornoway again. It was dangerous, but when the only option was to starve, they didn't have much choice but to brave the North Sea. The lease arrangement Robbie had entered into ended when they learned of his capture, so it was Sorcha's responsibility to pay the crew what she could from the profits, which they in turn gave to their families. The rest she spent on resupplying the boat and repairing the sails, but even then, it wasn't enough. Captain McDougall would have to use the additional funds she gave him to purchase extra stores en route.

When she wasn't dealing with matters pertaining to her boat, Sorcha was with the fishwives at the harbour. Working in groups of three, the women would bait the lines, some holding up to fifteen hundred hooks. After these were stored on board the inshore boats and the men were carried out and rowed away to loud farewells and wishes for a good and safe catch, the fishwives would turn their hands to first mending the nets from the previous day's catch, then fakin' them — folding them in a to and fro manner so they ran smoothly from the deck once the boats were out in the ocean.

The children were responsible for collecting bait in the shallows and among the rocks, usually mussels, which they either shieled or put in a scaup — a shallow rock pool where they could remain fresh until such time as they were needed. With their buckets they gathered cockles and other sea creatures for their own tables, sharing what they found. If the weather held, the more experienced fishwives, Sorcha among them, would collect salt and place it in barrels, ready for the fish on the men's return. The cloots, the strips of fabric they wrapped around their fingers, offered some protection from the cuts of the sharp fins, the swift action of the knives, and the sting of the salt. It had taken three nicks of the knife before Sorcha found her old rhythm. Once the fish were prepared and ready for sale, the women would load their creels and head off into town or along the coast or even inland to nearby farms to sell whatever they could. It made for long days, but also a good night's rest. Something that, until she returned to Pittenweem, had eluded Sorcha ever since Davan died.

As the weeks flew by, the foreboding she had felt the night Isobel Adam bowled into her house came to nothing. In fact, on New Year's Day there'd been many fisherfolk, shopkeepers and villagers having a good laugh about what happened to the young seamstress, the gossip having spread as it was wont to do. It was dismissed in exactly the manner Nettie and Sorcha had: all due to McGregor being in his cups.

No great doom had befallen Sorcha and, as spring approached and people flooded into town for the twice-weekly markets, buying fish from her as easily as they did from any other vendor, she was able to mock her foolishness. She'd allowed the superstitions and malice of old to affect her. It was what Pittenweem did, cast a spell that made you view the world and those within it in a different way. It was easy to forget what had befallen her when she was with the fishwives, especially those she counted as friends. Doing her best to avoid those who weren't, it was only on Sundays, when almost all the village went to the kirk, that she was forced to confront them and listen to sermons intended to shame her and any other fishwives who didn't conform: those who remained single, working hard to earn coin, raise their families — with or without husbands — and contribute to the town. None of that seemed to matter under the self-righteous stares of those who hung on Cowper's every word — words he claimed over and over were God's.

'I think the reverend forgets God always said blessed are the weak, and what are we women if not weak in His and Cowper's eyes?' Janet whispered loudly as they stood in the kirkyard one Sunday after a particularly long delivery, rocking from foot to foot to stave off the cold.

'It's the meek and Jesus said it,' corrected Sorcha wryly, sharing a smile with Captain Ross who was standing close enough to overhear.

'Aye, well, meek and weak, that's me,' said Janet. 'Praise be to God.'

They all burst into laughter, earning wrathful looks from first the Crawfords then the Cooks, Cleilands and Vernours — the families of the town bailies — as well as getting a dire stare from Cowper. The last thing Janet could ever be considered was weak, let alone meek.

Uncaring of the opprobrium they'd attracted, the women went back to Sorcha's cottage for a meal, joined by Beatrix and Isobel Adam.

And so the days melded into each other like a gentle roiling mist and Sorcha's nightmares dimmed. The memories the cottage held ceased to scorch her each time they intruded, retreating into a fuzzy warmth that was more akin to basking under the sun in a yellow-flowered field. She could finally touch them without getting burned.

When poor Margie Strang, the young wife of one of the fishermen, was attacked by a soldier in the streets after dark, it was Sorcha who brought the deed to the attention of Captain Ross and demanded redress.

Though the accused soldier denied Margie's accusations, the captain upheld her version of events and the man was sent to Edinburgh for trial. Weeks later they learned he'd been transported.

There were many among the fisherfolk who were grateful to Sorcha for what she did, and many said that without her intervention, speaking directly to the captain, justice would never have been served. Most ignored the blether that went around afterwards about the real reason the captain had listened. Sorcha McIntyre might be many things, folk would whisper, but a whore she wasn't.

Aware of the rumours swirling around about her and the captain, Sorcha reasoned this was why he was foremost in her thoughts most days. Much to her bemusement, rarely did a day go by when she didn't see Captain Ross. He would oft stir from the house where he was billeted — a large one on the Eastern Shore close to Nettie's husband's and owned by the collier, Malcolm Moray — as the fishwives made their way to the pier each morning. Standing on the stoop, he would greet the women and flash a smile. Arms folded, he'd watch them through a cloud of tobacco smoke. After he appeared several days in a row, Nettie whispered to Sorcha, 'He's only started doing that since you came back, you ken. More so since the bad business with Margie.'

Sorcha did know. She just didn't want to think about what it might mean. Yet, she did. In fact, Captain Ross began to occupy the space in her thoughts once taken up by the other men in her life: her da, her brothers, Andy and Kennocht. For all she tried to prevent his intrusion, thinking about the captain, who was neither dead nor an unwelcome memory, wasn't an unpleasant way to witter away time. She wondered if he missed his home on Skye and what he really thought of the Weem. One day when the chance arose, she might even ask him. The very idea made her blood sing. It wouldn't be that difficult either. Ever since that day he'd escorted her back into town and then, a few weeks later, helped bring the culprit who hurt Margie to justice, they'd taken to meeting. At first Sorcha thought it was a happy accident that he'd appear just when she was walking back from the harbour after she'd finished sorting the catch, or returning from Anster way with an empty creel. Sometimes she was with another fish-wife, but more often she was by herself. They would fall into step and talk as if they'd known each other for years rather than being recent acquaintances.

She learned he'd been stationed in Pittenweem eight months, having arrived not long after she left last summer. He didn't expect to be there much longer, what with the war escalating, and was merely waiting to be sent to join the Duke of Marlborough's men. The idea he might be leaving soon affected Sorcha more than she had a right to be. She convinced herself it was because he really did protect the Weem women. How could they be assured the officer who took his place would be so solicitous?

When on two occasions he was riding the back roads as she was returning from the farms over St Monan's way, she began to think it was more than a coincidence. What reason would he have to be visiting St Monan's? She didn't have the courage to ask — not about that — though she did ask about her brother.

'I hate to bother you, Captain Ross,' she began one day, 'but did you get a chance to ask your superiors about my Robbie?'

It was a drackie afternoon and the combination of fog and low clouds made the day dim early. Shivering as a frigid wind snatched at her cloak and bit her exposed skin, she raised her face to his.

'I wrote the day you asked, Mrs McIntyre. Alas, I've heard naught. Not that it means anything,' he added quickly, seeing her disappointment. 'It takes a long while for letters, let alone information, to arrive. War disrupts everything. But I ask you not to lose heart.'

Grateful for his efforts, she made a solemn promise she would do her best not to relinquish hope.

Once, when they were walking back from Anster way and the weather closed in, he lifted her onto his horse so they could reach their destination faster. Pressing herself against his back, her hands around his waist, she'd enjoyed the feel and smell of him, conscious of her breasts squashed against his coat, her inner thighs moving against him. She was aware of the way the muscles in his back responded to the movement of his arms, how his legs looked so very fine in their tight breeches where they rubbed against her skirts. That day, the wind blew against them, unravelling Sorcha's hair so it alternated between whipping and embracing them.

When Captain Ross deposited her at the door to her cottage that day, she was tempted to invite him inside, only she knew she'd never hear the end of it from Nettie or from Reverend Cowper, whom she'd seen lurking in the graveyard as they rode past. Reverend Cowper would ensure the villagers knew and the type of gossip that would attend her would be worse than ever. Instead, she made a show of saying goodbye, being sure to thank him prettily in a voice that carried.

Why she cared, she wasn't sure, only she did. She didn't want the captain, or their burgeoning friendship, tarnished.

That night, a pair of jet-black eyes and a dimpled grin disturbed her sleep, as did the memory of a pair of strong thighs and arms and the sensations they aroused.

After that, not only would Captain Ross wait for Sorcha and the fishwives to pass by each morning, sometimes she'd see him atop the western braes observing them at work on the sand or fossicking among the skerries. It was the same place she sometimes saw the reverend, only, unlike Reverend Cowper, who would move away as soon as he was certain he'd been seen, the captain would remain, uncaring, bold as you like. She took comfort from his presence.

She even saw the captain leading his men in a march down the High Street one afternoon. As she hurried out of a shop, he'd doffed his hat.

'Mrs McIntyre,' he called above the stomp of boots and clop of his horse's hooves.

Folk turned at the sound of his voice, noting with great interest who he was hailing.

'Captain Ross,' she replied formally, uncaring of the stares and whispers as his men moved in formation towards the sea, their muskets slung over their shoulders, their chins held high. He looked so grand, so in command riding beside his men; a fine figure in his uniform, even if it had seen better days. Aye, it was just as Nettie said, Captain Ross had brought order to the soldiers and to Pittenweem. What Nettie didn't know was the disorder he'd brought to Sorcha's mind.

NINE

You'll get the claw.
(You'll get punished.)

As she arrived at the shore with Nettie and Janet early one morning in March, Sorcha paused where the harbour wall met the ocean.
Salt spray kissed her face, the tang of seaweed made her nose twitch,
and the ballet of gulls on the thermals delighted her eyes; the cries of
the terns and shearwaters, and the steady sucking of the tides, were
a welcome chorale. It was hard to credit that over two months had
passed since she'd returned. Behind her, women were busy drying the
wives who'd carried the men out to the boats. Wet stockings were
held before a fire as they all downed a dram or two before starting
work.

Sorcha left her friends to help the other wives and jumped off the
harbour wall and wandered along the shore. She headed towards
the skerries, kicking the occasional rock, throwing up the coarse sand
with the toes of her boots. With the arrival of spring, the snow was
gradually ceding to frost and sea-driven fogs, even allowing the sun its
brief moment on the stage. Today, the sun had no such impediments
and tentative fingers yearned across the heaving Forth to bathe her with
their warmth, a warmth that didn't reach her insides. Damn Captain

Ross. Just when she'd started to think he was different to other men, he acted in a manner that turned all her feelings into a maelstrom.

She picked up a pebble, weighing it in her palm, and flung it as far out to sea as she could. She watched the splash it made without satisfaction. Why did she care so much? Why did her chest feel so heavy and her eyes burn? It was because of what had happened to Bel — Isobel Courie.

Bel was a single woman about whom the reverend had spoken in harsh terms due to her predilection for the soldiers stationed about the town. A week ago, Bel had told Sorcha and Nettie she was pregnant. Worse, it turned out the father of her unborn bairn was a Corporal Robert Varner who, she'd just learned, was already married. Sorcha wasted no time seeking out the captain and encouraged Bel to confess all to him.

Expecting the corporal to be punished for using and abusing Bel, Sorcha discovered that far from disciplining the man, Captain Ross, on the advice of the kirk, sent him away. Robert Varner was rowed out to a man-o'-war late one night, never to be seen again. Furious at what she saw as his lack of accountability, last night Sorcha had marched straight to where Captain Ross was staying. She felt she owed it to Bel to say something. Anyway, hadn't the captain told her she could ask him anything? In her mind that included telling him things as well — including things he mightn't be so inclined to hear.

Much to her chagrin, he was more amused by her anger than apologetic.

Invited to step inside, she'd refused to move beyond the entry hall. He waited till she'd spent her fury before he responded.

'Mrs McIntyre, I assure you, Isobel Courie is much better off without the likes of Corporal Varner in her life.'

'Easy for you to say,' snapped Sorcha, 'being a man. You no more care about a woman without a husband, without a father for her bairn, never mind means of support, than you do where you put your quhillylillie.' She flicked her hand in the direction of his groin.

Appalled that her tongue had run away with her and she could speak to him using such language, her face coloured. It didn't help that what she said was true. Kennocht and so many other men of her acquaintance were living proof — men who were ruled by their cocks. Her hands curled into fists by her side.

Aware the owners of the cottage and their servants were likely listening, she lowered her voice. 'How will Bel manage? The man should have been made to own his mistakes.'

She waited.

'One cannot force a person to own anything, madam,' said Captain Ross dryly. 'Much less what you consider a mistake. It's hard to credit now, but Miss Courie and the bairn will be much better off without Corporal Varner and the kind of support he might offer. We all will be.' He regarded her with such kindness, she found her rage hard to maintain. Anyway, it wasn't him she was mad at so much as mankind. If she was honest, Bel wasn't exactly innocent in all this, it was her wee bairn who would suffer, and that infuriated Sorcha.

Without a word of farewell, she'd stormed off up the street, ignoring those who hailed her, almost knocking over Widow Adams as she barged past the costermonger.

Later that evening she learned from Nettie that the captain had arranged for some of the corporal's pay to be set aside for Bel. She also discovered from Janet, who heard it in the tavern, that while Corporal Varner may have been married, Bel wasn't the first lass he'd left with a bairn.

Well, thought Sorcha, I hope she's his last.

Now she owed Captain Ross an apology for her behaviour. What right did she have to ask him for aid, then to rebuke him when he rendered it? She'd no reason to expect anything of the man, and yet she did. Apologising might be the correct thing to do, but was it wise? Given there was already talk in the village about her and the captain, to seek out his company again would only fuel further gossip.

Sorcha pushed thoughts of him from her mind, and instead she focussed on the silhouettes of the larger ships dotting the coast, returned at last and bringing with them goods from distant shores and, just as important, news.

Out on the water, smaller boats from the Weem, Anster and beyond surged against the currents, the men on the oars until they could raise a sail. She regarded them for a moment, admiring how they came together like dancers in a reel, marvelling at their united purpose to achieve a common goal. Why couldn't people always be like that?

The rise and fall of voices forced her to turn around and head back. Small groups of fishwives sat together on upturned barrels, their hands as busy as their mouths. Shucking off the melancholy thoughts Captain Ross had engendered, knowing what she must do, she hitched her skirts and joined them, picking up a net and perching on a barrel.

Chatter washed over her. There was talk of how the men who'd returned from a long voyage days before looked and how they were behaving. The fishermen were always a little strange when they came home, walking with a rolling gait, inclined to sleep heavily and drink that way too, seeking each other's company as if being trapped aboard with the same men day in day out wasn't enough. Some of the wives despaired when their husbands returned, urging them out of the house even while they were grateful for the wages, companionship and tales they brought with them. Others, like her father and brothers, clung to home and its comforts as if they might slip away like a fish from a hook. Though what Sorcha's da worried about most was that his wife would disappear.

Sorcha was thinking about her da and wishing she'd been able to give the crew on his boat — *her* boat — more money, when Beatrix Laing appeared and flopped onto an upturned creel beside them with a dramatic groan. She dropped her bags on the ground and folded her arms beneath her heavy breasts. Her face was the colour of yesterday's storm.

'What ails you, Beatrix?' asked Janet, wielding a needle as if it were an extra digit.

'What ails me?' repeated Beatrix loudly. 'I'll tell you what ails me. Bairns that have too much to say for themselves, that's what.' She pouted.

Sorcha caught Nettie's eye.

'Who's earned your wrath this fine day, eh?' asked Nettie, returning to her mending. 'I'd have thought you'd no one left to reckon with, having said your piece to most.'

That raised a few chuckles. Like Janet, Beatrix had a reputation for telling people what she thought of them.

Beatrix grunted. 'Patrick Morton's lad, Peter, that's who.'

Sorcha tried to picture Peter Morton. Like his father, he was a black-smith. A strapping youth, he had dark brown hair and startling blue eyes. Working the forges and hammering metal had given him a broad chest and shoulders. His da, being close friends with the reverend and the Crawfords, was one of those less than happy to see Sorcha return, but Peter had given her a warm smile and even warmer greeting. When he caught her eye in the kirk her first Sunday back, he'd even dared a wave. He seemed a nice lad, even if Beatrix begged to differ, but then it didn't take a great deal to upset Beatrix, much to everyone's amuse-ment. Given her contrariness, Sorcha half-believed the reason Beatrix had made a show of being friends with the McIntyres was simply to annoy the reverend.

'Och, what's that spit of water done to upset you?' Janet put a piece of yarn in her teeth to rethread her needle, focussed on her task.

'He refused to sell me nails, that's what.' Beatrix slapped her leg in disgust. 'Nails my William needs if he's going to fix our door. It's coming apart and if he doesn't repair it, we may as well live in a cave. Cheeky little bastard refused to part with any, even while dozens sat atop the shelves, right in my line o' sight. You'd think I'd asked for gold without a penny to pay for it the way he carried on.'

Sorcha hid her grin. 'I heard he's making nails for Thomas Whyte's ship.' She nodded towards where it lay anchored. 'It can't sail till the deck's repaired. If the lad refused you, Beatrix, it wasn't anything personal.'

'I don't care if he's making them for the King of France, he needs to be looking after all of us, not just bailies like Whyte. All I wanted was a handful.'

Sorcha put down the net she was restoring and rested her fingers on Beatrix's arm. 'I know it's frustrating, Beatrix, but a handful to you might be the difference between the ship remaining in port or putting out to sea. Without a working craft, the men cannot sail, the fish can't be caught, purses remain empty, and we all go hungry.'

Beatrix stared hard at Sorcha for a minute before throwing up her hands and shaking her head. 'Stop being so bloody sensible, Sorcha McIntyre. Just like your da. I think I liked you better when you weren't here.' She produced a smile to show she didn't really mean it. 'Look, I ken you be telling it true being a boat owner and all, but it's the boy's manner that sticks in my craw. He wouldn't listen to reason or curses.'

As one, the fishwives stopped what they were doing and raised their heads.

Nettie sighed heavily. 'Tell me you didn't curse him, Beatrix.'

'Well, not much,' said Beatrix, with a twinkle in her eye and a lop-sided grin.

Janet shook her head. 'They'll be the death of you one day, those curses of yours, you mark my words. They trip off your tongue like prayers from Cowper's lips. Remember what happened when you cursed the Todd lad?'

Beatrix waved a hand dismissively. 'That was nine years ago. Even Cowper was forced to let the petition against me go — there was no proof. Anyhow, I didn't *curse* the Morton lad,' she objected. 'I threatened to make a charm against him.'

Sorcha couldn't help it, she gave a gasp of mock horror. 'But that's exactly what Mr Todd accused you of doing to his son.'

'Charms mean harm — isn't that what Cowper says?' piped up Nicolas who, along with two other fishwives, had been listening to the conversation with no small measure of alarm. 'Don't mock. He doesn't mean harm from the spell, he means the harm that comes to those who cast them if he finds out.' She waited for her words to sink in. 'He says they're the devil's work.'

Beatrix puffed in disparagement. 'Do I look like a devil to you? I meant nothing by it. I told Peter if I have any say in the matter, he'll get the claw — punishment. If not from me, then someone else. You ken what the lad did? Laughed. Right in my face.' She folded her arms again, brooding.

Nicolas shook her head gravely. Janet rolled her eyes. Slowly, they picked up the nets and resumed their mending.

'On second thoughts,' said Beatrix after a moment, 'maybe a charm *is* what I need. Not to get those nails for my William, but to remind young Peter of his manners.'

'And you think a charm is the way to do that?' asked Sorcha lightly, needle poised mid-air.

Beatrix pushed her hands onto her knees and rose to her feet. 'For an auld woman like me, it's the only way. Lads and lassies these days, they've no respect for their elders, not any more. If I can't get it by fair means, I've no choice but to use what's available to me, even if it be foul.' Her eyes lost focus and she scratched her neck.

'Aye, well, you be careful, Beatrix,' warned Janet. 'Just because you got away with it before doesn't mean you will again. Problem with charms and curses, once you make them, you never know how they'll turn out. They've a power of their own and shouldn't be used lightly.'

'Och, I'll not be using it lightly,' said Beatrix. With a last wave, she hirpled her way back to the High Street, a sack of vegetables and a bag of grain flung over her shoulder. Sorcha hadn't noticed her limp being so pronounced before. Some said Beatrix broke her ankle chasing her husband with a broom after he refused to do something she told him to. Beatrix always said it was running from his advances. That had been years ago and Sorcha knew which version everyone believed. Beatrix had a terrible tongue, but as she said, she meant no harm by it. It simply ran away with her.

As she watched Beatrix leave, Sorcha also noted her friend's bent back, how her hair was now more white than burned copper. Beatrix might be using what she felt was her only option to teach a lad civility, but Sorcha feared it wasn't only Peter Morton who'd learn the lesson.

TEN

When a woman thinks alone, she thinks evil.

— *Malleus Maleficarum*, The Hammer of Witches

The following afternoon Sorcha was returning from a long day down by the shore. It had been a poor haul — mostly herring and a few cod — but a larger ship had sailed through the nets, tearing them mercilessly. It had taken all the fishwives working together with a couple of the old fishermen who no longer went to sea to repair them. One of the men, Thomas Brown, had been a mentor to her da and, after her father's death and Robbie was taken prisoner, became one to her, advising where to send her boat and when, which men to hire, who to let go after a run. As she and Nettie fed the nets to him, pointing out where the worst of the damage was, Sorcha noted how easily his thick knuckles and twisted fingers moved to patterns he'd followed all his life. While they worked, he shared news from the other boats; what the fisherfolk down Anster way and beyond were saying. There was nothing they hadn't already heard, and soon the conversation switched to Thomas's daughter and her baby son. They enjoyed Thomas's company so much, neither Sorcha nor Nettie complained when they were late leaving the foreshore to sell the catch.

Adjusting her creel as she finally headed home, Sorcha thought Thomas was beginning to show his age. Why, he must be almost eighty. Tall and thin as a fisherman's rod, her father used to say that when Thomas was young if he stood still on deck, the gulls would mistake him for the mast. Sorcha gave a whimsical smile. Not any more now his back was bowed and his eyes cloudy, though you wouldn't know from the speed with which he worked. For an old man, he still had plenty of energy. Not even the hacking cough that occasionally racked his frame seemed to upset him.

Sorcha might be younger than Thomas Brown by some decades, but she was exhausted and looking forward to a whisky, a meal and bed. Nettie had decided it was time to visit her husband for a few days and so had taken some of the catch to cook for him. It was weeks since Sorcha had the cottage to herself and she was relishing the thought. Lost in planning her evening, it took her a moment to notice someone walking close beside her.

It was none other than Peter Morton.

Squashing the disappointment that it wasn't someone else, she swiftly concealed her surprise that the lad they'd been discussing by the harbour only yesterday should suddenly manifest.

'Evening, Mrs McIntyre,' said Peter, touching his cap. 'Can I take that for you?' he asked, nodding at her creel.

'Nae, lad, but thank you. It's not very heavy. I've only enough in here for myself; managed to sell the rest on the High Street.'

'I saw you,' said Peter, jerking his thumb over his shoulder. 'Thought I'd take the chance to see how you're faring now you're back. I see you in the kirk, but we haven't had the opportunity to chat.' He gave her a wide smile, his eyes holding hers a bit too long. For someone so young, he had a way about him that belied his years, a confidence and strut that made her a tad uneasy.

'I am faring very well considering, thank you, Peter. How about yourself?' she asked, putting some distance between them on the road. She nodded to the McKenzies as they came out of the tavern, their dog at their heels. Peter beamed at them and touched his cap.

'I be grand today, Mrs McIntyre. Not only did I just deliver the nails Bailie Whyte had me make for his ship, but now I have the pleasure of your company.'

Sorcha didn't quite know what to say.

'I'll be the envy of all the lads,' said Peter, stepping closer to her and acknowledging the men loitering outside the tavern. 'There's no one who wouldn't want to be in my shoes, walking with the bonniest lass in town.'

Sorcha stopped in her tracks. 'Are you flirting with me, Peter Morton?'

Facing her, Peter put his hands on his hips and winked. 'Aye,' he said, a cheeky grin splitting his face.

Sorcha couldn't help it, as uncomfortable as she felt, there was something disingenuous about the lad. Anyhow, what harm did it do? Why, he was sixteen if he was a day, and what was she? An old widow of twenty-five. She could indulge him his fantasy. She was only practice, after all. As for him being the envy of the men for being in her company, more likely they'd be wanting to bathe him in holy waters, touch cold iron or perform an exorcism.

They matched pace, Peter holding out his arm for her to take. Aware the eyes of those outside the tavern were lingering upon them, she altered the position of her creel and looped her arm through his, wondering what his da might say, let alone Reverend Cowper should he see them. She knew the Cowpers and the Mortons were close. No doubt word would get back. Recklessly, she drew him closer. She listened as Peter told her all about making nails. He even mentioned Beatrix trying to buy some, though he omitted the part where she lost her temper. She liked him better for that.

They came to the Mercat Cross and paused. 'I go this way,' said Sorcha, indicating Kirkgate.

'Aye, I ken where you live. But —' Peter glanced at her shyly, 'if you could just step into Routine Row with me for a bit, I could show you the smithy.'

Thinking how gallant the lad had been and how it wasn't really much out of her way, Sorcha relented. 'Very well, but I can't stay long.'

Peter's smile was worth her concession. Linking his arm through hers again, he almost dragged her the short distance up the street. She could see the Morton house with its red-tiled roof and the large building to the side with its own chimney to allow the smoke and heat from the forge to escape.

'Da bought some new bellows,' began Peter. 'You have to hear them; they put auld man —' Peter pulled up short and dropped her arm.

Sorcha took a couple more steps before she realised he'd stopped, and turned around. Peter's face was chalk-white. He was staring at a wooden bucket propped just outside the large double-doors to the smithy. A thin column of grey smoke rose from it.

'Peter, what is it?' asked Sorcha, concerned when he didn't speak. 'Peter?' She touched his shoulder gently.

He lifted his arm and pointed a trembling finger.

'It's a bucket, Peter,' said Sorcha. To prove it, she stepped towards it, nudging it with the toe of her boot and peering inside. There was some water and a fire coal floating on the surface. Sorcha did her best not to flinch. It was a sea charm — one cast to control the waves. An odd feeling began in the pit of her stomach. If she didn't know better, she'd say Beatrix had put it there.

'Look,' she said as if she'd not a care the world. 'It's naught but a bucket and a bit of water. It's nothing to be afr—'

Peter let out a blood-curdling scream and, before Sorcha could prevent it, collapsed to the ground, thrashing, his head striking the road hard.

'Peter!' Sorcha flung off her creel, the fish slithering across the ground, and bolted to his side.

Falling to her knees, she tried to stop his flailing arms and legs, protect his head, but her efforts were useless. Stiff-limbed, he kicked and jerked and threw his hands about, screeching fit to raise the devil. The skin broke on his knuckles as they struck the ground, blood splattering on his clothes, on Sorcha's apron, her face.

'Help!' shouted Sorcha. 'Help!'

She tried to prevent him injuring himself further as he squirmed and twisted, his eyes rolling back until only the whites showed. He was strong, his heels pummelled her legs, he threw off her hands.

People came running from their houses but halted a few feet away and stared, not knowing what to do, afraid. 'It's Peter Morton!' cried someone. 'Fetch his da,' yelled another.

There was no need. Out of the house next to the smithy bowled Peter's father and his two eldest sisters. Throwing themselves beside Sorcha, they stared helplessly as their son and brother quaked and shrieked.

'What happened?' shouted Patrick Morton, trying to be heard above his son's haunting wails. A huge man, he had a great dark beard and small beady eyes that failed to meet others'. His large hands hovered above his son's body, too scared to touch him. His daughters began to sob.

'I don't know,' said Sorcha, trying not to let panic overtake her. 'Help me hold him still, please. He's hurting himself.'

Reluctantly, Patrick wrapped his hands around his son's arms, pinning him to the ground. Sorcha took his ankles and leaned all her weight on them. The lad arched his back; the veins on his neck were cords. All she could think was, please don't die. Please don't die.

'What happened?' repeated Patrick Morton through gritted teeth.

Sorcha tried to answer as she battled against Peter's unnatural strength. 'One minute we were walking up the street, the next he stopped and fell to the ground.' She looked over her shoulder; the wooden pail was still there, but the smoke no longer rose above it, thank God. Turning her attention back to Peter, she felt his movements weren't quite as violent. His screams had transformed into dreadful heavy breathing, much like she imagined the bellows he wished to show her would have sounded. His neck was stiff and his eyes wide open, his pupils huge.

'Let's get him inside,' said Patrick and, with his shovel-like hands, scooped up his son, throwing Sorcha back onto her heels. He carried him to the house. Scrambling to her feet, Sorcha followed. So did the rest of the folk. 'Someone get the reverend. Now,' ordered Patrick, pausing outside his door.

Seumas Cowper, the reverend's oldest son, a rangy lad in his twenties, with thinning hair and narrow lips, who'd appeared when the screaming started, raced towards the kirk, casting a dark glance in Sorcha's direction as he did so. 'Fetch the doctor, would you, Mrs McIntyre?' said Patrick over his shoulder as he kicked open the front door. Blocking entry momentarily, he waited for her acquiescence. He didn't want her coming inside his house.

'Of course,' said Sorcha and, forgetting her creel and the bucket, ran back towards the High Street, aware of the whispers and pointing fingers of the Mortons' neighbours, many of whom simply poured into the house behind Patrick, his now rigid, silent son and weeping daughters.

She hadn't even reached the corner when she heard words that made her heart sink. 'What's that bucket doing there? Och, what mischief is this?'

As she spun around, she saw Mrs Crawford waddling towards the bucket, Mr Roberts and Mr Baker heeding her call. Upon their heels were Cowper's two eldest girls, frowning and whispering behind their hands before raising their heads and staring at Sorcha with granite eyes.

She didn't wait to hear what they might say, but ran, the feeling in her stomach transforming into a leaden weight.

ELEVEN

Keeping' the stick in the wud man's e'e.
(Keeping an argument going too long.)

*I*t was late before Sorcha was finally able to go home. The sun had long since set and the wind had picked up, bringing with it a touch of frost as well as the melancholy sigh of the ocean and the smell of peat, fish and other reminders of comfort. An argument erupted from within a house, a lone bird shrilled. Smoke obscured the stars, but Sorcha knew they were there. It was the first night in ages there were no clouds. If she was up to it, she would try and see the starlight later, offer a few prayers for her family and the poor lad who lay stricken.

Sorcha had raised the doctor, but returned to the Mortons only to be denied entry. Joining the curious throng waiting outside for news, she was there when the reverend forced his way through and was admitted immediately. To her dismay, the bucket had been removed — to where, she dared not ask. Gossip was rife already. Talk of a wicked charm spread. Some of the folk had been inside and seen Peter laid on his bed. Sorcha didn't need to ask how he fared, it was on everyone's lips.

'His face was unrecognisable,' said Hetty Collins, the butcher's wife, rubbing her gnarled hands together. 'All twisted and ferocious.' She pulled her mouth and widened her eyes to demonstrate.

'Aye, and his chest was like a barrel, fit to burst.'

Sorcha couldn't see who was speaking, only hear the glee.

'It isn't natural,' said Hetty, shaking her head, clutching her little girl to her skirts.

'Soon as the reverend heard,' said young Rachel Johnson, a friend of Cowper's eldest lass, 'he declared it the result of malice, as God is his witness, he said.'

'Maliss?' asked Hetty's daughter. Sorcha tried to remember her name. 'What's that mean, ma?'

'Witchcraft, Mary,' whispered Hetty, the colour draining from her face just as excitement filled her eyes. 'Witchcraft.'

The mutterings and murmurs became a solid roar. Sorcha refused to listen. Instead, she waited for news of Peter, anything that might reassure her he was going to be all right. But as evening fell, the word spread and more people gathered, many clutching candles and lanterns. The chatter about witchcraft grew, until Sorcha could bear it no more. When Hetty and Mary went home, she departed as well, quietly, keeping to the shadows.

Exhausted, she hooked her creel over her shoulders. Grateful no one had seen fit to steal the catch as it lay on the street for a couple of hours, she no longer cared it wasn't fresh and bore traces of dirt. She was famished and heartsore. None of this boded well.

For the first time that day she wished Nettie was staying the night so she might discuss what had happened. What she knew she must do before the sun rose, no matter what, was warn Beatrix. The charm the woman must have placed at the smithy to frighten Peter Morton had done more than intended. If it was discovered Beatrix was responsible, there'd be hell to pay.

Malice, the reverend called it. Nae, it wasn't malice, nor the witchcraft Hetty and others believed it denoted. Just a foolish prank played by an old woman designed to teach a lad civility.

She'd only just reached her road when a voice came out of the shadows.

'I thought I told you, it's not safe to wander the streets at night.'

Startled at first, Sorcha was relieved when she saw Captain Ross approaching. Her hand dropped from her breast. 'You're making a habit of alarming me, captain.'

'Not half as much as you scared me the last time we spoke. I swear there were lightning bolts shooting from those eyes of yours.' He reached her side. 'Once again, I'm sorry if I unnerved you, it wasn't my intention.'

'Nor was it mine to frighten you,' said Sorcha quickly, before she could change her mind. 'I apologise for what I said the other day. I was just so angry — not at you, but at the corporal, at the situation. I forced my way into where you're staying and… and…' She searched for words. 'I'm sorry. I didn't know you'd already seen to it that Bel and the bairn would be taken care of. I should have known you'd do something like that. Please forgive me.'

Captain Ross smiled at her. 'You were forgiven before you'd even finished, lass. You were right to be mad — at me. Corporal Varner was my responsibility and I should have watched him more closely.'

'Aye, well, Bel Courie should have thought twice before bedding an incomer, a soldier as well.' She shook her head. 'It's the bairn I really feel for… And now there's this —' She nodded in the direction of Routine Row.

They both stared up the street. The glow from the candlelight vigil outside the Morton house could just be seen, a faint aura above the rooftops.

'I saw you coming away from there and wondered if you knew what was going on,' said the captain. 'The villagers in the tavern are full of talk. Something about the Morton lad and an evil charm.'

Sorcha sighed. 'Aye, well, I think it's a bit more complicated than that.'

'It usually is. Here,' said the captain. 'Let me take that.'

Before she could protest, he lifted the creel, helping her with the straps that sat across her shoulders. Free of the weight, Sorcha rolled her neck. 'Thank you. It's heavier now than it was a few hours ago, but I think that's because there's now a greater weight in here.' She touched her heart.

Captain Ross followed the direction of her hand then quickly looked away.

Embarrassed lest he think she tried to draw his gaze deliberately, Sorcha began to walk again. The captain fell into step beside her. Whereas Peter Morton had been of a height, the captain was much taller. She was aware of his broad form, a wall between her and the darkness beyond. When she didn't immediately talk, he touched her gently on the shoulder. 'You know, Mrs McIntyre, I find a burden shared is one halved. I'd be honoured to help lighten what you evidently carry.' When she didn't reply, he bent his head. 'A complication can oft be made simple once described.'

Wanting to explain what had happened, even if only to herself, she quickly filled him in on Peter's fit, omitting the part about what she knew the bucket contained and who she strongly suspected had put it there. She told him what the villagers were already saying, the conclusions they were leaping to. He listened without interrupting.

When she finished, he nodded gravely. 'And do you think there is a charm involved?' he asked.

Sorcha forced a smile. 'I don't really believe in such things.'

'If that's so, then why are you so worried? Why do you fear a complication? Surely there'll be others see it as you do?'

They'd reached her door. Already dreading being alone, she was tempted to invite him in so she might pour out her heart, share her qualms; but she couldn't afford to attract more gossip and innuendo, not now. She needed to think about what to do about Beatrix and the charm; think about how she, Nettie and the others could counter any accusations against her.

'I hope so, captain, but the Weem be a place where superstition is sown, not just into the soil, but flows in the veins.' Shaking herself, she remembered where she was and to whom she was talking. 'I thank you for your kindness, for listening to me. I'm simply worried about Peter; he's clearly very ill. He hurt himself badly when he fell. As for talk of a charm…' She looked towards the kirk, then in the direction of the Mortons' house. 'It's a nonsense. The boy was beset with apoplexy or some such thing. There is no malfeasance involved.'

'I never credited it for a moment,' said the captain. 'I've been here long enough to know that while malice may not have been intended, it's often how others read these things. The folk here seem to have a fascination for bewitchment and such — as you say, it's in the blood. There's a history of it in Pittenweem.'

'Aye, there is — of accusations and burnings, though not for a number of years, thank the Lord. Nevertheless, some make a habit of seeing malevolence where none is intended. It suits their purpose, whatever it might be.' She glanced towards the kirk once more before averting her eyes, fearing she'd already said too much.

They stood outside her house. Light from the neighbours' windows allowed her to see the crags and planes of the captain's face. He was a foreign country, a mystery part of her wished she could unravel. Gazing up at him, she exhaled quietly. Dear God, but the man invited peculiar thoughts into her head. Next, she'd be writing poetry or singing songs to dead lovers.

Dead lovers. Aye, well, she had one of those, only — was Andy really a lover? Loved, well, she'd loved him as much as she could. But he was not what she ever imagined a lover could be.

She shook herself out of her thoughts, wishing the heat that rose inside her would dissipate, and recalled what the captain just said. He was right. It was how Reverend Cowper and the rest of the Weem would read the bucket and coal that would dictate the fate of the person who put it there — they and Peter Morton, who, as they stood talking, lay in his bed, sickened.

Or, as others believed, bewitched; the victim of malfeasance...

'Thank you for seeing me home, captain. And thank you for your kind offer. If ever I need to share another burden, I won't forget it.' What he didn't know was she'd no intention of telling him anything more. He was an incomer and, as her da always said, fisherfolk stuck together — through good times and bad. Only, she couldn't recall the last time things were good.

'Be sure you don't,' said the captain.

She wished she could think of something else to say, a reason not to go inside. While she didn't want to share her fears for Beatrix, she was enjoying his company and would keep him there. But there was no reason. With a small curtsey, she went to the door.

'Mrs McIntyre,' said the captain.

Sorcha turned. 'Aye?' He was right behind her.

'I can say something to Mrs Laing if you wish — tell her what's happened.' He jerked his chin towards the dim light.

'Mrs Laing?' Dear God, why did he raise Beatrix's name? She hadn't mentioned her, had she? If the captain knew she'd placed the bucket and coal outside the smithy, then so must half the village. 'Why would you wish to tell Mrs Laing anything?' She hoped her dread wasn't apparent in the question.

Captain Ross stood so near, she could smell him. A hint of whisky, sweat and a musky odour that made her think of bathing in the ocean, drying before firelight and hazy summer days.

He lowered his face towards hers and for one mad moment, she thought he might kiss her. Her heart beat frantically against her ribs. Her cheeks burned. 'Because,' his breath was hot against her ear, 'I saw her talking to the Morton lad only yesterday and she didn't seem very happy.' He drew his face away slowly and gazed at her intently. 'I wasn't the only one. I thought it might be good for her to know what's happened, lest people read something they should not into their conversation.'

'I see.' Sorcha's mind whirled. The sooner Beatrix found out what had occurred, how Peter reacted to her charm, the better. It might be too late by morning. God knows what the reverend might do. Might make others do. And, if Sorcha was seen talking to Beatrix, what conclusions would then be drawn? Before she could change her mind, she gripped his hand. 'Aye,' she said. 'Aye. It would be grand if you could tell her. Now, if that's possible.'

'Consider it done,' said the captain.

'But please,' said Sorcha, her grip tightening, 'don't let anyone see you.'

'If I don't want them to, they won't.' He made no effort to leave.

She felt he'd more to say. She waited. The evening enveloped and protected them; the ocean whispered. The stars she'd longed to see sparkled above; the moon floated into view, casting its radiance over everything. Would that they could remain there forever, locked in moonlight and shadows, caressed by the salty breeze from the sea while the world outside passed them by.

Before she could think of a reason to detain him, he stepped away, forcing her fingers to drop, bringing her to her senses. He bowed and turned, swallowed swiftly by the darkness.

It was just as he promised. No matter how hard she tried, she couldn't see him.

TWELVE

You're in for a calahesion.
(You're about to get into real trouble.)

*T*hree days had passed since Peter Morton was bewitched. At least, that's how Reverend Patrick Cowper described the lad's affliction. The useless doctor might have tried to give an alternate explanation, but there was no doubt in the reverend's mind that the old bitch Beatrix Laing had put one of her charms upon the boy because he hadn't given her the nails she'd demanded. And it was no coincidence that the full power of the charm fell upon the lad when he was with Sorcha McIntyre. Och, she might deny it all she liked, she and the other fishwives, but the reverend knew a witch when he saw one and if those women weren't a coven, well, the devil could take his soul, too.

He had barely stirred from Peter's bedside since he was first fetched, and then only to deliver his Sunday sermon. Patrick was pleased to see the lad was at least lying quietly now, the paroxysms not coming upon him quite so frequently, even if their intensity had increased.

Dear God, when Patrick first arrived at the house it was akin to a marketplace with the boy being watched and commented upon by a crowd like he was a news seller or one of those theatrical troupes putting on a play. The place was filled with clash-bags, young lasses, lads and nearby vendors telling Mr Morton what they'd seen, what he should do, what the best cures were and all sorts of other rubbish.

At least Peter's da had the sense to call for him. He could scarce believe it when his lad, Seumas, came a-huffing and a-puffing into the kirk with the story. When he finally saw Peter stretched out on the bed, his back arched as if he were about to break in two, his neck so distended and corded with veins, his eyes set to pop, he knew what he was witnessing and did not fail to name it: malice. Was it not his godly duty to smite witchcraft and all who practised it lest they harm good Christian souls? It was. And so he named it and made sure, despite the doctor's call for caution, that the word spread.

Malfeasance had returned to the Weem.

Even though the day was cool, the lad was pale and sweaty against his pillows, his dull eyes fixed straight ahead. Patrick reached for his hand. As he held it, the lad blinked and tried to say something.

'There now, Peter, be not afeared. God is with you, and so am I.'

'Th… th… thank you, reverend,' said Peter hoarsely.

'Don't speak. Not yet. Let me get you a drink.' He fetched a cup of milk and put it to the boy's mouth, tipping it gently. As he did so, he thought about all the lad had said since he'd taken ill. He'd blethered about a charm, about the pain in his limbs, as if a thousand rats were biting him with sharp teeth. He said he could hear voices in his head, chanting, whispering, luring him into a dark space where the light went to die.

Patrick knew God had sent him a challenge. It was one he accepted with grace and pride. He would find who was responsible for this devilment and fell them. And this poor lad, this once hale fellow whom he'd known for years, would help him.

Having slaked his thirst, Peter fell back on the pillows. 'Thank you, reverend.'

Patrick smiled and brushed aside the appreciation. ''Tis naught, lad, 'tis naught. There's no need to talk, I want you to save your poor wee throat. But it's important I ask some questions. I have to ken what happened, find out who's responsible. Your ma and da are relying on me to get to the bottom of this. Are you up to that? Nae. Don't speak. All you have to do is nod or shake your head. Can you do that?'

'Aye —' began Peter, then pressed his lips together and nodded.

'Good lad,' said Patrick approvingly. 'Tell me, do you still hear the voices?'

Peter thought for a moment. He shook his head.

'Do you still feel the pain in your legs and arms?'

Peter hesitated, then nodded.

'May I take a look?' asked Patrick and lifted the blankets when Peter acquiesced.

There wasn't a mark upon the lad, just his sinewy legs and pale arms dusted with dark hair. He was a fine-looking young man, strapping and strong. It pained Patrick to see him brought low. To see that a curse wielded by ancient, devil-cursed witches could bring down such a one.

With great tenderness he touched Peter's neck, then his shoulders, asking if he hurt. When Peter shook his head, Patrick frowned.

'Can you tell me what caused you to fall that day, Peter?'

Peter stared, his eyes bulged, his lips contorted.

'Aye, you can talk now,' said Patrick, trying to keep the impatience out of his voice.

'Nae, reverend,' Peter croaked. 'Though I did see a charm before the smithy. As soon as I laid eyes upon it, the feeling came over me.'

'The feeling?'

'Of a mighty powerful dread. Like my body was no longer in my possession. As if someone else had control.'

'You mean like a puppet whose strings were being pulled?'

'Aye, by an unseen hand.'

Patrick regarded Peter closely, then leaned back in the chair. Holding his narrow chin in his long fingers, he continued to study the boy carefully. 'I see. Can you describe the charm?'

''Twas a bucket and it had smoke rising from it.' Peter's lips began to tremble. 'I ken what that means, reverend. 'Tis a water charm that conjures up a storm, bringing ill-luck upon those who spy it. I felt it strike me straight away, as if I'd been bludgeoned.' He paused and raised his eyes to the reverend's. 'Do you believe me, sir?'

'Aye, I do, lad. I do.'

Peter's eyes filled with tears and he squeezed the reverend's hand in gratitude.

'You see,' said Patrick, leaning on the bed and tilting towards him, 'this wouldn't be the first time someone like yourself has fallen victim to the wicked ways of those who are in league with the devil.'

'But why me, sir?' asked Peter in a small voice.

'You might well ask that. The devil likes to terrorise the innocent in the hope of converting them to his dark doings, using fear to force them to do his bidding. He recruits souls into his evil army. The more he recruits, the greater his force and the harder it is for others to resist. You wouldn't be the first and you won't be the last.'

Peter stared in horror. 'There's been others?'

'Many. You heard tell of Mrs Dore from St Monan's? She burned as a witch, as did Maggie Moran over fifty years ago. But there are others and younger than yourself.' He let go of Peter's hand, pleased to see the boy had reached for him before his fingers retreated under the covers. He rose and shut the door, then settled back into his chair. 'Have you ever heard tell of the lass Christian Shaw, from the Bargarran Estate to the west of here?'

Peter frowned then shook his head.

'Och, well, let me tell you what happened to that poor wee lassie.' The reverend gave a crooked smile, sighed deeply, and took his time. 'Christian was only eleven years old when a group of witches cast a terrible spell upon her. Like you, her body twisted and contorted. She shook like a trapped coney, flapped about on her bed like a fish brought to land and there was naught anyone could do to stop it.'

'W... why not?' asked Peter, bunching the blankets in his fists.

'At first, because no one knew what caused such fits, and she became worse. The doctors could do nothing. She lost the power of speech, she couldn't hear what was being said and even went blind briefly.'

Peter gasped. Patrick drew himself up. 'After a while, she began to vomit up the feathers of birds, hair, coal cinders the size of chestnuts, and even bones.'

'Bones?' squeaked Peter.

'Aye.' Patrick paused, allowing the lad to absorb what he said. 'She couldn't bear to have clothes upon her body, for beneath them, she was being pricked and bitten by unseen imps who'd been called upon by the devil to torment her. Her body was marked by scratches and bites, terrible marks that sent her into agonies.'

'But... why?'

'Why indeed. 'Twas a spell, a charm cast upon her by ungrateful servants — witches by any other name — who together summoned up a demon, or even a few demons, to possess her and torment her until she was deceased.'

Peter swallowed. 'She died?'

'Nae, lad, brave Christian Shaw lived and does even now as we speak. But those who tormented her are dead. They were burned to death, as all those in league with Satan should be. As all witches must be to protect others from their evil.'

'You think what's happening to me is because of witches?' Peter's knees were drawn up, he clasped his hands together as if in prayer.

'I've nae doubt.'

Peter gulped. 'But, sir, there be no witches in the Weem.'

'Nae?' Patrick Cowper stared earnestly at Peter Morton. 'There have been in the past. Why not now? Think carefully, Peter. Did you not tell me yourself that Beatrix Laing cursed you when you wouldn't give her any nails?'

'Aye, but —'

It was all Patrick could do not to crow. Beatrix Laing was considered a knabbie woman for a spinner of wool. By Weem standards she was very wealthy indeed, with a fine house, a husband who was a tailor and had once been town treasurer. And what about her daughter? Wasn't she married to a fisherman who crewed on an Anster ship? Didn't Beatrix help look after the wee bairn? What was her name? Elise? Emma?

'Does not Mrs Laing have a reputation for cursing and making charms?'

Peter frowned. Patrick could tell he was reluctant to name her. Never mind, they'd time.

'And what about those she regards as her friends?' continued the reverend. 'Janet Horseburgh, the one they call Nettie, was she not once labelled a witch?'

Peter's eyes widened. He nodded. 'Aye. She was. Once. Years ago. But da told me it was never proven.'

The reverend made a scoffing noise. 'What of Nicolas Lawson who dabbles in potions? And what about the auld scold, Janet Cornfoot?'

Peter's eyes rolled in his head. 'I... I don't know, sir.'

'Well, I do. Though it was never official, there were those who made accusations. About both of them. Many times.'

Peter pressed himself into his pillows. His face had grown even paler. Sweat poured down his forehead, his hair stuck to his temples.

'They are workers of malice, Peter. They've a history of it — the lot of them — and there are others will tell you it's so. They got away with it before and they seek to do so again. They've set their sights on you, lad.'

Peter began to shake.

The reverend laid a comforting hand over his. 'We have to put a stop to it.'

Peter fixed his eyes on the reverend. 'You'll help me, sir?'

'Aye, lad, me and God.'

'Thank you, reverend. Bless you, sir.'

'But, Peter, in order to stop these women working their evil, in order to rid your body of the demon that's been conjured, we have to identify *all* the witches involved. If we miss even one, then your torment won't end. The entire village will remain at risk. Do you understand?'

'Sir,' said Peter, terror pinching his face.

'Can you think of anyone else who might have worked malice upon you, lad? Apart from Beatrix Laing?'

Peter's brow furrowed. He half-lay, knees drawn, hunched, quiet. The reverend remained silent. Peter hadn't corrected him when he mentioned the Laing woman. Good.

Outside, the voices of those waiting for news were a dulcet song. A dog whined and the shrill cries of gulls carried as they fought over food. A cart bumped along the cobbles, pausing outside the Mortons' door. Within the house, Patrick could hear the low murmurs of one of Peter's sisters and his ma, and the deep, short notes of his father's voice. There was the smell of meat cooking. Patrick was hungry. A door opened, then closed.

'I think maybe Mrs Wallace did curse me once,' said Peter softly.

'Margaret Wallace? The fishwife?'

'Aye, that be her. My ma calls her Lillie.'

'Good, good, Peter. Can you think of anyone else?'

Peter frowned deeply but finally shook his head.

Drawing his chair closer, Patrick whispered, 'What of Sorcha McIntyre?'

Peter recoiled. 'Nae. Not Sorcha. She be no witch.'

The reverend relaxed back into his chair. 'But was she not with you when you were struck down?'

'A... aye. But da told me Hetty and wee Mary said she did all she could to stop me hurting myself. She didn't —'

'She made sure you saw the charm, lad,' said Patrick abruptly, slapping his hands against the arms of the chair, causing Peter to jump. 'Did she not come with you up this very road and stop right where the charm lay, so you might be the first to set eyes upon it?'

In answer, Peter screwed his eyes up tight.

The reverend waited. Was the lad trying to remember, or trying to shut out the very thought of Sorcha McIntyre and the intoxicating spell she cast over every man she met?

Patrick recalled her as he last saw her, the bronze hair threaded amply with burnished copper, her eyes translucent blue-green like the sun on the Forth, that pale northern skin and the lush full mouth, more often drawn back in a smile that was never for him.

'Like the others, she is a maker of malice,' whispered the reverend.

'Nae... I can't believe it,' whimpered Peter.

'They're witches, lad, every last one of them. Sorcha McIntyre too. Open your eyes. Open your heart. You must see the truth for us to bring it to light. In doing so, everyone else will see it too.'

Blinking rapidly, Peter opened his eyes. 'B... But Sorcha would never do anything to hurt me. Nor would Mrs White, or Mrs Wallace.'

'Are they not friends of Beatrix Laing? Did you not tell me that she cursed you?'

Peter turned his face away.

'Peter,' said the reverend softly. His voice was like warm honey. ''Tis a sin to lie, just as it's a sin to curse and weave spells. You'll not want to be like those who would cause harm, would you? And yet if you tell falsehoods, if you protect them with a still tongue, then you do the devil's work for him...'

The reverend paused.

'Aye, Mrs Laing did curse me.' Peter's voice was barely a whisper.

'And what type of being is it that offers curses, Peter?'

'A witch.'

The reverend took a deep breath, trying not to let triumph infuse his tone. 'So, Peter, tell me. What does that make Mrs Laing?'

Peter raised hollow eyes. 'A witch, sir. It makes her a witch.'

Patrick enveloped Peter's hand with his own. 'Exactly. She's much more than a bad-tempered auld crone — she seeks to corrupt your soul. Force you to her will. She and the others. You're not the type of lad to let yourself be forced by women, are you?'

'Nae, sir,' scorned Peter. He tried to sit up straight.

'And, while you can likely defeat a spell cast by one witch, as we have seen, they rarely work alone. They stick together — there's unnatural strength in their numbers. Once they choose a victim, they turn their wicked spells upon him and never leave him alone. They torment him forever and ever.'

Before Peter could pull his hand away, the reverend closed his other over the top, sealing it between his thin cool ones.

'Do you want that to happen to you, Peter?'

Unable to speak, Peter's eyes grew round. He yanked his hand out from between the reverend's and grabbed at his throat.

'Do you?' insisted Patrick Cowper, compressing Peter's other hand harder betwixt his own.

Peter tried to speak, but nothing came.

'Ah, lad, it starts again.' Dropping his hold, the reverend stood and went to the window, making a show of staring down upon the street. 'They ken you're speaking to me, and through me to God. You're learning how to protect yourself and to prevent that, the witches have stolen your voice.'

He swung back to the bed. 'Don't let them win, Peter. They're not your friends, they're your foes. All of them are wicked, wicked women, every last one of them. One has only to hear what happened to Christian Shaw to see that. She endured for months, but she endured. Despite what they did to her, she triumphed over the devil. Do you remember what I just told you about that wee lassie?'

With both his hands now wrapped around his neck, his face turning red, Peter shook his head wildly.

Patrick tried to prise the lad's hands away. When he couldn't, he settled for resting his own over them. 'I think I'd better tell you her story again. It's a way of arming you lest this curse work further evil.'

He peered into the lad's face, so close their noses almost touched.

'Aye, reverend,' said Peter, finding his voice at last. 'I think you should too.'

'Good lad.'

The reverend sank back into his chair and began to tell Peter exactly what the curse made Christian Shaw do, down to every last detail.

THIRTEEN

That's anither day an' anither dinner.
(We'll leave that for another time.)

*I*t was a fresh spring day carrying with it a hint of the warmth of the summer to come. The waters were relatively calm and the sun shone upon the Forth, turning the usually grey expanse into a glittering pool of silver. Birds hovered over the boats that dotted the sea, marking their location the way a group of clouds indicates rain. Gulls and terns heckled those who worked upon the shoreline, ever-watchful lest a fishwife drop a mussel or an oyster.

Sorcha would have enjoyed the break from the cold and rain had it not been for what preoccupied them all: the condition of Peter Morton. It had been three weeks since he fell ill and, according to gossip in the streets and Reverend Cowper himself most Sundays, he wasn't improving. Another doctor had been sent for from Anster and, when nothing he did worked, physicians from Edinburgh came calling. Baffled by what beset the lad, nothing they suggested improved his condition, not their purges, potions or ghastly medicines. Not even the prayers of the kirk or the reverend, who attended him daily. On the contrary, his fits had grown worse and the pain increased. It was said that red marks scored his body as if unseen hands and mouths tormented him.

While the physicians were at first sceptical of the reverend's suggestion of bewitchment, they were soon to be heard uttering the word, albeit reluctantly.

It was all the town could talk about. Where there was witchcraft, there were witches. It had happened before. Folk began to look askance at each other, to whisper behind their hands and look suspiciously upon the actions of their neighbours. It was difficult to ignore the growing disquiet. Beatrix ridiculed their fears, the wild imaginings of the townsfolk, but Nettie, Janet and Nicolas grew introspective and cautious. They remembered what had happened in Paisley only seven years ago, when six servants from the Bargarran estate were strangled and burned as witches. The accuser had been an eleven-year-old girl, Christian Shaw. A child who held the power of life and death over those who'd served her family faithfully.

Then there were those in the west of the country who had been accused only two years later. They too had been sent to their deaths. As Thomas Brown reminded them, in the last one hundred and fifty years or so in Pittenweem alone, at least two dozen had been called witch and put to the flame.

Huddled together, baiting lines, mending nets, working in threes, the fishwives sat close to each other, drawing comfort from proximity and their shared concerns. So caught up were they in exchanging news and pondering what might happen next, they only noticed Katherine Marshal, a seamstress and one of Beatrix's friends, when she was almost upon them.

'Nicolas! Nettie, Sorcha!' cried the woman, holding up a hand to attract their attention as she staggered down the sands, her chest heaving. 'They've taken Beatrix!'

The women stopped what they were doing. The net Sorcha was mending rolled off her thighs and pooled onto the sand as she slowly stood.

'Who?' asked Nettie. Her voice was thick. 'Who has taken Beatrix?'

The other women put their work aside and waited impatiently while Katherine caught her breath. The old men who sat outside the cottages lining the harbour walked across the road and jumped down onto the sand so they too could hear what she had to say. Thomas Brown tilted his head towards Sorcha in an unasked question; she pressed her lips together and shook her head.

Bent over, her hands still upon her knees, Katherine raised her freckled face. Her cheeks were red, the broken veins around her nose and along her chin prominent. 'The constables,' she gasped. Hands flew to mouths. Wide-eyed looks of shock were exchanged. 'They came to Beatrix's house and marched her to the Mortons. They said the bailies want to question her.'

'At the Mortons?' asked Nicolas, confused. 'Why there?'

'What about?' asked Thomas.

'What do you think?' asked Nettie sharply. She glanced at Sorcha, untied her apron and slipped it over her head. 'Come on. I'll be damned if I'll sit here waiting to hear what's going on. I'm to the Mortons.'

'Me too,' said Sorcha, taking off her apron and throwing it on a creel. She raised a quizzical brow at Nicolas.

Nicolas refused to meet their eyes. 'I'll wait. Someone should be here when the boats return.' Sorcha knew what she wasn't saying: *Best not be seen together.*

'Aye, no need for us all to go,' said the oldest of the fishwives, the kindly Therese Larnarch, bending back to her work. The others swiftly agreed.

'I'll wait with the lasses,' said Thomas, picking up a needle and joining Therese.

Nettie frowned at them in disapproval. Fearing her friend might say something she'd later regret, Sorcha grabbed her by the wrist and pulled her away. 'Let's go. Sooner we find out what's happening, sooner we'll be back.'

By the time they reached Routine Row, they were simply part of a throng heading for the Morton house. Linking arms, Sorcha, Nettie and Katherine pushed through those gathered outside, until they were in their midst.

Sorcha's heart sank as she heard the way people in the crowd were talking about Beatrix.

'She cursed me, I tell you,' said a woman behind them. Much to Sorcha's dismay, it was Mrs Robertson, the cooper's second wife, someone who'd known Beatrix her entire life. 'The words that came out of her mouth were like none I ever heard before.'

'Then you can't have been listenin' too hard to the others,' mumbled someone nearby. 'Since when has Beatrix Laing had a good word to say about anyone?' There were chuckles. Sorcha began to relax a little.

'All the bailies are inside,' said the brewer, Graham Donaldson.

'They've called the pricker and all,' said the man beside him, the tavern-owner, Michael Bruce.

'They'll get a confession out of the auld bitch,' said Widow Agnes.

'You mean witch, don't you, Agnes?' said Michael. 'Time to call her what she is.'

'Och, prickers would get a confession out of anyone. They'd get one outta me,' said Graham, thumping his considerable chest. 'And I be no witch.'

'You sure, man? Perhaps we need to ask your wife.'

Those nearby guffawed.

After that, Sorcha wasn't sure who spoke, but the gist was the same. Everyone believed Beatrix was being questioned on suspicion of witchcraft. But that wasn't possible, was it? Then again, the authorities had attempted to prosecute Beatrix before. But back then young James Todd hadn't succumbed to fits, nor had there been any evidence of a charm; it had all come to nothing.

What was clear was that once again Reverend Cowper had been the one to lay the charge. Only this time he had demanded Beatrix be brought here, to the Morton house. Sorcha wasn't sure if that was a good sign or a bad one. They would soon learn.

Around them conversation rose and fell. The sun, which had been shining, became occluded by clouds, and pockets of cold shadow passed over them. The smell of burning peat and smoked fish floated in the air; the endless plash of the waves breaking on the shore could just be discerned.

They didn't have to wait too long before the door opened and, in the company of two constables, Mark Smith and Simon Wood, Beatrix was escorted from the house. She looked old and frail. Dwarfed by the constables, she could have been anyone's harmless grandmother. Raising her head, her sharp eyes took in the crowd, the leers, the curious, hungry stares.

'Piss off, the lot of yers,' she screeched. 'There'll be no burning today — or any day, if I've my way.'

There were jeers, some laughter but mostly dark mutterings. Honestly, thought Sorcha, Beatrix could be her own worst enemy.

Throwing off the men's hold, Beatrix used her elbows to force her way through the mob. Hurling abuse if people stood in her way, they began to jump aside lest she touch them or, worse, lashed them with her tongue. It wasn't until she saw Sorcha, Nettie and Katherine that she changed direction. Rather than acknowledge them while everyone was watching, she indicated the seashore with a jerk of her head. Stomping off down the Row, she darted into South Loan before anyone could stop her. Sorcha wondered where she was going. Would she dare head home or did she have another destination in mind?

The constables began to hurry the crowd along, but not before Sorcha saw who else spilled from the house. Sure enough, there were most of the bailies, Cook, Whyte, Bell and Vernour, along with men Sorcha knew were close to the reverend. Of the minister, she saw no sign.

But at least they'd released Beatrix. The talk of her being tried and a pricker being summoned appeared to have been exaggerated. Why then did Sorcha feel a terrible tension, like a rope about to snap?

It didn't take the women long to get back to the harbour. There was no sign of Beatrix, and since the boats had returned, there wasn't the chance to ask if anyone had seen her or even to exchange much news. Not that it stopped the fishwives — or Thomas, or the arriving fishermen — wanting to know what had occurred. What could they say? They barely knew anything, except that Beatrix had been taken to the Morton house and brought into the presence of the bailies and let go.

'They wouldn't have released her if she was guilty, right?' said Nicolas hopefully.

'I wouldn't have thought so, lass,' said Therese, trying to reassure them.

Sorcha didn't know how to respond. It's what she hoped, too, but Janet's stories of the Bargarran trials echoed in her mind. Those men and women had been freed only to die — one by his own hand and the rest later by the flame.

It wasn't until Lillie Wallace, who'd been working the lines as long as Sorcha could remember, wandered over from the boats and whispered, 'Meet in Katherine's house when you're ready,' that Sorcha understood whatever Beatrix and her temper had started was by no means finished.

The weather had turned by the time those Lillie had approached gathered in Katherine's cottage, a small, draughty place that over-looked the sands. Her husband was away on a long voyage, so the women had it to themselves. Katherine made some tea and found a dram to share, and they all sat in front of the fire; some on stools, the rest on cushions on the wooden floor. Wrapped in her shawl, head bowed, Beatrix sat in the centre.

For all she was trying to keep up a brave front, Beatrix was badly shaken. The men had come upon her in the High Street and before she could object, marched her to the Mortons.

'They waited until William was away in the city, didn't they? Not one word of explanation was I given. Just carted away like a common criminal,' she grumbled. 'They took my basket and all.' She clasped it tightly to her chest lest someone snatch it away again.

'What happened once you were at the Mortons?' asked Nettie, pris-ing the basket away from her and placing a mug of tea in her hands.

Beatrix stared at her drink for so long, the steam wavering before her face, Sorcha thought she must have forgotten the question. 'I was taken into the main room,' she said finally. 'It was full of folk I knew, like it was my wake or something. There were the older of the Cowper children — the lads only, you ken. There were the bailies, and other important folk — MacDougall was there, MacDonald and Frost, the nosy bastard. There were so many I knew... Or thought I did.' She took a deep breath. 'The reverend was there as well.' Her eyes narrowed and she folded her top lip over her bottom one. Thinking. 'He didn't say anything at first.' She chewed her lips for a full minute. No one dared interrupt. 'Then, in front of all these men, the bailies began to question me.'

'What about?' asked Sorcha softly, though she knew.

'The bucket with the coal in it. They wanted to know if I set it at the smithy door.'

The women waited.

'What did you tell them?' asked Sorcha eventually.

'That I did.'

Sorcha's heart lurched.

'And?' prompted Nettie. 'What did they say to that?'

'Say? They wanted to know *why* I put it there.'

'What did you answer?'

'Naught. I said naught. Well, that's not exactly true. What I said was, I'd no reason for doing it except a fancy to be putting my bucket there and placing a coal in it.' She raised her chin and grinned at them before taking a slurp of her tea.

Unable to find any humour in the situation, Sorcha sat very still. Nicolas clicked her tongue and folded her arms, shaking her head. Katherine looked grim.

'What?' said Beatrix. 'What did you expect me to say? I knew what they wanted. They wanted me to own that I put it there to charm the lad.'

'Didn't you?' asked Katherine crossly.

'Aye, but not so he sickened. The charm isn't supposed to work like that. I had no part in *that*. That was something else altogether.'

Before anyone could respond, there was a pounding on the door.

They froze.

Katherine slowly rose to her feet and cast an anxious look at the others; she put her finger to her lips, warning them not to speak. 'Who's a-knocking?' she called.

'It be myself,' said a familiar voice. 'Thom White. I'm told my wife is there and I need to see her.'

Nettie jumped up, put down her mug, drained her dram and brushed her skirts. 'I'm coming, Mr White,' she replied. Placing one hand on Beatrix's shoulder and the other on Sorcha's, she bent over. 'You are walking a dangerous path, Beatrix,' she said quietly. 'And I am afeared where it will lead you. But stick to your story. They can't prove intent, no matter what they claim. Intent is in the intender and they can't wrest that from you unless you give it to them. You hear me?' Swooping, she kissed the top of Beatrix's head, then Sorcha's.

Katherine held the door ajar.

Nettie turned to regard them one by one. 'It be nothing but a storm in a bucket.' She tried to smile at her joke, but it was weak. 'And, like a storm, no matter how wild, it will blow over. We just have to stay strong. You, Beatrix,' she jabbed her finger in the woman's direction. '*You* need to stay strong.'

'Och, don't you worry about me, lass. I be sturdier than a Dutchman's ship.' Beatrix raised her mug to her.

As soon as Nettie left, Katherine poured another dram for each of them. The room felt bigger without Nettie in it, so large was her presence. Sorcha dragged her stool closer to Nicolas, who remained with her arms folded, her expression fixed. The sea was loud in the cottage, not so much the gentle breath she was accustomed to, as a roar. It was unsettling to say the least. The wind had also picked up and brought with it a right blash — sheets of rain slapped the windows, roof and sides of the cottage hard. They were being menaced from all directions.

Katherine took her seat and stared at Beatrix over the rim of her cup. Beatrix gazed at the fire, lost in thought.

'I can't believe you were fool enough to cast a charm, Beatrix, not after what happened to you the last time,' said Katherine.

'Nothing happened,' grumbled Beatrix, daring anyone to contradict her.

'Nothing except you were called a witch,' corrected Nicolas. 'A name that's haunted you and all those you associate with ever since, for all you pretend it hasn't.'

Lillie Wallace nodded in grim agreement.

Beatrix went to say something, then closed her mouth tightly.

They sat in silence, the wind and rain serenading their dark thoughts.

'Did you see the Morton lad at all when you were in the house?' asked Nicolas finally. She was pale but fierce, her dark eyes glimmering with unshed tears.

Caught mid-swallow, Beatrix shook her head, coughing and thumping her chest a few times. 'Nae, but I could hear him and they told me what ails him. A bloated stomach, rigid limbs, spewing and choking. He's stopped eating, too.'

Nicolas buried her head in her arms.

''Twasn't me, I tell you,' protested Beatrix. 'But I ken what did it all the same.'

Katherine sat forward on her stool and looked from Sorcha to Nicolas and then at Beatrix. 'What? What do you ken?'

'Why, his own ill-tongue is what brought an evil spirit to torment him. An auld evil spirit who, like me, thinks the young should pay their elders more respect.' She burst into cackles of laughter.

Katherine looked at her in sheer dismay. 'That's not funny, Beatrix. None of this is funny. You shouldn't be saying such things.'

'Katherine's right,' said Nicolas, unfolding her arms and lifting her shawl over her hair. 'You're a right fool to have done such a thing. Did you not realise what harm you were doing, intended or not? Did you not think about the trouble you'd make for yourself and for those you call friends?' She stood and glared.

The barely repressed fury in her voice rendered Beatrix momentarily speechless.

'I would never harm my friends. You ken me better than that.'

'Do I?' asked Nicolas. 'Do any of us?'

Before Beatrix could respond, Nicolas swept past her, wrenched open the door and stood watching the downpour, trying to breathe against the howl of the wind. The fire fought the cold air, guttering and bursting back into life. With one last look over her shoulder, Nicolas ran into the street, slamming the door behind her.

Sorcha began to shiver. Katherine and Lillie stared at Beatrix. Beatrix stared at the floor.

'Time for me to be getting home, before it gets dark,' said Sorcha finally, breaking the silence.

'But the weather —' began Katherine, then pressed her lips together. As Sorcha suspected, she wanted her gone. She wanted them all gone.

'Och, I don't mind a drookin'.' Drenched she'd be, walking through town in this weather. She glanced at Beatrix. She should offer to walk her home.

'What about you, Beatrix?' asked Katherine, catching Sorcha's look, clearly keen for the woman to leave. 'Shouldn't you be getting home?'

'I haven't far to go, lass, don't you worry. I'll wait for Sorcha and Lillie here to leave, then you'll be rid of me.' She reached over and patted Katherine's knee. There was no resentment, no attack, only a deep understanding and, if Sorcha read her right, apology. Beatrix never meant for this to touch any of them.

Sorcha also understood Beatrix didn't want to be seen with her. If she was so determined she'd done nothing wrong, and today had been the authorities flexing their might, then why was she protecting them? What was Beatrix not telling them?

Farewelling Katherine, Lillie and Beatrix, Sorcha headed up the High Street lost in thought, only dimly aware of Captain Ross hailing her and responding with a half-hearted reply.

What were the bailies and Reverend Cowper really up to? And, if they were convinced Beatrix, on her own admission, cast a charm, why on God's good earth did they let her go?

FOURTEEN

The proof o' the pudding's the preein' o't.
(Don't form judgements without some knowledge.)

Sorcha was dreaming of her mor. Her long barley-coloured hair was unbound and she was standing at the water's edge, arms outstretched, laughing, facing the Forth. Her smile was wide, her pale blue eyes sparkled, making her look like one of her Nordic goddesses descended from the sky. She was calling to her, but the gentle murmurs of the ocean and the wind stole the words from her mouth and transformed them into cloudy wisps. Sorcha wanted to share her mother's unexpected joy, fly into those arms, feel the loving embrace she'd always imagined. But as she tried to make her way forwards, her mor's face changed. Those eyes the colour of a summer morning widened in terror. Her beautiful mouth pulled back in a grimace of sheer horror. The sea, so hushed before, transformed into a mighty swell. A giant wave, starting beyond the Isle of May, became a solid wall that raced towards the Weem, towards her mor. She shouted a warning, screamed as, instead of fleeing, her mother lowered her arms, raised her chin and shut her eyes. The wave, a tower of deadly might, soared up and up before it folded, down, down, down, crashing upon the sand, the darkening shore, upon her mor, and in great, greedy gulps took all of Pittenweem with it...

'Sorcha, for God's sake, wake up.'

It took her a moment to cease flailing, before she understood her mother wasn't being swept up and drowned, the village wasn't being destroyed. She was in her bedroom.

'Nettie.' Sorcha sat up, untangling herself from the covers, looking around blinking. 'I was having a dream...'

'Dream?' said Nettie, propped on the edge of the bed. 'Was a nightmare if you ask me.' She appraised her friend. 'What are you doing asleep at this time of day?'

Sorcha rubbed her eyes. 'I didn't sleep much after yesterday, what with Beatrix and all. And we were up so early this morning and then the catch...' Her voice trailed away. Intending to simply rest her head when she came home, she could scarce believe she'd fallen into such a deep sleep.

'Aye, it was a sorry showing,' said Nettie, standing and throwing Sorcha's skirt at her. 'Now, get dressed, you sloven.' Nettie went into the main room.

Sorcha heard her rummaging around with the pots.

'Come on. I've news,' she called.

Sorcha ran her hands through her hair and plucked her shift away from her body. She was sweaty and her heart was still racing. Aye, it was no dream she had. Dreams were what you held close to keep away the sorrows of the day; they were not meant to make the reality of living worse. Try as she might, she couldn't rid herself of the image of the destructive wave, how it took out the whole town...

Throwing back the covers, she went to the dresser and plunged her hands in the icy water, splashing her face. Whipping off her shift, she dragged a wet cloth over her body, her skin goosing, her nipples hardening.

'Can you stoke the fire?' asked Sorcha, drying herself and searching for a clean shift and the clothes she'd been wearing. Still shivering, she pulled her skirt off the bed and climbed into it, fastening the button at the back.

'Already done,' answered Nettie. 'I'm heating some milk for you.'

Sorcha bundled her hair and pinned it back into place. Gazing at herself in the mirror, she noted the haunted look she'd borne when she first arrived had all but gone. Even if she didn't feel like it, she was looking more like her old self — not the self Andy wed or the one who lost Davan, but before her da, Erik and ma died. Before Robbie went as well. Older, aye, but hopefully wiser, and able to weather the storms that came with living in the Weem.

She sensed one brewing now. That was the message her mor was giving her. The purple crescents under her own eyes and the glint of uncertainty behind them told her the same.

'What news do you have?' she asked as she left the bedroom. There was a soft afternoon light. She'd slept for longer than she thought. At least the drizzle had ceased.

Passing her a warm cup of milk, Nettie indicated a stool by the hearth. 'You need to sit down.'

Sorcha's ribs grew tight. 'What is it? Beatrix?'

Nettie sat opposite her and gave a terse nod. 'Aye. We need to be prepared.'

'What for?' asked Sorcha, her mouth growing dry but unable to drink. The lone cry of a shearwater broke the stillness.

'The worst,' said Nettie bluntly. 'Katherine's spoken to the bailies.'

A lance of dread pierced Sorcha's chest as she held the quaich of warm milk Nettie had poured her. 'The *bailies*? What for?'

Nettie shrugged. 'To report what Beatrix told us yesterday.'

'What? Why?' Sorcha's mind galloped. A shadow passed the window, there were voices. Did folk know what Beatrix had done? Was her name on everyone's tongue?

Nettie let out a long sigh. 'There was nothing Beatrix said while I was there that was worth reporting to anyone, let alone the authorities. But, Sorcha, Katherine Marshal went to Cowper, who summoned the bailies and made her repeat what she'd told him.'

'What did she tell him?' asked Sorcha quietly.

Nettie's eyes locked on her. 'That's why I'm here. What exactly did Beatrix say to you about Peter Morton after I left that made Katherine run to Cowper?'

She tried to recall what was said. 'She... she said that Peter brought his sickness upon himself — that it was his ill-tongue that attracted... *Dear God.*' Sorcha gasped, her hand flying to her mouth. She stared at Nettie in despair, then slowly lowered her fingers so she could finish. 'That attracted an evil spirit.'

Nettie's head fell into her hands. After a moment, she raised her face. 'You ken what this means?'

Beatrix had admitted that Peter Morton was bewitched; that a malevolent spirit possessed him. And now Cowper and the bailies knew.

'Aye.' Suddenly, Sorcha saw her dream for what it was, a premonition of the worst kind. 'Will they arrest her again?' she asked.

'If they haven't already. It's only a matter of time.' Nettie reached over, scrambling for Sorcha's hand. She didn't need to say more. Sorcha heard her as clearly as if she'd said it out loud. It was only a matter of time for them all.

'Why'd she do it?' asked Nettie.

For a moment, Sorcha was uncertain whether she meant Beatrix or Katherine. Sorcha shrugged. 'Maybe she thinks it will help Beatrix?' Nettie shot her a look of disbelief. 'Maybe she thinks it will remove any suspicion from her. I don't know. I don't have the answer.'

Snatches of conversations, images of Beatrix, her anger when Peter wouldn't sell nails to her, the bucket, the coal, Peter collapsing, and Reverend Cowper paraded through Sorcha's mind. Then they were replaced by one of a tall man on a grey horse, with dark eyes and a captivating grin. It was Nettie who once told her the captain was there to protect the women of Pittenweem — not from rogue waves rising out of dark depths, but from the men. She'd meant the incomers, the billeted soldiers. And he'd done that. But what was to stop the captain from protecting them from their own? Had he not invited her to share the burden she was carrying when he found her after the Morton lad was struck down?

As much as she was loath to do so, perhaps it was time to take him at his word and ask him for help again.

'Nettie,' she said, standing. She finished her milk and left the cup by the hearth. 'We have to find Captain Ross.'

'Why? What can he do?' said Nettie. Her shoulders were slumped, her face pinched.

'What he's sworn to do — protect us.'

Nettie began to laugh, but there was no humour in it. 'No one can protect us from Cowper. Not even God. As the reverend reminds us every kirk session — God is on *his* side.'

Sorcha swung her shawl around her shoulders, checked the pins in her hair and gave a grim smile. 'Maybe he can't protect us from Cowper's God, but perhaps he can protect us from the man himself. But we won't know if we don't try. Haven't you always said as much?'

She stood before Nettie and held out her hands.

Reluctantly, Nettie placed hers in them and allowed herself to be hauled to her feet. 'I have. I do. I just pray I'm not made to eat my words.'

As they left the house in search of Captain Ross, Sorcha prayed for that too.

FIFTEEN

Keep the heid.
(Stay calm, don't get upset.)

When Captain Aidan Ross saw it was the lovely widow Sorcha McIntyre who wished to speak to him, he regretted he'd no news of her brother to share. He'd written to the civic officials in Edinburgh, and even sent missives to an old friend fighting in France. Thus far he'd heard nothing. He knew the chances of Robbie McIntyre being alive were slim, especially since he'd been taken prisoner four years earlier. No one he knew survived that long in a Bavarian prison, let alone a French one. A swell of pity rose for the woman who, he understood from some of the Weem folk, had never given up hope. With what she'd suffered, it made him admire her even more, marvel at her resilience. There were so many in this small fishing community like her. Hardened by a life dependent on the whims of the sea, yet not above compassion; deeply superstitious, yet accepting of God's will, too. He'd thought he'd hate every minute he spent in this seaside town with its strange sea-customs and oft unwelcoming folk, but he'd come to know and respect what they did and what they stood for — most of them, anyway.

He invited Sorcha and her friend Janet Horseburgh, who everyone bar her husband and the reverend called Nettie, into the main room of the cottage where he was quartered.

The women studied their surroundings. He noted how the light from the windows caught Sorcha's eyes, turning them into pools of turquoise that reminded him of the lochs in summer on his family's land back in Skye. More often wreathed in mists and rain, it was a wild place that encouraged tales and songs, much like Fife. He wondered how they fared, his folk. Whether the fish that swam in the lochs were more plentiful than those in the waters lapping the Weem. Listen to him, he sounded more like a local every day rather than the incomer he'd been made to feel by almost everyone — except for the fishwives and fishermen. Except for Sorcha McIntyre.

What had brought them here? Sorcha was fiercely proud and Nettie more independent than most women of his acquaintance. He smiled at Nettie, admiring her fine profile as she examined the paintings on the walls.

Some looked askance at Sorcha and Nettie, but there were many who respected them for what they did. He was among them. Respected and, truth be told, desired to get to know them better. Sorcha especially.

Much better.

'What can I do for you?' he asked politely, standing near the hearth so they might take the two seats. A servant quickly went to make tea.

'Captain Ross,' began Sorcha, standing with her back to a chair, but not sitting. 'We need your help. Again.'

'Whatever I can, lass, if it's in my power, I will do it.' He indicated for them to sit and they did, smoothing their skirts, pulling at their cuffs.

The tension that had made Sorcha's shoulders square and her face pale seemed to recede a little. She glanced at Nettie, who gave a curt nod, and ventured a smile. His heart skipped to see it. 'Thank you, I hoped that's what you would say. Though you may alter your mind when you hear what kind of help we're seeking.'

He waited.

Taking a deep breath, she intertwined her fingers in her lap, fixed her eyes on his face, and began. 'You know of the sickness that has afflicted Peter Morton and how the reverend and others are attributing it to witchcraft? We had some discussion about this the day Peter fell ill.'

Aidan nodded. 'I do. And I hear they've found someone to blame for casting the spell that bewitched the lad.'

It was hard to keep the sarcasm out of his voice. Aidan had no time for fear-mongering or those who talked of witchcraft. He'd seen it when he fought on the continent and witnessed the consequences, how people used such accusations to rid themselves of those they considered nuisances, or were jealous of, or from whom they wished to acquire something — mostly property, and mostly from women. Women who dared to assert authority or challenge those who had it. That this kind of reckoning had come to Pittenweem disturbed him more than he liked to admit. It wasn't the first time practitioners of witchcraft had been found in the town. The last time anyone was declared guilty, and that had been decades ago according to the men in the tavern the night before, the outcome had been catastrophic. He shouldn't be surprised fear of malice was being stirred up again. The stain of bewitchment lingered in the earth long after the spell was broken, the root uncovered and removed. Even on Skye they'd heard about the Paisley trials and how seven souls were burned. Later, the girl at the centre of the accusations, the one named — the irony — Christian, whom some in authority doubted even then, was termed the Bargarran Imposter and her denunciations deemed false. Too late to save those who died.

Aware the women were staring at him, he frowned. 'Sorry. Could you repeat that?'

Sorcha gave a little sigh. Clearly, whatever he'd failed to hear had taken its toll. She was on the edge of her seat, as if she would run from the room at the slightest provocation.

Before she could reiterate, they were interrupted by the arrival of the tea. Silent while it was poured, Aidan watched as Sorcha took the proffered cup and, instead of drinking, gazed out the window. People were passing on the street, baskets over their arms. A cart was wheeled by, two skinny dogs ran beside it, tails wagging. Out on the waters, the sails of three large ships from the city ports further up the firth headed for the ocean. Flocks of gulls wheeled above the craft and the swells, many winging towards the Isle of May. Heavy clouds slunk over the horizon, hinting at late showers.

The maid had only just shut the door when Sorcha suddenly swung towards him. 'A few weeks ago, you were kind enough to warn Beatrix Laing about what happened to Peter Morton.'

Aidan recalled leaving Sorcha's cottage and going straight to the Laing woman's house; the whispered conversation just inside the front door; how hard the woman tried not to show her fear. Careworn, with a pronounced limp and a deep, no-nonsense voice and manner, she'd grimaced when he finished. He liked her even before she expressed concern, not for herself, but for her friends.

Sorcha lowered her head briefly. 'We fear —' she indicated Nettie, 'that matters have got out of hand. That Beatrix might be accused of witchcraft.'

The captain nodded grimly. He'd already begun noting events for his superiors. What good it would do, he wasn't certain, but he felt it was important that someone impartial (if he could be called that), recorded everything to do with Peter Morton and this so-called bewitchment.

'She be no witch, sir,' said Sorcha. 'Just a foolish old woman with a sharp tongue.'

'She can no more cast a spell than I can ride a broomstick,' added Nettie.

Sorcha shot her an appalled look.

'Perhaps that was a poor choice of words,' conceded Nettie, looking closely at what remained in her cup. 'There are some would argue I do. Ride a broom, that is. But you ken what I mean.'

'I do. And it's a terrible thing to be so accused,' said Aidan. How could he express the repugnance he felt, the deep uneasiness at what he sensed was afoot? He didn't want to alarm these women. Sorcha.

But they had to know. 'I'm not sure how to tell you this, but a short time ago the bailies ordered the arrest of Mrs Laing and the constables took her to the Tolbooth.' Sorcha's hand covered her mouth. Nettie shook her head.

'We feared she'd lose her liberty.' Sorcha looked to Nettie for confirmation. 'We didn't realise the bailies had already acted, nor had her taken to the Tolbooth…'

Aidan cleared his throat, anything to prevent himself from moving to Sorcha and offering her the comfort he so desperately wanted to provide. She was a loyal friend to this Beatrix — both women were. But did she understand, did either of them, what they were risking by coming to him and even discussing — let alone defending — their friend? Aye, they did. His heart swelled — with pride and a deep, deep concern.

'I understand that's where the bailies — your council — have their offices as well?' asked Aidan. 'On the top floor of the Tolbooth?' He knew the answer, he simply wanted to remind them.

The women exchanged dire looks. 'It is,' said Nettie.

'Is there *anything* you can do?' asked Sorcha.

'I'm sorry,' said the captain. 'I've no authority over their decision. I've no authority over anything that happens in Pittenweem unless it directly affects my men.'

Sorcha's face fell.

'Surely,' Aidan said quickly, 'once they question Mrs Laing, they'll see what you claim: that she's simply an auld woman with a sharp tongue.'

'I take it you've not met the reverend before?' Nettie cocked a brow at him.

Aidan went to speak then fell silent. Of course he knew the reverend. He also knew what Nettie meant.

'They *know* Beatrix, the type of woman she is — the whole village does. She's done this kind of thing before and, much to the reverend's disgust, was cleared of charges. But the bailies — and God knows how many others — are under his thumb,' said Nettie.

'That,' added Sorcha, 'and they're afraid of incurring his wrath.'

'They'd be fools if they weren't,' said Nettie wryly. 'As the reverend likes to remind us, he talks straight to God.'

How could Aidan caution these brave women they'd do well to be afraid too? 'Aye, well...' Aidan's hands were suddenly useless and the fire in the hearth became fascinating.

Jumping to her feet, Sorcha crossed the floor until she stood so close to him, he could smell the sea upon her, the scent of roses, the coolness of the breezes that blew through the streets. The effect was heady, distracting.

'Captain Ross,' began Sorcha, regarding him earnestly, waiting until she met his eyes. 'I fear you're wrong about not holding authority. The people here respect you and, while you might not be the law, you are Her Majesty's representative. You help keep the peace and, God knows, with Beatrix's arrest and what she is accused of, that's about to be disturbed in ways that make me quake in my very soul.' She urged Nettie to support her. 'It should make you quake, too — for yourself and your men.'

Nettie rose and joined them.

'Sorcha is right, captain. We need you to come with us and appeal to the bailies and the reverend — if not to their sense of justice, then to their common sense. We're afraid they'll make an example of Beatrix, regardless of what she might have done — or not done. They've wanted to for a long time. At least, the reverend has. I think if the people see you, see that you understand what Beatrix really is, just a foolish auld gilly, you'll bring some balance. Then she'll at least get a fair hearing.'

'If not fair, a hearing at least.' Sorcha looked to Nettie for support. 'We're concerned —' she gave a bark of laughter at how inadequate the word was, 'that if something isn't done, Beatrix will be tried and convicted before anyone can defend her, before the authorities in the city can act. For isn't it true, Captain Ross, that in a case like this, Edinburgh should not only be involved, but have the final say?'

'Aye, when it comes to witchcraft, that is so.'

'Then please, at the very least, help us ensure that happens.'

He'd never noticed how pellucid her eyes, how smooth and pure her complexion, the way the light plucked out seams of fire in her hair.

Unable to help himself, aware he was being manipulated into something that was not mere gallantry but interference in a local dispute and against everything he'd been ordered to do while stationed at the Weem — that it was utter foolhardiness — he nonetheless relented. His superiors had warned him never to become involved in local politics or customs, no matter how disturbing, but he couldn't let this rest. Not when he feared for the women requesting his help.

'Very well,' he said, before he could change his mind. 'I'll do what I can, but I can't promise too much.'

In a move that startled him, Sorcha took his hands in hers. He felt the pressure of her fingers, the cool dryness of her skin, the calluses hardened over years of baiting lines, repairing nets, and gutting fish. He liked the way they felt. These were hands that knew what it was to work. Were they also hands that knew how to love?

Heat filled his body, and he found himself squeezing her fingers in return, meeting those crystal eyes and smiling.

'All we ask is that you come with us and do your best,' said Sorcha. Nettie made a noise of affirmation.

'When?' asked Aidan, praying his best was good enough.

'Now,' said Sorcha.

SIXTEEN

She deigned to be avenged upon him.

— A Just Reproof to the False Reports and Unjust
Calumnies in the Foregoing Letter, *1705*

'*R*epeat what you just said, Mrs Laing,' said Reverend Patrick
Cowper. 'I didn't quite hear you.'

Beatrix Laing sat with her back to the window on the top floor of
the Tolbooth. Seated in one of the five chairs placed in a semi-circle
around her, Patrick wished they could hurry proceedings up. After all,
it was just a formality.

It was getting late, the room was growing cooler. He'd no chance to
eat his dinner before the constables brought the woman to his house.
Gazing out the window, he could glimpse deep blue sky and scud-
ding clouds. They'd been forced to close the window earlier, due to
the commotion on the street below, the shouting of those foolish folk
protesting the Laing woman's arrest, as well as those praising it. The
noise had been a terrible distraction. But now the chamber stank. The
woman's fear was ripe, as was her obstinacy.

The weak sun beamed behind her slumped figure, but where he sat
there was no heat, only the cold stone floors and walls; the eternal damp

reached out to grip him in an icy vice. Repressing the shivers that began to rack his body took all his will, but God forbid he'd show weakness by wrapping his arms about his sides and rubbing them, even though he longed to do so. This was about Mrs Laing's shortcomings. Mind you, he'd make her pay for his discomfort. As God was his witness.

She was proving to be more stubborn than he'd thought. He knew the other bailies felt the same. They'd been here since before the clock struck one and all they'd managed to get out of her was what she'd readily admitted the day before in the Morton house: that she'd left the bucket and coal by the smithy, but there'd been no admission of it being a charm. Not yet.

Despite the shut window, raised voices carried into the room. The words were muffled, but their intention wasn't. He'd seen the crowd gathered outside the Tolbooth. Among them were Sorcha McIntyre and her friend Janet Horseburgh. What he hadn't expected was to see Captain Aidan Ross standing beside them. The officer had even thumped on the main door and demanded to speak to the bailies.

Under orders from the reverend, the Tolbooth keeper refused to admit him; after all, he'd no rights here. Patrick was surprised the captain remained. Astonished any of the crowd did, for that matter. Their persistence simply lent strength to his cause. This woman, *these women*, he reminded himself as an image of Sorcha and Nettie rose in his mind, were nothing but troublemakers.

Dear God in heaven but he resented this farce. They all knew the old witch was guilty as sin — sin that even now spilled from her thin, wrinkled lips. It was his duty to protect his congregation, indeed all the Weem, from the dangers of such as her — and her accomplices. It was because of people like the Laing woman that he had answered God's calling in the first place. He was a soldier in His army and he would fight to the end, God willing.

'I... I... said,' began Beatrix, her lips parting with difficulty. Her mouth was parched; her lips cracked. She was having trouble speaking. One of the constables stepped forward to offer water, but the reverend waved him back. Let the biddy thirst.

Flicking the reverend a look that made Bailie Cook shudder, Beatrix snarled. Patrick fell back in his chair, his hand flying to his heart. Why, he felt that! It was as if the wily crone had punched him.

Bailies Cook and Vernour tore their eyes from Beatrix and studied him with concern. Bailie Bell, his thick white hair ruffled because he repeatedly dragged his fingers through it, stared at the ceiling, his mouth moving. Bailie Cleiland, his ruddy cheeks withered and veined, looked up briefly from the notes he was making, uncertain what had just taken place.

'Go on,' said Patrick finally. The words cost him and he made sure everyone present knew it. He rubbed his chest, took a deep breath, and continued slowly. He was not above some theatrics if they served a purpose. And what better purpose than God's? 'Tell us again how you never intended the bucket and coal to be a charm, even though everyone in the Weem knows this is precisely what such instruments signify. A sea-charm used by witches to conjure up storms, cause havoc and drive men mad. Is this not what you intended, Mrs Laing, when you lay the charm by the smithy? To smite young Peter Morton and summon the devil to torment him?'

Beatrix gave a hollow chuckle. 'You seem to have great knowledge of what I intended, reverend. If I didn't know better, it would be easy to believe you set the charm yourself.'

This time the bailies gasped. Patrick, recovered now, jumped to his feet. With three strides, he loomed above her, his lank frame casting a shadow over her bent one. He raised his arm as if to strike her. Beatrix lifted her chin and locked eyes with him.

'Go on, lad. I dare you,' she whispered.

He lowered his arm, stepped back and gestured to one of the constables. 'We've wasted enough time. The woman needs to learn to speak the truth.'

'I *am* speaking the truth,' shouted Beatrix. 'It's you that won't listen.'

Patrick stood aside to make room for the constable. Moving behind Beatrix, the man elevated a stick above his head and brought it down across the back of her shoulders.

The old woman cried out and would have fallen off the chair if she had not been tied to it.

'God demands the truth,' Patrick shouted. 'If we have to knock it out of you, we will.'

'And it's what He *has* been given,' yelled Beatrix. 'You be naught but a slimy bit o' fish guts, tangling my words and my meaning.' Turning her head one way then the other, she tried to locate the constable who'd struck her, even as she twisted in her seat to try and dodge the next blow. 'Hit a feeble auld woman, will you, Angus Stuart? Well, I've had worse and from better than you.' She began to laugh. It was hollow. Dry. Broken.

Patrick knew where she found her voice, her courage to resist. 'Twas the devil.

He faced the bailies. Only Vernour looked at him directly, his thick lips pursed. William Bell had turned aside, refusing to watch proceedings. Of all the bailies, Patrick was least certain about him. There was a time he'd been a friend to the McIntyres, defending Astrid to the villagers, aiding Charlie in his endeavours, encouraging Sorcha to step out with Andy Watson. But with Charlie's passing that bond had frayed, until the drowning of the Watson lad had given it cause to unravel. Surely, now, any sympathy he might feel for Sorcha, for her demon-touched friends, would be sundered for good.

If not, he would have to ensure that was the case.

'Time, sirs,' said Patrick, straightening his shoulders, 'to use whatever means we have. It's the only language the devil understands.'

Not waiting for their assent, he spun around and, making sure Beatrix saw him, nodded to Angus Stuart.

The stick landed again and again. Across Beatrix's shoulders, stomach, legs. There was an exclamation of dismay swiftly stifled. Patrick could have sworn it came from Bell. He waited for an objection. There was none. Only the noise of the constable's ponderous panting echoed about the room. Not even the Laing woman made a sound. Twice the constable slapped her face so hard her head snapped back. Blood spattered her cheek. A tooth ricocheted off the wall, rolling into a crevice beside the shelves that held the council records.

At first, Beatrix remained defiantly silent. But slowly, as the blows kept raining upon her, some softer than others, as if the man delivering them was weakening, she tried to speak even if only to hurl insults. When, at the reverend's order, another constable took the first one's place and commenced with renewed vigour, she began to whimper then wail.

Outside, voices cried out in protest as Beatrix's fractured screams pierced the thick walls.

'For godssakes, Patrick,' said Bailie Bell, half-rising out of his chair as blood poured down Beatrix's cheek from a laceration on her temple.

'It's for God's sake and the sake of this town I do this,' cried Patrick. Bailie Bell looked to the other men for support. When none was forthcoming, he slowly sat back down. The constable continued.

When the stick landed on the hand clutching the arm of the chair, breaking two fingers, Beatrix shrieked like the banshees in the tales the Irish sailors told.

Patrick signalled for the constable to cease.

With the exception of Robert Cleiland, the bailies squirmed in their seats, unable to look at the battered woman. Deep in his heart, Patrick despised them for their lack of fortitude. But then, he reminded himself, they didn't understand what it was they faced. This was no ordinary woman but the devil's own disciple. Pacing around Beatrix, he paused to pat the constables on the shoulder, whisper reassurances, remind them of the good work they were doing. The Lord's work.

As he signalled it was time to start again, Patrick made sure Beatrix saw his gesture.

Only then did she beg for mercy. Quietly at first, so softly that Patrick had to lean over so his ear was close to her split lips, then in great ragged gasps.

Fists hammered the door below, their echoes resounding up the stairs.

Holding up his hand, the reverend made a show of preventing the constable from attacking again. Beatrix's keening halted. Almost simultaneously, whoever was pounding the door also stopped. There was an unnatural quiet except for Beatrix's laboured breathing.

She let out a cry of utter anguish that dissolved into thick, indistinguishable words.

'You've something to say?' asked Patrick, kneeling before her. 'Speak clearly, woman. You have to make sure we can all hear, mind. Bailie Cleiland needs to record what you say.'

Cleiland made a strangled noise that could have been agreement.

The mottle-haired bitch was a muddle of stained rags; her defiant face a mass of swellings, blood and bruises. Her bent back had folded over. Her hands were twisted knots of flesh. Patrick tried not to smile. No woman of her age could withstand such a beating and live. This was all the proof he needed that this was no ordinary person they faced, but a witch. A witch with the devil inside her. The devil wouldn't last long in such a worn-out shell. If Patrick didn't destroy him now he would seek out other bodies, other willing collaborators. That must not be allowed to happen. He was already losing his hold over the town; the devil would wrest control from him altogether if he had his foul way.

'Aye,' croaked Beatrix, her chest rising and falling with the effort. 'You're right. You've been right all along. I made a charm.' She paused, taking long, arduous breaths. 'I was angry at the lad for not making me some nails and sought to be avenged upon him for his defiance.' Tears flowed down her sunken cheeks. A great trail of snot ran from her nose, over her swollen, bleeding lips and down her chin. It was all Patrick could do not to recoil.

Instead, he used his most persuasive Sunday voice, the one his wife used to say was like clotted cream. 'Go on.'

Closing her eyes, Beatrix raised her chin. The sun struck the flesh, making it appear like parchment — delicate, fragile, torn. 'I asked the devil to teach the lad a lesson for his ill manners to me.'

'I see.' Patrick glanced over his shoulder. The looks of reproach and doubt that had begun to set on the features of the bailies were transformed into curiosity and more than a little fear — even Bell's. They teetered in their chairs, leaned on their forearms to catch her every word. Bailie Vernour gave a nod that was as good as a concession. What did the methods being deployed matter if they extracted the information they needed? If it protected the town?

Patrick hid a smirk and turned back to the woman, stroking her uninjured hand. She tried to move it, but because of the ropes binding her wrists to the arms of the chair, could not. He continued to caress it, despite her flinching.

'And how did you know the devil to summon him with such ease?' he asked.

There was not a sound in the room. Outside, the hushed notes of birdsong bid the last of the day adieu. The voices below the window had dropped to murmurs, a melody to the birds' faint chorus. The light had dimmed, the sky was a pale mauve and strawberry pink, much like the markings on Beatrix's battered face.

'Because… because…' Her head fell forwards making her next words indistinguishable.

'What was that?' asked Patrick, tipping his head until his ear was close to her face. 'Did I hear you say you renounced your baptism?' he coaxed. 'That you made a pact with the devil?'

Bailie Cleiland's quill scritched and scratched.

Beatrix nodded. The bailies began to mutter, hurriedly, words laced with disbelief and alarm.

Patrick used Beatrix's chair to lever himself upright. He faced the shocked bailies, triumph on his face and in his heart. 'How many years ago was this? Five? Seven? Ten?' He waited between each number.

Beatrix shook her head to each one.

'Twelve?'

'Aye,' she whispered. 'Twelve years ago, I entered his service.'

'And what did he bid you do, your devil master, Beatrix? Tell me, confess your sins to God; free your soul from this darkness.'

'He did bid me to make an image of Peter Morton out of wax so he might torment the lad on my behalf.'

'How did you let the devil know where to hurt Peter?'

'I stuck pins in the image so the devil knew where to make the lad feel pain.'

Patrick nodded sagely. 'And were you alone in its making?' He moved to the side of her chair, one hand pressing against the shoulder that had borne the brunt of the beatings.

'Aye.' Beatrix tried to wriggle away, but when she couldn't, began to cry. 'Nae, nae,' she said and he eased the pressure.

Patrick's eyes shone. 'I see. Well, Beatrix, God will forgive you if you share the names of your accomplices with us here and now. Share them, and all this — the pain, your suffering, will come to an end.'

She shook her head. 'There are none. There are no accomplices. It was just me.' He pressed her shoulder harder, causing her to cry out once more. Bailie Bell swung his body around so he wouldn't have to watch.

'Was it Sorcha McIntyre?' asked Patrick.

Beatrix hesitated and then shook her head.

Patrick blanched. He leaned on Beatrix heavily, so she bore his entire weight. 'Was it Nicolas Lawson?'

'Aye, aye.' Panting, she was whimpering freely now.

'And what did Nicolas do, Beatrix? Did she make the image with you?'

Unable to speak, Beatrix nodded.

'And stuck it with pins?' He forced his weight upon her again.

'We both did,' howled Beatrix. Then she fainted.

Patrick no longer cared. He had what he needed to begin to unite folk and cleanse the village of the terrible evil that had been brought in on a tide of darkness. A tide, he couldn't help but think, that flowed with the return of Sorcha McIntyre.

'Did you write down all she said?' He snatched up the document before Bailie Cleiland could reply.

Holding the paper aloft triumphantly, he turned to the constables. The one who'd administered most of the beating, Angus Stuart, was flexing his fingers, the other, his brother, Gerard, nursed a bloodied stick in his hand. Patrick blazed with triumph.

He carefully put down the record of Beatrix's words, found a blank sheet among those on the table, snatched the quill out of Bailie Cleiland's fingers and scrawled a few words. Signing with a flourish, he then passed the document and the quill to the other councillors, waiting as one by one they read his words and added their names to his. Once they'd all signed, he pressed the council's seal upon the page. When it had dried, he passed the document over to Angus. No one had said a word the entire time.

'You're to apprehend Nicolas Lawson immediately, lads. Bring her here.'

'Wait,' said Bailie Bell, rising from his seat so fast it almost toppled over. A frown knitted his brow. 'You can't do that. Not until we have proof of what she says.' He nodded towards Beatrix's unconscious form.

'Proof?' snapped Patrick. 'What more do you need than the name from a witch's mouth? Did this… this woman not say she renounced her baptism? Did she not say she made an image of the boy and pricked and prodded it to torment him under guidance from the devil?' He glared at Bailie Bell, who in turn stared at first Bailie Vernour then Bailie Cook, willing them to speak. Their heads remained lowered. Bailie Cook coughed into a fist, his fleshy cheeks wobbling.

Patrick persisted, 'Did she not admit Nicolas Lawson was her co-conspirator?'

'Aye, she did,' agreed Bailie Bell. 'But look at her.' He gestured to Beatrix, but failed to follow his own command. 'The woman was under duress. She was… suffering —'

'Does not Peter Morton?' replied Patrick. 'Does he not lie there day after day, racked with pain and filled with torment?'

'Aye, but —'

'But? But?' Patrick spat, his face puce, his eyes bulging. His hands were balled by his side. 'But what? Do you not want to put a stop to this before we lose control? Before the devil and his witches run amok?'

'But you heard the protests outside. The calls for a greater authority than us to wield judgement.'

'I heard no such thing,' said Patrick, trying to regain his composure. Och, he'd heard them all right and he knew the voices — Sorcha McIntyre, Janet Horseburgh and that damned Captain Ross among others. If only Beatrix had named *those* women… He could not think on that, not yet. He mustn't move too fast. He needed the support of these men, either that, or their fear. What he didn't need was their doubt, their enmity.

'I did,' said Bailie Cook quietly. Bailie Bell clamped a hand on his shoulder.

'As did I,' said Bailie Bell firmly, raising his head to meet the reverend's cool gaze. 'Just as I heard what Captain Ross said to the Tolbooth keeper. He has a point. As Bailie Whyte keeps reminding us,' he glanced meaningfully at the man's vacant chair, its occupant conveniently called away on business that morning, 'the courts in Edinburgh don't look too kindly on local authorities administering justice, especially in cases of this nature.'

'Let's call it what it is,' said Bailie Cook, moving slightly so Bell was forced to remove his hand, 'a case of suspected witchcraft.' He frowned as he looked at the unconscious woman, a look of pity dawning on his face.

It wouldn't do. Patrick huffed and folded his arms, moving to stand between the bailies and the broken Beatrix Laing. 'What do you suggest then?'

Bailie Bell took a deep breath. 'I suggest that before we proceed any further, we search Mrs Laing's house for this image. Hers and Mrs Lawson's. In the meantime, we send to Edinburgh. If there *is* witchcraft at work here as Mrs Laing claims, then at the very least we need advice on how to proceed. How to work within the law.'

Seeing the man would not be moved and that Bailie Cook, if not Vernour as well, was inclined to support him, Patrick relented. 'Very well. The constables can search for this waxen figure. But if they find it, then we proceed as agreed. We'll send for the pricker and find out how much more Beatrix Laing is hiding. For I've no doubt she's withholding information. There are more involved in this evil business than just her and Nicolas Lawson. One has only to see Peter's suffering to know this to be true.' He turned towards Beatrix, the other men following his gaze.

At that moment, Beatrix opened her eyes and raised her chin. She smiled; her missing teeth and bloodied mouth and lips made her look like she was wearing a devil-cast mask.

Patrick shuddered just as the other men recoiled. He stepped towards them and lowered his voice. 'But think on this, gentlemen.

We've no need for Edinburgh's involvement — not yet anyhow,' he said quickly, before Bell could disagree. 'The woman has confessed and that's a grand start. We must handle this ourselves for as long as we're able. Otherwise, we might never put an end to it.'

Beatrix continued to stare at them, not understanding the significance of what they were saying. The men studiously avoided her gaze and glanced at each other, undecided.

Patrick was fed up with their ambivalence. Much like the constables who'd beaten Beatrix Laing, he knew where to aim so it hurt. 'After all,' he said, waving a cavalier hand, 'which of us can afford to pay for the presence of advocates from the city? Pay for lawyers' advice? Their upkeep while they eat our food and drink our whisky? Is it you, William? Thomas? You, Robert? For I tell you now, gentlemen, I can't afford the luxury of Edinburgh magistrates and neither can the town.'

That decided it. They all agreed Patrick was right. The bailies would rather see an old woman beaten bloody and pricked to uncover her accomplices than part with coin. A search would be mounted — first for the wax image and, if that was found, or even if it wasn't, then, with the help of a pricker, for anyone else who might have aided and abetted Beatrix Laing.

Beatrix Laing who, of her own admission, was a witch in league with the devil.

SEVENTEEN

Duntit f'ae dowg tae devil.
(Pursued by misfortune.)

Sorcha stormed into her cottage, followed more sedately by a crest-fallen Nettie and a resigned Captain Ross.

'They won't find it,' said Sorcha, swinging around to face them. 'Not in Beatrix's house or Nicolas's. How can they when, like this pact with the devil, a wax image is just something the men forced her to admit in order to justify arresting her?'

Nettie shooed Captain Ross further into the room and shut the door.

Sorcha fell into a chair and dropped her head into her hands. She could barely think, she was so angry, so despondent. She'd not felt so powerless since... since... Davan died. Back then, as she held his little body in her arms, unable to breathe life into his wee blue form, make his sweet heart beat, she'd made a promise to never again allow herself to be in a situation she couldn't control. Yet, here she was. Sometimes, no matter how much you wished to alter things, they simply were. It was like what old Thomas Brown would say, 'You canna hold back the tides.' It was so unfair. Raising her head, she stamped her foot.

Nettie knelt beside her, prodding the fire back to life. She placed a comforting hand on Sorcha's leg and gave it a squeeze. 'I know, lass, I know. This be madness. But we can't let it affect us. We need to be calm, to think. Let's have a drink and discuss what to do next. We have to be smart. Beatrix and Nicolas are going to need all the help they can get.'

'And friends,' said Sorcha, pulling the scarf from her hair and letting it fall in her lap. 'And friends.'

'Aye,' said Captain Ross. Sorcha had almost forgotten he was there. He stood by the window, his back to them, looking up and down the street. He turned to regard them. 'It seems your bailies and the reverend want to handle this matter themselves. Made no difference how many times I mentioned Edinburgh, reminded them of the law, legal procedure, they were having none of it.'

'But,' said Sorcha, taking the dram Nettie passed to her gratefully, 'I thought the law states they have to notify the city magistrates in instances of witchcraft. They may have dealt with it themselves last time there was an accusation, but what happened at Bargarran changed everything. Edinburgh did not come out of that affair well.'

'Let's pray none of them forget that,' said Nettie quietly, offering a drink to Captain Ross.

'Thank you,' he said.

'Please, captain, sit down,' said Sorcha, remembering her manners. 'I'm not being a very good hostess. I can barely think straight. I could scarce believe what Alick told us at the Tolbooth.' Alick Brigstowe was the Tolbooth keeper, a man with a large belly, bent legs and a gnarled hand — his other one having been amputated after it became caught in the rigging on her da's ship. Unable to fish with one arm, Alick had been given the job of managing the Tolbooth thanks to her father, who had used his influence as a boat owner to arrange it. There was no love lost between Alick and the reverend; Alick was one of those led astray by the soldiers and more likely to be found drinking ale on a Sunday than attending kirk. He refused the coin the captain offered him when they first knocked on the door of the Tolbooth and demanded to speak to the bailies, and instead reported back all he could hear through the door. It was his information that allowed them to leave before the constables and warn Nicolas.

'They beat her,' said Sorcha then downed her drink in one gulp. 'They beat poor auld Beatrix.' She shook her head as if to banish the thought.

'I'll never forget the sound of her screams. Thank God her William wasn't there to hear them.' Nettie shuddered. 'The bastards. And now we know exactly what she's been accused of, thanks to Alick.'

Sorcha stared at the fire as it took hold. Wind whistled down the chimney, blowing smoke back into the room. Squinting through the worst of it, she went over what Alick had revealed. 'You don't think Beatrix was telling the truth, do you? That she renounced her baptism?' She raised her limpid turquoise eyes to Captain Ross, then Nettie.

'Nae,' said Captain Ross. 'I think she was telling the men what they wanted to hear.'

'I agree,' said Nettie. 'Anything to stop being hit. In naming Nicolas, she named someone she knew would be strong against the reverend. Against these base accusations. Nicolas laughed when we told her, bless her. Unlike Beatrix, it's not worth their while to imprison her.'

'What do you mean?' asked Captain Ross.

Nettie whirled her whisky as she considered how to answer him. 'You're not so ignorant as to miss my meaning, are you, captain? Once someone's named a witch, then the town council is entitled not only to fine them and their families, but also to take a huge portion of their wealth — something like two-thirds or at least a half. Beatrix has means. Nicolas, on the other hand, is as poor as a kirk-mouse, not worth arresting, not really. I'm not sure what the reverend or the bailies hope to get out of questioning her, except perhaps something to help convict Beatrix, who, of course, possesses both property and coin.'

'Purge the village of sin, unite them in a quest to renounce the devil, that's what the reverend said according to Alick,' added Sorcha dolefully. 'As if it's only auld women or the likes of Nicolas who sin in the first place.'

'What you both say might be true,' said Captain Ross carefully, 'but what if, like today, Mrs Laing and Mrs Lawson are... persuaded to name more women as witches? Women with more to lose — or, should I say, to give to the council?'

Nettie and Sorcha shared a look. Sorcha nodded grimly.

Nettie gulped. 'It's what we're afeared of, laddie.'

'They tried to wrest the boat and house from me once before, after mor died, and failed,' admitted Sorcha.

'What she means, captain,' added Nettie, 'is the reverend tried — by marrying her off to one of his sons, no less.'

Sorcha grimaced at the thought. 'Needless to say, I declined the proposal. But surely, accusing any of us of witchcraft is a step too far even for the reverend and bailies.'

Sorcha looked around the room with an objective eye. There wasn't too much of value here, though the garret was a different matter, filled as it was with nets, creels, ropes, iron and so much more. Memories to her, they'd make good coin if they were to be sold. And then there was the cottage itself, not to mention the boat...

Regretting he'd frightened them, the captain tried to change the subject. 'Push it out of your minds for now. I could be wrong. In the meantime, don't let the whisky go to waste.'

'You're right,' said Sorcha, refilling their cups. She tipped some more into her own and waited for the other two to lift their quaichs to her. 'Here's to Beatrix and Nicolas. May God be on their side for a change.'

'To Beatrix and Nicolas,' echoed the captain and Nettie. They drained their drinks.

'Now,' said the captain, drawing his stool closer. 'Let's discuss our next step. We know from Alick that the reverend and bailies have no intention of informing Edinburgh at present. But what's to stop me writing to my commanding officer and notifying him what's going on? What's to stop him letting the authorities in the city know?'

Sorcha felt a smile begin. 'Why, nothing. The reverend's made it clear you have no influence over what Weem people do. Which means, in essence, he has none over you.'

The captain gave an insolent grin. 'My thoughts exactly. I'll leave here shortly and attend to it at once. But if I might make a suggestion?'

'Go ahead, captain, please. We need all the advice we can get, unlike the bailies or the reverend,' added Sorcha.

'I think it would be wise if you and Nettie, and perhaps some of the other fishwives, tried not to be seen in each other's company for a while.'

Nettie and Sorcha looked at each other and burst out laughing.

'What?' asked Captain Ross. 'What's so funny?'

'I see what you're about, captain,' Nettie said through her chuckles. 'But that would raise more suspicion than it would subdue rumours.'

'We always work together,' explained Sorcha. 'Nettie's right. If we ceased to do that, then talk would fly.'

'Like a witch,' said Nettie, her eyes sparking with mischief.

'So,' said Sorcha with a shrug, 'we've no choice but to place our faith in Edinburgh. And in you.' Their eyes met. Sorcha forgot to breathe.

She lifted her glass in a toast before realising it was empty. Glad to be given something to do so she didn't have to look at the captain again, she stood and poured.

Captain Ross held his quaich steady until the others were filled. 'Here's to the authorities in the city,' he said.

'May they see justice done,' said Sorcha and they knocked cups and drank.

'I'd best be going.' Captain Ross put down his quaich. 'I want this missive away by first light. The sooner we contact Edinburgh about Mrs Laing, the sooner something can be done to prevent what promises to be a travesty.'

Sorcha followed him to the door. As he stepped outside, she grabbed his arm. 'I cannot thank you enough, Captain Ross. There's not many in your position would do what you have.'

'What's that?' he asked.

'Get involved.'

He smiled. Not for the first time, she wondered what he was thinking behind those dark eyes. 'Don't thank me yet, Mrs McIntyre. Let's see what comes of this.' He placed his hand over hers. 'You should be prepared lest nothing happens. The authorities in the city may decide to leave Mrs Laing to the Weem council; especially after what happened in Paisley. As you correctly pointed out, the outcome there did the reputation of the city magistrates no favours.'

Sorcha looked grave. 'I know that whatever we try may make no difference. But at least we will have tried. What they decide to do once they've been alerted is on their conscience.'

They stared at each other for a long moment. Above the captain's head, clouds scudded across the sky; a flock of gulls floated in the thermals, dark against the sun's glow. The wind whipped his black hair about his face, across his mouth. She looked at his lips, aware he was staring at hers.

'Come away in or shut the door, will you?' called Nettie. 'The fire's guttering.'

They broke away from each other, their momentary closeness interrupted. With an apologetic smile and curtsey, Sorcha stepped inside. Captain Ross placed his hat on his head and, with a small salute, strode down the road.

Sorcha closed the door and leaned against it, her hands clasped behind her. She grinned.

'Look at you,' chuckled Nettie. 'Giddy as a wee lassie, and with all that's happening too. I told you the day you returned he was a good 'un, didn't I?'

'You did, Nettie. Even so, I thought he'd never go.'

Peeling herself away from the door, Sorcha went to the fire. She pulled a small doll-like figure from her pocket and studied it. Nettie joined her, so close she could hear her breathing. Made of wax, it had a head of brown wool hair, disproportionate limbs and bright blue beads pressed into its tallow face for eyes. It looked like no one they knew, but they both understood who it was meant to represent. Sorcha had found it beneath Beatrix's pillow when they'd raced to her cottage after Alick revealed what was happening. The captain had waited outside while the two friends did a quick search of the premises. Shocked to find it, agreeing it meant nothing but a poor attempt at punishment and humour, Sorcha had stuffed it in her pocket. Why they kept it a secret from Captain Ross she wasn't sure, but she knew it was the right thing to do. The man was risking enough for them already.

'Here's to Beatrix and Nicolas,' she said, holding the small wax figure aloft. What on earth Beatrix was thinking to do something so foolish, so reprehensible as to make a figurine of Peter Morton, she couldn't fathom. Never mind, no one would find it now.

She threw it on the flames and put an arm around Nettie, drawing her close as they watched the damn thing become engulfed by flames before it swiftly fizzed and melted.

EIGHTEEN

*About the beginning of May, his case altered to the worse, by having such
strange and unusuall fitts, as did astonish all onlookers...*

— Annals of Pittenweem, Being Notes and Extracts from the
Ancient Records of that Burgh, *13th day of June, 1704*

$\mathcal{P}$eter Morton found it hard to remember what it was like to live
without pain. Each day the stiffness in his neck and limbs seemed to
grow worse. His stomach, unable to hold down anything but watery
broths for weeks now, was bloated and sore. Admittedly, it was mainly
when Reverend Cowper came to visit and they spoke of the torments
experienced by Christian Shaw that his agonies increased. The reverend
would become almost ecstatic, holding his hand, murmuring prayers,
calling on God and asking Him for the names of those causing Peter's
affliction. Strangely, as the days wore on, each time the reverend asked
God to reveal the people responsible for Peter's fits and contortions and
recited possible names, Peter's pain intensified and he would cry out.

The reverend was so pleased with Peter whenever this happened, he
would hold him and pray for him and speak to him as his father never
did. Whereas his da seemed almost embarrassed by what was happening to his son and was unable to remain in the room with him, the

reverend gloried in it. He visited every day, brought cakes, cheeses and other temptations to try and whet the lad's appetite. Reverend Cowper would settle in the chair beside the bed and read from the Bible, as well as stories from the city newspapers, and from a book about Christian Shaw, replete with detailed descriptions of her suffering. On two occasions he'd read accounts of events in a place called Salem in the New World. It was a small village in a territory Peter couldn't pronounce, let alone try and spell, but all the same, it resonated. It was in the colonies, which just went to prove that witchcraft, as the reverend said, knew no bounds. Whereas his da rolled his eyes and snorted when Peter tried to keep him by his side and share what the reverend had told him, Reverend Cowper was never so dismissive. When his da demanded his son rise and return to work, saying he'd had enough of his idleness, the reverend scolded his father thoroughly. After that, his da was banned from the bedroom.

Apart from some of the bailies and their wives, and members of the kirk the reverend trusted, Reverend Cowper was his main visitor. He would sit close to the bed, run his fingers through Peter's hair, not caring if it wasn't washed or combed, and call him a 'good lad', a 'brave and bonnie man', and a 'child of God'. Together, he promised, they'd expose and oust the devil and his assistants from the Weem. He said over and over that he, Reverend Cowper, and God, needed Peter's help. Ever since, Peter feared to disappoint him.

When the reverend asked to see his legs so he could comprehend why he was experiencing such pain and saw nothing, Peter knew the man was frustrated. He didn't stay long, nor did he read or praise him that day. So the next day when Peter cried out each time a name was mentioned, arching his back, twisting his neck and huffing and puffing as if he'd run from St Monan's to the Weem, Peter was pleased to reveal his limbs when the reverend lifted the covers. Covered in red marks like scrapes from a fine needle, crusted in blood, deep at the ends, shallow in others, the gashes were shocking to see. When the reverend asked who put those marks upon him, Peter denied knowing how they got there, only that they added to his terrible torment.

That day, the reverend stayed by Peter's bedside for hours, reading and talking to him, reminding him over and over how like a son he was. The following day, Peter showed him his arms and stomach. There were bite marks as well as deeper wounds, some bleeding so freely the reverend was forced to ask for an unguent and bandages, but not before he'd invited in the bailies and the doctors from Edinburgh (who were thinking of leaving the town) to inspect his patient.

When Peter was in the midst of his fits, there were men who would try to still him, lift and bend his legs, turn his head. Even the strongest of them was unable to do so. Likewise, when they saw the gouges on his legs, the bite marks, the imprint of fingernails and what appeared to be bruises from pinching, they could find no evidence of who or what had made them. No instrument was to be found in Peter's bedroom, and his parents and siblings denied harming him.

While Peter had days when nothing afflicted him, they were becoming rare. The more the reverend visited and spoke of Christian Shaw, Salem and other trials that found and punished witches, trials where the victim was hailed a hero by the good folk freed from bewitchment, the more frequent the attacks became.

The reverend told him Beatrix Laing had finally confessed to placing a charm upon him. Surprised to learn that Nicolas Lawson was involved too, Peter nonetheless dutifully reacted and shivered at the mention of her name, gratifying the reverend no end. Nevertheless, though the constables hunted for the wax image Beatrix claimed the two women had made, it could not be found.

When the reverend whispered to him that they would be bringing Beatrix Laing to his house on the morrow and into this very room so they could prove once and for all that she was indeed a witch, Peter knew his moment had come. The reverend was depending on Peter to help him prove to the bailies and any doubters in town that Beatrix Laing was in league with the devil. Only by doing this could he and Peter liberate Pittenweem from the curse this woman and her coven had brought upon them. A curse whose harm stretched beyond Peter's suffering.

'Look at how poor the catch has been of late,' the reverend reminded him in hushed tones. 'And what about all the drownings and poor crops? This isn't the work of God, but Satan himself. Will you help me, Peter my son?' His voice made Peter think of warm milk laced with whisky, of the sun-drenched fields beyond the braes in summer. Most of all, it made him think of the sweet lips of Sorcha McIntyre and what it would be like to feel them upon his own. If he helped the reverend to expel the devil and unite the town in Christ's love, then maybe he would.

'Aye, reverend. I will help you in whatever way I can. I live to serve the Lord.' And you, Reverend Cowper, thought Peter. And you.

NINETEEN

By the pricking of my thumbs, something wicked this way comes...

— Macbeth, *Act IV scene i*

*B*eatrix lay on the foul straw, watching the way the rain beading down the high window reflected strange patterns onto the walls. She tried to remember how many days she'd been locked inside the Tolbooth. Was it four or five? She could no longer be sure. From the moment the constables, acting under the orders of the reverend and the council, placed her inside this room beneath the chamber where she'd been first questioned then beaten, they'd determined to make her incarceration even more miserable.

Ensuring she didn't sleep, they stomped on the floor above, banged the door of her room at intervals or, when they saw her dozing off, would burst inside, lifting her to her feet and forcing her to walk around the room for hours on end. At first she couldn't work out how they knew when her eyes began to close and her head to nod. But before long she understood that what she thought were just marks on the ceiling were in fact strategic holes those in the council room above could use to watch her. Shamed at first that they saw her squat to piss or shit, after a few days she no longer cared, raising her skirts to bare her backside, thrusting her hairy quim towards them when she thought they might be looking. It made her feel better knowing they would be shocked or aroused when they knew they should feel disgust. The very thought lifted her heavy spirits. Dear Lord, she'd never felt so injured, so full of sorrow and fear. What must her poor husband think? Or her daughter, Cassie, and her sweet wee granddaughter, Elise? What had they been told?

Even so, these were small victories that she knew wouldn't sustain her for much longer. Her body ached with fatigue and hunger; she couldn't cease worrying her gum where her tooth had come out. All that before she considered what the pricking had done. Raising an arm to the dim light, she examined the marks the pricker, a young man from Leith with a pale complexion and mean pebble eyes, had left upon her. There were rows and rows of superficial and deep scratches. So many. Too many. Perhaps she'd been here longer than five days.

But it was over now. At least for the time being.

Rolling onto her side, wincing as the straw poked through her thin, filthy clothes, she caught a whiff of the bucket they'd left her. Told she was lucky to have it, especially after she threw the contents at the last constable to pass her some stale bannock and a watery kale soup, she knew it was because they were afeared where she'd shit if they didn't. From the smell of the straw, someone had already used it to piss in and not just the rats that scurried about at night.

She ran her good fingers over her broken ones. After that first day when the reverend's men had beaten her bloody and they'd decided to search her house and poor Nicolas's for the figurine she admitted making, she'd been left to suffer. If it hadn't been for the Tolbooth keeper, old Alick, she wasn't sure she'd even be alive. Bringing the medicines Sorcha, Nettie and Janet had smuggled to him, along with some cloths, he had splinted and bandaged her broken fingers together.

'This be a sorry business, Beatrix,' he'd said. 'I want no part in it.' He worked using his one good hand and his teeth, asking her to help with the fingers she could move, and deftly bound her digits together. He'd also given her some whisky Sorcha had sent him by way of thanks for what he was doing to numb her pain. It had worked that night — and for a few nights after. Bless him.

But that was before the pricker arrived. When had that been? She frowned. She recalled one of the bailies complaining about it being cold for mid-May. Not that it mattered in here. It felt like a lifetime ago. She still couldn't bear to have her breast brush against anything, not even the fabric of her shift. And as for her cunt…

What was the pricker's name? He'd told her. Ah, that's right, Mr Bollocks. Nae, that was what she called him every time she saw him to help reduce the terror he inspired. She refused to think of him as The Pricker. It was Bollard. That's right. How one so young could take so much pleasure from causing an eldren woman pain, she could barely credit. Cast from a devil's mould he was, and yet she was the one they believed possessed and recruiting others to an evil cause.

Yet they never found the waxen image. She could guess why. God bless her friends. Instead of releasing her, the reverend and bailies chose to inflict additional pain and deprivation upon her — in order to extract what from her? More lies? Lies to confirm their supposed truths? It wasn't right. None of this was right.

The first day Mr Bollard came to her room, he examined her. He rolled back her sleeves, lifted her skirts, pinched, pulled, poked, prodded, delighting when she yelped, frowning when she made not a murmur. Forcing open her mouth, he'd inserted his fingers, before making them crawl across her scalp. All the time, she was being watched by the council through the holes above. She could hear them, see the moving shadows as the light changed. Cowards. They should be in the room with her, with him. Hear, smell, look in her eyes and know her contempt. She'd shouted at them. 'If they burn me, then any woman who speaks her mind, contradicts you lot, is equally guilty and must burn also. Tell that to your wives, gentlemen…'

The shuffling above had stopped.

'Och,' said Mr Bollard, his mouth close to her ear. 'I like them defiant.' He raised his voice and tilted his head so he spoke to the ceiling. 'Means they take longer to break.'

She shuddered just thinking about it. The tears started then. She'd tried to resist, she really had.

When the constables, those foolish Stuart lads, acting under orders from Mr Bollard, stripped her naked in front of the reverend and two of the bailies, who'd been in the room all this time as if to undermine her accusation of cowardice, she knew she couldn't last much longer. She was bone-weary, so very sore and, as much as she disdained admitting it, terribly afraid.

When Mr Bollard showed her his special leather satchel with its set of needles designed to 'encourage' her to talk — bits of dull iron, inches long, brass tacks and other tools — any courage she had left fled. Pulling them out one by one, he'd run his long fingers up and down the shafts, caressing the metal as if it were a living creature, whispering something to each piece before placing it upon a table brought into the room for the purpose of displaying the instruments that would, she'd no doubt, shatter her.

Ashamed of her unclothed body, despite her bold actions of past days, Beatrix had hunched in the chair as best as she could with her hands and feet tied, aware of how pendulous her breasts, how shrivelled her stomach. As she'd stared at her wrinkly knees, she'd tried to think of anything rather than the high-voiced man with the clean-smelling clothes who'd until this moment, apart from playing with his needles like a lover his mistress, mainly threatened her. Now he held up his implements one by one, remarked on the differing thicknesses, the little cross-bar that prevented him from inserting them too deeply into her soft flesh.

In a loud voice he began to explain to the reverend and bailies what he intended to do, how he would proceed. She refused to listen. Rather, she allowed her mind to drift…

The first needle went in. Driving it slowly into her leg, above her ankle, it was the same spot Mr Bollard found yesterday after pressing and pulling her flesh in all sorts of places to get a reaction. Ensuring she was watching as he pushed it in further and further, he waited for a response. She sucked her breath in deeply. She knew she should have felt something, but because it was the exact place she'd injured her leg years earlier, it was most often numb. It was the reason she limped. Even so, it felt as if all he'd done was rest the cold cross-bar against her leg; as if only the very tip had broken the skin.

When it appeared he'd driven it in as far as it would go, he left it there and raised his face towards the bailies.

'You see, gentlemen. A normal woman would be prone with suffering. I have pushed it into her until it can go no further. What happens? Nothing.' He gestured with his hand, a showman with an act. 'A witch has no feeling. Look, this canny one studies the iron like a familiar.'

Too late, Beatrix understood she should have howled the Tolbooth down.

Before she could amend her error, Mr Bollard extracted the needle swiftly. There was a trickle of blood, but not as much as Beatrix expected, not even after he'd done this a few more times.

She should have cried out, struggled against her bindings. But she was too tired, her mind foggier than the Forth in autumn. It was absurd, the whole thing. How had it come to this? She dwelled upon her husband, dear, patient Mr Brown; her daughter and wee granddaughter; her friends, no doubt working down by the sea.

'This is why I needed her naked,' Mr Bollard intoned, interrupting her woolgathering, a teacher at his lessons. 'Yesterday, as requested, I examined her for devil marks, for those signs that indicate she is indeed a witch. There are a number, which I will reveal to you now.' Before she could protest, Mr Bollard grabbed one of her breasts and, lifting it, pointed to a large mole that sat atop her ribs. 'Here,' he said. 'This is a devil's teat upon which the beast will suckle. As you can see,' he weighed her breast in his hand, 'it has been well used.'

There were some chuckles.

'What rubbish,' said Beatrix hoarsely, wanting to slap his hand away, to cover her modesty. She could do neither. 'I've had that mark since I was a wee bairn...'

'Exactly,' said Mr Bollard and drove a needle into it.

Much to her shock, Beatrix felt little pain. Again, it was as if the needle merely grazed her.

'Look, sirs,' said Mr Bollard triumphantly, withdrawing the needle. 'No blood.'

The bailies murmured, but they didn't stop watching and leering. After a few more insertions, Beatrix understood what was happening. There were blunt needles, used to prove the so-called witch's marks didn't bleed, ones that retracted the moment they touched the surface of the skin, and long, sharp, painful ones designed to draw blood from the fleshier parts of her body.

Changing from one type to the other, Mr Bollard prodded and pricked again and again. Shafts of pain shot through her body, lodged in her throat. She struggled to breathe. Her body went rigid, her legs stiffened, her head rolled back.

Beatrix lapsed in and out of consciousness, unsure how long her torment went on. The light changed as clouds coursed across the sky. Grey, bruise-blue, silvery then pewter as rain began to fall. Before inserting each needle and withdrawing it, mapping her arms, legs and torso, Mr Bollard would repeat, in that reedy voice, 'All you have to do is name your fellow-tormentors and this will stop.'

She would shake her head, swallow her wails, her moans.

At some stage, the Reverend Cowper appeared by her side, adding his churned-butter pleas to Mr Bollard's, promising to pray for her, to help her seek salvation. He vowed to baptise her again so the evil spirit within her could be banished and she and anyone else she named would be welcomed back into the fold, into the Weem family, into his kirk.

It was tempting. Dear God, it was tempting.

When she spat upon his boots, the reverend said something to the pricker.

Thrusting his hands between her knees, Mr Bollard did the unthinkable. He pulled her legs apart. If she hadn't been lost in a nether world of agony, Beatrix would have keeled over with the humiliation. Her womanly parts on display, like she was a wanton, a whore. She began to cry, to protest, but it came out as gibberish.

'Behold. She speaks in tongues.' He spread her legs as wide as her bonds allowed. 'Look!' he cried. 'As I suspected, here is another one.'

Mr Bollard pinched the lips of her mull together, pulling at them and, before she could prepare herself, drove the needle through. This time, Beatrix screamed. It was like a cow bellowing. Blood flowed from the wound, hot and plentiful.

Cries rent the air, powerful, deep. Shockingly, she understood with a distant part of her mind, they were hers. She could take it no more — the pain, the utter abasement.

'Nae more. Please, please, nae more.'

Mr Bollard inhaled sharply. The reverend moved beside her. 'What?' he murmured. It was like manna to her ears.

'Please… no more. I can stand it no longer.'

'Do you confess?' asked the reverend. His voice was so very soft. An unguent, a salve to her hurting body, her aching soul.

'Aye. I confess, I confess,' she panted through ragged breaths.

There was an intake of breath. 'What do you confess, Beatrix Laing?' She heard the snapping of fingers and then a warm, wet cloth was run over her snottery face. It was so soothing, so nice. A sheet was draped over her body. The blood flowed between her legs, as if she'd given birth again. Aye, she remembered when young James came into the world. But he went to God soon after. Too many of her bairns went to the Lord…

'To what do you confess, Beatrix Laing,' repeated the voice. Harder this time. The wet cloth was taken away. The sheet began to slip from her body.

'I confess that I renounced my baptism…'

There was a noise of disgust. 'We know that already. Twelve years ago you renounced the Lord. What of it?'

'I… I… did that so I might enter into compact with the devil.'

'Did you now?' She could feel the reverend's sour breath on her cheek. He smelled of sweat — sweat and whisky. 'What did he look like?' The cloth began to pat her fevered brow, gently wipe her scorching cheek.

'A black dog…' said Beatrix, thinking how ridiculous she sounded. But she'd heard the reverend make mention of a dog the colour of coal. How it was the devil's hound. Had not others accused of witchcraft in the pamphlets the reverend read to the kirk said the same? Beatrix remembered the story about young Richard Dugdale from Lancashire... he made mention of a mongrel, did he not? 'He came to me only once. It was upon Ceres Moor and he wore the guise of a black dog.'

'Did you hear that, gentlemen?' crowed the reverend.

'I did,' the men said in chorus. Like they were lads in school. There were more mutterings. 'Dear God,' said someone loudly.

Dear God. Dear God. Help me.

'Tell me, Beatrix,' whispered the reverend, resuming his position at her feet. 'Who are your accomplices in this terrible bewitchment?'

Beatrix's eyes fluttered. Her lips moved.

The reverend came as close as he was able without getting blood upon him. Already the sheet was sticking to her body where Mr Bollard had plunged his needles in and out, in and out.

'Who, Beatrix, tell me who?' Behind him hovered the pricker. The needle in his hand caught the light. He was an angel with a flaming sword, waiting to plunge it into her flesh. She could bear it no longer.

Beatrix fixed her eyes on the reverend. Light shone from his blurry face.

''Twas all of them, Heavenly Father. 'Twas all of them.'

The reverend made a noise of frustration. He signalled the pricker to start his work again.

'Nae, please,' said Beatrix hoarsely.

'I need names, Beatrix. And I need them now.'

She felt the blunt edge of a long needle against her breast. It broke the skin as it was forced into her pliant, ageing flesh. She screamed. As she did, a slew of names spewed from her mouth. It wasn't her saying them, the reverend said. It was God. He plucked them from her head. And a few more she'd not thought of besides. He was All-Knowing, All-Powerful. He forgave her.

At some point, the needle was extracted. Blood was wiped from her throbbing breast. She was covered again. Her modesty preserved.

There was a lull as Reverend Cowper stood and stepped away. 'You heard her. We've no time to lose, we've already wasted a week.'

His voice had changed. Had God abandoned her already?

'Round them up,' snapped the reverend. 'Every last one, and do what we agreed. Take them to the Morton house and let's see if the boy can corroborate what the witch says. It's the least Edinburgh would expect.'

Beatrix heard rather than felt movement. The passing of shadows across her eyelids, the draught as their bodies sped away. Even the pricker left, thanks be to God.

They would all leave her in peace.

That was last night. Alick had untied her and, after washing her wounds, helped her back into her grubby shift. He even left her some food and a blanket before he departed. She'd fallen into the deepest of sleeps.

Now, with the cold light of early morning, the brief peace she'd felt deserted her. There was only dread.

Going over all that had happened, she could recall what that pricker had done, all his accusations. They were mere hurts to her body; to her reputation. It was what she'd said to Reverend Cowper that pained her the most.

She remembered the words as if they were seared into her soul.

When asked to identify her accomplices she'd shrieked seven names — the same number as those who'd burned in Paisley back in 1697.

She'd named Isobel Adam, Lillie Wallace, Nettie Horseburgh, Margaret Jack (how her name had come to her, she knew not), Janet Cornfoot, old Thomas Brown and, last of all, she'd said the name the reverend had been trying to get her to speak for days.

Sorcha McIntyre.

TWENTY

You claw ma' back, I'll claw yours.
(We'll see that we both get something out of this.)

They came for Sorcha less than a week after she burned the wax figure.

Down on the shore, sorting the latest catch of herring, cod and other fish into creels for sale later that day, she was unprepared for the constables or the orders they carried.

'Will you look at them,' said Nettie, jerking her head towards a group of men marching purposefully along the foreshore. Her arms deep in fish guts, Sorcha stopped what she was doing, wiped her hands on a cloth and watched as they approached.

Nicolas Lawson turned and did the same. All the women slowly ceased working and followed the direction of Sorcha's and Nettie's gaze.

'I don't like the look of this, Nettie,' said Sorcha quietly, coming around to join her.

'Me neither.'

'They appear angry,' said Lillie Wallace, joining them from over by the nets.

'Angry?' huffed Janet Cornfoot, standing up. 'I think they look afeared.'

Janet was right, thought Sorcha. There was a wide-eyed panic about the men, their tight-lipped mouths, the exaggerated swinging of their arms, the way they puffed out their chests, projecting a fierce determination not to be cowed by women or public opinion.

They'd heard how the constables had beaten Beatrix, a woman old enough to be their grandmother. One of them had copped a tongue-lashing from his own ma, so ashamed was she that he could lay hands on Beatrix, even if it was under orders from the reverend and council. He protested he hadn't hit her hard, as if that was a suitable defence. Sorcha doubted that was true, even while she wanted to believe it was so.

'At least the pricker not be with them,' said Nettie under her breath as the men jumped down onto the sand.

Sorcha shuddered. Alick had told Captain Ross — and Mr Brown, who, upon learning of his wife's arrest had abandoned what he was doing in the city and come home — what the pricker had done to Beatrix. While the captain had refrained from describing everything the poor woman had endured, his omissions, and the fact William Brown was prostrate with guilt and grief, spoke more loudly than words.

The four constables, lads Sorcha had known their entire lives, came to a halt directly before her and Nettie. All that lay between them and their batons and rope, the metal chains that hung from their shoulders, and the women was a trestle upon which lay the spilled innards of fish and a pile of netting waiting to be mended. Nine women stood the other side, their creels a row of makeshift battlements behind them, silently watching and waiting. Down by the shore, a group of children ceased their play and edged forward, the evident tension quietening them. It was telling that not one of the constables looked at the fish-wives, preferring to focus on the equipment, the dead fish, the sea.

The fishermen just returned from inshore paused in their swaying boats or upon the crumbling pier, waiting to see what would happen next. A couple tried to call the bairns to them.

'What can we do for you, gents?' asked Nettie light-heartedly. Sorcha could feel her arm trembling as it gently brushed against Sorcha's side.

Constable Gerard Stuart nudged his brother, Angus. Sorcha knew they were the ones who'd beaten Beatrix. Standing either side of the brothers were Mark Smith and Simon Wood. Simon had gone to school with her brother Erik, Mark with Robbie.

Clearing his throat with a sense of self-importance, Angus pulled out a piece of paper. 'We're here to take into custody one Janet Cornfoot, Lillie Wallace, Margaret Jack, Nicolas Lawson, Sorcha McIntyre and Janet White.'

For a moment Sorcha failed to register her own name as she wondered who Janet White was, before understanding they meant Nettie.

When she did, she gasped.

'On what charge?' demanded Janet Cornfoot, hands on hips.

'Conspiring with the witch, Beatrix Laing, to cause mal... male...' Angus stared at the words on the paper.

'Witchcraft,' growled Simon. He was the only one to meet Sorcha's eyes. 'Now, you can either come peacefully, or you can come in chains. It's your choice.'

Some of the women began to protest; Sorcha forced a laugh. Surely, this was a charade. Then she caught the expression on Nettie's face. After all, they'd taken the wax doll from Beatrix's house. Was that considered conspiring? How would anyone know what they'd done? Regardless, that was down to her and Nettie; the other women had nothing to do with it.

But the men were serious and the dubious smiles and objections swiftly died.

'I'll not be going anywhere quietly with you, young Angus, let me tell —' began Janet, before Nettie interrupted.

'This is ridiculous,' said Nettie. 'We're no accomplices — just as Beatrix Laing be no witch. Why, you've known us your whole lives, lads. Who was it gave you a taste of your first mussel, Mark Smith? And what about you, Simon Wood? Look at me when I'm talking to you, lad. Who was it brought fish soup to your ma when she was poorly? Who wiped your dirty arse when you had the squits?' The fish-wives snickered. 'Nicolas here even used her special remedies to look after your wee sister when she fell and broke her arm.' When Simon didn't respond, Nettie sighed and shrugged. 'Very well. That's how it is then. We'll come with you, lads, but only because you'll be escorting us back here before the tide turns, won't they, lasses?'

The women tried to mimic her flippancy. All but Sorcha failed. Untying their aprons, they passed whatever tools they were using to the remaining fishwives. The men at the boats had by now crossed the sand and, with the children by their side, were watching the proceedings with a mixture of rage and concern. Sorcha prayed they wouldn't do anything foolish lest the women be accused of bewitching the men to do their bidding as well.

Taking her lead from Nettie, she gave the fishermen what she hoped was a reassuring wave. 'It's all right, lads, kiddykins. We'll be back to finish before you know we've gone.'

Gerard came and stood on one side of her. 'Where are you taking us, Gerard?' asked Sorcha, praying it wasn't the Tolbooth, though at least if it was, they would see Beatrix.

'To the Morton house,' said Gerard and began to lead them away from the shore.

'The Morton house?' asked Janet. 'Since when has it become the place the council does its business?'

Mark gave the old woman a shove. 'Cease your blether. It's where we're ordered to take you. Now, move, *lasses*.'

The last word was said with such disdain, it was all Sorcha could do not to clout him across the ears. The men might have been ordered to take them into custody, but they could show some respect. But it was as if they'd changed — all of them. From former playmates and neighbours into burly, terse guards and the women were transformed into criminals. Nae, she knew what it was they'd suddenly become: witches.

Her stomach flipped and her throat grew dry.

Nettie fell lightly against her and whispered, 'This does not bode well, hen.'

As they were herded up the High Street, folk came to their doors, spilled out of shops to watch them pass. Most were silent. A couple spat, but whether at the women or the constables, Sorcha couldn't be certain. Some called out, asking where they were going, why they were being taken.

'Haven't you done enough to poor auld Beatrix?' shouted someone from a window. It was Emma Gilligan, her babe in arms, glaring at the men. 'Looking for more women to have sport with, are you? You should be ashamed of yourselves.'

The mutters grew and a crowd fell in behind them. The sky above darkened and the promised rain began to fall, a drop or two at first, before it became heavier. Surrounded by the constables, the fish-wives continued, heads bowed, their skirts getting wet, their neepyins drenched. What was a bit of water to them?

Sorcha searched the faces lining the street, some withdrawing indoors to avoid the weather, but she saw no sign of the one person she longed to see. Where was Captain Ross? There was no chance his notes to Edinburgh would have been answered yet, it was too soon. She prayed with all her heart he would hear of this and, if he couldn't prevent what was about to happen, he would at least record it so those in authority would know what was going on.

After all, if they didn't know, how could they stop it? But perhaps that was what the council wanted — to keep everyone in the dark until it was too late.

TWENTY-ONE

...when any of the women whom he [Peter Morton] accused touched him, and sometimes on their coming into the room, he fell into grievous fits of trouble, and cried out...

— A Just Reproof to the False Reports and Unjust
Calumnies in the Foregoing Letter, *1705*

When Beatrix Laing was brought into his bedroom, Peter Morton thought he was having a terrible vision. Who was this haggard crone with bruises upon her cheeks, a cut lip, terrible gouges along her arms and a bent, shuffling gait? And what was she doing beside his bed? She smelled worse than his chamber pot. Once the initial wave of panic subsided and he saw the bailies and their wives crammed against one wall of his bedroom together with the doctors from the city, the angry army captain and his good friend the reverend as well, he relaxed.

The reverend had warned him that Beatrix Laing and some other women were being brought before him and he must listen carefully to what was said and be sure to remember what to do. They'd gone over it last night, many times.

Aware of the reverend's eyes upon him, Peter gave the briefest of nods and turned his bleary gaze upon the woman.

Immediately, he felt his limbs tense, his neck became stiff. His stomach distended and his breathing became laboured. He began to wail — short sharp bursts at first, transforming into caterwauls. Some of the women in the room put their hands over their ears, whimpering at his evident distress.

''Tis she who cursed me, 'tis she!' cried Peter, pointing feebly at the beldam.

Beatrix lowered her head. Her shoulders slumped and, if it hadn't been for the two men holding her arms, Peter was convinced she would have collapsed to the floor. He wanted to feel sorry for her, but he couldn't, not when she'd used her vile powers to turn him into this wreck. His body was no longer his own; his thoughts were in disarray. He hurt all over. She might look and act like a feeble old woman, but she was evil.

The reverend signalled to the men, who marched Beatrix out of the bedroom. She'd been there less than a minute.

As soon as she was gone, Peter's breathing improved, his arms and legs co-operated and his stomach shrank back to its usual size.

'As I told you, ladies and gentlemen,' said Reverend Cowper, ensuring he scowled at each witness in the room. 'Peter is badly affected by the mere presence of the witch. She is still, along with her accomplices, casting a terrible spell upon the lad. The devil is powerful in her.'

Peter snivelled.

Captain Ross detached himself from the wall he had been leaning against. 'It proves nothing,' he said, daring the reverend to contradict him.

Minutes before Beatrix was shown in, he'd forced his way into the bedroom. The reverend had tried to have him expelled, but the captain, who'd sought out Bailie Bell and handed him a letter with an official seal upon it, refused to move. The bailie had read the letter, frowned, and passed it to the reverend.

Casting his eyes over it, the reverend shrugged. He explained to all present it was from a city advocate, ordering the council to allow Captain Ross to bear witness to events in Pittenweem so there might be a party to record what occurred on Edinburgh's behalf.

'Makes no difference to me or anyone here who observes. Or to whom you report, captain.' He stared meaningfully at the officer. 'God is the authority here, not Edinburgh, not me, and not some army official, no matter what rank.'

After that, the reverend turned his back on the captain and bent over Peter before ordering Beatrix to be brought in.

When she was led away, her knees buckling so she was practically carried, the captain stepped forward and objected. The reverend swung towards him.

'I don't know what you expect, captain, but to me, this proves everything the lad said is true.'

'Not if he is pretending to be afflicted, reverend.'

There were shocked mutters. The reverend's eyes narrowed. 'Pretending? You think the lad is pretending to twist his body into impossible shapes? To starve himself? You saw the size of his belly before. It was as if the lad had swallowed a whale, and now it would scarce accommodate a minnow.' The captain remained unmoved. 'Why, I'll have you know, sir, when the fits are upon him, not even the strongest of men,' he nodded towards Constable Smith, who had just entered the room, 'can lift him; nor can they straighten his neck or arms. It's not natural. It is the work of witchcraft, I tell you.'

'That may be,' said the captain. He was calm in the storm of the reverend's outburst; the nods of agreement from the witnesses. 'But if the lad can see those you've arranged to be brought forward, it hardly counts as proof. Why, he can identify anyone he dislikes, anyone against whom he bears a grudge. Anyone you have a mind to tell him to.'

There were gasps of outrage. Peter saw the reverend's face redden; felt his own change colour.

The captain continued. 'Have you forgotten the events in Paisley, sir? Because I assure you my superiors in Edinburgh have not.'

Comparing the soldier and the reverend, Peter thought how tall and regal the captain looked in his uniform. It might be patched and worn, but the man stood straight, he spoke with assuredness and power. Compared to him, the reverend looked small, thin and hunched; his hazy eye spasmed, the lid fluttering as it did when he was nervous. Peter willed his champion to stand straighter, to use his special voice.

'What do you suggest we do then?' asked the reverend. Peter detected a sly note.

'Cover the lad's eyes,' said the captain. 'Don't let those you've arranged to be here speak. Let them come forward and touch the lad anonymously.'

'Touch him?' The reverend looked appalled. 'What? Allow the witches to unleash their power and inflict further injury? I'll permit no such thing.' Reverend Cowper paused. 'That is, unless I may sit beside him and offer him the protection of the Lord.'

There was a noise in the corridor. Bailie Vernour excused himself from the room.

Captain Ross frowned. Clearly, he was unhappy with what the reverend suggested. The other witnesses nodded their approval with this arrangement.

'Aye, let the reverend sit with him,' said Bailie Cook.

Captain Ross raised a brow towards one of the Edinburgh doctors who nodded what appeared to be reluctant acquiescence.

'Excuse me,' said Bailie Vernour, squeezing back into the room. 'Those we ordered taken into custody have arrived.'

Peter heard noises outside, voices, the sound of shuffling feet. His heart began to pound. *Dear God, protect me from my tormentors; give me the strength to know who they are and help the good reverend bring them to justice so we might protect our village and all who live here.*

'I must insist you cover the lad's eyes,' said Captain Ross.

'And I insist that if Peter is to be blindfolded, I shall be his protector,' countered the reverend.

'The captain and reverend are both in the right,' said Bailie Bell finally, gesturing for everyone to stop talking. 'You're already overstepping the mark, captain. You've no authority but, as the letter you carried states, are here to observe. Do that. As a sign of goodwill, we'll do as you bid and cover the lad's eyes. Be sure to let your superiors know we were so obliging. The reverend can sit near him and ensure no harm befalls him.' He made a clicking noise and flapped his hands. 'Come on. We're wasting time. We must discover who exactly is responsible for causing Peter's terrible affliction.'

A cloth was found and placed over Peter's head. Propped up on pillows, the reverend made Peter comfortable and then sat beside the bed, holding one of the lad's hands in both of his.

'Are you ready, Peter?' he asked kindly.

Peter didn't trust himself to speak. He nodded, panicking slightly at how helpless he felt without his sight. This isn't what the reverend said would happen.

'Bring them in one at a time and in no particular order,' said the reverend.

Unable to see who was shambling towards him, Peter could nevertheless feel the tremors in the unknown fingers that lightly touched his, just as he could feel the reverend squeeze his other hand as tight as he ever had.

Peter waited a second, as he'd been instructed, then screamed.

TWENTY-TWO

By this your Lordship may see, it is only the weakest that went to the walls.

— A Letter from a Gentleman of Fife to his
Friend in Edinburgh, *1705*

*I*t was two weeks since Sorcha had been identified by Peter Morton in his bedroom and locked in the damp, bare rooms of the Tolbooth to await, so Reverend Cowper said, justice. She remembered the day it happened as clearly as if it had been yesterday. Dragged into Peter's presence, at first Sorcha didn't recognise the lad, so pale and thin had he become. His once bonnie cheeks were sunken, his dark hair lank and unwashed. A sour smell pervaded the space, a sickly odour that was overlaid by sweat and excitement. Unable to see Peter's eyes, which were shrouded by a cloth, she'd been told not to utter a word but, when commanded, to step forward and rest her hand on the lad's exposed arm.

Captain Ross started as she entered the room, and she almost exclaimed in relief upon seeing him. The fear that had been growing in her steadily as one after the other of her friends were hauled into the bedroom and then hustled back out through the front door to God knew where, subsided. He became a sturdy rope that tied her to a solid point when all around her was shifting. She met his eyes and saw what she first thought was confusion before she understood, with a lurch of her heart, it was terror — for her.

After all, he'd seen what had gone before.

Seated beside the poor lad, who was as still as a corpse beneath the covers, was the reverend. With a smile that never left his lips, he performed a mime for her benefit. She bent and gently traced a vein that ran from the base of Peter's wrist and along his now skinny forearm. It pulsed beneath her fingertips. Even through her hardened skin she could feel the power of his heartbeat, the vitality that to all appearances seemed to be draining from his body.

Somewhat reassured, she continued to stroke him. Dear God, he'd become gaunt. He made not a sound, not a murmur. The reverend grunted, the noise almost like words she couldn't quite catch. Puzzled, she almost forgot the command to remain silent when Peter let out an almighty cry. 'Take her away, take her away, it be the sea-witch, Sorcha McIntyre!' Horrified, Sorcha snatched her fingers back as if they were burned, swinging towards the captain in dismay.

There was only one person who'd ever called her a sea-witch... Before she could accuse the reverend of putting words in the lad's mouth, Peter started shouting.

'She seeks to torment me further!' He screamed again, his back arching so high, she thought he would snap in two. Her instinct was to render help. Constable Wood gripped her elbow and steered her away from the bed, but not before she'd seen the tears coursing from under the cloth and down Peter's neck. Was it from the pain he professed she was causing? Why would he claim she was doing such a terrible thing? Why use the reverend's name for her? She stared at her hands, turning them first one way then the other, shaking her head in disbelief, then raised her chin and looked at Patrick Cowper.

He stared at her, a glimmer of triumph in his eyes.

'Edinburgh will learn all that has befallen here, as God is *my* witness,' said Captain Ross as she was dragged away. He raised an arm, as if he would pull her back through sheer will power alone.

Marched up the High Street like a common criminal, along with three of the other accused women, she was thrown into a dank and dingy room on the first floor of the Tolbooth. She learned later it was where Beatrix had been kept. All it contained was a chair, a table and some fouled straw. When they were able to open it, the window let in light and air. She shared the space with Nettie, Isobel and Nicolas. According to Alick the keeper, Janet, Lillie Wallace, Margaret Jack, and even Thomas Brown had also been named. *Thomas Brown.* What had that kindly man ever done to stand so accused — apart from own shares in one of the larger boats. Alick said they'd been put in the cell on the lower floor.

The suspects were separated not only to fit them into the small, fusty rooms more readily, but to prevent them colluding — whether in innocence or malfeasance wasn't specified. All Sorcha knew was she should be grateful she wasn't on the ground floor of the Tolbooth. In her cell, they at least had fresh air. The window of the room directly below had a loose grate, and so was sealed shut lest the prisoners escape. When the rains were heavy, water trickled through the cracks and pooled on the floor. It hadn't stopped raining since they'd been incarcerated, as if the skies were lamenting their plight.

But it was poor Beatrix who was made to suffer the most. Taken from the Tolbooth first to the Morton house, she was later delivered to the dark and windowless hole beneath the church known as St Fillan's Cave, a former smugglers' storehouse. For her sins, Beatrix was to suffer in darkness and solitude. Her only visitors, apart from the guards who brought a little food and water, were the reverend and the bailies.

Mr Bollard, the pricker, was too busy for Beatrix. He was now concentrating on those locked in the Tolbooth.

Sorcha tried not to think about that.

Instead, she sent her thoughts and prayers winging to Beatrix. The cave was narrow and cold with a low, uneven rock ceiling and weeping walls. Sorcha's da had taken her there one time to fetch some tea and claret. Brought over from France by sailors wishing to avoid the usual excise, the goods had been hidden deep within, away from the eyes of the government officials who patrolled the coast, waiting to be resold to gentry and merchants on surrounding estates and in the city. It wasn't uncommon for locals to purchase some of the booty. Since Patrick Cowper's arrival, not only had the smuggling ceased, but the cave was used to imprison the worst offenders, to break them utterly. Rumour had it you could enter it from the church, so no one even knew you were there. Every night Sorcha prayed Beatrix would survive this, that they all would.

She prayed now, raising her head towards the ceiling when she'd finished. Not so much to see if her words went to God, but to try and spy the presence of those who spent a great deal of time peering through the holes in the ceiling to watch them.

Nettie saw where Sorcha was looking and shook her head. They were alone. It didn't happen often, as one or more of the town council, the guards or the reverend spied on them most days. Whether it was when they were being forced awake by having the large sounding horn blasted in their ears, or dragged to their feet and marched around the floor by a constable and volunteers from the kirk, pricked by Mr Bollard, or being shaved, stripped, having a shit or piss, eating what little they were given, the men would watch.

At first Sorcha had been self-conscious; the ignominy of being observed in the most private and vulnerable of moments had almost consumed her. But once Nettie said she thought that they'd been put in the top room because they were the younger of the accused and the men sought to get pleasure from viewing their bodies and the punishment inflicted upon them, she made a promise to ensure any delight the men had was short-lived.

It was the idea they were watching that kept her strong when her hair was cruelly cut then shaved from her scalp. As her long tresses floated to the floor to be scooped up along with Nettie's and Nicolas's dark ones and Isobel's golden ones, knowing the men would find them less attractive allowed her to forget her vanity and take a peculiar strength from her prickly naked skull. She discussed this with the women and they all agreed they would celebrate their new look, hold their heads high and feel no shame. If anyone should feel that particular emotion, it was the men who ordered it to be done, who observed as their orders were carried out.

That night, they'd chuckled about their appearance as they tried to adjust to their bald, itchy scalps, the way the cold bit at their flesh, stroking each other's heads, describing how odd they felt.

'Reminds me of Thom's cheeks when he kisses me,' said Nettie.

Isobel broke into a smile. 'Mine feels more like my grandpa's lips. When he offers me a tirl, it's like being stung by nettles.'

'You're lucky,' added Nicolas. 'Reminds me of my ma's.'

They'd all rolled around on the straw at that, cackling loudly.

Their confidence didn't last long, their determined defiance. Not once Mr Bollard came to visit.

It took only one session with the pricker for them to retreat to their stinking bedding, bleeding, crying quietly, to make a solemn pact.

After Mr Bollard attended, they ceased to wash, even when they were ordered to. They tipped over the bowls of cold water, cast the soap out of the window. Used the cloths meant for washing and cleaning their teeth to blow their noses, wipe their arses. They made sure their body odour was as foul as their surroundings, that their breath, when it hit their accusers was as putrid as their toilet bucket. They made sure the vermin that set up colonies in the straw and burrowed into their clothes, crawled over their bodies and their fuzzy scalps, were transferred to the men whenever the opportunity arose.

They might have been prisoners, might have been at the whim of these desperate zealots, but they weren't completely powerless. Not yet. Sorcha wouldn't allow that to happen. Nor would Nettie.

Reflecting upon how long they'd been there, wondering as she did every moment how much more of this hell they'd have to endure, Sorcha hauled herself upright, aware her legs pained her horribly and that her underarms were tender. She limped to the window and pushed it open as far as she could. The broken latch meant it wouldn't concede much, but at least she could breathe in the fresh air, push out her arm and feel the rain upon her flesh.

Dear God, she thought for the umpteenth time, how had it come to this? These wicked and patently false accusations. All because of a young lad. All because of a woman's imprudent tongue. Through Alick, they'd learned that Beatrix was inconsolable about giving up their names. When they learned how long she'd held out, exactly what had been done to her and then, shockingly, experienced it themselves, any anger they'd felt towards her dissolved.

No one should have such punishment inflicted upon them in the first place.

But that was the point. They would all be driven to the same precipice as Beatrix, where they would say anything, do anything, leap into the abyss and condemn themselves, if only the pain would stop. With a shudder, she pushed the idea to the back of her mind, tried not to think about the aches that worried her body, or the wounds marking her flesh. What strength remained she sent to Beatrix, alone in that cold, lightless hell-hole beneath the kirk.

From her vantage point, Sorcha could see the High Street. It was emptier than usual, despite the weather, but still she searched for the one figure she'd come to rely upon to be there most days. She wasn't disappointed. There he was. The captain. With a leap of her heart, she gazed at him as he sat upon Liath beneath the tavern shingle, staring up at the tower.

Upon seeing her, he lifted his hat and bowed his head, his sign that he saw her. Tears filled her eyes as she waved, making sure she put all the energy she possessed into the simple gesture. She would not let him, or any of the others who might be looking, see how much the action cost her. How moving her arm caused her shoulder to pain, her ribs to burn, the sores in her armpit to open. Thank goodness he was too far away to see her wretched state; the dirt that lay beneath her fingers, in the crook of her elbow, the dried blood. Thank goodness he couldn't inhale her scent. Her lips were cracked, her pricked belly sunken. She was mere bones dressed in filthy flesh.

Gazing at her slender arm, the bruises and bloodied scratches that tracked her skin like a pitted roadway mapped by a madman, she gave one last wave and withdrew, using the rainwater to wash away the dried blood, stifling her groans as she did so. She moved away from the window and joined Nettie, who resembled a nun without her cowl; almost beatific.

'Maybe they'll leave us alone today,' she whispered. A habit already honed.

'It's Sunday. Even we witches deserve a day of rest,' agreed Nettie.

'Don't call us that,' snapped Nicolas. Of them all, Nicolas suffered most. Mr Bollard had been crueller to her than the rest. After she refused to admit to any wrongdoing, despite being accused of fashioning a wax figure that was never found, he took even greater satisfaction from pricking her flesh, fondling her breasts, searching her maukin, her woman's parts, for signs of a witch. The more she sobbed and cried, the harder he stabbed and prodded.

If Sorcha had an instrument she could have turned on the man and used to end all their suffering, she would have gladly. Let them hang her for a real crime. But they were all bound when the pricker came. Their wrists were tied and, as they were taken one by one to the rooms above and forced into a chair, their ankles as well. It was the same when the reverend asked his endless, repetitive questions over and over; they were secured so they couldn't use their limbs to conjure demons, to enchant the men.

Thus far, despite what had been done to them, none of them had broken. Not yet.

Beatrix had told the men nothing else since she gave up their names; not even the worst Mr Bollard could do was as bad as confessing, surrendering to the pain and telling lies. She begged Alick to pass that piece of wisdom on to her friends. He had.

Upon that, they were agreed. They would not tell falsehoods; they would not condemn others to this miserable fate.

For that was what they were being asked to do: to tell lies, to give up innocent names. They were no more witches than the men who tortured them. Why would no one believe them? Why would no one come to their aid? Even Captain Ross's efforts had amounted to nothing... so far. But how far was that? There was a weight of anticipation in the 'so' — as if their circumstances could change. It seemed an impossible hope.

'Was he there?' asked Nettie as Sorcha gingerly lowered herself beside her, jerking her chin towards the window.

'As always.' Sorcha let out a long sigh and leaned the back of her head against the wall and shut her eyes. The stone was hard, cold. At least her head wasn't as tickly as it had been when they were first shaved. They'd only nicked her a few times, unlike Nicolas, who'd tried to resist and earned herself a deep cut above one ear for her efforts. It was when the men shaved their cunts that none of them had dared to shift. Cowper had supervised that part of their humiliation, entrusting the task to Simon Wood and Gerard Stuart.

Allowing the women to keep their skirts on, simply to hoist them, Simon had at least been embarrassed, careful. Perhaps it was because as he worked, Sorcha kept reminding him of the times they would frolic upon the braes as bairns; how they'd play jokes upon Widow Agnes and her father and then run like the clappers when the old man had chased them with his stick. Nettie added her own reminiscences of when Simon was a bairn. When the reverend understood the women were affecting the lad's work, he'd had their mouths stuffed with fabric. Gerard Stuart had become... excited by what he was doing, hamfisted, and had cut Isobel. After that, Cowper had taken the knife himself and shaved her then Nicolas, raining prayers and curses upon them for their womanly wiles and efforts to seduce men.

After that, the pricker had begun his work. Between Cowper's and the bailies' questions and Mr Bollard's instruments, they sought to have them confess, promising to end their agonies if only they would admit to being witches. These men must have thought them fools. Had Beatrix's suffering ended after she'd confessed? Confessed not only to being in league with the devil, but naming accomplices? It had not. They would not confess to what they hadn't done. To being what they were not.

Sorcha wanted to believe no one would, but now Alick was gone and she feared they wouldn't hold out much longer. The Tolbooth keeper's efforts to make their imprisonment easier by sneaking in supplies and passing notes from Captain Ross and other snippets of information had been discovered and he had been removed from the tower.

In the room below them, Thomas Brown and the other three women suffered greatly as well. The new guards, hastily recruited and posted to safeguard the lower room only last week, were refusing to give Thomas the food his daughter cooked for him, eating it outside the door with great relish so those inside might smell it and know what they were missing out on. Janet had managed to have a message passed upstairs by one of the other, older guards who felt sorry for them. From this they learned that Thomas had fallen ill and was becoming frailer with each passing day. Sorcha was scared for him. For Janet, too; for all she gave the appearance of being as tough as a seasoned milch cow, she was really just a grannie mutchie.

A noise outside the door drew Sorcha's attention. The key rattled in the lock. The women scrambled to their feet, meeting in the middle of the room and holding hands, drawing strength from each other. God, they were a sorry looking lot.

Who should enter but the reverend, fresh from delivering his sermon. So much for Sunday being a day of rest.

'Good afternoon, ladies.' The rain had plastered his hair to his skull. His smock was damp along the bottom. Grass and clumps of dirt clung to his boots. He smelled of the outside, of wood smoke and, goddamn him, whisky and mutton.

Behind him was Mr Bollard. Sorcha no longer had the energy to be afraid. Following them were bailies Cook and Vernour. There were others as well, the constables, a few town officials. The latter pressed handkerchiefs to their noses, gazing at the women with round eyes, their shock apparent. A couple coughed. One cleared his throat loudly.

'We've come to give you one last chance,' said the reverend amiably. Sorcha knew his words were empty, said for the benefit of the strangers. He said that every time.

Pulling pieces of paper out of the satchel he had slung across his shoulders, he came further into the room. He laid the papers on the small table and smoothed them out. A quill and inkhorn were also produced. 'If you would but sign these confessions then all this will stop.' His hand swept the room. 'You would be free to go.'

'Free?' snorted Nettie. 'For how long, reverend? For as long as it takes the constables to round us up again and set us to burn upon the Kilgreen like the witches of bygone days.'

The reverend shook his head. 'You're wrong, Mrs White. If you do but sign these papers then we can take your confession, seek to baptise you into the Lord's family again and banish the devil from your soul.'

'I thought you said I had no soul?' said Nettie. 'You told me I'd given it to the devil. So which is it, reverend? Do I have one, or not? 'Cause I wouldn't want you wasting your time trying to save what's not there.'

Sorcha bit back a grin. Nettie's defiance gave her strength. From the way Nicolas's grip on her hand tightened, it did her as well.

The reverend frowned. 'Watch your tongue, hussy. You're as bad as that Beatrix Laing and Janet Cornfoot.'

Nettie shot a sly smile at Sorcha. Their friends weren't beaten yet either.

'Very well,' said the reverend. 'Are any of you prepared to sign?'

In turn, the women shook their heads.

'God would not want me to lie,' said Isobel. Sorcha had never been prouder of her.

'If that's your final word?' asked the reverend and, without waiting for an answer, scooped up the papers, folded them and replaced them in this satchel. 'It's as I told you, gentlemen.' He bowed in the pricker's direction. 'They're all yours, Mr Bollard.'

He strode out of the room followed by the officials. The constables, Bailie Cook and the pricker remained.

The noise of their boots upon the stairs echoed dully. The men were ascending to the floor above to position themselves to watch.

'Come now, lassies,' said Mr Bollard after the door shut.

Removing his cloak and draping it carefully over the end of the table, he pulled his leather pouch from wherever he concealed it. He smiled. He had grey teeth, as big as tombstones. 'I thought you'd be happy to see me, considering we've gotten to know each other so well. Perhaps not as well as I'd like — after all, I haven't seen you for a few days. I think it's time to rectify that, don't you?'

He turned from where he'd conscientiously lined up his needles and other gadgets on the table; soldiers ready for battle. 'I think I'd like to refamiliarise myself with you first, Sorcha. If the rest of you would be so kind as to leave us alone? That would be grand. Constable, if you could take them?' He gestured towards Constable Wood who ushered the others out of the room. They'd be guarded temporarily in the room above, where they could hear enough of what was happening to understand what was in store for them.

'We love you, Sorcha,' called out Nettie, earning a deep frown from Mr Bollard.

When the door was shut again, Mr Bollard passed Constable Stuart some rope, and drew a chair towards the table.

It took all Sorcha's will not to shake, scream and resist. From past experience she knew it only made things worse. Holding her head high, fastening her eyes on the window, watching the way the rain crazed the glass, thinking of the captain upon Liath, she complied. Even while her mind shouted.

When she was tied down, the ropes checked, and the constable had retreated to a corner, Mr Bollard clapped his hands. 'Right, all is in order.' He extracted a long, sharp needle from the neat row he'd made. Holding it horizontally, he pressed it to his lips before showing it to Sorcha.

'Let's begin, shall we?'

TWENTY-THREE

It was upon his [Peter Morton's] accusation... the minister and bailies imprisoned these poor women and set a guard of drunken fellows about them, who by pinching and pricking some of them with pins and elsions, kept them from sleep for several days and nights, the marks thereof were seen by several a month thereafter. This cruel usage made some of them learn to be so wise as to acknowledge every question that was asked of them...

— A Letter from a Gentleman in Fife to his
Friend in Edinburgh, *1705*

Sorcha only knew it was the end of May because the month and date had been written on her confession. It was spring, the season of rebirth and renewal. She should have been outside, walking through mist-veiled morns down to the shore, breathing in the warmer air, watching lambs gambolling on the pastures between Anster and the Weem. Enjoying the seal pups making their way towards the rocks at the edge of the braes, their mothers floating anxiously nearby while bursts of puffins, little motes of black, white and sunshiny yellow and red, sprang from nests dotted all over the Isle of May. She should have been casting off her winter shawl, feeling the sun on her back, dodging hatchlings and fondling puppies as she strode up the High Street. Washing the curtains, scrubbing the floors and getting ready for the day when the hearthstone and fire could be properly cleaned. She should be roaming the markets. Instead, she, Nettie, Nicolas, Isobel and the others were interned in the eternal coldness of the Tolbooth, still subject to the whims of the reverend and the bailies. Dependent on the generosity or sympathy of the guards and those who could bribe them.

Food was scarce, but that was because even when the guards took coin to pass on meals prepared by family and friends, they more often ate what was provided. She couldn't blame them, not really; everyone was hungry, not just those for whom the food was intended. The catch was still meagre; the land hadn't recovered from the famine that ravaged it only a couple of years previously. Astounded by the generosity of those who sought to ensure the prisoners didn't starve, she worried that they did. The guards, clearly, had no such compunctions. Blankets and even clean clothes did find their way upstairs. It was a relief to dress in them, to huddle beneath the extra warmth, even if their bodies were foul, scarred and beaten.

What they all wanted more than anything, apart from this protracted nightmare to end, was information. Information about those in the room below, about Beatrix in the cave down the wynd, and about what the reverend and council intended to do with them.

Especially now that, with the exception of Thomas Brown, they'd all confessed.

Becoming weaker by the day, Thomas refused to confess or sign anything. Sorcha was in awe of his strength, his will. What she feared — what they all did — was it would outlast his body.

As Sorcha sat against the wall, her knees drawn up and her arms resting limply upon them, her chin sank towards her chest. For days they'd held out. Days and days. After all that, what had finally broken her, broken them all, was the incessant pricking. Allowing them short periods where they were left alone, lulled into a false sense that maybe the torture was over and real healing could begin, only made its resumption worse. Ruthless, endless, it wouldn't stop. Bollard would not stop. Awash with blood, delirious with pain, her mind wandering, she'd finally uttered the words the reverend was imploring her to say.

Believing that he and the pricker were responsible for the eventual admission of her sins, what Sorcha would never tell Patrick Cowper was that it was the spirits of her dead family who finally persuaded her to concede. Appearing before her in a vision after one terrible session with Bollard, they'd begged her to admit to what was being demanded. Weeping, her da and Erik, even her mor, had whispered they feared she would die if she did not. She must do what she promised and live — if not for herself, then for them.

It wasn't violence, but love that made her confess. By then, she'd lost her faith in God (no matter what she promised Him, He did not listen), in justice, but not in her da, nor Erik. Not even in her mor. Memories of them were strong, untarnished by current circumstances. They lived in guiltless perpetuity in her heart.

Without even reading what was written on the paper the reverend slid across the table, she did spy the month. Shocked so much time had passed, she held the quill in her shaking, twisted hand, repulsed by the long, filthy nails, and signed. What she'd confessed to she didn't find out until later.

Returned to her cell, she collapsed on the floor. It was over. Her ordeal was over. Nettie, Nicolas and Isobel crawled to her side. Wrapping their lacerated arms around her, their heads close together, they simply lay there. She couldn't speak; not because her voice was taken but because she didn't want to tell them what she'd done — not so much that she'd signed — they would have guessed — but that she'd given up.

One by one, the women were dragged out of their prison (for that's what it had become), before being returned hours later. Nicolas was so brutalised by the pricker she'd been carried. Just like Sorcha, the women had lain upon the cold, soothing stone floor, while hot tears and blood flowed. For the first few hours, they kept their backs to each other and, like Sorcha, stared at the blank wall. They were facing their weakness, their shame and, while forgiving it in others, hated it in themselves.

It wasn't until after Nettie was brought back, crawling on her hands and knees to close the distance between them and forcing Sorcha to turn around, that Nettie told her she too had signed.

Over the following days, they forgave each other their broken promise to withstand the men, the pricker, the reverend. Their promise to each other.

At least, Nettie said, they would be released now.

But as the days and nights passed and no one came to unlock the door, except to pass them vittles and messages, they began to lose hope all over again. This was the cruellest blow. At least in confessing, they'd been given a glimpse of the end of torture, of release. While the brutalising did stop, they remained locked in the cell. Too mortified to stand at the window and reassure friends and family they were alive, too weak to cry out for news, they lay or sat, talking quietly of what their lives had been before — when they were free. As if it was a shared dream, they spoke of their loved ones, the ocean, the currents, the slippery herring, the sweet faces of the seals and their hoarse barks, the prickly seaweed and raucous gulls, with wonder and longing. They took it in turns to describe each of the fishermen who worked the boats, the fishwives too, sometimes chuckling at their memories, how different they were. They shared confidences and aspirations.

More than ever, Sorcha found herself thinking of Captain Ross, hoping, praying he was doing whatever he could to see that justice was served, to liberate them from this hell. But in her bleakest moments, when the room was so black she could taste the darkness, she began to wonder if justice and freedom were even the same thing.

Beatrix ran her fingers over the gouges she'd made in the walls, trying to work out how long she'd been in this place. She knew she could light the stump of candle smuggled to her by Simon Wood, but didn't want to waste it. Anyhow, she thought, dropping her arm and feeling her way back to what passed for a bed, what did it matter? The reverend had won; he'd broken them and they'd all confessed.

Collapsed on the pile of stinking blankets, she reached around until her fingers found the lump of bread she'd saved from yesterday. As she nibbled on it, she knew the crumbs spilling down her front and onto the floor would mean the rats would pay a visit, but she was beyond caring.

As they so often did, her thoughts flew to her friends in the Tolbooth. They might have each other, they might have light and even fresh air to comfort them, but did they understand how cold that comfort was? They were all living on borrowed time.

Janet would know. Thomas, too. She prayed the rest of the lasses remained in ignorance.

Until yesterday, she'd been spared what Thomas and the women in the Tolbooth had been forced to endure — not merely the pricker and his sick hobby (dear God, she was grateful for that) but the vile utterings of the reverend.

When she heard the key fumbling in the lock last night, she'd assumed it was the guards bringing the daily ration of food and water, only the sound was coming from the wrong direction. In the semi-darkness, it took her a moment to realise the noise was coming from the kirk and the small door wedged under the overhanging bit of rock towards the rear of the cave.

For a wild moment, her heart leapt and she wondered if someone had dared to come and free her. Inwardly berating herself for allowing such a foolish hope to flare, she quickly leaned over and extinguished the candle, plunging the cave into darkness. Let whichever bastard disturbed her learn how to navigate their way around the hole like she did, skinned knees, grazed hands, broken tooth and all.

The reverend came alone, pushing the door open and holding a flickering candlestick aloft, blinking and peering. He looked like a badger emerging from its den. For a few moments, Beatrix had the advantage and she saw the reverend before he had a chance to adjust his features. He looked smaller than she remembered, older, but also, as the halo of light accentuated his cadaverous face, narrow lips and strange cold eyes, a man incapable of remorse. How had he ever come to God?

She'd no doubt Cowper was like so many of his ilk, attracted to the Almighty for the power his position afforded him, power he wouldn't otherwise be able to wield, despite being a man.

'Och, there you be, Mrs Laing. Cowering among the rags, where your kind belong.'

Beatrix knew better than to respond.

He studied her. 'I came to tell you that your sisters have joined you.'

What did he mean? She resisted the urge to look around, as if the others might manifest beside her.

Then it struck her. They'd confessed. God damn the arse.

She screwed her hands into fists, relishing the pain that shot up her arms. Keeping her eyes fixed on the reverend, she swallowed the words, the insults and threats batting at her mouth. She wouldn't give him the satisfaction.

'Mr Bollard's expertise was what was needed,' continued the reverend after a while, his voice oddly flat in the cave, 'to extract what law and the city officials require in order to put you all to trial — confessions. With the exception of Thomas Brown, everyone has now conceded they are indeed witches and that you, Beatrix Laing, are their leader.'

Beatrix's eyes glimmered as tears banked. She willed them not to fall. Not yet. It wasn't what he said that upset her, but what he didn't. What must have been done to the lasses to make them say such things?

'It won't be long before Thomas Brown also confesses. After all, how can he meet his Maker if he doesn't cleanse his soul?'

The reverend stared, clearly expecting her to ask what he meant, to seek further information. She wouldn't give him the satisfaction. She'd heard that Thomas was wasting away in the cell, unable to eat, drink or sleep; that at the reverend's insistence the pricker had been merciless with him, uncaring of his age.

Cowper's brow furrowed then cleared.

'It also won't be long before you're free of this place, Beatrix — all I'm waiting upon is word from Edinburgh, then this will be over. How will that feel, hey?'

Beatrix raised her chin. A tear escaped and slowly slid down her left cheek. Damn if the canny dede-doer didn't see it.

Raising the candle higher, the reverend leered. 'Imagine, the wind upon your face, the fresh spray of the sea, the smell of brine and weed and fish — the odour of Pittenweem. There'll be a nice view from the Green as well. You'll be able to see and inhale it all — that is, before the smell of smoke, fire and burning flesh consumes you.'

Before she could respond, he gave a crow of laughter, turned and wedged the door closed, leaving her in the dark once more. There was the jangle of keys, the abrasive scrape of a latch being drawn, then silence.

Beatrix sat still, breathing deeply. In and out, in and out. If she listened very carefully, she could hear the sea. She could almost feel it as well. It was like it surged beneath the floor, echoed deep in the walls. It had been her greatest comfort. Some days, her only one.

Though that wasn't quite true.

They might break her body, but for all they tried, they couldn't shatter her mind. Between them, the sea and memories of her husband, daughter, granddaughter and her friends sustained her. And, in its own strange way, so had the cave.

The one thing no one ever told you about the dark, even the inky blackness she now dwelt in, was that despite the absence of light and colour, it wasn't true that you couldn't see. You might not be able to fasten upon what was actually there — the uneven cave walls, the pitted, rocky floor, or the low-hanging ceiling, punctuated with crevices, holes, and all manner of shapes. But they were its illuminated dress. It wore another when there was no light, and Beatrix had come to appreciate its beauty. Despite the dark, or perhaps because of it, if she narrowed her eyes she could see the mauves and golds of sunset; if she opened them swiftly after screwing them up tightly, there were the scarlet and blues of a stormy morning. At other times white spots flashed across the undulating dome above her like the lighthouse on the Isle of May. Sometimes she could even make out the changing palette of the Firth of Forth upon the floor, as if it had washed into the cave and was lapping at her toes. Aye, the darkness had its own way of introducing her to a different way of seeing and that was before she considered the textures and smells of St Fillan's Cave. Nae. Not Fillan's any more. It was now Beatrix's cave and she knew it as well as her own sore and worn body.

It was to the blackness that Beatrix now surrendered herself as she thought of her friends in the Tolbooth. Lying down, she shut her eyes and, refusing to think about Patrick Cowper or his menacing words, allowed their bright beautiful images to parade across her night — burnished copper, roses, turquoises, greys and chestnuts, all accompanied by the golden strains of laughter.

TWENTY-FOUR

He speired the guts oot 'o of me.
(He asked too many inquisitive questions.)

Captain Aidan Ross entered the reverend's study gathering what remained of his forbearance. As he closed the door, he took in the room and the tableau of men before him. Rather than the austere space he'd been expecting, the reverend's study was luxurious, with polished wood, plushly upholstered chairs and thick curtains. The large hearth blazed despite the sunshine outside. Many framed pictures hung upon the walls, as did a large arras, and provided a sumptuousness he hadn't expected from the aloof, reedy man dressed in black who sat behind the big desk at the end of the room.

Aidan schooled his face and approached. Light filtered in from two windows to his right, framed by dark blue curtains. The road outside could be seen clearly as he crossed the floor, his boots soundless on the rugs. Almost everyone who passed glanced up at the Tolbooth. It had taken on a new significance in the past weeks.

The reverend cleared his throat and, rising to his feet, scraped his chair back across the boards. From the half-empty glasses and thickness of pipe smoke above the desk, the papers, ink and tidy pile of quill shavings upon it, the men had been deliberating a while. Aidan was determined to discover what they had been discussing.

On either side of the minister, looking as if they'd been peering over his shoulders before he interrupted them, stood bailies Cook and Bell, secular bookends for this holy man.

A less holy man, Aidan thought as he traversed the room and bowed, he was unlikely to meet. The skeletal face wore a blank expression and a wry smile curved the thin lips. The skin was sallow, broken veins crawling up hollow cheeks. The outlandish eyes missed nothing, much as they attempted to appear indifferent to having an officer of the Queen in his manse.

Patrick Cowper might appear to be pliant, but he was also ambitious and ruthless. Aidan had learned what he could about the man over the last few weeks. A widower, father of eleven children whom he dominated as he did his congregation, he was both feared and resented. He had the ear of the powerful, including some gentlemen in St Andrew's, most of whom, according to the fishermen he'd spoken to and the letters he'd received from his commanding officer, were too scared to go against him lest he turn on them. Moving to Pittenweem twelve years earlier, he'd set about changing the church from an Episcopalian to a Presbyterian one, establishing his authority swiftly. A proud Covenanter who supported English rule, he made a point of condemning Jacobites. Not that this changed how most in the Weem felt towards the one true King: the place was a veritable hotbed of Stuart sympathy. Which was also why folk followed Cowper — not because they shared his support of the English Crown, but in order to appear loyal to it. He oft threatened to unmask Jacobites and report them to the authorities, authorities who included his influential friends. In that regard, Aidan could understand and even forgive folk's compliance.

However, as Aiden discovered, despite the influence he wielded, the minister's ambition did not extend beyond the streets of Pittenweem, even though he was a moderator *pro tempore* of St Andrew's presbytery. His real interests lay mainly where he could see and be seen. Many believed he accepted the position in Edinburgh for the sake of the title, throwing it about to increase his standing in the Weem.

Most were unaware it meant he was merely a replacement for the usual moderator if ever he was absent. The position was as hollow as the reverend's heart.

In this small seaside kingdom, Patrick Cowper, minister, Covenantor, Presbyterian, and temporary moderator of the Kirk, reigned.

'Sit, sit,' the reverend said to Aidan as he resumed his own seat. Aidan pulled up the chair indicated and moved his sword to one side so he could perch on the edge of the seat. Bailies Cook and Bell took this as a signal to come out from behind the desk and find chairs. Bell acknowledged Aidan with a dip of his head. Cook ignored him.

'What is it you wish to see me about, Captain Ross?' asked the reverend amiably, picking up a glass and swirling the amber fluid. He didn't offer Aidan a drink.

'You know the reason, reverend,' said Aidan, equally affable. 'It's the same one we've oft had cause to discuss of late.'

A flash of displeasure crossed the reverend's face.

'Until the women and Mr Brown are released from the Tolbooth,' continued Aidan, glad he'd discommoded the man, 'or a reason accompanied by proof is given for their continued internment, I'll not have a different one.'

The reverend took his time, sniffing the whisky, as if he hadn't already drunk a great deal. 'Aye, well, this time, captain, I'm pleased to report we not only have a reason to keep the women and Mr Brown locked up, we also have this proof you keep demanding.' He shot a sly look at Aidan. 'I mean the authorities in Edinburgh. You're really only their mouthpiece, after all.'

Bailie Cook nodded smugly. The reverend smirked.

It was all Aidan could do not to flatten the man's thin nose all over his face. Choosing to ignore the insult, he persisted. 'You have proof? Of witchcraft?'

'As you ken, Captain Ross, that's what the prisoners are accused of, aye.'

Aidan clenched his fist, took a deep breath and waited. He learned long ago that people like the reverend didn't like silence and sought to fill it. He wasn't wrong.

'You, see, captain, these people you're so keen to defend, that you've stuck your neck out for, involving your superiors in Edinburgh, are everything we feared they were and more, aren't they, gentlemen?' He addressed the last question to the bailies.

'Aye, that they are,' said Bailie Cook, and was rewarded with an appreciative smile. There was a beat, then Bailie Bell grunted agreement.

'What proof can you possibly have?' It was all Aidan could do to keep the scorn from his voice. Pushing aside memories of Sorcha as he had last seen her leaning out the window of the Tolbooth, her beautiful bronze locks gone, the terrible marks upon her arms, the deep lilac crescents beneath her eyes, the sunken cheeks, he regarded the reverend calmly though a storm raged in his chest. 'You can hardly concede that anything said under the duress of pricking, let alone the other punishments you've ordered,' he included the bailies in his statement; Bell, at least, had the decency to look uncomfortable, 'counts as proof.'

The reverend raised his bony hand and rested it lovingly on a pile of papers to his right. 'Ah, but there you're wrong. These, sir, these papers. These ones right beneath my fingers. These are my proof. You ken what they be?'

Aidan glanced at them but didn't respond.

'Confessions, captain. They are confessions, each and every one signed by the witches themselves.'

Aidan did his best not to look shocked. He already knew the pricker claimed to have found witch's marks upon the women's bodies, marks the man no doubt carried himself but would describe differently.

The reverend noticed Aidan's change of demeanour and sniggered. 'Aye, they've each confessed — with the exception of Mr Brown, who still refuses. But give him time.' He glanced knowingly at the bailies. '*We'll* give him time.' Mr Cook seemed to find this very amusing.

'To what exactly have the women confessed?' asked Aidan, crossing his legs in an effort to appear more relaxed than he felt. It would also make it harder to draw his sword. He was afraid that if he could, he would run the man through, God help him.

The reverend brushed his hand against the papers before lifting one from the pile.

'Let's see then, shall we? Take Janet White, commonly known as Nettie Horseburgh.' He made a point of reading what was in front of him. 'After much… questioning, she admitted to joining with Beatrix Laing, Sorcha McIntyre and Nicolas Lawson, among others, with the sole purpose of committing malfeasance against one Peter Morton. Mrs White, Horseburgh, whatever she calls herself, and the others also confessed to renouncing their baptism and being in league with Satan.'

Aidan felt a cold so heavy descend upon him, he couldn't move. 'They *all* said as much?'

'Every last one. Condemned by their own mouths and signatures.' Putting the piece of paper down, the reverend's finger stabbed the place where a name, shaky but discernible, was scrawled.

'I see,' said Aidan calmly, though his mind raced. God knows what the poor souls had endured to force them to admit to such rubbish. What Sorcha had suffered. He clenched and unclenched his fists. 'And what are your intentions now you've… extracted these from the women?'

'As it happens, your timing is impeccable, captain.' The reverend rose and began to pace about the room, pausing before the fire. Above the fireplace was a painting of Jesus sitting in a field surrounded by children and cavorting lambs. The clouds were pale salmon and lavender, the grass a melange of soft yellows and green, the lambs like thistledown that might scatter to the winds should they be touched. Aidan marvelled that Cowper could stand before such a peaceful, loving image while discussing the torture of the women and Mr Brown. Surely such measures should offend a godly man, a Christian one. Not Cowper. It was then Aidan noticed the subject of another, larger picture on the opposite wall: the crucifixion. At its centre, on a huge, solid cross, was the frail, emaciated body of Christ, His bloody wounds weeping, sorrowful eyes raised heavenwards, pleading for His Father's forgiveness. Or were they pleading for His tormentors to release Him? Cruelty and suffering leapt from the image. Aye, that would be more to Cowper's taste.

As he waited for the reverend to continue, Aidan noted the row of books resting above the mantel, their leather spines cracked. There was a Bible and some other religious tomes; nothing to appeal to the imagination, the creative soul. The light fluctuated briefly. Folk passing by the window, their voices rising and falling, unaware a group of men sat inside this room, holding the power of life and death over the helpless.

Still Aidan said nothing.

'You see,' said Cowper, returning to his desk. 'The good bailies and I have just been drafting a request to Edinburgh.' He touched Aidan on the shoulder. 'Save you the effort.' He laughed at his joke. The bailies began to join in then caught Aidan's expression and stopped.

'And what does this request entail, sir?' asked Aidan politely.

'Here,' said the reverend and lifted the piece of paper he'd been studying when Aidan entered. 'Read it for yourself.'

Aidan scanned the contents swiftly, his brows arching. 'You're requesting the help of the Commission of the General Assembly and Privy Council in Edinburgh to bring the witches to trial.'

'Aye,' said the reverend. 'We are.'

Aidan hadn't expected that. He had believed that the reverend would do everything in his power to stop Edinburgh interfering. According to the letter, bailies Vernour and Cleiland were seeking an audience with the Commission. Aidan knew that less than a fortnight ago, on the first of June, bailies Bell and Cook had travelled to the city and had a meeting with Sir Thomas Moncrieff, justiciar to the regulatory of St Andrew's. Sir Thomas, along with the rest of the presbytery, must have given them permission to seek (or demanded they did) the aid of Edinburgh. Why, this was good news, wasn't it? With Edinburgh becoming involved, rather than merely being informed of what was happening by the Pittenweem council — or indeed by his own letters — and bringing in lawyers who were familiar with the vagaries of witch trials, suspicious of the motivations of those doing the charging, that would be a good thing, wouldn't it?

So why did he feel as if a flock of seagulls were trapped in his chest?

'May I ask when you intend to send this?'

'Tomorrow,' said the reverend simply. 'Why waste time? In fact, since you've been making so many trips to Edinburgh yourself of late, perhaps you'd be good enough to deliver the document on our behalf? You or Sergeant Thatcher? Once it's properly prepared and sealed of course. Consider this request a mark of our good faith in the correct legal procedure.' The reverend retrieved the document from him.

Aidan's mind galloped. Why was the reverend following due process now, when he'd been flouting it so recklessly before? Had an order come from the city? Had Aidan's superiors managed to pull the man into line? Somehow he doubted it. Thus far any appeals Aidan had made to them had been dismissed. Few wanted to interfere with provincial justice. Least of all his commanding officer, when there was a war raging. They'd more important issues to occupy them. Yet, if Aidan took the document to Edinburgh, he could ensure that the men who could make a difference knew exactly what was going on, not simply what his superiors or, for that matter, the council, chose to share. He'd tell them exactly what types of punishment Cowper had endorsed, what the pricker had done to extract these so-called confessions. But why was the reverend asking *him*? Surely he knew Aidan would take this opportunity to present an alternate view of the Weem council's 'facts'? He tried to study the reverend surreptitiously. What exactly was the man up to?

'Aye,' he said, careful not to show too much enthusiasm. 'I'll deliver it.'

'Excellent,' said the reverend, clapping his hands together. 'Then there's no need for you to tarry any longer. If you're to make haste to the city on the morrow, then you'd best get some rest. I'll make sure the finished letter is delivered to your lodgings as soon as possible.'

The reverend strode to the door and held it open. Rising, Aidan bowed to the bailies. When he reached the door, he made a show of putting on his hat.

The reverend waited for Aidan to acknowledge him. One of the reverend's eyes was almost opaque, as if it had a veil drawn across it. A faint scar ran from the corner of the eye to the top of his cheekbone.

'Let me tell you now, captain,' the reverend spoke so softly, Aidan was hard-pressed to hear, 'if you're thinking about telling the authorities in Edinburgh how we extracted the confessions, then it won't be me, the bailies or Mr Bollard who'll be held to account.'

Trying not to show annoyance that the reverend so accurately guessed his intentions, Aidan casually cocked a brow, crossed the threshold and paused in the hallway, spinning slowly on his heel. 'Nae? And who might be then?'

The reverend wrapped long fingers around his arm, forcing him to bend over so he could speak in his ear.

'Who else but the witches, lad? Who else but the witches?' His breath was hot, fumes of whisky wafted on it. He released Aidan. 'You say anything, the witches will be held to account. By me.' His face transformed from one of victory to one etched in contrition. 'And, God knows, haven't the poor wretched souls been through enough?'

Before Aidan could think of a response, the reverend shut the door.

TWENTY-FIVE

*One Thomas Brown, the only man accused by [Peter] Morton,
imprisoned by the minister and bailies, after a great deal of hunger
and hardship, died in prison...*

— An Answer of a Letter From a Gentleman of Fife, *1705*

God damn. God damn them all. Thomas Brown was dead. Found
in his cell this June morning, lifeless, cold, bloodied and bruised and
fucking well dead.

If only he hadn't ordered the guards to ignore the pleas for sustenance and medick the women imprisoned with the old man had
made. If only he hadn't made that sappie-headed fool Camron Mac-
Gille Tolbooth keeper after Alick's dismissal. If only the guards hadn't
been so precise in fulfilling their duties...

This wasn't his fault.

Patrick Cowper paced back and forth in his drawing room, trying
to think through the ramifications of this news, delivered by a breathless constable whom the reverend then demanded accompany him
back to the Tolbooth so he could see Brown's body for himself. Ordering Angus Stuart and the Tolbooth guards to remove the hysterical
women first, he'd waited until he was quite alone before examining

the corpse. Staring at the pale underweight body covered in cuts, bruises and scars, it was evident he was as dead as a fishwife's herring. He certainly smelled like one.

Squatting beside the cadaver, Patrick shut his eyes. If anyone blundered in, it would look as though he was praying. His mind worked swiftly. How could he turn this disaster to his and thus the town's advantage? Thomas Brown had lasted over two months in the Tolbooth only to drop dead now. Instructing Angus and Cameron to take the body upstairs to the council room, he'd waited until the doctor examined the cadaver and had given his verdict, then returned home.

Patrick thumped his fist against the mantlepiece in rage.

Pain shot through his hand and up his arm. Inhaling sharply, he cradled his fist in his other hand, feeling the heat rush into it. He breathed heavily to calm himself. Think, he remonstrated. Think! What to do? How to explain this catastrophe. He rubbed his injured hand absent-mindedly. The fucking witch wasn't meant to keel over. He was meant to be put to the flame before the town so folk could see that justice was served; that demons had been excised. That he, Patrick Cowper, had kept them safe.

What was he to do now?

Brown was the only man identified by Peter Morton. Worried the lad had misstepped, it wasn't until the Laing woman also named Brown as one of those who had made a pact with the devil that the decision to imprison him was validated. If she hadn't, then they'd be in more trouble than a Jacobite at Whitehall.

Running his hands over his face, Cowper took a few more deep breaths and began to feel better. It would be all right. They'd done nothing wrong. *He'd* done nothing wrong.

He sank into a seat and thought about Thomas Brown. Moderately well-off, it didn't hurt that he owned shares in a boat that were now, with his death, free to be bought by someone more inclined to divide them among the councillors. Could Brown's daughter be persuaded to sell the half she was entitled to? Maybe. Not immediately. She would be too angry, too caught up in grief. But perhaps later… They might even be able to seize all his property. After all, he died locked up as a witch. Admittedly, he didn't confess, but he was named an accomplice...

God. The authorities in Edinburgh wouldn't like this. Not at all and he didn't need that bloody soldier, Captain Ross, to tell him that.

Even so, news of Brown's demise shouldn't have surprised him. The man had fallen ill within days of being imprisoned. The pricking, beatings and enforced sleeplessness weakened him further. But it was that idiot guard — what was his name? Rab Burne — who not only over-used the witch goad, the paddle the men used to beat the prisoners to prevent them sleeping, but denied the man the sustenance they were by law required to provide. Brown wasn't only tortured (he winced as the word loomed in his mind), but was, according to the doctor, starved to death. Water, as Dr McLeod, a man prone to supporting Patrick's decisions in the past, had pointedly said, will only maintain life for so long.

Burne, the greedy fool, kept the meals Brown's daughter brought to the Tolbooth for himself, gulping them down within hearing of the prisoners. Patrick shook his head. He should have had Burne removed. Should have him whipped. Patrick could scarce believe the emaciated corpse was Brown, the man they'd interned. Not man. Witch. He must remember that. They may not have extracted a confession from Thomas before he died, but would have done eventually.

Anyway, what did it really matter? Brown had enjoyed three score years and ten or more. Testimony to his hardiness that he lasted so long. His death was inconvenient rather than a tragedy.

Running fingers through his thinning hair, the reverend stared out the window of his drawing room. Beyond the gravestones in the neighbouring kirkyard, the grey sea roiled. Wisps of mist hovered over the water. In the spaces between the stones he caught glimpses of the fishermen's boats bobbing, their nets flung wide, their lines unspooled. Gulls hovered above them, cawing and shrieking as the men hauled in their catch. Closer to shore, he could see figures walking along the sands. Some he recognised, more were unfamiliar. That had been an unexpected boon of this witch hunt. The number of strangers who, learning what was afoot, flocked to the Weem to see for themselves.

As word spread across Fife that Pittenweem had imprisoned witches, eight of them — well, seven now — folk travelled to town. These incomers brought much-needed coin. Already he'd heard how the tavern was selling more ale than it had since the war began. Local farms could scarce keep up with the demand for eggs, poultry, milk and cheese. Even the paltry catch was being sold before it landed. The inns were full for the first time in years, so full locals had taken to billeting people — even Anster and St Monan's were benefiting from the influx. If nothing else, witchcraft was good for business.

The thought aroused a real smile.

But he was wasting time and there was still work to do before the witches were brought to trial. He left the drawing room, almost bowling over a maid waiting to sweep the hearth, and went to his study, where he began to shuffle some papers, anything to take his mind off Thomas Brown, the women in the Tolbooth, the silent, glowering one in St Fillan's Cave. In the rooms beyond, he could hear his children talking. The low voice of his housekeeper urged them to be quiet because their father was working. They paid her no attention. Who could blame them? What a weak, mousy woman she was. Still, she was a Covenanter like him, godly, even if bedding her was like pounding a half-full sack of grain. He frowned. He shouldn't think about that. He shouldn't think about women at all and yet, if he were truthful, over the past couple of months he'd been obsessed by them.

Images of creamy breasts and thighs flowing with blood leapt into his mind. Dried mouths opening in hoarse screams, wet eyelashes stuck together against shiny cheeks, wide, fearful eyes. He felt his prick stir beneath his cassock. He reached down to staunch its hardening. When his fingers touched it through the coarse fabric it sprang to life. Gripping it through the cloth, he enjoyed the roughness against his flesh, how firm he felt. How manly. He began to think of Sorcha McIntyre, those wide lips, those full breasts with their rosy pointed nipples. He'd never seen skin like that on anyone before; anyone except that foreign mother of hers. Dear God, but there was one. A siren brought to land to tempt men to ruin. His wife, God bless her, had been possessed of red, scaly flesh that was abrasive to touch, prone to itching and patches of rawness. The housekeeper's was much the same. Sorcha's was perfect, like the cream of cow's milk. And as for her cunny, so pink and plump without its hair. He began to imagine pounding that…

When he'd finished, he sat in his chair. His cheeks were hot, his chest rose and fell in rapid pants, but his body was replete. No longer could he imagine Sorcha or the others, Nettie Horseburgh, Nicolas Lawson or young Isobel Adam as they'd been when they were first stripped by the pricker. Punishing him for the act he'd just committed, God reminded him why they were in the Tolbooth by placing pictures of what they looked like now before his mind's eye. Stinking, wretched creatures with tatty short hair, grey teeth, dirty faces and fingers. They weren't imprisoned so he could look upon them when he chose and assuage his lust with the memory of their lovely bodies, but so he could rid them of the devil that lurked inside each and every one of them.

After weeks in the Tolbooth, no longer were their bodies desirable with their differently shaped breasts, curves, marks and lines. They were bruised, beaten, torn, broken and befouled — and all at his command.

How had it come to this? How had *he* come to this? It was the witches. It was Sorcha McIntyre, the temptress, the devil's own bride. This — he stared at the damp stain on his cassock — was her fault.

Resting his elbows on his desk, he lowered his face into his hands. Sorrow for what he had to endure welled in his chest. Why did God ask so much of him, a mere man? Why did he have to suffer so?

A sob escaped, catching him unawares. At first, he tried to stifle it, but it wouldn't be stopped. Left with no choice, he let it come forth, a great howl, like a wild animal, it filled his ears, his head, the room. Grabbing the edge of his gown, he stuffed it into his mouth and unleashed his torment.

Forgive me, God, for my weakness, he prayed. *You called me to Your service and here I am baulking at what You ask of me. I must gird my weak body, my weak mind and heart and continue. Do whatever it is You ask of me.*

There was a timid knock at the door. 'Are you all right in there, sir?' It was the housekeeper.

Patrick pulled the edges of his robe out of his mouth, swiped the tears from his face, cleared his throat and sat up. His mind was clearer now.

'I'm fine.' His voice was loud and firm. 'Leave me be.'

Moments later, he heard her shuffle away. He let out the breath he was holding. She couldn't see him like this. No one could. Only God knew the doubts that sometimes racked him, the demons that cavorted through his dreams whispering lewd things, placing salacious images in his mind. Daily, guilt flooded his body before he forced it to recede, and not just because Satan tempted him — the witches tempted him. Weren't they one and the same?

The sounds from outside intruded as incomers walked towards the kirk and manse, up Cove Wynd, commenting loudly on what they saw. Stopping beneath his window, people pointed at the Tolbooth. He could hear them, hear the glorious fear and elation in their voices as they discussed the witches.

He knew then what he'd tell the men to do with Brown's body.

As a witch, Brown didn't deserve a Christian burial. Witches must be denied the everlasting peace of the hallowed soil of the kirk. Burying Brown in the cemetery would undermine everything he was doing, everything he was achieving. He and the Morton boy. He thought briefly of Peter. He was a good lad. A loyal one, too. To the curious, he was as much an attraction as the witches. Why, the incomers had been weaving their way through Pittenweem lanes and wynds like ants to their hills, begging admittance to the Morton house, even leaving coin just to set eyes upon him. Like the Shaw girl, Peter was a victim of possession, malfeasance, a wonder to behold. For his sake, Patrick had to make a lesson of Brown; for the sake of all that was yet to be done. To do otherwise would be to admit he was wrong, that God was wrong.

Finding the relevant piece of paper, Patrick dipped a quill in the ink. He wrote an addendum to Brown's death certificate and then signed his name under the doctor's with a flourish. Reading over his orders, he was satisfied.

The witch, Thomas Brown, would be flung upon the western braes and left for the corbies, scavengers, and the elements to consume. And if the incomers wanted to remain, to see what a rotting witch looked like and spend more money in town while they did it, then who was he to deprive them?

TWENTY-SIX

The curse of the first-footer.

14 June 1704

*W*ith a heavy heart, Sorcha watched Nettie being escorted out of their cell. Days earlier they'd learned that Captain Ross, along with bailies Bell and Cleiland, had ridden to Edinburgh to obtain a commission from the Privy Council to try them. Confused as to what this meant, why Captain Ross was with the councilmen, it was Sorcha who reassured the women that this latest development worked in their favour — if for no other reason than that if Captain Ross was with the delegation, he would ensure their interests were represented.

Yet, instead of officials from Edinburgh arriving (surely they would have heard by now?) or the captain returning, it was a group of dour-looking men from the presbytery of St Andrew's who answered the summons. Declaring they wished to see the accused witches for themselves and then report back to Edinburgh, they were brought to the Tolbooth.

Confused and exhausted, the women were now soul-sick and desperate. The news last week about Thomas Brown's death had been a blow from which Sorcha doubted they'd recover. It changed the terms of their imprisonment. It was no longer a case of if they'd ever be free again, but whether incarceration and torture would kill them first.

Not that Mr Bollard had attended them since they signed their confessions. They'd been told he'd returned home — wherever that was. Hell, said Nettie, and Sorcha was inclined to believe her. That at least was one small mercy. Now they'd only to endure the infection that set into the wounds and which their living conditions did nothing to aid. Even the guards, initially remote but now guilty about Thomas's death, changed towards them. Isobel said it was because they felt sorry for them. Not sorry enough to give them the food brought by friends and family every other day. But they did at least tell them when Thomas's body, which had been tossed on the braes 'like muck from a water closet' as one guard put it, disappeared.

'It had been pecked, you understand, pecked and partly eaten,' said Camron, the new Tolbooth keeper, a simple farmhand from Crail way who was perpetually hungry and in awe of the reverend, so unlikely to question his orders. What the reverend didn't see, but the women did, was the kind heart beneath the blank face and the loneliness that had made him accept the repellent position in the first place.

'And it stunk worse than me brother's shit. Not that it stopped people going to gawk at it or blathering 'bout his missing eye, the colour of his skin — blue and purple in case you be interested, especially 'long his arms and back.' Camron rubbed his belly. 'Och, you should have seen the marks on his body and the way his bones poked out like they were 'bout to puncture his skin.' That those he was telling bore the same marks, if not worse, escaped Camron altogether. Nor was he the type of man able to sense when his comments weren't appreciated and shut up. Unaware of the effect of his lurid descriptions, Camron stood in the centre of their cell, ignoring the stench and bleak conditions and blethered on. Sorcha was too scared to stop him lest he cease giving them any information, and forced herself to listen to his terrible tale. No one knew who had removed Thomas's body, but it wouldn't be too hard to guess. She hoped his family were not only careful, but that wherever they did inter Thomas, they offered prayers from her as well.

According to Camron, the sightseers who'd come to Pittenweem in droves from all over the country to see the witches were bitterly disappointed when Thomas's corpse vanished. Some attributed it to evidence of more witches (an idea that made Sorcha's heart plummet), or to Satan himself retrieving the body of a disciple. She could imagine them exchanging more vivid and outlandish ideas over ale in the tavern, the locals feeding the imaginations of the incomers. Camron said there were so many now, farmers were charging them rent to camp in their fields behind the village.

Sorcha and Nettie had thought there were more strangers clustering in the High Street outside the Tolbooth each day to await news or to catch a glimpse of the Weem Witches. That is what they'd become. A lurid novelty to attract tourists. Nicolas told them they were imagining things, but Camron's words and other whispers that came their way proved they were not. Nevertheless, the women ceased to oblige the people by appearing at the window. If it hadn't been so macabre and frightening, Sorcha thought it would be funny. She knew crowds gathered outside Holyrood and the great palaces in London to see the Queen or any member of the royal family, but to see her? She gazed across at Nettie, knowing she looked the same if not worse. Nettie's hair now covered her scalp, growing in uneven patches, much the way it had been shaved. Her teeth were foul, her skin so grimy it was streaked in shades of grey, her clothes were rags. Examining her fingers, Sorcha couldn't bear the thought of biting her long nails, so encrusted with dirt were they. Dirt and dried blood.

They all scratched ceaselessly because of lice and fleas, and the wounds from the pricking and the beatings never seemed to heal. Whereas they would once pace the cell and take it in turns at the window, describing what they saw, inventing tales, singing on occasion, or bathing each other's wounds and trying to care for them, they now mostly lolled on the hard floor, the straw too repellent to lie upon.

At least with summer arriving it was marginally warmer.

They'd been reduced to a grotesque spectacle. They were living versions of poor Thomas — something for folk to gawp at, judge, and ghoulishly revel in. They'd also heard their reputation was bringing much needed money into the town — something Cowper would be gloating over.

The thought of Cowper was almost more than Sorcha could bear. But bear it she must and use the idea of his triumph — a victory based on the cruel extraction of lies — to give her the strength to survive. That would be her greatest revenge, outlasting this. Whereas she honoured her family by living when they could not, she would have vengeance upon Cowper by doing the same. They all would, damn the man's soul.

There were times she wished she really was a witch and could cast a spell upon him. She would wish him to suffer all she and the others had endured tenfold. Nae, a hundredfold, for all eternity.

But when Nettie was taken out of the cell one day, just when they'd begun to believe all the separations and punishments were a thing of the past, all thoughts of revenge upon Cowper were replaced by dread.

What did the men want now? What more could they do to them? And why Nettie?

It wasn't only Nettie the men from the presbytery wanted to speak to, but all of them, one by one. Nettie wasn't even the first. That honour was given to Janet Cornfoot from the cell below. But Sorcha only discovered this when it was her turn.

Escorted into the room on the top floor of the Tolbooth, she was sat on a chair in its centre that was covered in dried blood and other stains she couldn't bear to think about. It was the same chair she'd been tied and pricked in. Sorcha eyed the grim-faced men seated in a semicircle around her. Strangers, their backs were to the window, which had been pushed wide open. She could see the grey, lumbering clouds, feel the breeze coming in. Inhaling the fresh air, she wished she was outside to enjoy the overcast day. Despite being closer to the window, many of the men turned away from her, wrinkling their noses, pushing kerchiefs into their faces. It took her a moment to realise it was because of her odour. Instead of being embarrassed, she relished that it caused them such obvious discomfort and silently wished they'd choke. Unable to prevent it, a smile formed. One of the men saw it and his eyes narrowed.

'Find this amusing, do you… What's her name?' he asked. His voice was booming; accustomed to whispers and quiet, it hurt Sorcha's ears.

'Sorcha McIntyre, sir,' said Reverend Cowper. She hadn't noticed him. Installed at the end of the semicircle, behind a table, his black robes folded around him like broken wings. Suddenly she understood who these men were and her heart sank. They were known to Cowper through his role as a temporary moderator at St Andrew's. They were friends, no doubt. 'She's the daughter of Charles McIntyre, and his Norwegian wife, Astrid Grimmsdatter.' There was some muttering, as always, at the fact her father had taken an outsider to wife. 'She's also, since her older brother, Robert McIntyre, is a prisoner of war, believed dead, the owner of the *Mistral* and in possession of a fine cottage in Marygate.'

There were raised brows and nods.

'She owns a boat?' asked another, his incredulity barely contained.

'Aye, that she does. A sturdy vessel,' said the reverend. 'Large enough to do longer voyages and currently in the North Sea.'

'She won't for much longer if these charges be proved,' said Mr Booming Voice.

Sorcha raised her chin. At least she'd learned where her boat was. She prayed the men stayed away until this was over lest their cargo be seized and they miss out on their percentages.

Papers with what she assumed were her details and earlier confession were passed among the men. With one exception, they conversed in low voices.

She could hear the muffled conversation of the women below. The holes in the floor enabled snatches of their words to enter the room and buzz about like summer flies. As they did when Nettie and Nicolas were being questioned, a hush would fall when her interrogation began. At least she knew from Nettie what to expect. The intention was she would not only repeat what was in the confession she made a couple of weeks earlier, but admit to even more wrongdoing.

What the Pittenweem councillors and the reverend hadn't anticipated was that, faced with a new audience, the women would retract their statements. Nettie told Sorcha this was what she'd done, because she'd learned from Camron as he escorted her upstairs that this was what brave and bold Janet Cornfoot had dared to do. Sorcha could scare believe her ears. Nor could Isobel or Nicolas. Hugging Nettie close, in awe of her courage, of Janet's, Sorcha felt something akin to joy, a lightening of her spirit for the first time in weeks.

'After all, hen, what have we got to lose?' whispered Nettie, returning the tight hold. 'Good auld Janet, hey?'

As she regarded the men and watched the scrivener prepare his quill and paper, Sorcha feared it was more than they could even begin to imagine. She determined then and there to refuse to let her anxiety show. They'd put words in her mouth once, but never again.

'Mrs McIntyre,' began a man with large, protruding eyes and fleshy cheeks. His accent marked him as from the city. 'We'll have you know that on this day, the fourteenth of June, in the year seventeen hundred and four, your accomplice, Mrs White, whom you ken as Nettie Horseburgh, admitted to having the devil say her name. She confessed to wishing ill upon Peter Morton and implicated you in this. You and the other women imprisoned here in the Tolbooth.'

Sorcha knew that, despite giving today's date, they were referring to Nettie's earlier confession of the twenty-ninth of May and that they were waiting for her to say the names of her so-called accomplices. She remained silent, waiting, watching.

'You also ken that the lad, Peter Morton, identified you and the others as his tormentors?' It was quiet except for the sound of a chair creaking under the girth of one of the men. 'Well, lass? I'm waiting. Do you ken?'

Sorcha took her time. 'At the start of April, Peter Morton did identify me and the others, aye. But I also know that he was mistaken.'

There were some grumblings, a cough, followed by an exchange of pointed looks. A couple of the men appeared annoyed, and turned briefly towards Cowper.

'Is that so? Well, you would say that, wouldn't you?' said the portly man. 'What do you have to say about casting a charm against Peter Morton?'

'I say I did not.'

'What do you say about Nettie Horseburgh casting a spell?'

'I say she did not.'

The man sighed and shook his head, his jowls quivering. 'What do you ken about Nettie Horseburgh saying you helped her cast the charm?'

'I know nothing of this, because I could not help her do something she did not do. Nor do I believe she bears me any malice that she would suggest I did such a thing.'

The man swung to look at the reverend, who flapped a hand for him to keep going.

The man used his kerchief to pat his slick brow. The room was warm, much warmer than the cell below. Lines of perspiration tracked the sides of their faces, dotted their upper lips and stained their shirt-fronts. 'What then do you say to the fact that Nicolas Lawson also named you?'

Sorcha took a deep breath, trying not to flinch as her ribcage ached. 'Again, I say that she could not. I neither cast a spell nor am I a witch.'

'I see.' The man gave the appearance of thinking, but Sorcha could tell the question was already prepared. 'Do you happen to ken a Mrs Jean Durkie?'

Sorcha nodded. 'Aye.' Of course she did. She was a fishwife and a good friend of Nicolas's. Her husband was a fisherman who, like others tired of the meagre drave, had become a soldier and been shipped to Flanders before Sorcha left the Weem. He still hadn't returned.

'She's close to Mrs Lawson?' asked the portly man.

'Aye.'

'And you, too, Mrs McIntyre, you are close to Mrs Lawson?'

Where was this line of questioning going? 'Aye. All the fishwives are close,' she replied. There were exceptions, those who were surly or kept to themselves, but the men didn't need to know that.

Reverend Cowper cast a long, shrewd look at one of the other men who nodded and nudged the gentleman next to him.

'So, it's not too far a stretch then to assume that like Mrs Durkie, you too were receiving lessons in witchcraft from Mrs Lawson?'

Sorcha felt a frisson of panic. 'Lessons? From Mrs Lawson? Nae. I do not understand how Mrs Lawson could teach something about which she has no knowledge.'

'Nae? I find *that* strange since Mrs Durkie knew well that Mrs Lawson was a witch and admits she asked the woman to teach her to cast spells.'

This required a careful answer lest she incriminate both Nicolas and Jean. Sorcha's head hurt. 'I would assume that if Mrs Durkie indeed made such a claim, asked such a thing, then it was done in jest. She oft said she wished her husband was back, so perhaps she said something akin to that — she wanted her wish to come true and who would not in her position? I say again, sirs, Mrs Lawson is not a witch. She could not teach Mrs Durkie anything nor bring her husband home — Jean would have known this.'

'What of the wax image it's claimed you helped form?' snapped one of the other men. Sorcha turned her head to regard him. He was a sprauchle of a man, puny, and wore a pair of tiny wire spectacles that made him appear owlish. 'An image that was used to inflict great suffering and torment upon the lad. How did you ken to make that? Did not Mrs Lawson teach you? Or was it the Horseburgh woman?'

'Again,' said Sorcha patiently. It was becoming hard to stay upright in the chair. The room, at first so refreshing with its breeze, was now stuffy. Even above her own odour, she could smell the men. Their whisky-breath, their sweat, their horse-soaked clothes. 'I say I know nothing of a wax image. I know nothing of witchcraft, never have and have no desire to, sir. I would argue the same for the women whom you have named.'

The man stared at her for a long moment, gave a loud harrumph, then rose from his chair and walked over to one of his peers, removed his glasses and began a frantic, whispered conversation. When it finished, he gave a nod before replacing his spectacles and looking at Sorcha carefully. She returned his gaze steadily, even while her heart thundered. The other men talked quietly among themselves.

There was the clatter of cartwheels on the street, the persistent whine of a dog, the shouts of children. A normal day in the Weem, though this was anything but normal.

Resuming his seat, the man eventually spoke again. 'Do you have anything to say for yourself, lass?' His tone was not unkind.

Sorcha dared to fancy. 'I desire, good sirs, along with the other women you have seen and who are confined in a parlous state in this Tolbooth, to recant my earlier confession that —' The men erupted. There were cries, shouts. Fists thumped the table, chairs were rocked, papers swept to the floor. Her questioner tried to calm them.

'What?' shouted one man. 'How is it they're all recanting?'

'Cowper, what have you to say? How can you explain this?' raged another.

Before the reverend could respond, the portly man interrupted. 'Sit down, Mr Smith, Mr Walker. All will be addressed in good time.' He waited for them to resume their seats. 'We came here with the express intention of hearing from the witches themselves to see if there was a case to be trialled. This includes hearing the unexpected, which must, in due course, be addressed.' He turned to Sorcha. 'Please, continue, Mrs McIntyre.'

Relief began to flood her body. Was Nettie right and this was to be a fair hearing? A just one? As yet, apart from Janet, they didn't know how those below them had fared, or poor Beatrix who was still in St Fillan's Cave.

'Thank you, sir. I wish to recant my previous confession because it was extracted from me, as confessions were from the others, under duress. We were pricked, beaten, starved and made to endure night after night of sleeplessness. We all confessed not only to make our punishment cease, as was promised, but to please the reverend and the bailies.'

With each description of what she had gone through, the discomfort of the men grew. Some exclaimed. Others shook their heads. All cast looks of reproach at Reverend Cowper who simply sat, hands clasped in his lap, watching Sorcha. What he was thinking, she couldn't tell.

'I see,' said the portly man finally, waiting for the outrage to die down. 'These are terrible things, unjust and harsh indeed, and not what should be inflicted upon any Christian soul.'

It was all Sorcha could do to resist turning to the reverend and poking out her tongue.

'A witch, however,' continued the portly man, 'is a different matter. For a start, she's not in possession of a Christian soul.'

Any confidence Sorcha was starting to feel dissolved. It fled from her body faster than a dogfish from a net. The reverend sneered.

'As God is my witness, good sirs, I am a Christian, and I deny I am a witch or have ever known one with every last breath in my body.'

'Aye, well, if it's proven you are one, Mrs McIntyre, then you may yet have to,' said the portly man and, with a snap of his fingers, indicated she was to be taken from the room.

But not before she heard the order given that Janet Cornfoot, as punishment for retracting her statement in the first place and thus encouraging the other lasses to do the same, be placed in solitary confinement while the matter was thoroughly investigated.

'It's clear,' said the portly man, addressing the others, 'these arrogant, disrespectful women are as guilty as sin itself. What must need happen is —'

The door closed.

As the guards took her back down the stairs, Sorcha's head reeled. While she'd never really believed in the myth of the first-footer, she started to think that maybe Nettie had been right.

Isobel Adam, the first to cross her threshold that year, a young woman possessed of fair hair, had brought deadly trouble on them all.

TWENTY-SEVEN

Corpus deliciti.
(Body of evidence.)

*P*atrick Cowper stared at Captain Ross, absorbing the man's words. He resisted the urge to whoop with triumph. He was vindicated. Edinburgh had at last seen sense. They agreed there was enough evidence to bring the witches to trial. Patrick put down the glass he'd every intention of topping up once the captain left his study and, without appearing too eager, reached across the desk and took the offered missive to read it for himself.

'The details are in there,' said Captain Ross and, without waiting for an invitation, sat.

Patrick delayed breaking the seal and pretended to examine the outside of the letter while surreptitiously scrutinising the officer. The captain looked weary, and not only from travelling back and forth to the city on an almost weekly basis or writing countless fruitless letters on the witches' behalf. It was the kind of weariness that came from understanding all your efforts were for naught. Was it unchristian of the reverend to feel a frisson of pleasure at that?

In this instance, he knew God would forgive his lack of charity.

Unable to remain still, Patrick stood and took the letter over to the window, as if to make use of the light, but really so he could allow the inner joy he felt to burst through in a wide smile. Resting a shoulder against the window frame, he pulled the curtain aside slightly. The sun had begun to set, tossing threads of translucent clouds about the sky, while its amber warmth remained long enough that people lingered in the street. Swill-bellies gathered outside the tavern, soldiers among them, he noted, choosing not to allow their bad influence on his parishioners to dampen his pleasure on this occasion. Women with children on their hips stopped beside the costermonger and outside the apothecary's; a couple of fishwives wandered past, their creels hooked over their foreheads and shoulders, selling what remained of the day's catch. Fewer than before and not only because of those interned, but because others had chosen to leave the Weem and chase the summer drave and the work it provided. Still, the fishwives he could see gadding about didn't look half as intimidated as they should. After all, it was the one occupation that produced the greatest number of practitioners of malfeasance. They should be worried, not flaunting their independence, the coin thrust into their palms, throwing their heads back with mirth, winking at all and sundry and calling out greetings. Look at the newly minted widow, Jen Hazell, whose husband fell overboard only three weeks ago. Instead of locking herself away to grieve, there she was, pausing to exchange gossip with the jocks on their stoops while she cleaned some whitefish for a customer. Didn't matter she had a living to earn, a child to feed, it wasn't right. It wasn't godly. Those fishwives had too much to say for themselves, too much to say to others. Surely they understood their time had come? Anyone associating with them should tremble in fear lest they too be tainted by witchery, not encourage them. This was something he would raise in his next sermon — warn good folk away, remind the fishwives and those sympathetic to their libertine ways of what could happen.

His eyes danced over the street and he noted with no small measure of delight that woven among the locals were still plenty of incomers, and many were stopping outside the Tolbooth in the hope of catching a glimpse of the now infamous witches.

Patrick couldn't but be pleased with himself. He'd helped put Pittenweem — and, indeed, the Kingdom of Fife — on the map again; put money back into the town's coffers. If he could ensure there was still plenty of drama to keep the strangers fascinated and entertained, they might even make enough money to repair the ruined pier completely. And when the women *were* found guilty, there would be even more profit for the council and the kirk. Not only would hundreds flock to see them burn, but there was the disposal of the women's property to consider. Not that the lasses were worth much. The only exceptions were Janet White — Nettie — and Sorcha McIntyre, though Beatrix Laing had a penny or two. Dear God, White's husband's health was failing and in no small measure due to what had happened to Nettie. He was unlikely to be around to make any claims on her wealth. She owned that lovely house in Anster Easter that she regularly leased. Sorcha was even better pickings with the cottage in Marygate and the *Mistral*. Imagine what he could do — what the village could do — with the monies earned from that boat, especially once the pier was fixed and ships could unload on Weem docks again. What if they found a wealthy merchant in the city, someone who traded with the north, to buy the vessel? And the new owner used their port to load and unload goods? The fees they'd accrue, the taxes. If that didn't work, maybe they could find someone in London to sell it to. A lump sum would go a long way.

Thomas Brown's daughter may have refused to sell the shares in the boat she inherited upon her father's death, but that was small stakes compared to what Sorcha and the Horseburgh-White woman could potentially offer. After all, it was easier to dispose of a woman's lot and while Mr White might kick up a fuss, he was a very sick man with a confessed witch for a wife. And as for Sorcha, she was alone in every sense of the word. Well, except for this stubborn captain from the west who seemed to have taken a shine to her. He wouldn't be the first, Patrick thought, remembering Andy Watson — his own son as well

— but he might be the last. The idea filled him with such righteous goodness, he had to grip the windowsill lest he keel over.

God would be smiling upon His Pittenweem son this day.

Aware he still hadn't read the document from Edinburgh, the reverend took a moment to compose himself and stem his glee. The captain didn't seem to notice. He was sitting still, his eyes focussed on the painting of the crucifixion. That was Patrick's favourite. A reminder of the suffering good Christians must endure to earn a place beside their Holy Father. If nothing else, by the time Patrick had finished with the witches, they would not only have repented, but be cleansed of their sins and able to join God in heaven once more. And if not, well, they'd burn in hell.

The thought made him feel very warm; very satisfied.

Breaking the seal, catching the bits of wax and placing them on the sill, he unfolded the pages, noted the date — the twenty-first of July — and began to read. As he did, any joy he'd taken from the captain's brief summary of the contents was staunched.

This couldn't be right. Aye, the witches were to be tried, but not in Pittenweem as requested. Instead, the letter was most clear about it: Sir James Godtrees, the Lord Advocate, who was based in the city, was to initiate the process against the said witches. This could take some weeks. In turn, when notice was given that all was in readiness, Sir James had ordered the Earl of Rothes, the Sheriff of Fife, to organise for the women to be transported to Edinburgh. There was an offer to pay for transporting them there. But no more. That was it.

Weeks! Why, not only were the village and the local burgh officials, which included him, the bailies and other councilmen, to be denied justice, denied the right to try the witches themselves and pass sentence here in Pittenweem, but they must pay the cost of keeping the women in the Tolbooth for an indefinite period until Edinburgh was ready, never mind while they awaited trial in the city itself. It was more than the town coffers could bear.

Damn. Patrick thought he was to be rid of the women once and for all. He believed this letter would give him the permission needed to conduct his own trial, ensure God's justice, and have everyone in Pittenweem see it served. Everyone in Pittenweem and all the visitors...

He returned to the letter. There was mention of what happened to Thomas Brown — his death while in custody and how it didn't reflect well on the local burgh. Ha! What would those city gents know, locked away in their fine offices, mutton and oysters for breakfast and dinner, whisky and ale by the barrel? They didn't understand what it was like living here, thinking about little but where your next meal was coming from. Eating fish, mussels, neeps, slurping kale soup and munching brittle bannocks day after day. Didn't reflect well? They didn't see Peter Morton, what had been done to the lad.

Curse the captain. He knew the contents of the letter and had deliberately misled him, made him believe Edinburgh had capitulated to his demands. Ignoring his warnings, he'd clearly told them about Thomas Brown. Either that, or he'd written another damn letter. He'd heard how the captain, styling himself as a 'Gentleman of Fife' had penned numerous letters to the Privy Council. Clearly, some had borne fruit.

Fury swept him. Fury and a desire to crush the man. He'd warned him what would happen, who would pay should he interfere... again.

Once more Patrick was forced to compose himself before he returned to the desk, only this time the emotion he stifled was quite different.

He sat down, topped up his drink and drained it in two gulps. Through slightly bleary eyes, he regarded the officer.

'You managed to convince them to hold the trial in Edinburgh.'

The captain didn't respond.

'Why is it that bailies Bell and Cleiland didn't inform me of this when they returned?' On the contrary, they too had allowed him to think that they'd won.

'The decision hadn't been made then. The men you mention were...' Captain Ross paused, 'keen to get back, I believe, so didn't wait around to hear the outcome of your request.'

Patrick slumped into his chair, folding his arms and frowning. His mind was working swiftly, trying to find ways this decision could work in Pittenweem's favour. Goddamn the captain. Goddamn Bell and Cleiland. This was not only going to cost the town money they could ill afford — though the incomers' coin would offset that to a degree — worse, it could cost his reputation. A reputation he'd worked so hard to shore up. Just as he was winning more and more of the townsfolk to his side.

He picked up the letter and read it again, flicking through the pages, aware of the captain watching him with those dark Spanish eyes. Eyes that drank in the light. He wished the captain would go away so he could think. Nae. Truth be told, he wished he could have him thrown in the Tolbooth. Wouldn't be hard. He consorted with witches, didn't he? At the least, he defended them. Imagine what the Queen would say if Patrick did that? Imagine what kind of ransom would be paid to have an officer of Her Majesty's army released…

That was it. Patrick sat up. That was the solution — well, one — to his problem. A way of ensuring that the captain understood he meant what he said. He put the letter down, smoothing out the creases he'd inadvertently made when he crumpled it in his fist, and fashioned a smile.

'I did warn you what would happen should you stick your nose in where it's not wanted. But I'm not an unreasonable man. While I'm mighty disappointed the women can't be tried here in the Weem, among their own, I also don't think it's right to hold them in the Tolbooth until Edinburgh sees fit to dispense justice, do you? Reading between the lines here,' he waved a hand over the letter, 'it could be months before a trial is held. I think the witches have withstood enough.'

Aye, that was the line he'd take. It would deflect any criticism he'd been inappropriate in his dealings with the women. It would also help people forget what happened to Thomas Brown. If he showed some clemency, it would silence his detractors. After all, how could they say he was playing God or being unreasonable if he was the one insisting the women be freed until their trial?

Captain Ross straightened. He edged forward in his seat. Ah, Patrick thought, he'd taken the bait, now to reel him in.

'What do you propose to do with them?' asked the captain, daring to place an elbow on the desk.

Patrick could smell anticipation on the man. He resisted the urge to reach across and shove his arm off the wood.

'What I propose,' said the reverend, lowering his voice until it was almost a whisper, 'is to release them.'

'Release them?' The captain blinked. He was so eager, so ready to believe. 'You mean, let the women out of the Tolbooth?'

'Seems the right, godly thing to do, don't you think?'

'When would you be looking to do this, reverend?'

Patrick could almost hear the calculations being made in the man's head.

'Och, well, it's not up to me entirely.' They both smiled at the absurdity of the statement. Aye, even the captain, an incomer, knew who had power in the Weem. It was all Patrick could do not to preen. 'But I think I can get the council to agree to this.' He paused, watched the captain's face. 'Only, there'd be a proviso.'

The captain slid his forearm off the desk and sat back in his chair, putting distance between them. 'What might that be, reverend?' The question was cold.

'It's only fair that the women pay a bond. After all, we can't afford to have them flee, can we? A bond is their guarantee they'll remain in the district until they're brought to trial.'

This time it was the captain's turn to dissemble. Patrick sensed rather than saw it. 'I see, and how much mo— How much do you think might be asked of these poor women?'

Patrick knew the captain had been about to say 'more' but stopped himself in time. 'Taking into consideration the severity of their crimes, the fact they've confessed —' He didn't mention their retractions. 'How fearful everyone will be if they're released, I think five hundred marks not be out of the question.'

'Five hundred?' The captain did a quick calculation. 'Why, that's not unfeasible...'

'Each,' finished the reverend.

There was silence. A bee buzzed outside the window. A tic in the captain's jaw pulsed in time with the clock. Patrick couldn't tear his eyes away from the man's face.

'You know that will be impossible for them to pay,' said Captain Ross finally. 'They've been locked away for months, unable to draw a wage. They've used up all their savings. They're not healthy. They need time...'

The reverend stood up and stretched. 'That's not my business, is it? If they can't find the bond, then they'll have to remain where they are.' He made a show of folding the letter and pressing down what remained of the wax seal again. A thought struck him. 'Or, perhaps,' he said, coming around to the other side of the desk and clasping the captain's shoulder in a friendly gesture, 'they could conjure the money.' Laughing at his own joke, he moved to the door and opened it, waiting, aware the captain was using every ounce of will not to lash out.

The man stood. Dear God, but he was maucht. Tall, sinewy and broad, like a highlander. If he came at Patrick now wielding a claymore and shouting unintelligible words, he wouldn't have been surprised. Just terrified.

Scooping up his hat, without a word of farewell the captain marched from the room.

Patrick watched the captain's retreating back, his sword swinging against his hips. He heard the maid usher him out.

Patrick may have won that battle, so why did he feel like he was on the losing side?

TWENTY-EIGHT

If a' tale is true that's no a lee.
(Indicates scepticism.)

12 August 1704

*T*he last thing Sorcha expected upon being released from the Tolbooth was the crowd waiting to greet them. As she stepped into the muggy, mizzling summer's day, holding the door frame with one hand, the other shielding her eyes from the brightness, aware of the guards close behind her, there was a cheer.

Blinking back tears, Sorcha gave a watery smile, trying to find words to thank those who'd come to welcome her for their faith, their efforts and, most of all for the money few could afford to part with but so many had given regardless.

When they learned from a note penned by Captain Ross, and passed to them by Camron, that the reverend and council had put a price of five hundred marks each on their liberty, she thought she'd never see the outside of the Tolbooth again. But she hadn't considered the Weem's generosity, Nettie's wealthy friends, or the families who were dependent on the *Mistral* for their income. It may have taken a few weeks, but they'd raised the required sum.

Not even a spittering kept them away. Sorcha raised her face to the sky, relishing the droplets on her cheeks, the feeling of space, light and fresh air. Inhaling deeply, she sent a swift prayer to the God she'd briefly rejected, the God she'd started to believe only looked out for the likes of Patrick Cowper, and thanked Him.

Aware she looked and smelled terrible, even though the women had tried to wash and tidy their appearance when they learned they were to be released, it didn't stop folk crowding around her. Some touched her gently on the back, others, mainly the fishwives like Jean Durkie, Therese Larnarch and Jen Hazell, pushed themselves forward and, dragging her off the doorstep, threw their arms around her, uncaring of her odour or the holes in her skirts, and wept into her neck.

Questions were thrown; offers of food, shelter and so much more. It was hard to take in. All the noise, the flesh, the smells, the warmth of the day after the relative quiet and cool dampness of the Tolbooth, let alone the fall of rain upon her skin. She turned one way, then the other, not really seeing anyone, unable still to find words. She hoped they understood.

There was a movement behind her and then another cheer went up as Nettie appeared. Like a queen before her subjects, she lifted her chin, gave a wave and grin, her teeth stained, her lips dry, though her cheeks were wet. Linking her arm through Sorcha's, she drew her away from the Tolbooth entrance as if she was afraid they'd be sucked back inside its dark doorway. A commotion immediately in front of them revealed Nettie's husband shouldering people aside. He was chalk-pale and appeared as if he too had been in the Tolbooth, he was so thin. Letting go of Sorcha, Nettie hobbled across the cobbles and fell into his embrace.

The sight of them together, locked in a hold, crying openly, made Sorcha's eyes fill again.

Watching Nettie reunited with Mr White, seeing the husbands or brothers of Nicolas, Beatrix and Lillie Wallace among the crowd, not forgetting Margaret's sister and even poor Thomas Brown's daughter, who offered the saddest of acknowledgements, it struck her that she had no one. No one to really care what happened to her, no one to be grateful she was free and welcome her back properly. She was alone.

Sorrow welled. In all the months she'd been locked away, it had never occurred to her what it would be like to be free, how much she longed for someone to ache for her, to want her, to fight — not just for justice, there were so many doing that, God bless them all — but just for her. Not even Dagny had been able to put aside her anger and offer support, let alone a welcome. Dagny's absence hurt her more than was right.

Casting aside self-pity and determining to put on the brave face that was needed, that they all deserved, she found a smile.

Then she saw him.

Standing apart from the others, over by the Mercat Cross, Liath beside him, was Captain Ross. Their eyes fastened on each other. She saw a look pass over his face — aversion? Anger? She wasn't certain, she only knew it wasn't directed towards her — before he gestured to his mount and invited her to join him.

With a deep, deep sigh that came from the soles of her boots, carrying within it a great promise that she dared not examine, she weaved her way through the mob. As each woman emerged from the prison, there was a burst of noise behind her, making her twitch. Fixing her eyes on the captain, afraid if she looked away he'd vanish, she became aware her gait was uneven, her clothes were rags hanging from her scrawny frame; her shorn hair, which had regrown to at least cover her head in a bronze cap, needed a wash. Nonetheless, she didn't stop. Not until she reached his side.

Uncertain what to do, what to say, she stood and stared at him, taking in his worn coat, the damp hat, but more importantly, those black, black eyes and the way they drank her in.

He took her hand in his large warm one and, much to her utter astonishment, raised it to his lips.

'I'm glad to see you, Mrs McIntyre.' Though the press of his warm mouth against her cold skin was gentle, the heat of rage and something else burning in those coal-black eyes was not. Something within Sorcha broke. She staggered and, before she could fall, he swept her into his arms and, pressing her to his body tightly first, lifted her onto his horse.

She cried out in pain as he gripped her beneath the arms and again as her legs, unprepared, struck the saddle.

'Dear God, what have they done to you?' His voice was hoarse, his eyes as they left hers to gaze at some point over her shoulder, were murderous.

Unable to explain, not really wanting to lest she relive the experience all over again, she shook her head and stayed mute. He placed his large hand over where hers rested on the pommel and didn't move it. She didn't want him to.

Shivering now, she clung to the saddle for dear life, enjoying the feel of his flesh against hers, the security it offered. When he said no more, she followed the direction of his gaze.

There were others besides those gathered directly outside the Tolbooth. Clustered in groups of two and three, they stood further down the wynd and at the crest of the High Street. Some looked upon the reunions with healthy curiosity. Others pointed towards her, then Nettie, and leaned in to whisper among themselves and nod sagely, as if measuring fish for sale. Each time a woman came out of the Tolbooth, their mutters grew. There were faces she didn't recognise, some in fine clothes, others draped in unfamiliar plaids.

Her extra height atop Liath allowed her to see another group just beyond the Tolbooth in Cove Wynd, close to the kirk entrance. This disturbed her the most. They were people she knew and who, even as she acknowledged them, turned aside. There were the Crawfords, standing shoulder to shoulder, arms folded tightly and, beside them, the Mortons — all except Peter. Bailies Vernour, Crawford and Cleiland were there. Of Bailie Bell, she could see no sign. But the rest, aware she'd noticed them, shook their heads in disapproval that left her with a cold, hollow feeling.

In the centre of the group, the small space around him making him easier to see even in his black robes, was Reverend Cowper. Despite the distance between them, she could still feel the power of his stare, the loathing he brought with him, as if it were alive, a virulent sea-creature with long tentacles, reaching out to draw her closer.

It took a monumental effort to redirect her attention.

'How… how long have they been waiting for us?' she asked, finally finding some words.

'As soon as news of your release spread, people came. Your supporters,' the captain jerked his head towards the Tolbooth, 'and detractors.' He didn't need to indicate who they were. 'They keep a length from each other.' He nodded towards another group Sorcha had failed to notice until that moment. It was Sergeant Thatcher and at least a dozen soldiers spread out around the edges of the crowd. In full uniform, they carried weapons. 'I could at least see to that. I didn't want you having to deal with any scuffles.'

'There's been fights?'

'Aye, a few. Mainly since Thomas Brown died, and then again after your bail was posted. It galvanised folk, his dying, the unfairness and cruelty of it. But today is not a day for quarrelling. Sergeant Thatcher and my men will make sure of that.'

Unable to find words as her throat became suddenly thick and her vision swam, she simply nodded. She knew who it was motivating folk, who encouraged them to speak up about the injustices; and who was partly responsible for the brawls. She would thank him later.

The rain became heavier; thick, powerful drops that presaged a dowsing. Pulling a blanket from one of the panniers draped across his horse, Captain Ross wrapped it around her. She wasn't even aware she was trembling. It wasn't cold, not really, not the weather. Rather, it was the realisation that what had happened while she'd been locked in the Tolbooth, all the suffering and accusations she and the others had been forced to endure, had divided the village.

For that was what she was witnessing now. Those who stood with the accused, welcoming them back, taking them in their arms and leading them away, and those who stood with Cowper, watching, as if to memorise the names and faces of those offering succour to use against them later. Surrounding them were armed men ready to prevent any violence.

At that moment, Isobel Adam appeared in the Tolbooth doorway. Dear God, she was so thin. How had she not noticed before? Bruises circled her wrists, her cheeks were underpinned by dark hollows, as were her eyes. She stared about uncertainly, seeking a friendly face, not understanding that those in front of her were that and more. A cry went up at her appearance, and she recoiled as if struck, the noise quickly dying before it reached full volume. It was only when her father came forward and enswathed a shawl across the lass's shaking shoulders that Isobel fell to her knees and began to sob.

There were grim mutters from the folk around Cowper, looks of disdain cast in the direction of the young lass, as if Isobel had given a performance. Did they not understand this was no ploy to garner sympathy? That the poor woman could scarce stand?

It was more than Nicolas could do. Carried out in the Tolbooth keeper's arms, she was deposited directly into those of her husband. Having been away south helping with the harvest, he'd come home to news of his wife's imprisonment. Along with Nettie's man and the captain, he'd fought for her release — to no avail — until now. There were gasps of horror as Nicolas's skirt rode up and exposed the injuries to her legs. A mass of deep scars and bloodied swollen holes oozing pus and blood, they were shocking to see.

Mr Lawson quickly pulled her skirt down, as Nicolas, weeping softly, buried her face in his chest.

It was then the mood began to turn. Some of the folk began to shout. 'You should be ashamed of yourself, reverend.' It was Therese Larnarch.

'Aye,' came cries of agreement. Someone spat.

'And you too, bailies,' yelled one of the men. It sounded like Mr Lawson. 'You are as much to blame for this as anyone — you and your damn pricker.'

'This is what you call justice?'

Sergeant Thatcher raised his musket and looked towards Captain Ross who subtly shook his head.

Further down the High Street, outside the tavern, men's heads shot up as the racket grew and the mood changed. They rose from their stools and trundled towards the Tolbooth, rolling up their sleeves, exchanging ominous looks. Sensing a fight was brewing, women pulled their children close, grasped their baskets tightly, and followed at a distance.

The circle around the reverend grew tighter. The faces stubborn.

Still, Captain Ross bade his men wait.

Lillie Wallace, pale, shrunken and dirty like them all, finally surfaced from the Tolbooth to weak cheers as more accusations were hurled at the reverend. Rather than joining the throng, Lillie waited atop the step, one skinny arm raised to attract attention. Noticing her stance, there were nudges, calls for quiet. One by one the voices stilled. When there was complete silence, she spoke.

'Today, with the exception of dear Thomas Brown, may God rest his soul, those falsely accused of witchcraft walk free.' There was a roar of approval as well as some dissent. 'All but one.'

Sorcha tightened her grip on the pommel, felt the captain's fingers close over her own.

'All except Janet Cornfoot.' Lillie screwed up her eyes, searching for someone. 'Under orders from our council, from the Reverend Cowper, they're not releasing her.' Her voice cracked. Someone handed her a small flask, which she raised with a shaking arm. Much of the liquid bubbled over her lips as she drank. Coughing and spluttering, she wiped her mouth and handed the flask back. 'We've been told Janet's to remain imprisoned but not why.'

There was an upswell of anger, of confusion.

This time, the sergeant moved his men into position. Townsfolk parted to let them through, most grateful they were there.

Lillie waited for the reaction to her news to die down, and leaned heavily on the building. Spying the reverend, she raised a finger. 'This be your doing.' Her voice was quiet at first, but as she continued it grew louder and more confident, filled with a repressed rage at what she'd endured, at the treatment of her closest friend. 'Call yourself a man of God? I ken who's your master.' Before she could say any more and incriminate herself, Sergeant Thatcher strode forward and gently coaxed her from the steps. She was passed to one of the soldiers and swiftly led away.

Sorcha almost tipped from the saddle. She didn't know Janet was to remain; Janet, Lillie, Margaret and Thomas had been confined in the room below, and communication between them had been sporadic and down to the goodwill of Camron and the other guards. This decision must be sudden. No wonder Lillie was in shock. Poor Janet.

Their freedom came at an additional cost after all. Not just the outrageous bond, but an old woman's liberty.

The crowd's mood became uglier.

'Where's Janet?' The question could have come from anyone, but was clearly directed at the reverend.

'Why isn't she being let go? Her bond's been paid,' cried Jen Hazell.

There were catcalls and clamour. Someone began to bang a drum.

Jostled by his supporters, who sought to shield him, the reverend moved towards the soldiers. He said something to Sergeant Thatcher who cleared a path and led him to the Tolbooth door. The crowd shifted to allow them passage.

Sorcha couldn't help but admire the reverend's bravery. She doubted she'd walk so calmly through such a furious gauntlet, even with the sergeant and his men to protect her.

The reverend's face was hard to read as he waited for quiet. Ignoring the rain that drummed against his head, his dark robes a contrast against the pale grey and brown stones of the Tolbooth, he was more like a statue than a human, a gargoyle akin to those Sorcha had seen carved on the churches in Edinburgh.

''Tis true,' he began. 'Mrs Cornfoot's bond's been paid and will be held in trust for her until such time as she is freed.' There were jeers. The reverend raised his hands for silence. Accustomed to obeying him, the crowd eventually hushed.

'The Edinburgh magistrates have shown great clemency in releasing any of these w… women.'

There were hisses.

'As I said,' he repeated. 'Great clemency has been shown. These women have been charged with a capital offence. The magistrates have taken a great risk in freeing them. What you don't seem to understand, my friends, is that you have as well.'

There were some scornful noises. 'What risk are they to us? Have you not seen the state of them?'

'Believe what you like,' thundered the reverend, his patience gone. The rain was heavy now. His hair was flattened to his scalp. Seeking shelter, the incomers started reluctantly to disperse. They weren't the only ones. With Nicolas in his arms, Mr Lawson turned his back on the reverend and pushed his way past the soldiers to the High Street. Isobel, head bowed, followed with her father.

Undaunted, the reverend continued. 'What was done to these women was done to protect *you*. It was done to protect them —' he pointed after Nicolas and Isobel, 'so they might recant their allegiance to Satan and be returned to our Christian community.'

There was muttering and much shaking of heads. More people began to move away. They either didn't want to listen anymore or wanted to avoid being soaked.

'These women are not innocent. They are charged — out of their own mouths, by their very own confessions.' Realising he was losing his audience, he began to bluster. 'They are still a threat — to us, to you — and it's only out of the goodness of our Christian hearts and the imprudence of the magistrates in Edinburgh they're being allowed back into the community — lest we forget, there's still a trial pending.'

Bellows of agreement rang out. The reverend's supporters had shifted into spaces left by those who'd taken the prisoners away.

The reverend raised his arms again. 'Listen to me,' he shouted above the rain. 'The women might be at liberty, but they're *not* free. You must all treat them with caution — including those of you who refuse to see what they are. Watch your backs lest what happened to Peter Morton also happens to you.'

The Mortons and the Crawfords raised a cheer. It was all but drowned by the heckling of the women's supporters and the increasing rain.

Cowper dropped his arms. A path opened for him and he strode through the crowd, his followers falling in behind him.

There was more muttering, a few yells of defiance, but not as many as before. Most simply watched him depart.

'Come,' said Captain Ross, sending a signal to his sergeant. 'I've heard enough. This helps no one.'

Lacking the energy to resist, Sorcha allowed the captain to lead her away. There wasn't far to go, but it felt like the longest of journeys. Her mind fizzed and burned. She was shocked by what their incarceration had done to the village; it was something she hadn't foreseen. Pittenweem had always had its rifts — families falling out with one another, neighbours arguing, deaths, marriages. But this was different. The town was rent. She wondered if it could ever be whole again.

What the reverend and council had succeeded in doing when they arrested eight innocent souls was to cause a schism so wide only a miracle could heal it.

That, or something catastrophic.

PART TWO
August to November 1704

Your eyes bewitched my wit, your wit bewitched my will,
Thus with your eyes and wit you do bewitch me still
And yet you are no witch, whose spirit is not evil,
And yet you are a witch, and yet you are no devil.
Oh witching eyes, and wit, where wit and eyes may read,
A witch and not a witch, and yet a witch indeed.

— Nicholas Breton, 'My Witch', circa 1545–1626

Our Presbyterian ministers are showing great zeal in discovering witches and they
think they have fallen luckily on a cluster of them in Pittenweem.

— *A True and Full Relation of the Witches at Pittenweem, to
which is added by way of prefix, an essay for proving the existence of
good and evil spirits, relating to the witches of Pittenweem, now in
custody, with argument against the sadducism of the present age*, 1704.

TWENTY-NINE

She be a brazen besom.
(She's a shameless woman.)

Captain Ross stood aside as he opened the door of the cottage, allowing Sorcha to enter first. As soon as she was inside, she leaned against the wall, her legs aching, her head reeling. She was home.

A fire crackled in the hearth and Sorcha could detect the unmistakable odour of mutton cooking. Nausea rose in her throat and she put the back of her hand against her mouth in an attempt to quash the sensation. She took a couple of calming breaths, waiting for the wave of sickness to pass, and stared around in disbelief, noting the tidy shelves, the polished table, how dishes had been placed where they didn't belong. There was a book she didn't recognise on one of the side tables near the armchairs. Clearly someone (and it didn't take much to guess who) had been living here in her absence. Not knowing whether to feel umbrage or gratitude, she continued her survey before turning to regard the captain quizzically.

Sorcha knew curious passers-by wouldn't fail to gossip about the fact that both she and the captain were inside. Instead of launching into questions, she waited for him to close the door and explain.

Unbothered by her regard, he removed his hat and placed it on a chair, picked up the poker and prodded the fire, then squatted to check the bubbling pot set to one side of the burning peat, lifting the lid and inhaling the smell, a satisfied look on his face. 'Hope you like mutton. Widow Browning sold me some yesterday and I made this.' He replaced the lid and stood, dusting his hands. 'You need to eat. You are all skin and bone.'

Sorcha resisted the urge to wrap her arms around her middle. She feared it would only confirm the captain's assessment.

'I gather you're responsible for this as well?' She gestured to the room, noting anew how clean it was — unlike her. She'd expected months of neglect and dust and instead — this.

'Aye.' He undid his coat and shrugged it off, folding it neatly and laying it over the arm of the chair where his hat rested. Sorcha watched in bemusement; it was as if she were the guest and he the host.

He then dragged a large pot, one she usually reserved for boiling sheets, onto the fire. Water splashed over the edges. 'We'll get this heating too, hey?' he said.

Folding her arms, she waited.

Understanding she wanted a fuller answer, he began to busy himself in the kitchen area. 'I thought that since you and Mrs Horseburgh were in the Tolbooth for an indefinite period, leaving your cottage empty, it would be best I stayed here awhile. Protect things. I wasn't sure what might happen to your belongings given the uncertain mood in the village.' He looked around. 'I hope you don't mind.'

'Mind?' Sorcha felt a laugh flicker to life. She recalled the conversation they'd had, how long ago was that? Felt like years. About how the reverend and council would do anything to resolve the town's debts and fill the coffers. At the time, she hadn't seriously thought her property or Nettie's was under threat. But that was before an accusation of witchcraft was levelled against them. Now she wondered if she or her possessions would ever be safe again.

Her heart swelled at his consideration and a lump formed in her throat. 'On the contrary,' she said hoarsely. 'I'm very grateful.' Through the open door to the bedroom, she could see a shirt draped over the end of the bed, a blanket she didn't recognise covering the mattress. 'You've made yourself at home.'

'Aye and nae. I merely watched over things with a view to surrendering all as soon as you were set at liberty.' He moved to the dresser and took down a couple of plates, laying them on the table along with spoons and knives.

Sorcha thought how comfortable he appeared. Much more comfortable than Andy had ever been...

'Sit, lass, sit,' said the captain, waving towards a stool as he produced a loaf and began to carve it.

A loaf of bread! How long had it been since Sorcha had tasted that? How long since she'd had a decent hot meal and the comfort of a chair, the warmth of a fire? Not to mention being in her own home? As for a man tending to her needs rather than cruelly denying them...

Tears filled her eyes and she quickly wiped them away. She didn't want the captain thinking she was weak, even though it took all her strength to remain standing.

Aware she hadn't moved, the captain glanced in her direction before resuming his task. 'I'm not going to ask if you be all right, because I ken the answer. But, please, Mrs McIntyre, take a seat and allow me to at least ensure you have a decent meal before I leave you in peace.'

Peace. What a funny word. She hadn't felt peace for years. Would she ever know it again?

When she still didn't move, he abandoned the bread and, taking her by the arm, led her to her da's old chair.

'Wait,' said Sorcha, wrenching her arm free and standing her ground. 'I can't.'

'What is it you can't, lass?' asked the captain so very gently, his great black eyes reflecting the flames, radiating kindness and such empathy it made her want to weep all over again. 'If you can't bear to have a man near you, I'll understand and make myself scarce. I see now I shouldn't have touched you and for that I'm very sorry.' He held up his hands as if in surrender. 'I'm worried about leaving you in the state you're in. All of your friends have someone to care for them, the townsfolk made sure of that. And I said I'd look to you. So, please, let me, then I'll be gone.'

Sorcha's shoulders slumped and damn if she didn't begin to sob. 'Nae… nae… That's not it.' She shook her head. 'You don't understand.'

'Nae. I don't,' agreed the captain.

'I can't sit,' Sorcha cried.

'Is it something else those bastards did, lass? I know some of it, but not all.' He drew himself up to his full height.

If Sorcha hadn't been so upset, she would have smiled. Would she ever be able to talk about what *was* done to them? The terrible humiliations and pain? She doubted it. All she wanted was to forget those things ever happened.

'It's quite simple, really. I don't want to sit or eat while I'm so filthy. While I smell like the Tolbooth. I feel like I don't belong here — at least, not like this.' She glanced down at her grubby skirts in dismay.

The captain smacked his palm against his forehead. 'What was I thinking? I'm readying some water for you to bathe in, lass, but I thought feeding you was more important.'

Sorcha's eyes glimmered. 'I need to be clean.' *To be cleansed.*

Misunderstanding the source of her trembling, he ushered her closer to the fire then left her standing there. Crying freely now, wondering if the others felt like her, so dirty that a bath was their priority, Sorcha was vaguely aware of a tub being rolled into the middle of the room, the captain moving backwards and forwards across the floor, out the back, the gurgle of water being poured, before the smell of lavender and roses wafted towards her.

By the time she'd dried her eyes, hiccoughing gently now the tempest had subsided, it was to find a steaming bath awaiting her. It was enough to make her cry afresh.

'Och, lass,' said the captain. 'Please don't weep. I'll leave you to wash and come back later to make sure you're fed.' When she didn't move or answer, he gestured to her mor's chair. 'The drying sheets are there along with fresh clothes… I wasn't sure what to get you, but there's a clean skirt and shirt and underclothes. If you leave what you're wearing by the hearth, I'll take them to the laundress who does my clothes on the morrow.'

'Burn them,' said Sorcha, staring at the tub with longing. How she'd dreamed of immersing herself in hot water. Of soaping her body, her hair. If it was within her capacity to do so, she would have peeled her skin away, turned it inside out and washed it as well.

'Are you sure, lass?'

'I never want to see these ever again.' With a desperation she didn't know she possessed, she began to undo her shirt, pulling so hard, the ties snapped. Ripping at the sleeves, she tugged her arms free.

'Whoa there, Mrs McIntyre,' said Captain Ross, turning his head away and holding up his palms. 'You must wait till I go.'

'Go?' Sorcha froze. The thought of being alone filled her with dread. 'Why would you go? Who will wash my back? Help me wash my hair?' She ran her hands over her head. 'What remains of it.'

'Madam,' said the captain, stepping forward and gathering the two pieces of her shirt together and pulling them over her breasts, 'just as I protected your cottage, I would protect what remains of your reputation. Your modesty.'

Sorcha threw back her head and laughed. It was a low, dark sound, filled with bitterness. 'Och, captain, you of all people know I've no reputation left to protect and, as for my modesty, it has been trammelled these last months by men who have no honour. You think I care if you see me naked? It is the very least of my concerns. Worse men have, why not you who seeks to help me, to see to my well-being? I've no maidenly blushes, sir, no shame that has not been felt.' She took a deep breath. God damn it. She had no pride... or perhaps it was pride that gave her the strength to ask. 'I would you stay.'

She waited until his eyes met hers.

'I don't want to be alone. I've been pricked, poked, and beaten bloody. I've been watched while I shit and piss, while I vomited, bled, writhed in pain and succumbed to nightmares. Having you remain while I bathe is nothing to what I've been forced to tolerate; what I'd no choice but to endure. So, I ask you to stay. Please. Not just while I bathe. I would also you stay... longer. This is my wish if you could but grant it to me.'

His hands dropped and he stepped away.

She became aware of how drab she was, how she must stink. The water they'd been given to wash in wasn't clean, nor the cloths, certainly not after all four women had used them. God, she could smell herself, smell the reverend, the pricker and his searching grubby hands and filthy implements. Smell the blood, the pain, the infections, the humiliation.

Maybe the captain couldn't bear to be near her. She'd misread his kindness as tolerance of her state. Maybe he had to leave because for all his chivalry, she disgusted him. Heat rose up her neck. Her cheeks began to burn. Turns out, she still had pride after all.

'Forgive me. You don't have to stay, captain... I... I'm being selfish. God, I can barely stand to be in my own presence.' Her arms swept her body and encompassed the room. 'You've already done so much for me, for the others as well. Go. Go do your duties, with my blessing and thanks. I will manage.'

The captain moved towards her and gently spun her around. He began to tug at the ties that bound her skirt at the waist. 'Aye, I ken you'd manage. You always will, won't you, Mrs McIntyre? But this time, you don't have to manage on your own.' Her skirt fell in a puddle at her feet and she stepped out of it. Uncertain what to do with her arms, her hands, whether to shield her womanly parts, explain the marks that covered her body or not — more for his sake than her own — she let them hang by her side.

Sensing her ambivalence, the captain continued quickly. 'I should probably tell you there's not much I haven't seen, what with being at war and tending wounded soldiers and civilians — women and bairns as well. Seeing them maimed and worse, all the times I carried one of my men back from a tavern and saw them to bed. Then, there's the help I gave as a lad with calving and lambing back on Skye. And that's before I blether 'bout my sisters. Och, the stories I could tell you about those two and my ma and me bathing and dressing those wee grubs...'

His tone was solemn, but also teasing, temperate, as he helped her divest herself of her shirt. As she tried to tug her shift over her head, her arms wouldn't co-operate as it clung to her body. She had to rely on him to peel it over her head. The entire time she was being undressed, he talked.

Standing before him naked, aware of how thin, bruised and scarred she was, she nevertheless held her head high. Captain Ross had not once looked away from her face.

Falling silent, he took her by the hand and helped her step over the lip of the tub, holding her steady as she lowered herself into the steaming waters.

Shutting her eyes as the level rose around her, relishing the feel of the scented liquid lapping her flesh, the sting as it touched her wounds, she sank deeper and rested her head against the edge, releasing a long, contented sigh.

Uncaring that he saw her at her most vulnerable, bore witness to the cruelty that had been inflicted upon her physically, she opened her eyes and brazenly watched him as he knelt beside her, sleeves rolled up, a cloth in one hand, soap in the other. For all the world as if he was his ma and she one of his sisters. He kept his eyes fixed on the body part he was administering to, being careful not to let his shock at her state, the numerous wounds, the still-healing scars, show in his expression. He'd a task to perform and he would do it. As he worked upon her body, he distracted them both by humming a tune, a wild, sweet refrain. It made her think of grass blowing in the wind, seagulls bobbing on the water, and the way the clouds would sometimes dance across the sky. Any nervousness or anxiety fled. At one level, she'd lost all sense of humiliation in the Tolbooth, but at another, she'd found the strength to demand what she wanted.

She wanted a bath, aye, to be clean and thus cleansed. But, as the captain carefully lifted her other arm and began to soap it in gentle circles, rinsing and then repeating before moving to another part of her body, she knew deep in her heart, she wanted this man too.

THIRTY

My Lord, this is not the tenth part of what may be said upon this subject…

— A Letter from a Gentleman in Fife to
his Friend in Edinburgh, *1705*

When Sorcha woke the next morning, she was at first confused. What was she lying on? What was that sweet smell? The quiet but steady breathing? She was so warm, so comfortable… Not daring to move lest she disrupt the dream, she lay still, her fingers resting against the sheets. Sheets! Slowly, her memories of the previous day returned.

She was in her cottage in Marygate. She was free of the Tolbooth. She was clean. Never again would she have to endure the pain and suffering of the last months. Her thoughts flew to the others, to Nettie, Isobel and Nicolas. How were they faring? And what of Lillie, Margaret, and poor, poor Janet? Her heart flipped as she thought of Janet Cornfoot, exchanging places with Beatrix in the cold dampness of St Fillan's Cave; for some reason, she'd been selected to pay for all their sins. Beatrix had survived. In what condition she was yet to learn. Hopefully, Janet would as well.

Then she recalled last evening.

Turning her head slowly, she studied the man sleeping beside her.

After bathing her yesterday, a bath that saw three changes of water before Sorcha was satisfied, he'd given her a cloth for her teeth, then helped her dress before serving a rich meal of mutton, fresh bread, kale and neeps. Unable to eat much, she nonetheless downed what she could, slowly fighting her stomach's urge to rebel. Understanding she was struggling with eating and talking, the captain filled the silence with quiet conversation, telling her more about his life until, about an hour after the meal was finished and they were seated by the fire and she'd enjoyed her first dram, she begged him to tell her about what had happened while they were locked up. What happened when he went to Edinburgh all those times. How he'd finally succeeded in getting the Privy Council to order their release.

'I didn't do much, Mrs McIntyre,' he said.

'I think, captain, the time for you to address me as Mrs McIntyre has passed, don't you?'

Colour flooded his cheeks. 'Aye.' He cleared his throat. 'In that case, please, call me Aidan.'

The sun had set and Aidan lit a couple of candles. Not because they needed them, but because after being denied something as simple as candlelight for so long, Sorcha wanted it. Seated in her parents' old chairs, Sorcha wondered what her da, her mor, would make of Aidan Ross, an incomer, and couldn't help but think they'd approve.

'I couldn't do as much as I would have liked,' he added, bringing her back to the present.

'But what you did — the letters, the representations — they made a difference. Camron MacGille overheard the bailies saying as much. Sometimes we could hear bits of what the men in the room above were saying and would try to make sense of them. It was evident your involvement changed things. Not only did it mean the authorities couldn't ignore what was happening here, it had us released.'

'I think I played a small part. Once my commanding officers reminded the advocate and the Privy Council that by law, witches — sorry, lass —'

Sorcha dismissed his words. Apologies weren't necessary from this man.

'— are not meant to be tried by locals or in the jurisdiction where they live, they understood something had to be done. There have been too many tragic outcomes in the past to tolerate it any longer.'

'You're thinking of Bargarran and Christian Shaw.' Sorcha repressed a shudder. To think they could have suffered the fate of those accused.

'Aye, and others. Once I managed to reach my colonel and remind him of this, he spoke to his cousin, the Earl of Rothes, and that's when things really started to happen.'

Though he had powerful connections, Sorcha had no doubt the captain was underplaying his role. She knew it was because of him, and those in the village who'd never ceased in their support and agitation for the women's dispensation, that this had happened.

Yet what of the reverend and his followers? A spark of fear seared her ribs, made her heartsore and uneasy.

'It's not over yet though, is it?' she asked.

The captain poured her another dram and then topped up his own quaich.

'I'm not going to lie to you, lass. Nae. It's not. You'll have to appear in Edinburgh. They've ordered a trial and that's what they'll insist upon. The good news is they'll not allow those they see as legally untrained and thus ignorant to pass sentence upon you — that means your bailies and minister. The Pittenweem council. Reverend Cowper will do all he can to overturn the order and have you tried here in the Weem and by himself and the bailies — he's said as much and not just to me. He'll go looking for more evidence to prove the charges against you all and thus bind the lawyers in Edinburgh into an agreement — one where he sets the terms.'

Her eyes slid from the captain's face as she thought of Peter Morton. She hadn't even asked after him, the lad whose sudden illness had started this in the first place.

'What do you think will happen to Janet Cornfoot? Will you be able to appeal to your colonel for her release too?'

Captain Ross shrugged. 'I'll alert the colonel to her situation and pray that he in turn will let his cousin know.' He hesitated. 'It's my belief the reverend's punishing her because she recanted before the Queen's Advocate who, you understand, still seeks to try you. When the rest of you followed her lead and did the same, you humiliated him before his betters. Worse, before his peers and the town. Despite what Cowper says, he'd no real choice but to set you free for the time being. He can't hold each of you, but he can Mrs Cornfoot — for all your sins.'

'Has he not done enough?' asked Sorcha sadly.

Stretching out his long legs, the captain sighed then gave a short, sharp laugh.

'What? What's so funny?'

'I was just thinking. The reverend isn't going to have it all his own way.'

'What do you mean?'

'Unbeknowst to him, young Peter Morton is about to be summoned to Edinburgh to appear before the Privy Council.'

'But...' Sorcha sat up, alarm writ on her features. 'If they see how afflicted he is...' Images flashed before her. Peter writhing on the ground, his hands spraying blood as they struck the stones, his distended stomach, bulging eyes. His emaciated body.

'For some time now Peter Morton has shown no signs of bewitchment. Something the gentlemen who interviewed you weeks ago noticed as well.' The captain swirled his whisky then tossed it back, smacking his lips in appreciation. 'Aye, the reverend may have coached the boy while he was... sick, but if he does it again, it will do naught but arouse suspicion. I've a feeling the Morton lad's days of conning the townsfolk are over.'

Relaxing into her chair, Sorcha sighed wistfully. 'I hope you're right, Aidan, I really do. I just wish I knew why Peter did it in the first place. What did he hope to gain?'

Aidan shrugged. 'Notoriety? Approval? Sympathy? Who knows why people do such wicked things.'

Sorcha dwelled upon the captain's words. Would the lad dare to perform for an Edinburgh audience?

As she stared at the captain now lying beside her on the bed, his head on the pillow, she thought how young he looked with his eyes shut, his face in repose. It was a strong face, all angles and planes with a dark growth along the jawline and upper lip. His lips were full; his mouth upturned. Tearing her eyes away and quashing the thoughts that rose unbidden, she resisted the urge to push a stray lock from his forehead. What a gentleman he'd been last night. Not only had he bathed her with measured thoroughness and helped her dress, he'd fed, entertained and reassured her and then, when he helped her to bed, acceded to her wish that he remain alongside her — on the mattress.

'Not for any other reason than the security of your company, Aidan,' said Sorcha, though she wasn't sure why. It was clear he neither found her attractive nor much of a woman. Who could blame him? She was like a scarecrow that had hung all season, barely withstanding flocks of crows, pecked, bitten, pulled, weathered and beaten.

Running a hand down her hip, she marvelled at how thin she'd become. She thought back to how Isobel looked upon the Tolbooth stoop, how Nettie appeared. Seeing them back in the community, outdoors with light and rain striking them, it was as if she saw them with transformed eyes. No doubt others observed her the same way. No wonder there was so much anger directed towards the reverend. It was easy to believe they were witches deserving of dire punishment when they were locked away, out of sight, a bunch of stubborn, evil women who wouldn't confess their sins. A danger to all of Pittenweem.

In broad daylight it was a different story. They were exposed for what they were — ordinary women, wives, daughters, sisters, friends, and, above all, victims of the reverend and the council's superstitions and panic.

Holding back a sigh, she studied the captain once more. Last night, as they lay side by side unable to sleep, they'd whispered in the dark. He, about his sister, Bridie, who'd died when she was but four years old, trampled by a horse on the road that wound to the town of Portree. She'd insisted on accompanying him when he went to buy stores, and had demanded to be set down from the cart so she might pick some flowers in a nearby field. Paused by the side of the road, Aidan had taken the chance to adjust the horse's harness and, believing his sister still occupied, didn't think to caution her as a rider fast approached.

Excited by the blooms she'd gathered, Bridie had run across the road, failing to heed the galloping horse until it was too late. Her last words were Aidan's name... The memory was painful, his voice broke more than once. No wonder he'd never spoken of her before. She was part of the reason he'd left Skye as soon as he was able, his father purchasing a commission for him in the Queen's army. Sorcha had reached for his hand and twined her fingers through his; she'd felt him squeeze them ever-so-gently in return.

Was it the darkness or his sharing of such a terrible loss that prompted her to tell him about Davan? She was uncertain. All she knew was that as she told him about her son, her wee boy who never breathed, never saw his broken-hearted mother, she felt altered. The grief was still there, but it wasn't like an archer living in her chest releasing quiver after quiver into her heart. Nor was it an anchor ready to weight her with blackness. It was simply there. A part of her that would help shape who she was becoming.

But what was that?

A survivor. A woman who'd lost her entire family, but lived to remember them. A fishwife who had been accused of witchcraft, shamed, shunned, pricked, tortured, threatened and lived to tell the tale. Death had knocked on her door, and she'd barred it against him. Partly because of this man. This magnificent man who still shed tears in memory of his little sister...

His face was so close to hers, if she leaned forward just a wee bit, she could kiss those shapely lips, feel them against her own. God, it had been so long since she'd felt a man's mouth, a loving, desired touch. Never again did she want to experience the kind Mr Bollard or the guards bestowed. Nor the illicit kind of Kennocht, or the rather per-functory kisses and clumsy groping of Andy.

Her body, her starved, wounded, aching body wanted to know another type; even in this wretched state, it, she, wanted something more...

Inching closer, her mind whispering she was almost denied this chance, who knew if circumstances might snatch it away, if death would come for her next time, her lips connected with his. She closed her eyes, melting into his warmth and softness, pressing closer. The beauty of such sweet contact made her insides burn so hot, she moaned.

The sound made her jerk back in horror. What had she done?

A pair of sable eyes gazed into hers. 'Good morning, Sorcha,' growled the captain, touching the corner of his mouth. 'Do you oft wake your guests in such a charming way?'

Even in the dim light of the bedroom, his devil-eyes twinkled.

'I don't know what came over me. I'm sorry. So sorry.' She buried her head in her hands momentarily, before moving them away. She would confront what she'd done. Face him. 'I don't know what I was thinking…'

With barely any effort, he drew her into his arms. She didn't resist. 'Och, lass, I think you do.' He pushed his nose into her cheek and then ran it down the side of her neck. She shivered as she felt his warm breath upon her skin. His mouth trawled across her jawline, hovering above her lips. 'And just so you ken, I'm thinking the exact same thing.'

Before she could protest, he kissed her.

Gentle at first, as she opened her mouth in response to his liquid tongue, pushing herself into him, his lips became firmer, wilder. One of his hands cupped her face, the other held the back of her head. Daringly, she twined her arms around him, tugging his shirt from his breeches so she could stroke his skin.

It was smooth, warm, and he shuddered beneath her touch, groaning into her mouth. In a single move, he rolled her onto her back. She hissed with pain. He lifted himself onto his elbows, pulling away slightly. 'Are you all right, Sorcha? I didn't mean to —'

With a click of annoyance, she reached for him and arched her back to keep the link with his body, to feel his strength, his hardness against her. Pushing aside her discomfort, she focussed on her need.

'Are you sure you want this? You'll not regret it after?' he asked softly.

Sorcha pushed her fingers into the thickness of his jet black hair, and clenched it tightly. 'I'll only regret it if we don't. But what about you, Aidan? Will you regret it?'

'Regret what I've dreamed of since I first saw you? I don't think so.'

Sorcha smoothed his hair from his face. 'Ah, but I'm a very different woman from that one.'

'Not to me,' said the captain. 'To me, you're more beautiful than ever.' He began to pluck at her shift, tugging it up over her legs, her stomach, exposing her torso.

He bent his head and dropped long, slow kisses on her breasts, travelling down her body, using his mouth and tongue to explore her flesh, every single cut, scar and bruise.

It was all Sorcha could do to lie still. The pain, the pleasure. Little fires were being lit all over her body, stoked until she became a furnace.

Parting her legs, he ignored her light objection and ran his nose and cheek up the insides of her thighs, speaking words that singed her flesh, sent a trail of goosebumps from her centre to her throat. She tossed her head to one side and back again. Helpless, yet powerful, too, Sorcha trembled all over.

She reached down and scrambled at his breeches, meeting his busy fingers as she rid him of the last of his clothes. She could feel and see his hardness. Dear God, he was the beautiful one. And he wanted her.

Sorcha held his head, felt his tongue, his mouth against her centre, molten, then firm. Waves of glorious pleasure overrode any pain as she lost herself in a place of starlight, moonbeams and the crashing of the ocean.

When she cried out, her body stiffening before releasing, he didn't stop, but held her as she shuddered against him again and again. Tears streamed from the corners of her eyes, down her neck. Tears of joy and utter wonder.

This, she thought, this was how love feels.

Dear God... *love*? Did she love this man?

As he crawled up her body, a rain of light kisses scorching her flesh in his wake, she knew in her heart she did.

With a wicked grin, he kissed her mouth once again, lingering upon her lips, tugging her bottom one with his teeth. Gently, he lowered himself onto her. 'I'm not hurting you, am I?'

'Och, aye,' she said, imitating his speech. 'And it's this kind of hurting I be wanting.'

'Are you sure, Sorcha?' he asked, staring into her eyes, holding himself back. 'Because I tell you now, it's the loving kind I want to give you.'

In their dark depths, she saw what she'd always hoped she would — desire, compassion, respect, fierce protectiveness and, above all, passion. It was what she felt too.

'Aye, Aidan, I'm sure,' she murmured and, as he entered her, she knew her search for the type of love she'd longed for was over.

After a time, she slid down his body, ignoring the pinch of healing wounds, and whispered, 'Now, let me love you the same way too.'

THIRTY-ONE

Back tae auld claes an' parritch.
(Back to old familiar things.)

*A*s she stared out the window of her cottage one bright September dawn, Sorcha's thoughts ran inwards.

She was both astonished and relieved that the division she'd felt so strongly in the community when she was freed five weeks earlier had not erupted into violence. At least, not yet. Instead, it surged beneath the town like an underground torrent, searching for release.

From the moment Sorcha returned to the harbour, a mere week after leaving the Tolbooth, the fishwives and fishermen rallied to welcome her and Nettie. Some of the shopkeepers made a point of greeting them when they passed on their first day back, as did the wives of the men away on long voyages. Emerging from their houses, waving and, on two occasions, bringing food to share while the fishwives worked, they'd been eager to show support. In their kind looks, forced laughter and sly references to the reverend and the bailies, she knew they were letting her, Nettie and others like Beatrix, who also came to the shore, know whose side they were on.

The week she remained at home, some of her neighbours made a point of calling by, bringing soup, bannocks, and occasionally a dram to share. While there were those who pretended not to want to know what happened in the Tolbooth, the fishwives weren't so tactful. They were keen to learn every single detail. Mainly because they wanted to add to their growing list of complaints against the reverend. Sorcha was reluctant to share anything, but Nettie felt no such compunction.

When Sorcha warned Nettie against saying too much lest it came back to bite her, her friend explained that telling the fishwives made the entire nightmare more akin to the tales her da had regaled her with as a bairn. In the telling, *she* owned the story. She took it from the men who inflicted the pain and suffering, the officials who allowed it to happen and kept records, and made it hers.

Unable to bear what had been done to his wife or to cope with her gruesome recountings of it, after a couple of weeks, in an uncharacteristic show of authority, Thom White reasserted his husbandly rights and insisted Nettie not only remain with him, as she had since she left the Tolbooth, but since the tenants had now vacated, that they shift into her house in Anster together. Letting him believe he had complete mastery, Nettie confessed to Sorcha she was relieved to escape the Weem for a time.

'I understand why you went to Dagny, hen, even knowing it wouldn't be a joyful reunion. Sometimes, you just need to put distance betwixt yourself and a place — mainly because of the memories it tosses up like wreckage after a storm.'

What Nettie also admitted was her grave concern for Thom's health. The cough he'd developed before she went into the Tolbooth had worsened and he'd lost a great deal of weight.

'You'd think he was the one who'd been locked away,' Nettie grimaced, her eyes filled with disquiet as she gazed at him standing beside the cart that would carry their belongings to Anster.

Even with Thom ailing, Nettie found it hard to stay away too long and would often visit. Taking advantage of the long summer evenings, when it was still light enough to roam the coastal path, she'd wait until Thom was tucked in bed before making the journey. Without warning, she'd knock on Sorcha's or Beatrix's door and stay for a meal, sharing news. After a couple of weeks, with Thom rallying, she grew bored in Anster, so donned her fishwife's apron and neepyin and returned to working down at the harbour, going back to her husband upon eventide.

As for Beatrix, there wasn't a day went by when she didn't call on every one of them — including Nettie. It was a way of assuaging the terrible guilt she felt at having given up their names in the first place. Holding herself responsible for all their misery, and for Thomas Brown's death and Janet's current situation, she couldn't stop apologising or trying to make amends. Didn't matter that no one blamed her. They knew Beatrix had experienced all their suffering and more. While some said it was remarkable that Beatrix had recovered so well, especially after being in solitude in St Fillan's Cave for such a length of time, Sorcha knew she hadn't. None of them had. But by focussing on her friends, Beatrix could get through, just as Nettie dealt with it by turning their terrible experience into macabre tales.

Then there was young Isobel, still able to eke a living as a seamstress. Much to Sorcha's relief and the reverend's wrath, she learned to trade upon her new-found infamy. Sorcha was afraid that just as it had before, the villagers' mood would swing faster than the northerly winds that swept down the coast. The majority might be with them for now, but when the drave lessened again as autumn fell upon them with cold cruelty, and the reverend kept raging about witches from the pulpit each Sunday, using Janet Cornfoot as an example of utter infamy and malice, she feared the town could turn against them again. It was as if she was holding her breath, waiting for it to happen. When she mentioned this to Nettie, her friend shook her head sorrowfully.

'If you keep waiting for something to happen, you'll likely will it into being, hen.' Cupping Sorcha's face in her hands, she kissed the tip of her nose. 'It's over. For us at least. For poor auld Janet, never mind Nicolas with her terrible hurts, it's still ongoing.'

Every few days after they'd sorted and sold any of the catch that wasn't going to market, a few of them would meet and walk to Nicolas's cottage, bringing supplies and gossip about what was being said around the Weem. Her health was slowly improving, but it would be a while before she'd be her old self again. The doctor advised her to lie in bed and keep her legs wrapped. He'd lathered her limbs with all sorts of pungent salves, swearing by their efficacy. Once he'd gone, Nicolas would order her husband to carry her to the ocean and prop her by a rock pool. Peeling off the bandages, she immersed her legs in the salt water. She persuaded Sorcha and Nettie to do the same; they were reluctant at first because the pain was so very great. Nicolas told them to dangle their legs for a minute at a time, to allow their bodies to get used to the cold and the sting. Within a few days, they were able to leave their legs in for longer and the dreadful welts and holes began to heal, the pus to dry up. After that, Beatrix and occasionally Isobel, Lillie and Margaret would join them, dipping their arms in the sea as well, amazed and grateful to Nicolas and her healing knowledge as their remaining wounds mended.

Once, daringly, they'd even soaked their entire bodies. Slowly, the marks left by the pricker began to scab and turn pink. The infection that had entered so many of the lacerations disappeared.

But it was the unseen scars that ate away at tranquillity, that entered dreams to tear away good memories and hope. Those would take longer to heal.

Most nights, Aidan shared Sorcha's bed. She marvelled that such a man had come into her life; so ardent, so understanding. Oft she'd wake with his arms around her as he comforted her out of a terrible nightmare. He never demanded she tell him what she relived, and for that she was grateful. How could she explain that even her nightmares didn't compare to the reality? Instead, she'd snuggle against his bare chest, feel the heat of desire rise within her, and stir her limbs to relish the life and passion in him as well.

As for poor Janet Cornfoot, even weeks after they'd been released, she still languished in St Fillan's Cave. The moment she retracted her confession before the legal representatives of the Crown, Mr Ker of Kippilaw and Mr Robert Cooke from Edinburgh, her fate was sealed. It was nothing but cruel and petty punishment and all in the Weem knew it.

Once they'd recovered from the worst of their injuries, the fish-wives determined to do what they could to change that.

Every evening after they returned from traipsing about the countryside with their creels, those who were able gathered outside the door
to the cave. Uncaring who else heard, they'd shout to Janet, hoping
and praying she did. They spoke of the day, the fishing, the tides,
sunlight, rain, heat and lately the cooler winds and frosty morns. They
told her about the tailor, Angus Riding, who became so drunk he fell
asleep on a gravestone, frightening the grieving Mrs Tyler who'd come
to pay her respects to her father and ran screaming when she thought
he'd risen from the dead.

They shared the tale of Mr Butterworth of Crail who, on advice
from the doctor, came walking along the coastal path, his only company a bottle of medicine he'd been given by a French pirate who swore
it would aid his melancholy. Finding the medicine made him feel quite
hale, he'd downed the entire contents before he'd even left Anster, only
to fall from the harbour wall. The tide was high and the current strong.
Being a good swimmer, he'd struck out for what he thought was the
shore. A Pittenweem boat picked him up almost drowned, halfway to
the Isle of May. Turns out, the medicine he was drinking was a rough
Irish spirit made from potato skins. The poor man was delirious and
swore it was selkies who rescued him when it was really the strapping,
thick-haired McDonald lads. Afeared these ungainly water faeries had
come to claim him, as soon as he set foot on land, he'd bolted before he
could be tended, running into the hills never to be seen again.

It didn't take long for the guards from the Tolbooth to come marching down the wynd, hollering at the women to be on their way and
threatening to lock them up again. They knew it was the reverend
who sent them, as his children would hang over the kirk walls watching, the younger ones even throwing rocks and sticks. The fishwives
would pelt them with fish heads or clods of peat they'd collected to fill
their creels, laughing when one hit its mark. The children would jump
down and run away, screeching for their da.

Rather than frightening the women, the guards trooping towards
them, fists and pikes raised, emboldened them. The day Nettie
hitched her skirts and showed Angus Stuart her pale skinny arse was
one Sorcha wouldn't forget in a hurry. Flustered, the man had stopped

and stared, colour draining from his cheeks before he recalled where he was and ran at them, scattering the laughing women in all directions. When Therese Larnarch flung fish guts at Simon Wood, Sorcha thought she'd wet herself at the sight of the lad blinking through blood and slimy entrails, spitting and coughing even as he tried to bluster. Whenever the guards appeared now, the women would flee, running back to the shore road, cackling and shrieking, hoping Janet could hear both their defiance and their forced joy.

Just below the surface of their bravado was a terror so great that Sorcha feared it could swallow them. Facing it, laughing defiantly at those who aroused it, enabled them to control it. They never admitted as much to each other. It was a dangerous game, but it was all they had. It was all Janet had, too. Sometimes they fancied they could hear the hollow ring of her mirth, the echo of her approval. Sorcha prayed it wasn't just a fancy. Sometimes she worried that when the door to the cave was finally opened, they'd only find Janet's bleached bones propped against the far rocky wall, arms limp by her side, her sightless skull yearning towards the opening.

They'd begged leave to see her. Many of the other Weem folk had as well, even those who'd stood with Reverend Cowper on the day Sorcha was released. Whereas once their inclination had been to side with the man, when they saw what had been done to the women with their own eyes, how thin, ashen-cheeked and raddled-eyed they were, how utterly filthy and beaten and pricked, their feelings changed. When the released witches showed no propensity to harm anyone and Peter Morton's symptoms vanished, any sympathy or apprehension the reverend stirred began to abate.

Even the incomers, who were still drifting into the village to hear the stories and see the witches for themselves, began to dry up.

At first Sorcha was pleased, but then she remembered what Aidan had told them: the incomers had spent a great deal of money in the Weem and in Anster, Silverdyck and beyond. If they ceased to come, this source of funds would cease to flow. He was concerned the reverend and the council would seek another means to lure folk back and make money, even if it meant discovering more witches.

'But there aren't any,' insisted Sorcha for the umpteenth time.

'*We* know that,' said Aidan one night, pulling at the short strands of hair on her head. Now her hair was thicker and growing longer, she liked him playing with it. 'But where there's a yearning to see them, and money to be made through their appearance, there's a way to produce them.'

A chill entered her heart. A chill that not even this inviting autumn day so full of promise could disperse.

Only thoughts of Aidan had the ability to do that. So, as Sorcha tore herself away from the window and prepared to go to the harbour, the sky transforming into a palette of rose and violet, she lost herself in thoughts of the captain, her love.

Truth be told, her reason for living.

THIRTY-TWO

You are just menseless.
(You want far too much.)

$\mathcal{P}$eter Morton skulked along the narrow lanes inside the crumbling town walls, doing his best to avoid anyone, wanting nothing more than to find a private place where he could lick his wounded pride and think about what had happened to him in Edinburgh.

Ducking behind a coop in an untended garden, he waited while a group of soldiers led by brawny Sergeant Thatcher went past, arms swinging, weapons bouncing against their hips, voices low. What they were doing up this end of the Weem, God only knew. That officer of theirs was determined his men not remain idle, so sent them out of town to local farmsteads to offer themselves for work, or made them practise with their swords and muskets on the fields between Anster and Pittenweem.

As the soldiers disappeared around the corner, Peter re-emerged cautiously. It was a glorious autumn day, warmer than usual for November. The sun shone, bees buzzed and starlings and lapwings cavorted and sang. Above a hedge of hawthorn, butterflies performed a ballet and Peter stopped to enjoy their merry antics until the events of the last two days flew back into his head.

Summoned to the city by none other than Her Majesty's advocate and questioned thoroughly by the Earl of Rothes, Peter knew he'd let the reverend down. The reverend and all those in the village who'd supported and prayed for him the entire time he was afflicted.

Nae, bewitched.

When he was abed with tremors, cursed, a victim of malice, folk had listened when he said it was witches who caused it. While he knew there were those among the townsfolk who doubted, as time went on and even the doctors who'd come from Edinburgh to examine him were inclined to believe it was malfeasance, they'd been persuaded as well. Never before had he been showered with such attention, such compassion. It made him giddy just remembering it.

When he was first called to the city to give evidence, he was glad of the opportunity to tell how afeared he'd been. Travelling by the coach the reverend organised, dressed in his finest clothes, he imagined the men would commend him for his courage and how, by identifying the witches, he'd prevented others from being harmed. What he hadn't expected as he sat in the stuffy room lined with books and documents on the second floor of a huge stone building, the smoke-wreathed light above the men's heads making them appear otherworldly, saintly almost, was scepticism.

It was like a heavy blow; even now he struggled to recover from it. He wasn't yet ready to face his family. Or the reverend. Insisting the coach leave him outside Anster, he'd wended his way back to the Weem, crossing fields to avoid encountering anyone. Favouring rarely used paths, he approached the village from the north, where he was less likely to be seen. Thank goodness the soldiers had gone.

He made his way towards the western braes, knowing he'd have to head home soon. His ma would be expecting him. So would Reverend Cowper. He'd made it clear he wanted a full reckoning the moment Peter returned. How could he explain about the earl and the other gentlemen who'd questioned him as if he were the culprit and not a victim? From the moment they began, the men challenged the reports the reverend had written about Peter's affliction. When they asked how they were to credit such tales when he looked so hearty, he told them the truth: his symptoms had disappeared about three months prior, as mysteriously as they'd begun.

Red-faced, uncomfortable, shocked by their lack of faith, he felt their scorn as surely as if they'd struck him. And that was before they offered alternative explanations for what he had been through.

How dare they suggest he'd feigned his illness! They weren't there; they didn't see the charm, feel its effects, hear his cries, his moans. They didn't know how his body wouldn't allow him to control it, how afraid he'd been. They didn't know what it was like to live with witches as neighbours. But when the Earl of Rothes went so far as to call him a villain, Peter felt a deep resentment begin to burn. They thought being from the city, with their fine clothes, their peculiar way of speaking, their ability to read and write, made them better; they thought their understanding greater than his, the tawpie lad from a small place. Anger surged through Peter and he kicked a drystone wall, uncaring of the pain that shot up his leg. Fury towards those evil beings who'd made him suffer in the first place — the agony of the curse and now this latest humiliation — made him kick it again. A ewe bleated on the other side, sending him on his way.

He picked up a clod of earth and flung it down the wynd, feeling gratified when it exploded in a shower of dirt. Instead of being praised for his role in uncovering the coven as he'd anticipated, as the reverend had alluded, he'd been sent home in disgrace. All the while, those who caused his misery were free to wander where they pleased. Where was the justice in that? What reward did he get for naming the devil-loving hizzies but a flea in his ear and a father who could scarce look at his own son any more?

Just as well not all the villagers felt that way. Ever since he'd risen from his bed, there had been those who congratulated him — not only on his recovery, but for identifying the witches in the first place. Keen to use his services, the smithy soon rang once more. He'd only to step in the tavern and men crowded around to slap him on the back, buy him an ale, blather over a dram. Aye, there were many who knew what he'd saved them from…

Only, the reverend believed they weren't saved at all; they'd merely been granted a reprieve.

Peter prayed he was wrong, but a part of him prayed he was right. Then those boldinits in Edinburgh could eat their words.

Any remorse he felt at the role he'd played in gaoling the women was swept aside in a mixture of rage, pride and bravado. He'd done a good thing. One couldn't allow witches to run around the place cursing all and sundry and corrupting good Christian souls, could they? That's what the reverend said over and over.

It was only when he thought of Thomas Brown that the seed of guilt planted all those months ago sprouted once more. Not that it was his fault the auld souff died, of course.

The man's death had not gone to waste. Despite his daughter's protests, his property had been confiscated and sold. The money had gone far: beautiful timbers and stone to commence repairs upon the pier had been delivered to the foreshore only a couple of weeks ago. Many would benefit from that and not just those hired to do the construction. The exception was Mr Brown's daughter, Ellie. Left with a few measly pounds to remember her father by, she'd gone to live with relatives in St Monan's. He was glad. He didn't think he could face her.

There were a few he dreaded seeing again, even though God was on his side. God and the reverend. The very first day he left his house he'd seen Beatrix Laing, the foul auld gilly. She'd pretended not to see him as she hirpled up the High Street, leaning on her husband. He'd been shocked to see how small and lean she was. In his mind, she'd taken on the proportions of a giant. Still, her hands were like claws even if they were stuck on stick arms. Her face was shadowed by a bonnet, but it looked like she'd grown a beard, so dark was a patch on the side of her face. With ever-expanding horror, he realised it was a large bruise.

After that, he'd been prepared for how Nettie Horseburgh, Lillie Wallace and the others appeared. But the one he most dreaded to see again was Sorcha McIntyre. Of all the women who'd been imprisoned in the Tolbooth, it was Mrs McIntyre who haunted him.

Unable to forget how she was so kind to him that day they walked to the smithy, how she'd laughed and given him a smile that made him feel warm deep inside, as if he were the man he knew himself to be, she'd continued to disturb his dreams. Not in the way he claimed the witches did. Nae, Mrs McIntyre was altogether different.

He cringed at the thought of setting eyes upon her again, not so much because he was remorseful for what he'd done, but because he feared she'd resemble the other women — all angles and horrid, painful-looking scars. Sunken eyes and cheeks, colourless and defiant. He heard she'd been poorly treated and the idea made him shrink inside. But what had he expected? When the reverend insisted Sorcha was a witch and that it was his godly duty to name her and protect the village, Peter knew that she would be punished. Reverend Cowper told him it was long overdue. Mrs McIntyre, he whispered, was a wicked woman, a brazen besom, who swept men off their feet using bewitchment. She manipulated them for her own ends.

The reverend had a point when he spoke of the men in Sorcha's life. They were all either dead or missing — even her wee bairn had died. Peter's illness had fallen upon him when he was with her. To the reverend, this proved she was in league with Beatrix Laing, a known witch. Just like her other associates. As much as he was reluctant to concede this, Peter knew there was some truth in what Reverend Cowper said. Why would Sorcha tolerate such company if she was not of a similar mind? If they were not part of a coven working towards a common goal, a common evil? And Isobel and Beatrix weren't even fishwives...

At the top of the braes Peter stared out over the Forth. It was good to be home. At least here you could breathe, feel the wind, the earth; smell the sea, not be choked by chimney smoke and tobacco or tromp on hard, stinking cobbles, inhale horses' shit and human feculence or have your ears assaulted by endless noise and blather. Here you could spin with your arms out wide and touch the sky. In the city, you were lucky if it could even peek between tall buildings. Peter twirled around now, remembering how it had felt to be pushed and carried along in a tide of humanity, all smelly clothes, sharp heels, odorous breath and deafening shouts.

Coming to a halt, he shut his eyes until the world stopped spinning, then opened them again. Small whitecaps rippled across the water as the wind fanned its surface. Boats were putting back out to sea, wanting to take advantage of the gloaming, a time when the fish would bite, if they were about. There were people milling on the harbour and the beach to help them, enjoying the unusually balmy weather. He saw children splashing around in the incoming tide, a couple of dogs chasing gulls, barking in joy.

With a deep sigh, he clambered down the rocky slopes, away from prying eyes, intending to explore the tidal pools. There was no one to see him this side of the braes or to stop and ask how he'd gone in Edinburgh. Checking he had his knife, he rather fancied a mussel or two. Perhaps he'd even bring some back for his da. Their relationship had never been the same since that day by the smithy.

Peter was so busy looking for mussels, he didn't see the woman at first. But he heard her. A sweet voice singing a sailor's ditty. He almost turned around and headed back towards the cottages, only something convinced him to remain. Approaching the sound cautiously, he squeezed between two large rocks. The tide was turning but the skerries were still exposed, creating numerous pools — some no bigger than a key hole, others so large a few people could sit in them and not touch. Peter used to love exploring them when he was small, gazing into their translucent depths, reaching in to poke the starfish and other creatures, watching the way the tendrils of seaweed swayed to unheard music. Much to the amusement of the fishwives, he'd tell them it was an entirely different world down there, populated by tiny magical beings. An upside-down world, where water was the air they breathed, the lapping waves their wind. Transfixed, he would lie on his belly and wish himself into the place he'd created, where no one went hungry, everyone was friendly, God walked among them and fathers never, ever beat their sons.

Following the siren song, he squatted next to a wet boulder and peered around. The swollen sun had gone behind a cloud, transforming the light into a silvern glow. A woman sat on the edge of one of the larger rock pools. At first he thought she was a mermaid, as he couldn't see her legs. Her face was turned away, her song a gift to the sea. Able to view her without being seen, Peter drank in the vision. The long neck, the cap of bronze curls, the soothing melody.

Unaware of him, after a time she hauled herself out of the water, hitching her skirts high, and he saw the terrible marks upon her limbs. What he first thought were tricks thrown by the water, he now knew were the scars of torture. The shorn hair, the lacerations, the voice. His heart skipped. It was the widow of the sea, Sorcha McIntyre.

The sea-witch.

Dear God, what he wouldn't give to fall under her spell. But wasn't that exactly what had happened? He'd named her and in doing so declared himself a victim of her malice.

But how could a woman who looked like that, sounded like that, be malicious? God, she was a beauty, even with the lesions upon her body and the cropped hair. More slender, more frail, she was like a goddess of old; ethereal. A woman like that needed a man. To protect her — even from herself. And what was he, if not a man? Forget what the advocate said, calling him a foolish lad and all but accusing him of lying. He was a man fully grown with hair upon his face, his chest, and a man's needs. What was Sorcha but a woman to fill those? Why, before he'd fallen ill, she'd all but made her intentions clear.

He glanced over his shoulder one last time, checking there was no other soul in sight. Just the murmur of the incoming tide, the caw of gulls and the dizzy dance of terns. Crabs scuttled across the rocks, a large beetle rolled into the water, making a tiny splash. Flexing his shoulders, puffing out his chest, aware of a disturbing warmth, Peter reached a decision.

He got to his feet and was about to reveal himself when another voice forced him to freeze.

'I thought I'd find you here.'

Skipping across the rocks as if he were born to it was the officer from Skye. What was his name? Och, aye, Aidan Ross.

Sorcha dropped her skirts and turned towards him, breaking into a smile that took Peter's breath away. She'd never smiled like that for him.

The captain caught Sorcha in his arms, lifted her off her feet and spun her around. Arching her back so her body melted into his, Sorcha laughed, the sound an aphrodisiac that set Peter's heart racing so hard, he fell against the boulder. Lowering his mouth to hers, the captain and Sorcha shared a long, deep kiss.

Peter knew he should look away as heat crawled across his cheeks and neck, but he was transfixed. He'd not seen two people kiss like that before, with such wanting, such... devotion. That was a word the reverend oft used when he spoke of God, Jesus and the power of faith. What Peter saw now, that was devotion. The way they reluctantly ceased, their lips parting as they held each other, gazing into each other's eyes.

A dreadful ache seized Peter. Starting near his heart, it radiated to his groin, across his chest and into his throat. Anger marched through his mind, making it blaze before it turned freezing cold, leaving him hurting, wanting, needing.

Taking Sorcha's hand, the captain picked up her stockings and boots and led her away from the rock pool. Understanding they were going to pass his hiding place, Peter ducked back and retraced his steps as quietly as he could, grateful for the sounds of the waves and wind disguising any noise he made. Squeezed between the rocks, he stood still, praying he wouldn't be seen in the shadows. Water lapped at his boots.

They stopped almost in front of him. The captain kissed Sorcha again, deeply. Her fingers reached up and twined themselves in his long, heavy hair. Peter could hear their breathing, they were so close. He could smell them; their excitement, their evident passion. It excited him, too; excited him into wanting to do something rash...

'Will I see you tonight?' asked the captain, resting his forehead against hers.

'I'm counting on it,' said Sorcha, a little breathless, then, with a laugh she kissed the captain once more. She took her stockings and boots from him, ran across the rocks and disappeared around the headland.

The captain waited a while, his eyes fixed on where she'd gone. Only when he saw her reappear on the sands did he turn.

Peter didn't dare move.

Pausing a moment, the captain looked in his direction. Could he see him? He shut his eyes only to find when he opened them, the man had vanished. Where to, he couldn't tell.

Peter waited a few more moments before emerging from his hiding place, his boots thoroughly soaked, and began the climb back up towards the braes. His mind sizzled and whirred. He couldn't wipe away the image of the two kissing, touching. It sickened him. It filled him with yearning. It made him furious.

He wondered what the reverend would make of it, Sorcha McIntyre and Captain Ross. What did it signify?

What it told Peter was that the reverend was right all along. Sorcha was a brazen besom who played with men's feelings and led them on with only one purpose — to enact mischief.

Sending a prayer of thanks to the good Lord that he was saved from bewitchment this time, he began to wonder what Sorcha intended to do with the captain. More importantly, what tasks had he already performed on her behalf? There were the letters he'd written that had caused no end of strife... but what else had he done? What else was he being primed to do?

With renewed purpose, the shame of Edinburgh and desire for Sorcha burning in his heart, Peter set out to find the man with all the answers: Reverend Patrick Cowper.

THIRTY-THREE

I never let dab.
(I told no one.)

$\mathcal{P}$atrick Cowper ignored his eldest daughter's entreaties to join the family for supper and retired to his study, a bottle of whisky in one hand, a plate of bannocks and hare in the other. Until he heard how Peter Morton fared in Edinburgh, he wouldn't be able to sit still, let alone tolerate mindless blather.

When the knock came shortly after six of the clock, it took all Patrick's willpower to remain patiently behind his desk and pretend an indifference he didn't feel.

As he watched Peter cross the floor, he noted the redness of his cheeks, the sweat that beaded his brow. Had he run from Edinburgh? The lad was alive with a simmering intensity, keen to speak, but why could he not meet his eyes?

'Sit, lad, sit,' said Patrick, rising to his feet, coming around the desk and clapping Peter on the back as he took a seat. He noticed his boots were wet, his stockings as well. His hair was tousled and he smelled of sweat and seaweed. By which route had he come?

'You'll have a dram with me?' asked Patrick and, without waiting for an answer, collected another glass, poured and passed it over.

The lad gulped the drink, coughing and wheezing, rubbing his chest.

Patrick waited for him to regain his composure. 'Well,' he began, easing himself into his chair, fingers spread on the desk as he fixed his eyes upon Peter. 'Tell me what happened, tell me everything.'

Peter did.

Patrick resisted the urge to swear when Peter related how the earl, the advocate and the other gentlemen had treated him. He forced himself to remain calm. So what if those puddocks didn't believe the lad? They weren't from here. Hadn't seen what those women had done. What they were... But they would. God help him, they would.

When he finished, Peter sat quietly. Patrick's mind raced. Now he had to deliver another blow. News had come that Isobel Adam, the first of the women to be sent to Edinburgh for questioning by the Privy Council back in October, had been set free. No longer was she on a bond awaiting trial. Despite her confession, Edinburgh had ordered that every charge against her be dropped. She would not face trial. It had been all Patrick could do not to tear the missive bearing the news into shreds and shove it down the messenger's throat.

It was clear what had happened. Those ridiculous men had paid no account to what he and the councillors reported, or the gents from St Andrew's who believed the women guilty despite their recanting; nor to the confessions signed by the witches or eyewitness accounts of Peter's afflictions, or indeed the word of the lad himself. Instead they took the word of a pretty young lass. A pretty young lass and an interfering captain...

What had Councillor Cleiland told him? Turned out, the captain's commanding officer, a Colonel Leslie Johns, was a cousin of the Earl of Rothes. How bloody convenient. Seemed the captain had bested him after all. The reverend had no doubt that now Isobel's charges had been dropped, those against the remaining women would be as well.

Patrick poured himself another dram, ignoring Peter's plaintive look into his own empty glass.

Silence filled the room, broken only by the spitting of the fire and the voices of passers-by. From elsewhere in the house came the irritating sound of a child crying. Drumming his fingers against the desktop, Patrick chewed his lip.

This would not do. Those women could not go unpunished. It wasn't right or righteous. Didn't the Bible say, 'Thou shall not suffer a witch to live'? Yet here were Edinburgh and the Queen's representatives ignoring God's commandment. Ignoring him, Reverend Patrick Cowper.

Yet what was he to do? He'd tried to keep the good folk of the Weem safe and what happened? Many had turned against him. Turned against him even as he was trying to save their souls from perdition.

It was that fucking captain who ruined everything. Him and his endless letters and entreaties to those in power. Him and his connections.

Was there nothing to be done about him?

Unaware he'd spoken aloud, the reverend jumped when Peter replied, 'But I think there is, sir. That's what else I have to tell you.'

'Och, and what's that, Peter?' said the reverend, only half-listening as he tried to formulate plans of his own. Peter was a good lad, but simple. He'd obeyed him in every regard and it still wasn't enough.

Peter quickly told him what he'd witnessed at the skerries. How it was evident Sorcha and the captain were lovers.

The reverend watched the lad carefully, noting how jealousy thickened his words and clogged his throat. How his cheeks flooded with deeper colour; the way the lad moved a finger around his neck, loosening his scarf. How he shifted in the chair a few times. He buried a smile in a cough. The lad was so transparent. But maybe, just maybe, Peter's clear affection for Sorcha McIntyre could work to his advantage. It had been hard to get the lad to incriminate her... but he had. Unwillingly. Maybe now she was so clearly involved with someone else, an incomer responsible for their current tribulations no less, it would be different.

If only he were able to remove the captain for a time, or better still, for good. That would make things a great deal easier. The reverend stared at his whisky, swirling it in the glass, watching the way the light turned the fluid into a whirlpool of umbers and gold. Aidan

Ross wasn't the only one with connections. He had them too — in St Andrew's, no less. Why, that was almost as good as Edinburgh.

He began to think about the latest news of the war. The Duke of Marlborough had enjoyed a mighty victory earlier in the year at the battle of Blenheim on the Danube. There were reports he was rallying troops to march into France and needed extra men. Surely a captain of Aidan Ross's standing would be of more use over there rather than babysitting soldiers here.

Patrick sat up. He may not have networks in the military, but he knew someone who did. Not insubstantial ones either. A word here, a hint there, a mention of the fine work Captain Ross was doing in Pittenweem and how he was wasted in a small coastal town when a war was being waged on the continent. One never knew what might happen as a consequence.

He smiled at Peter who, astonished, returned it as the reverend half-rose over his desk and gave the lad's glass a generous splash of whisky.

'You did well in the city. It's not an easy thing to face men like those as you did today. You should be proud. If nothing else, it will prepare you for what you have to do next.'

A flash of concern crossed Peter's face. 'What's that, sir?'

Patrick smiled. 'Just be ready to help me trap some witches, lad. Together, we'll save the village.'

'Does it still need saving?'

'Aye,' grinned the reverend. 'It just doesn't know it yet.'

The boy nodded and sipped his whisky. Patrick appreciated that. Gave him time to think. More than ever, he knew how important it was he didn't let folk forget about the threat that witchcraft and its practitioners posed to their very souls.

He picked up his quill, dipped it in the inkhorn and began to scratch some notes for his next sermon.

As he wrote, his mind drifted. After the lad left, he'd write to his friend in St Andrew's, someone who was also a proud Covenanter. A colleague and like-minded gentleman who also happened to be the brother of General Overkirk, the man responsible for mustering troops in Holland. Surely the general could use the services of a fine officer? And if not the general, then perhaps the duke himself?

The reverend didn't know why he hadn't thought of it sooner. He'd make sure to praise the captain highly, point out all the attributes that he'd previously resented but now saw would work to his advantage.

Chuckling inwardly, the reverend abandoned his sermon and instead wrote 'brave', 'maintains order', 'inspires loyalty', the list of Captain Ross's qualities growing with each sip of his drink. Let the captain believe his witch was safe; that this battle was over. The sappie-headed jock didn't understand who or what he was dealing with.

It wasn't just a small-town cleric the captain was fighting, but the devil himself, the devil in the guise of a woman. A woman who'd bewitched him, just as she did all who came within her ken.

He regarded the lad on the other side of the desk morosely. Just as she had bewitched Peter Morton.

Only now, through God's good grace and Patrick Cowper, the lad's eyes were about to be opened.

THIRTY-FOUR

I'll sowther her ower.
(I'll calm her down.)

At last it was official. Those Peter Morton had named as witches, who Reverend Cowper and the bailies had arrested, imprisoned and forced to suffer, had been pardoned by the Privy Council in Edinburgh. It had taken until the middle of November, but now Sorcha had the papers to prove it.

She placed the documents safely in her da's old sea chest, closed the lid and slowly lowered herself upon it, praying she'd never have to look at them again.

Where was the relief she expected to feel now it was all over? Perhaps in her heart she knew it wasn't finished. As long as Reverend Cowper kept preaching against witches, against those he felt had unjustly escaped his clutches, and as long as folk listened, it never would be.

She leaned back against the wall and thought over what had led to this moment.

Two days earlier, the rest of the accused witches — with the exception of Isobel Adam, who had gone earlier, and Janet Cornfoot, who remained in St Fillan's Cave pending additional charges (which was really just an excuse to punish her further and keep her locked up) — had travelled to Edinburgh and faced the sheriff, the Earl of Rothes, the advocate and other officials. Nettie overrode the earl's arrangements for transporting them and insisted on paying extra, hiring a coach for the journey, as if they were grand ladies and not a bunch of recuperating prisoners. Dressed in the best clothing they owned, they still bore the marks of their confinement, albeit much faded. At least Nicolas could now walk unaided.

They were to leave husbands and family at home and undertake the journey with only a couple of constables as outriders representing Weem officialdom and each other for company. It was how they'd endured in the Tolbooth, and how they would face the city authorities.

That morning they'd met at the Mercat Cross then quietly walked to where the coach and mounted constables waited. Dawn had not yet broken and the last stars were glimmering in the heavens, a nippy breeze snapping at their cloaks, threatening to dislodge their hats. Arms linked, they'd kept their heads bowed, trying not to start when a rat scuttled across their path or a rooster crowed.

It wasn't until they saw the coach, a dark silhouette against the lightening sky, that they knew they weren't to travel without friends after all. Aidan, Sergeant Thatcher and two corporals were on horseback, talking to the driver and the constables in low voices.

Upon spying them, the women stopped. Sorcha wriggled free of the group and approached.

'Aidan,' she said, nodding to the driver and the soldiers. 'I thought we agreed. You don't need to do this.'

'I'm not going for you, lass,' said Aidan, looking down at her, his breath a plume of white. 'I've been summoned to Edinburgh again.'

Sorcha's heart skipped a beat. For all he pretended otherwise, she knew he was really doing it to ensure her safety — hers and that of her friends. 'Do you know why?'

Aidan shook his head. 'Nae. But, as I explained to the constables here —' he gestured towards Simon Wood and Mark Smith, who acknowledged the women before looking away, 'it's in our mutual interest we travel together, isn't it?'

He beckoned the other women forward and, dismounting, he and the sergeant assisted them into the coach, ensuring their legs were covered with blankets, the windows sealed against the cold. As he went to close the door, Sorcha gripped his hand. 'Thank you.'

Aidan dipped his head, but she caught his smile.

The women barely spoke as day broke, dull and grey with heavy clouds. They knew there'd be words aplenty once they reached Edinburgh. What they secretly prayed was that words would be all that was asked of them. As they rocked from side to side, bumping shoulders and hips, Sorcha noted how Nettie would absent-mindedly rub her wrists; how Nicolas winced any time they met a pothole. Margaret and Lillie remained mute but wary. Beatrix closed her eyes, but from the way her lids moved, it was clear her mind was busy. God knew, Sorcha couldn't cease ruminating.

On arrival they were ushered one by one into a dim room in a large building, its cold corridors filled with dark-coated men carrying voluminous files. The interviews, which Sorcha had been dreading and they all secretly feared, despite Isobel's reassurances, might involve Mr Bollard and more beatings, were swift. Unwilling to show any sympathy towards the women, the men weren't entirely contrary to them either, but at least, the women agreed later, the questions were not nonsensical.

The journey back to Pittenweem, without Aidan, who was ordered to remain in the city, was a different affair to the restrained one of the morning. Within the confines of the coach there was much laughter and the relieved blether of those who'd been spared. Nettie and Nicolas spent most of the trip imitating Lord Rothes, who had the most unfortunate lisp, while Beatrix, Margaret and Lillie revelled in the fact they'd been able to retract what they'd confessed under duress and were believed.

That was the part that gratified Sorcha the most — that they could explain what had been done to them and how, unable to endure any more pain, they'd admitted to anything the reverend or the bailies suggested, including pacts with the devil in a variety of guises. The men had tried to hide their discomfort at the women's revelations, but

Sorcha could tell they were appalled. The scribe taking notes in the corner was so disturbed by Sorcha's evidence, at one stage he'd ceased to write.

Upon returning to the village, Sorcha and Nettie had wasted no time but had gone straight to Bailie Bell's house and presented him with their pardons. The following day, the constable, Simon Wood, had rapped on their doors, handing over a note from the town council declaring that if they wanted their pardons properly acknowledged, they were to pay a fine of eight pounds each.

Knowing this had nothing to do with Edinburgh and everything to do with putting more money in the town's coffers as well as being punitive, Nettie and Beatrix had wanted to refuse. Sorcha persuaded them against this, even though Isobel, Nicolas, Margaret and Lillie would struggle to pay.

'I'll help,' said Sorcha; anything to prevent them getting into more trouble.

While Sorcha had assets to her name, ready cash was a different proposition. Not only had Cowper and his associates damaged their reputations immeasurably with their false accusations, they'd also taken away their ability to earn money for an extended period. It was hard to make up the shortfall that six months of no income created. The *Mistral* was due home any day and it was only the guarantee of its cargo and the coin that would bring that enabled Sorcha to borrow enough to help those she'd promised. After Isobel, Lillie, Margaret and Nicolas sold linens they'd saved for their winding sheets — and thank goodness they'd no use for those at present — and Nettie and Beatrix had added what they could, they'd enough.

As a group they went to the council rooms and handed over their fines to the treasurer, Bailie Whyte, who, if they hadn't known him better, might have been described as shamefaced.

When Sorcha said as much afterwards, Beatrix had cast her a long look. 'Aye, and William's really my selkie lover.' They'd burst into laughter.

Alone in her bed for the first time in ages, that night Sorcha tossed and turned, praying her boat would reach port soon. Once more the

Pittenweem community had rallied behind them and, if there weren't quite as many folk to champion them as when they were first released, it was reassuring to know not everyone had been swayed by Patrick Cowper and Peter Morton.

Not yet.

It was mainly because of the reverend that they decided to celebrate their release. Forced to attend the kirk each Sunday since they'd been freed — not to go would attract fines they could ill afford and would be seen as an admission of guilt in the eyes of the reverend and his followers — they had to endure his sermons. Every week he warned people against witchcraft, decried the monsters and evil spirits who, he claimed, walked among them. He maintained the devil was loose in the world, even quoting from a sermon given by a Salem preacher, Cotton Mather, published in *Wonders of the Invisible World*, a book Sorcha knew well, as it had done the rounds among those who could read as soon as it was published. As he spoke, there were some who stared pointedly at the fishwives, craning their necks and casting them looks of fear, pity and even anger. Having to put up with this made Sorcha, Nettie, Beatrix and the other fishwives more determined than ever to defy the man and invite those so inclined to join them for some food and drink to mark their pardon.

Sorcha was brought back to the present by the voices of Nettie and Beatrix. Folk would be arriving soon. She calmly rose from the chest and went to help. Together, they'd spent the morning baking bannocks, stewing some fish they'd hoarded from the last catch, and cutting cheese bought from the farms. Lillie and Margaret had collected oysters and mussels, Therese Larnarch had cooked a coney pie and brought some slices of mutton she'd managed to barter from a farmer out St Monan's way. There was also a steaming plate of neeps, eggs, and a custard. Bottles of whisky and some wine from France — no doubt courtesy of Thom White and the smugglers — were also among the booty they'd managed to rustle up at short notice.

As she watched her friends laying everything upon the table, she couldn't help but admire not just the feast, but the defiance that had led to it. Not that she really wanted to celebrate, especially while Janet still languished in St Fillan's Cave, though she knew the woman wouldn't begrudge them some festivities — on the contrary, she would have been the first to suggest them. Sorcha, Aidan and the others had done what they could, but neither the council nor Edinburgh were prepared to say what the new charges were that justified Janet still being held. All avenues of appeal were, for the moment, closed. Janet's liberty — just like the repayment of their bond money — was at the discretion of the Pittenweem council. Part of Sorcha was afraid that celebrating their pardons would rouse Cowper to be harder on Janet than he already was.

All too soon, guests began to arrive. Mrs Fraser was among the first, along with Crabby. Pipes and fiddles appeared and music started. Food and drink were downed and conversation rose and fell, laughter sprinkling it like early winter snow. Despite the general air of gaiety, Sorcha couldn't escape the feeling that maybe, just maybe, they were counting their fish before the catch.

As the light began to fade and evening fell, she also wondered, as people came and went, some reflecting soberly on what had happened, others less so, where Aidan was. Since she'd left him outside the sheriff's offices in the city, all she'd had was a hastily scrawled note, promising he'd return as soon as he could.

Why did her heart quicken painfully when she thought of those words? Was it because his notion of soon didn't match hers? Or was it the feeling of foreboding they conjured?

Almost as if she was a witch and sensed an evil spell had been cast.

Curled in her da's armchair, Sorcha cupped her quaich and gazed dreamily into the fire. Outside, the wind howled and rain smacked the windows as if a pagan god was wielding a whip. Between blows, Sorcha could just detect the reassuring rumble of the ocean. She tried to gather her thoughts, aware she'd drunk too many drams to do this altogether successfully.

The detritus of the evening's festivities was scattered around her. Glasses, quaichs, greasy platters, half-eaten bannocks, crumbs littering the floor. A lump of cheese looked most unappetising melting by the fire; what remained of the bowl of neeps had turned grey. Next door's chickens would appreciate what remained. Remembering the way Crabby had snuffled along the floor, licking up scraps, they were lucky there was anything left to toss their way. The memory of the dog's golden head and wagging tail made her smile. Content to roam between legs, accepting pats, all Crabby really wanted was some attention and a full belly. Like most men, Sorcha thought. Most men except for one.

Her mind drifted back to Aidan and she marvelled that such a man had come — nae, ridden — into her life.

For some reason, thinking of Aidan made her conjure an image of Reverend Cowper. There was another man who wanted more from life, but whereas what Aidan wanted was based around love and helping others, what Cowper most desired was all about power and controlling people.

Squinting, she looked at the clock on the mantelpiece. It was well past midnight, now Sunday — no longer, in her mind, the Lord's day, but Cowper's. She wondered what treats he'd have in store for his congregation, how he would seek to malign the fishwives and link them to witchcraft this time. Would he know about their wee party? What was she thinking? Of course he would.

Finishing her drink, she was disappointed to find only a few drops remaining in the bottle. She'd really had enough. Not enough to push thoughts of Cowper away and not nearly enough to send her to bed. How could she sleep when she still hoped and prayed Aidan would arrive?

She turned to look out the window again. Gusts shook the house and rattled the glass, though the rain had eased. It was a wild night. No one in their right mind would be abroad, certainly not navigating the roads between here and the city.

There was a raspy cough, the jingle of harness. Sorcha sat up, the room temporarily spinning.

The door opened and in swept Aidan. Drenched, his hair was stuck to his face, his coat sodden. As he plucked at the buttons, Sorcha could see his full-dress uniform beneath. It at least was dry. Instead of taking his coat off, Aidan strode towards her, gripping her hands and pulling her up into his arms.

'You're all wet!' exclaimed Sorcha, laughing but not really objecting as he held her close. When he didn't speak, didn't release her immediately, she grew still.

She placed her hands on his chest and pushed herself away slightly, searching his eyes. 'What is it? What's wrong?'

'Wrong, why would anything be wrong?'

'Och, I don't know,' she said, extracting herself from his arms and gesturing to his apparel. 'Maybe the fact you're drookit and dripping on my floor, or that you've ridden that damned road,' she pointed in a vague direction, 'in the middle of the night in this weather. Risking your neck. And then you have that look.' She stood on tiptoe, screwing up her eyes and bringing her face close to his.

'You're drunk,' he said, swallowing a grin.

'Damn right I am. What else would I be? I'm all alone since Nettie escorted poor Thom home. I wanted to be awake in case you turned up, so made that bottle —' she jabbed the air with a finger, 'keep me company.' She swung away from him, her arms flailing momentarily. 'I'll get you a drink and we can celebrate my freedom together now you're here.' She found a quaich, sniffed it, peered inside and tipped what remained into a bowl. Finding a bottle of whisky that wasn't drained, she poured. Most of it went into the cup.

'Here,' she said, thrusting it towards him, licking the back of her hand as a wave of liquid splashed over the rim.

Aidan took it.

'Now, sit, sit. Drink. Tell me why your connel —' she giggled, 'col-o-nel wanted to see you.'

Putting down the cup carefully without touching the contents, Aidan took Sorcha's hands. 'That's exactly what I've come to do.'

There was something in his tone, in the gentle way he held her hands, that made Sorcha's heart beat faster. The sensible part of her began to work against the treacle in her mind. Why was Aidan in dress uniform? Why was it dry when his coat was so wet? Where was Liath?

She glanced over his shoulder, but could see nothing of his horse in the darkness outside.

Propelled to a chair, Sorcha waited while Aidan brushed the crumbs from it before she sat. He knelt beside her. Pushing her hair from her forehead, he gave a sad smile. 'I'm afraid, Sorcha, I've some news.'

'You're not here to tell me Edinburgh want to lock me up now, are you?' She folded her arms and pouted.

'Nae.' He smiled softly and found her hands again, unfolding her arms. 'Nothing like that. I'm here to tell you I've been posted.'

'Posted? Like a parcel?' Sorcha heard the word and refused it. The sister of a soldier, she knew damn well what 'posted' meant.

Aidan didn't answer, but tilted his head and ran his thumb over her lips. She shivered.

Sober now, the clouds of whisky and thick memory swiftly thinning, she kissed his thumb then covered the hand that cupped one side of her face with her own. 'Where?' Her heart was so loud in her ears, she felt sure he must be able to hear it.

'I'm to join the Duke of Marlborough's forces in Bavaria.'

'Bavaria?' Sorcha felt as if she'd been punched in the stomach. It was hard to breathe. 'When?' she whispered.

Aidan tried to take her in his arms, but she resisted. 'When? Tell me.'

'At dawn. We sail with the tide.'

Her vision swam. Instead of Aidan, it was Robbie, proudly announcing to her and their mor that he was off to fight for the duke in Flanders. Darling Robbie, the last of her brothers. Her brother whom she never saw again...

Pulling her knees up to her chest, she buried her face in them, wrapping her arms around her legs to prevent him coming near. She was a fortress.

Instead of moving away, Aidan's arms encircled all of her. 'Sergeant Thatcher and I rode from Edinburgh as soon as my orders were signed. I wasn't meant to leave the barracks, but I had to see you, explain in person.'

She could feel his breath against her, the pulse in his neck where it rested against her forearm.

'Why now? I thought you were needed here, in Pittenweem.' *I need you.*

'Apparently there's a treaty being negotiated and they require officers accustomed to dealing with the French, the Spanish too.'

'Why you? There must be others.'

Aidan gave a self-deprecating laugh. 'Och, there are, lass. And I believe my name cropping up was no accident, nor was the approval for this new posting. I think someone arranged for this to happen. The order was from on high. Not even my superiors knew from whence it came, but I have my suspicions.'

Sorcha raised her head and met his eyes. The answer was writ large. 'Cowper.'

Aidan grimaced. 'I've no evidence, not yet, but that's what I think. I don't ken who he knows or how he did it, but I'll get to the bottom of it.'

'Not that learning how he did it will change anything, will it?'

'Not this time.'

Sorcha frowned. A sour taste rose in her mouth that had very little to do with all the whisky she'd consumed. A sour taste tinged with needles of anxiety. 'The bastard. He's paying you back for what you did for us, for me. For alerting Edinburgh, for writing all those letters and ensuring justice was served.'

'Aye. Or —' Aidan hesitated.

'Or what?'

Half-standing, Aidan lifted her into his arms just as he slid onto the seat, depositing her onto his lap. Waiting until she rested her head against his chest, and he was able to stroke her hair, he continued. 'Or… and, Sorcha, this is what I fear most, the reverend is planning something and wants me out of the way.'

Sorcha raised her head and gazed at him. 'What could he possibly be planning?' She didn't tell him he was merely saying what she suspected. She didn't want to alarm him. Not now, when he was about to leave and could do naught. Her heart ached. For him, for her. Oh, how she would miss him. *Please, God, if You be there, keep him safe.*

Aidan shook his head. 'I don't ken, lass. But I want you to promise me you'll be careful. You, Nettie and the rest. He is a wicked man, Cowper, and I wouldn't put it past him to try something else. He's angry about those pardons. He's angry and his pride has been bruised. He'll take it worse than a personal slight. He'll see those acquittals as being against God and something it is his religious duty to correct.'

A sea of sorrow churned in Sorcha's breast. 'I hope you're wrong, Aidan.'

'Aye, me and all, lass. But in case I'm not, promise me you'll be cautious.'

Sorcha twisted in his arms and put one hand on his chest so she could study him properly. 'I promise, Aidan. But there's something I would ask you to promise me.'

'Anything.'

'Promise you'll come home.' Her vision swam. Her throat became thick. 'That you'll come home *to me*.'

There was a beat as Aidan swallowed. Sorcha felt her ribs tighten.

'Och, lass, I promise that and more.'

Sorcha couldn't speak, so curled herself back in his arms. She couldn't look at him. She was afraid she'd see in his face what they both knew to be true: that he'd lied.

THIRTY-FIVE

*... how hard it is to root out bad principles once espoused by the rabble,
and how dangerous a thing it is to be at their mercy...*

— A Letter From a Gentleman of Fife to
his Friend in Edinburgh, *1705*

Sorcha didn't sleep — neither did Aidan. They chose instead to lie in
each other's arms and talk softly as the night deepened and grew colder,
the house creaking as the relentless wind pushed and prodded and the
sea crashed and moiled in the distance. Oft times they clung without
speaking, their hearts murmuring what their mouths could not.

When Aidan donned his uniform before the embers of the fire that
frigid, windswept dawn, Sorcha watched him from the bed, admiring
his perfect, lean form. The broad shoulders, the dark hair so fine and
neat across his chest, as if a barber had cut it to order, or a farmer had
scythed it. She loved nothing better than to run her fingers along it,
revelling in its softness against the hard body beneath. As she studied
him, her heart tender, tears threatening to spill as she thought of the
farewell they would all too soon be making, she tried to imprint him
on her memory. Curling her arm around his pillow, she brought it
close, inhaling the scent of him, wondering if, like her mor, her da and

brothers, that would be all she'd have left — fragmented memories of intimate moments, the fragrance that was peculiarly his, until that too faded.

Not wanting his last memory of her to be of red, swollen eyes and a miserable mouth, she pushed her sorrow away, climbed out of bed and warmed some milk for him, adding the last of the whisky to his cup.

When the time came to say goodbye, they stood in the middle of the room and said nothing. They simply cleaved to each other — Sorcha, as if she were drowning and he her only chance of salvation.

His kiss, when it came, was chaste and warm, soft, yet in it were a thousand promises, and she knew in her soul he intended to keep them all. Kissing him back, she made sure he knew she felt the same. Her body was pliant against his, but her mind was unyielding as she railed against God and the fates that once more someone was being taken from her, that her love was being cruelly tested. She wanted to shake a fist at the heavens, rain curses upon Him and any who professed Him good, but was afraid that if she did, Aidan would be punished.

While she might deserve the wrath of the Lord, he did not.

Just as he had the first night she met him, almost a year ago, he disappeared into the gloom. If he looked back, she didn't know, but stayed by the door all the same. It wasn't until she finally went inside and stood by the fire that she felt cold.

Cold and alone.

As she dressed for kirk the last Sunday in November, two weeks after Aidan departed, Sorcha wondered, as she did every moment of every day, what he was doing. Had he reached Marlborough's forces yet? Not knowing exactly where he was to join the general, she had no idea of the distance he had to cover or how long it would take. In her mind, he was with the great man, drinking whisky, enjoying a coffee, safe and warm in a tent, Liath and a corporal with him. The one blessing in all this was that Sergeant Thatcher had remained and been placed in charge of the troops until a replacement arrived; she knew Aidan had asked him to watch over her.

She wished Nettie was here to help lace her best dress — an emerald green and turquoise creation her mother had made for her. Her mor always said it reflected her eyes. Smoothing the skirts, she ran a comb through her curls, winding her locks into orderliness at the nape of her neck. Pinning a scarf over her head, she studied herself in the looking glass.

Her skin was smooth again, the marks that she'd borne out of the Tolbooth were gone. Though the drave was still meagre and farmers were charging hefty prices for their produce, her diet was much improved. Her body had slowly healed and she'd lost the stick-thin, waif-like look they'd all worn when they emerged from captivity. Nettie looked as though nothing had happened to her. It was only if you caught her face in repose and saw the darkness behind her eyes that you realised this was a woman with bleak secrets. A raging anger, too. It was the same with Beatrix, and it didn't take much to make either of them snap and utter words that could be misconstrued. So afeared were Lillie Wallace and Margaret Jack of being found guilty again by association that after Sorcha's celebration they'd left the Weem to look for work in another port town — the further afield, the better. Who could blame them? Not now Cowper's sermons had become more pointed than ever. It was as if Aidan's departure had shaken something loose in the man, something beyond reason.

And today she had to listen to another of them. God, if only she could plead a megrim or, better still, claim Dagny needed her in St Andrew's. But she was neither sick nor needed, least of all by her sister. If anyone needed her it was Nettie, Beatrix, Isobel, Nicolas, Janet and the other fishwives, and the women and men who refused to be bullied by a furious beast wearing a clerical collar and his threats of God's wrath.

Glancing at the clock, Sorcha sighed. The service would start soon. She must be there lest Cowper fine her or worse, use her absence against her. With one last look around the room, ensuring the fire was a warm glow, she grabbed her shawl and headed outside.

Reverend Cowper's sermon was worse than Sorcha anticipated. Seated at the back of the kirk, she'd come late and was squeezed between Callum Gregson, a former councilman and mercer, his widowed daughter Caitlin, and the village doctor — a title generously bestowed rather than earned. Everyone understood that anything of use Duncan McLeod knew he'd learned from his mother and not the university he'd attended for less than a year in Edinburgh.

Grateful for the cold air coming in from the rear of the kirk, which meant the doctor's terrible body odour and the reek of wine from Mr Gregson were at least bearable, Sorcha looked for Nettie among the parishioners. Against the Anster doctor's advice, Thom had gone away on business, so Nettie was coming to stay again. It was a moment before she spotted her, halfway down, Isobel on one side and Beatrix on the other. So much for keeping their distance in public...

Contemplating the women's refusal to be pushed around by the reverend or to bow under the weight of the parishioners' judgement, Sorcha was torn between admiring their courage and being afraid lest it come back to torment them. Thus preoccupied she didn't immediately focus on what the reverend was all but shouting from his pulpit. Accustomed to his booming tone, she was well able to cancel it out. Rather, it was the way first Mr Gregson and then Dr McLeod stiffened beside her then tried to move away, whereas earlier they were practically on her lap, that drew her attention.

'Let not the wrath of God fall upon you, for He sends these monsters to earth to test us. He waits to see who will fall into temptation and become possessed, allowing demons to take their bodies, and who will resist, who will fight.' The reverend slammed his fist on the lectern. The first few rows jumped. It would have been funny had his words not been laden with deadly portent.

Sorcha's heart drummed in her ears. Her hands became knots in her lap.

Lowering his voice, Reverend Cowper gripped the sides of the pulpit and leaned forward. 'Who can forget the agonies inflicted on one of God's own by the devil's very servants? Who can forget the suffering of Peter Morton?'

There was a wave of murmurs. A few turned to regard Peter where he sat, eyes downcast, in the middle of the kirk.

'Think on this,' continued Cowper. 'The very same people who share this kirk with us, who walk the streets beside us, with whom we break bread and so much more, are responsible for what happened to the lad. It doesn't matter what those far away in Edinburgh declare. The women are guilty from their own mouths, by their own signed admissions. I cannot forget that. Can you?'

There was a wave of loud chatter, some shaking of heads.

Sorcha's heart sank. Nettie's glance swept the room.

'Nae. We can't forget. Nor must we. The good Lord tells us, we must remain vigilant. We must look to each other, be wary of those who would do us harm even as they work to hide their nefarious intentions.' Again, his eyes searched the crowd, only this time they lingered on Nicolas, on Beatrix. Sorcha began to slide down in her seat.

'You see, not only does Satan create witches, but he creates doubters. He fashions those who refuse to believe in witchcraft, something we all ken to be true. They are like the Sadducees of auld and would tear us from our faith, from God. Why? So they too can recruit us into Satan's army.' He gave a bitter smile. 'Have we not seen this for ourselves? Together, the witches and their associates, the doubters, sow seeds of malice in little towns like ours. They turn loved ones against each other, friends become foes. In the meantime, witchcraft and its foul practitioners thrive unpunished. Is this right? I ask you. Is this what the good Lord intends?'

There was a murmur of 'Nae,' which quickly rose to a crescendo. Some shifted in their pews, looking askance at their neighbours. The gap between Sorcha and the men was growing. Dr McLeod looked as if he would stand in the aisle.

Reverend Cowper paused, his chest heaving. 'It isn't right. And if we needed more proof of Satan's work, look at the poor drave. Where are the fish? Where is the sea's bounty? Why is His briny larder, which has sustained us for centuries, being closed to us in the Weem now? What is God telling us?'

Sorcha wanted to protest, point out that the drave had been bad for seasons and it wasn't only Pittenweem feeling the pressure.

'And what of our crops? The poor crofters and farmers who are forced to plough ruined fields, sow what they'll never reap? They too are starving. Those we once relied upon to feed us when the sea was barren can barely feed themselves.'

The murmur grew to a roar.

'And what about the weather?' called one parishioner. Sorcha couldn't see who.

'I don't remember it being like this in November before,' added another.

'If it weren't for your wife forever hailing you, you couldn't remember your name, Hamish Fletcher,' countered someone. Sorcha could have sworn it was Therese. There were a few chuckles.

Rather than silencing his flock, the reverend relished the commotion.

When there was a lull, he continued. 'And then there be the deaths from war.' Sorcha's heart leapt. 'We have always paid dearly for our service to the English Crown, no more so than now, as many of you here are all too aware. May God bless your sacrifice.'

Sorcha's head spun. Not only was the reverend treading close to treason with these words, pretending a Jacobite sympathy he'd never possessed, but what did he know? He couldn't have heard anything yet, not from Bavaria. He must be talking about France, about the losses they'd sustained in other wars, before even Robbie went. Nettie turned in her seat and caught her eye. She shook her head. Sorcha understood. It was enough to calm her. The reverend was merely blaming any ill-fortune, even deaths that were years old, on witchcraft — on the women. Couldn't the parishioners see what he was about?

'The officials in Edinburgh said the lasses weren't responsible for what befell Peter Morton,' cried out someone else. It was Moira Fraser, God bless her. Not all were being gulled.

The congregation quietened. The talk softened. There were some nods, timid smiles.

'That be true, reverend. They were found not guilty of malfeasance.' Much to Sorcha's surprise, it was Nicolas's husband who spoke. There were grunts of agreement. Someone leaned forward and squeezed Nettie's shoulder. Dr McLeod took his foot out of the aisle, sliding back towards Sorcha. Mr Gregson relaxed.

'Aye, that's so,' said the reverend amiably. 'The women we locked in the Tolbooth, from whom we extracted confessions, were found not guilty of malfeasance towards Peter Morton and released.' He gave a scoffing laugh. Some joined him. As quickly as his laugh began, it ended. 'But I ask you all to dwell on this.' He drew himself up. 'While the officials said there was no *firm* proof they harmed the lad, at no point did they say the women were innocent. They never said they *weren't* witches.'

He allowed that thought to take root.

'And if we let but one witch go unpunished, then we are no better than the Sadducees. Like them, we condemn our Christian souls to hell. Beyond this,' he continued without drawing breath, 'remember, it is against the law and a capital offence to help — even unknowingly — or consult a witch. What constitutes help? Well, it comes in many forms, from providing comfort in times of woe to giving sustenance, even the kind that is purchased. Help can be a friendly smile, assistance carrying a heavy load, or even offering a sympathetic word. Think on that, think on that.'

By seeding doubt, the wily bawbag was warning people not to sell goods, even food, to those believed to be witches — or to buy it from them. To turn their backs on them in every regard, to deny them common courtesy or risk being condemned.

There was a deep silence broken only by the sound of the sea.

Casting around to see if anyone wanted to add anything, the reverend continued, asking for God's forgiveness of the Weem, offering a prayer for the fishermen and the soldiers fighting for Queen and country before a last hymn and dismissing everyone to their Sunday.

Sorcha resisted the urge to bolt from the kirk. Striding past the reverend and his eldest daughter with barely a greeting, she waited for

Nettie and Beatrix on Cove Wynd. Clutching her shawl against the cold wind and the icy blood in her veins, she noted that fewer people than ever acknowledged her. Some even went so far as to turn in the opposite direction, even though she knew their houses lay past where she stood. Others lingered around the kirk door, aligning themselves with the reverend.

Her heart sank into her gelid, worn boots.

When Nettie and Beatrix finally emerged, Nettie was stopped by the reverend who, resting his hand on her arm, whispered something. At first, Nettie gave a derisive sound that might have been mirth, but when he continued, her face paled and she staggered. Beatrix, who was standing next to her, wagged an angry finger at him, eliciting a mocking laugh while the other parishioners recoiled in shock. Instead of remaining together, the friends parted ways without a farewell.

Before Sorcha could ask what was wrong — aside from the obvious — Nettie took her arm and propelled her towards the cottage.

'What is it?' asked Sorcha quietly.

'Not yet,' murmured Nettie. 'Wait.'

The Robertson family turned aside as they passed, pretending they hadn't seen them.

'Good day to you, Mr and Mrs Robertson, and your bairns,' said Nettie pointedly.

Sorcha greeted them as well. They might ignore her, but she wouldn't disregard people she'd known her whole life, no matter what they were thinking. No matter what the reverend encouraged them to do.

It wasn't until they were inside Sorcha's cottage that Nettie spoke. Hefting her burlap onto a chair and turning her back to the fire, she faced Sorcha.

Her eyes were blazing, her cheeks grey.

'Nettie? What is it? What did he say to you?'

'That bastard,' spat Nettie. 'Can you believe how he twisted the Edinburgh verdict?'

'Aye,' said Sorcha contemptuously. 'I can. And before the entire congregation. I also witnessed how many were prepared to accept his version.'

Nettie closed her eyes briefly and sighed deeply. When she opened them again, she offered Sorcha a hopeful look. 'Do you have any whisky left, hen?'

Sorcha peered around. She'd had a wee tipple the night before, enough to know all her supplies were drunk.

'Nae bother,' said Nettie. 'Though I fear we're both going to need some after I tell you what the blaggard dared to say to me and Beatrix.'

Sorcha sank into a seat and waited for Nettie to do the same.

'He said he's going to do his duty by God and his flock to save the Weem. When I asked, "What from?" he said, "The likes of you and your witch friends." I started to laugh, Sorcha, even though his words felt like hoarfrost in my blood. That's when he grabbed my elbow and said, "Enjoy the cold while you can, Mrs White, for where I am sending you, it is damn hot."'

Nettie rubbed her arm and stared mournfully at Sorcha.

'He's up to something, hen — and it's not just trying to convince the parish our pardons are meaningless, I tell you. Just when I thought this was all over and we could return to our lives, he's planning another salvo in this war.'

Sorcha reached for Nettie's hand and held it tightly. 'A war against *us*. Not witches, but women.'

'Aye,' said Nettie. 'Only this time, I'm afraid he's going to win.'

With a sinking heart, Sorcha knew she was afraid, too.

PART THREE
November 1704 to 30th January 1705

They asked her how she came to say any thing that was not true; she cried out 'Alas, alas, I behoved to say so, to please the minister and bailies;' and in the meantime, she begged for Christ's sake not to tell that she had said so, else she would be murdered.

— Privy Council Minute, at Edinburgh, 15th day of February 1705, *The Annals of Pittenweem, Being Notes and Extracts from the Ancient Records of that Burgh*

Thou shall not suffer a witch to live.

— Exodus 22:18 *King James Bible*

THIRTY-SIX

He be a muckle sumph.
(He is a stupid person.)

$\mathcal{A}$lexander McGregor was a simple man. A fisherman for as many years as he'd been alive on God's good earth, he did his job, went to the kirk regularly and, if he enjoyed more than a dram or two each night in the tavern and within his own four walls, God would forgive him.

All the same, he couldn't help but think on Reverend Cowper's words that Sunday. For months now, the reverend had spoken of witchcraft and witches as if they were striding the streets of the village day and night. As if it was just a matter of time before the likes of Janet Cornfoot or those others who'd been accused ran amok and they were all killed in their beds — or worse, recruited into Satan's dark army to wreak havoc. The very notion made Alexander shiver and pull the thin blanket tighter across his shoulders.

Still, what the reverend said that day made sense. Alexander couldn't remember the drave ever being so poor. Admittedly, in years gone by the catch had been so bad they'd been forced to take the boats into the deeper waters, risking storms and high seas. But doing that made little difference any more. Inshore or out past the Isle of May, the silver darlings, cod and other fish were scarce. No wonder some of the fish-wives had taken it upon themselves to wander the coast, seeking work where they could find it. They had to make a living too, didn't they? There was barely enough work to sustain those who remained — those fishwives who'd no choice but to gut, sort and mend the nets beside the suspect witches. He shuddered at the thought of the danger those women were in.

His stomach growled. It did no good thinking about fish, about food. It reminded him of how empty his larder, his belly. Pouring himself another dram, he poked the fire, the peat crumbling and send-ing sparks and smoke into the room. At least he was warm, which was more than could be said for some. And there was the reverend, asking for donations to repair the pier again. What they'd managed to fix with the money gained from Thomas Brown's seized property and the incomers gawking at the witches barely made a difference. And now that had dried up. Christ, folk could barely put food in their pots let alone part with coin to save rotting wood and crumbling stone, much as the village might need the damn pier fixed.

What if the reverend was right and all this ill-fortune wasn't God's will but Satan's? What if witches *were* causing it, all while living and working beside them, pretending to be affable and godly while under-mining everything with their charms and evil spells? Taking another swig of his drink, he thought about the women who'd been impris-oned in the Tolbooth. Some said they'd suffered greatly. He recalled how Beatrix Laing looked when she emerged from St Fillan's Cave. He didn't recognise her, so shrunken and pale had she become. Hard to believe it was the same carline who'd bark at you if you dared look at her twice. Nicolas Lawson had been carried out of the Tolbooth, the damage to her legs so great, some said she'd never walk again. Yet she did. How did she recover so well when he knew fishermen who'd been bitten from the frost to lose their limbs?

Filling his cracked quaich again, Alexander dwelled on the women. Why, that Sorcha McIntyre, for all she came out a bag of bones with her hair shorn, in a matter of weeks she looked bonnie again, bonnie enough that the captain bedded her — or so rumour had it. Same with Nettie Horseburgh. Nor had a spell in gaol softened that woman's sharp tongue. According to Camron MacGille, it hadn't blunted Janet Cornfoot's either. She'd harangue and abuse whoever came to the cave to bring her sustenance. Mind you, if she was eating like him, kale and neep soup day in day out without the comfort of a fire, bed or whisky, no wonder she gave the guards a tongue-lashing.

He'd heard from the eldest Cowper lad that Margaret Jack and Lillie Wallace had left the Weem. Gordon Jack had gone with his wife and taken his long lines with him — a loss that would be hard to bear. Was that the witches' intention, to make everyone in the Weem suffer? To make everyone blame God and each other before turning to their Dark Master? That's what the reverend believed.

There was a shout outside followed by a short sharp scream. One of the Browning girls by the sound of it. She was always crying now she was wed to Gavan Wright. Fond of his ale and using his fists was the story. Another wail pierced the walls. He wished he could stopper up his ears. Maybe another dram would help.

Downing it quickly and refilling his cup, he stared at the amber fluid, aware of the fire burning on the periphery of his vision. A movement outside his window forced his head up. There were hushed voices. They reminded him of something…

Rain began to fall, gently at first, then it hammered the window, turning the sky dark, blocking out the light shining from the house across the way. The fire guttered briefly and shadows loomed. Not long until Hogmanay again. The last one had been bitter as well. And there'd been showers — right plouts as he recalled. What he didn't remember was being quite so hungry, so cold and maudlin…

He'd invited Isobel Adam to come to his house last Hogmanay to mend some of his shirts. Difficult to credit she was one of the witches, pretty little golden-haired thing. She'd been in the kirk today and all. He'd caught her staring at Peter Morton, a peculiar expression on her face. An expression that plucked at his memory…

Alexander sat up suddenly, whisky spilling over the lip of his cup. He sucked it off his hand. Try as hard as he could, he never remembered opening his door to Isobel. First he recalled was waking to find her standing over him. He'd grabbed her. She'd screamed and run out before he could reassure her he meant no harm. She'd just frightened him, that's all.

But what if it was more than that?

Isobel had been holding a needle and a piece of fabric. Screwing his eyes shut, he was sure what she'd actually been holding was a doll, a doll bearing his likeness that she was about to prick with that long needle.

His eyes opened.

She hadn't just screamed, had she? Words had spilled out of her mouth. Frantic, hurried words that, try as he might, he couldn't follow nor understand. Gibberish, it was. With a thundering heart, he remembered... there were coal-black figures cavorting behind her. He'd assumed it was the fire throwing shapes against the wall, but what if there was another explanation?

He became ice-cold before a raging heat filled his veins. She'd been casting a spell on him. That was why nothing had gone right for him all year, or for the rest of the crew on the boat that employed him. If he thought about it, he wagered he could pinpoint all the bad in his life to that night — Hogmanay.

Hogmanay and Isobel Adam.

Alexander leaned forward and stared at the smouldering peat, trying his hardest to recollect everything. Reverend Cowper's words from a Sunday a few weeks ago overlaid the images that were dancing about his head; they mingled with the warnings the reverend had repeated that very morning. 'Nae person shall seek any help from or consult with any users of witchcraft... on pain of death.'

Leaping to his feet, Alexander finished his drink and reached for his coat. He had to tell someone what he now knew to be true. His ill-fortune and that of the Weem *was* because of witches. It was because of Isobel Adam and all those she consorted with. She'd ensorcelled him in an attempt to lure him into her demonic ways. He'd woken in time and thus broken the spell and saved himself.

It was time to save others. To save the Weem. Just as young Peter Morton had tried to do. As Patrick Cowper tried even now. God bless them.

As he wrenched open the door, he heard the sobs of young Joanna Browning. Folk were peering through their windows and standing on their stoops despite the cold, not knowing whether to go to her aid but hoping to prevent worse happening. He ignored them all and strode down the wynd towards the manse. He had to tell the reverend. If he didn't, then just like Cowper said, he was the same as those who aided and abetted the witches — he would be seen as one of them. A conspirator.

If he didn't reveal what he now remembered as clearly as if it were yesterday, then he would be punished just as Reverend Cowper said — as a witch.

Punished unto death.

THIRTY-SEVEN

A drew gaun aboot.
(An unidentifiable illness attacking people all over town.)

$\mathcal{W}$hen Patrick learned Alexander McGregor was at the door asking to see him, his first instinct was to send the ragabash away. It had been a while since he'd last enjoyed time alone with Peter Morton. God knew, the lad wanted to forget what happened in Edinburgh — they both did.

Not even his weekly entreaties from the pulpit about witchcraft had yielded the results he'd wished, never mind what the congregation's reactions had promised. He knew folk were fearful and, as winter loomed and their food supplies shrank and the old parts of the pier continued to fall into disrepair, he hoped they'd be keen to attach the blame to someone. They always had in the past. This time he intended it would be the witches.

But McGregor had never come to the manse to seek him out before and, despite the lateness of the hour and his young companion, Patrick's curiosity was whetted. When the fisherman was brought to the study, reeking of whisky and the musty smell of damp clothes seldom washed and dried by a fire, all tinged with the odour of fish and the ocean, he wondered what had dragged him out on a night like this.

Wringing his cap in his hands, eyes darting, feet shuffling, McGregor was as disoriented in the study as the reverend would have been on his boat.

The reverend rose from behind his desk and crossed the room to direct his visitor towards the fireplace. The last thing he wanted was to have the malodourous man dripping all over the furniture.

'Well, Alexander,' he said, as the fisherman stood with his back to the flames, gazing in bewilderment at the picture of the crucifixion on the wall opposite. 'What can I do for you this dreich night?'

Mesmerised by the painting, Alexander seemed lost for words. Nae, thought Patrick, looking at him closely, it wasn't so much he'd lost the power of speech, as he was afraid of what he had to say.

'Come, lad,' said the reverend, though Alexander was of an age with him. 'Anything you say to me is as if you were speaking to the Almighty Himself. Whatever ails you, you can share.'

Alexander's eyes widened before they slid to Peter sitting quietly in front of the desk. 'It's not you I be worried about talking in front of, reverend, so much as the laddie.'

'Whatever you have to say to me can be said before Peter. He's as trustworthy as the sea is cold. He's been forged in the hottest of fires and emerged unscathed.'

Alexander raised a brow.

'The fires of witchcraft,' said the reverend solemnly.

Alexander swiftly moved his hands from the small of his back to clasp them over his belly, his cap strangled between them. 'It's upon that very matter that I'm here, reverend.'

The reverend's heart quickened. 'Oh?' He hoped Alexander couldn't see how thrilled he was.

Peter sat up in his chair.

'Come, come,' said the reverend, walking towards his desk. 'Why are you standing over there? Make yourself comfortable. Take a seat, take a seat.' He led Alexander to a chair. 'Don't worry about a bit of water upon your clothes. Peter, pour the man a wee drink.'

Once Alexander had a glass in his hand and had downed at least half the contents, the reverend propped himself on the edge of his desk, folded his arms, and tried to appear casual. 'Now, what is it that you wish to tell me?'

As Alexander voiced what had happened last Hogmanay, how he woke to find Isobel Adam casting a spell over him, Patrick wanted to shout with joy. At last. Here was the proof he needed.

The more Alexander spoke, gleaning the grave interest of the reverend and Peter Morton, it was evident he began embellishing. He said how he understood, in light of what the reverend preached in the kirk that morning and many more Sundays besides, that Isobel and her accomplices had summoned a demon to dispatch him or worse. 'Do to me what was done to you, Peter,' said Alexander, looking at the lad. 'But when her efforts failed, she must have done something so I couldn't remember. Not until today. Not until your words, reverend, juddered the memory free.'

Patrick wasted no time but found a quill, inkhorn and paper. Pulling up another chair, he sat beside Alexander, glancing occasionally at Peter, who was working not to show his relief. If Alexander was tormented by the witches as well, then it cast a whole new light on what had happened to him.

As he questioned the fisherman carefully, Patrick made sure to catch the details. It was remarkable what, with a little prodding, the man could recall.

'There were others with Isobel, Alexander?' asked Patrick softly as the man finished, staring into his empty cup.

At a sign from the reverend, Peter swiftly refilled it.

'I... believe so, reverend, but I can't be sure who they were.'

'Was Nettie Horseburgh one of them? She's a good friend to Isobel after all. You might remember, they were locked in the Tolbooth together.'

'And sat near each other in the kirk today,' added Peter. Patrick cast him an approving look.

'Aye, aye,' nodded Alexander. 'She was there. I remember now.'

'And what of Beatrix Laing?' asked Patrick. Peter nodded encouragingly. 'It's unlikely Isobel would dare do something without that auld witch to guide her.'

'Beatrix was there too.' Alexander gave a violent tremor. He then named Lillie Wallace and her friend Margaret Jack — they'd been imprisoned in the Tolbooth. Why? Because they were witches. Witches stuck together so as to use their collective powers to cause harm — wasn't that what the reverend said?

Patrick wrote the names down. 'And what of Sorcha McIntyre? Did you see her, Alexander?'

Peter's eyes flickered. Patrick knew the boy was torn. But whereas Peter, in his foolish young heart, still carried a torch for Sorcha and wished she could be his, Patrick wanted to rid himself of the temptation she posed, not only to himself, or Peter, but to all the men of the Weem.

He also saw how the love the lad thought he felt for the fishwife had twisted upon itself. So long as Peter didn't learn that Aidan Ross had been sent to war and, most likely, his death, he could use this jealousy to his advantage.

Time to put it to the test. 'Did you not say Sorcha was one of those who tormented you the most, Peter?' asked the reverend.

Peter raised his chin and gazed steadily at Patrick. Doubt marched across his face and Patrick could see he was recalling her lovely features.

'Does she not enchant men, Peter, and use her female wiles to bewitch them?' The reverend waited. Rain pummelled the windows. Something thudded deep within the house.

'Did you not tell me, Peter,' added Patrick, 'that she has bewitched a soldier so he has no choice but to do her bidding and that of the other witches?'

Peter took a deep breath; a flicker of annoyance drew his brows together.

Patrick knew he was treading on dangerous ground, revealing a secret like that, but he had to risk it.

'I did say that,' said Peter reluctantly.

'Do you not think she could have been trying, along with Isobel and the others, to bewitch poor Alexander here? That he might have been the first of their victims, even before you? What if the truth is that they waited until Sorcha McIntyre returned to the Weem and then pounced? Imagine what the men in Edinburgh would say to that. How differently they would regard you once that information came to light.'

Alexander was gripping his glass so tightly, his knuckles were white.

Peter wriggled his legs, shifted on the seat as if something uncomfortable was upon the cushion. His lower lip thrust out. 'All I ken is that Sorcha McIntyre be no ordinary woman. She be —'

'Aye, aye,' cried Alexander, his fist thumping the arm of his chair. He slammed down his empty glass. 'She *was* there. I remember. I remember everything. They came together, all of them, Thomas Brown among them, and burst into my cottage. They called upon the devil to do me harm. They thought I was asleep, but I was in a trance and saw them. I saw them all.'

Patrick stopped writing. He put down the pen slowly and stared at Alexander McGregor. Why, this was far better than he had hoped. The muckle sumph even named Thomas Brown. How could his death be deemed unlawful if he was a witch? If he was among those hellbent on tormenting McGregor? This would clear both him and the bailies of any wrongdoing in either his imprisonment or death. Patrick wanted to cheer.

Reaching out, he held Alexander's shoulder reassuringly, much as a proud father would a son. 'What you have done here tonight, Alexander, is a brave thing. 'Tis righteous.' Alexander's cheeks suffused with colour. 'God will reward you for this.'

The reverend regarded Peter, who stared at the floor, his face unreadable, then the fisherman, whose bloodshot eyes shone with unshed tears. Rising to his feet, he removed his hand from Alexander's jacket.

'Between you both, you've saved not only your own souls, but the souls of every person in this village. God be praised.'

'God be praised,' said Peter and Alexander in unison.

With a grim smile, the reverend went behind his desk and found a fresh piece of paper. He sat and began to write again.

'What are you doing, reverend?' asked Alexander, pushing his glass along the desk, a clear signal of what he'd prefer to be doing.

Without looking up, the reverend answered, 'I'm writing to the bailies.'

'The bailies? What for?'

'To do what must be done.' He raised his head. 'It's clear that I was right all along. Edinburgh was swift to judge, not the witches, but me. The council. Swift to judge you, Peter. Now, with Alexander's testimony, we will be vindicated and the village saved.' Signing the page with a flourish, he read over what he'd written and sanded it.

Peter poured himself and Alexander another drink.

Patrick tipped the candle and watched as wax dropped onto the back of the folded paper. He waited for it to cool slightly, then pressed his seal against it and gave a satisfied look. 'Take this, lad,' he said to Peter. 'Go straight to Bailie Cook's house and make sure he reads it now.'

'May I ask what it says, sir?' asked Peter, putting down his glass and sliding the letter beneath his jacket.

The reverend stood up and stared past the men, through the window and into the night.

'It's an order for the arrest of Isobel Adam. She's clearly the chief tormentor here and thus the one we must break. Once we've questioned her and extracted the names of her accomplices — those you've revealed, Alexander — then we can move on them.

'This time, there'll be no one to help them, no one to plead mercy on their behalf. This time —' his eyes took on a faraway look, 'they'll not escape the Lord's justice. Nor will they escape mine. Unlike some, I'll not suffer a witch to live.'

THIRTY-EIGHT

Isabel Adam... in pursuance of a quarrel which Beatrix Laing, formerly
mentioned, had with one Alexander McGrigor, a fisher in town, made
an attempt to murder the said McGrigor in bed; which was prevented by
his awakening and wrestling against them.

— A Just Reproof to the False Reports and Unjust
Calumnies in the Foregoing Letter, *1705*

Sorcha was by the harbour, watching as her father and brother
prepared the boat to leave the Forth and sail into deeper northern waters,
following the whitefish. Wind whipped hair into her eyes, the ocean
spray stung her face. Gulls swooped overhead, the men were checking
lines, folding nets and hammering nails into some loose decking...

Dull thuds interrupted the image, making it quiver before it slowly
dissolved.

Stirring, Sorcha lay still upon the bed, trying to bring it back.
The pounding began again; this time, she heard her name. 'Twas no
dream. She pushed back the covers and scrambled for her shawl in the
dark. She collided with Nettie in the main room as, half asleep, they
fumbled their way to the front door.

Sorcha reached it first and wrenched it open. In the dim light of the embers in the fireplace she could just make out Mr Adam, Isobel's father, and Nettie's daughter from Anster.

'Rebecca!' exclaimed Nettie, any sign of sleep vanishing as she reached for her daughter's hand and dragged her across the threshold. 'What are you doing here? Come away in.'

'Mr Adam,' said Sorcha, moving to allow Rebecca past. 'Come away in too, please.' It was raining steadily and both visitors were sodden. Peering out the door, Sorcha couldn't see anything; just the rain, and the bleak stone wall of the graveyard opposite. The ocean rumbled and rolled. By the time she'd closed the door, a protesting Rebecca was peeling her coat off and Nettie had stoked the fire.

Sorcha quickly lit some candles. Mr Adam was pale and deeply agitated.

'Here,' she said. 'Let me help you with your coat. You're drookit.'

'Nae, lass,' said Mr Adam, raising a gnarled hand to prevent her. 'I not be staying. I came to warn you both.'

'Warn us?' asked Nettie, flashing a look at Sorcha as she draped her daughter's coat over a stool. Rebecca gave up trying to retrieve it. 'About what?'

Mr Adam pinched the bridge of his nose, as if focussing his thoughts. He took a deep breath. 'Earlier this morning, the guards and Bailie Cook came for Isobel, before the cock even crowed. Marched her off to that damn Tolbooth. Again.'

Sorcha gasped. Nettie's hand flew to her mouth. Rebecca appeared stunned.

'Why?' asked Sorcha. 'She was pardoned. We all were. What are they accusing her of now?'

'What else but witchcraft,' said Mr Adam then, much to her dismay, buried his face in his large, nobbled hands and began to weep. Sorcha put an arm about him and led him to a chair.

'Is this why you're here?' Nettie turned towards Rebecca.

'Nae,' said Rebecca, clearly shocked at the news. 'It's pa. He's back from the city ports, ma, and I fear he's very poorly.'

Nettie gave an exclamation of despair. Thom had been ill for a long time, eating little, coughing ferociously, claiming whenever asked it was naught and dismissing Nettie's concern. Sorcha knew living and working in Pittenweem was a way of keeping Nettie's mind from his troubles as well as helping to earn enough to cover the cost of his treatment. Seeing the way colour fled her face and tears welled, this was a bitter blow. For all her independence, she loved her husband dearly.

'I said I'd come and fetch you. I ken naught of what Mr Adam is saying. It's just a coincidence we arrived together. But, ma, he needs you.' Rebecca snatched up her coat and began to put it back on again, leaving a trail of water across the floor.

'Give me a moment, lass, and we'll be on our way.' Nettie shot an apologetic look at Sorcha.

'Go. Go,' said Sorcha. 'I will send word once I learn exactly what this is about.' She squeezed Mr Adam's forearm reassuringly.

Nettie dressed swiftly, throwing some extra garments in her burlap and dropping a kiss on Sorcha's head. 'I'll return when I can.' She opened the door. 'If Isobel has been arrested, I've nae doubt who's behind this,' she said grimly.

After kirk yesterday, they'd had a long discussion about the reverend's latest sermon.

'Ma, we have to leave,' pressed Rebecca, trying to push her mother out the door.

'I pray Thom will be all right,' said Sorcha, hugging her friend tightly.

With a grunt, hoisting her bag, draping her coat over it and ensuring her scarf was tied tightly, Nettie signalled to Rebecca she was ready and, with one last wave, left.

'It's just you and me now, Mr Adam,' said Sorcha gently, waiting until the women's voices had faded. Finding a bottle of whisky, Sorcha poured a dram and pushed it into Mr Adam's hands. After he'd taken a couple of sips, she sat beside him, her knees almost touching his.

Raising bleary eyes to Sorcha's, Mr Adam surprised her by grabbing a hold of her hand. 'Just when I thought this malice nonsense had been put to bed, it starts all over again. This time, they're saying my lass cast a spell on that drunk Alexander McGregor and sought to murder him in his bed.'

'Alexander McGregor?' Sorcha's head reeled. If there was one thing their arrest had taught them all, it was to only keep company with folk they could trust, who wouldn't turn on them because of an ill word or misunderstood action. As far as Sorcha knew, Isobel had been nowhere near the likes of Alexander McGregor. Not since the night Sorcha came home and Isobel had burst into the cottage claiming the man had scared her witless.

Oh dear God…

Sorcha leapt to her feet and began to pace. 'When was she supposed to have done this?'

'Last Hogmanay.'

Sorcha stopped and made a scoffing noise. 'But 'twas Isobel who fled from McGregor. As a matter of fact, she came here, to me and Nettie.'

'I ken what happened. Isobel told me. But McGregor now swears she was casting a spell and if he hadn't woken and interrupted her, she would have killed him with witchcraft.'

'It's a complete nonsense.' Sorcha began to wear a path between the fireplace and door.

'The reverend didn't think so when McGregor told him this last night.'

Sorcha's heart skipped a beat. 'He told the reverend?'

'Aye. 'Twas the reverend who ordered her taken to the Tolbooth so she might be formally questioned — and we ken what that means.'

Sorcha began to worry her nails. Mr Adam sipped his whisky, his frantic arrival settling into something less now he'd shared his burden.

Pressing her hands against her cheeks, Sorcha tried to think. 'Isobel ran away from McGregor — others saw her. There are witnesses.'

'Isobel said as much.'

'The reverend didn't listen?'

'Nae, lass. Not him nor the bailies. That's why I'm here. I have to warn you. The others as well.'

Sorcha stared at Mr Adam. A needle-like pain began to prod and prick. Starting at the base of her neck, it travelled the length of her spine, running in bands around her ribs before lodging in her breast. 'What about?' she asked breathlessly.

Mr Adam rose and put down his drink. 'Isobel wasn't the only one McGregor named as present in his house that night.'

Even though Sorcha knew what he was going to say next, she had to ask. She had no choice. 'Who else did he name?'

'Among others, you, Sorcha McIntyre. He named you.' Sorcha's stomach lurched and she lost focus. 'And you ken what that means, don't you?'

Sorcha blinked Mr Adam back into existence.

She did. All too well.

It took less than two days for the reverend and council to extract a full confession from Isobel. Rumour had it she wasn't tortured, she simply blathered the moment the reverend and the bailies appeared in her cell and mentioned the pricker, names and details spilling from her mouth. Beatrix was identified as head of a coven who conspired to murder Mr McGregor in his home. Isobel claimed it was because McGregor refused to rent one of Beatrix's houses.

Sorcha didn't doubt what Isobel had confessed, or who'd put the ideas into her head. All it would take was the threat of punishment to have any of them who'd been interned before to confess to anything.

Not sure whether she should sit and wait for the guards to come and arrest her or flee the village like Margaret and Lillie, Sorcha returned to work. If she ran, it would be an admission of guilt and she refused to give the reverend the satisfaction, not over such ridiculous claims. At least while she faked the nets, collected bait and hooked the lines, sorted, gutted and sold the few fish that were caught, her body was occupied, if not her mind.

It was down at the harbour that she heard the gossip. Whereas Edinburgh had thought the evidence upon which she and the others had been interned in the Tolbooth was flimsy and the interrogations dire, the reverend believed that not only would McGregor's testimony and Isobel's confession change the minds of city officials, but vindicate him and the council. Thomas Brown's death would now be seen as just: God's will made manifest.

Whereas there'd been many in Pittenweem in agreement with the Crown authorities who thought Peter Morton was as great an imposter as Christian Shaw from Paisley, they now expressed fury that the poor lad had not only been disbelieved but mocked. Peter enjoyed a wave of sympathy and support reminiscent of when he was first afflicted.

Sorcha could hear women and old men clecking on their stoops, reminding each other how the lad had suffered and asking what those toffs in the city would ken. They hadn't seen the way his neck twisted or his belly distended. And what about when he coughed up all that hair and other strange objects? The stories grew wilder, more assured with each telling. Details were added and embroidered. Sorcha grew more despondent.

What had once been a murmur of discontent about the way Peter and, as a consequence, the reverend, the council and the entire town had been treated by Edinburgh, ridiculed and ignored when they were in the gravest of peril, in a matter of days had transformed into a blame-filled fury.

Alexander McGregor's testimony was little more than kindling to an already burning flame; a flame about to erupt into a conflagration.

What unnerved Sorcha most was the way attitudes towards her altered from one day to the next. Even after she'd been released from the Tolbooth in autumn, there'd been folk prepared to risk the wrath of those who still believed she was a witch and not only greet her and celebrate her freedom, but continue to defy the reverend and buy their fish from her. No more. Doors were closed in her face. More often she would knock and wait, but no one would answer. It didn't matter if she called out or smoke belched from the chimney, a curtain was quickly rearranged or a bairn's cry muffled — she was stranded on the stoop.

With the few fish she did sell, she tried to buy milk, neeps and eggs, but found each farm or shop had suddenly run out. Likewise, when she sought to acquire some needles, and even take her boots to the cordwainer for repair, service was refused.

Dejected, she'd gone to Beatrix's house to find she told the same story, only worse. Word had spread that Beatrix was leader of a coven and she was not only being shunned, but threatened. There were rumours she was going to be hounded out of town — she and Nicolas, whose once much sought-after homemade remedies were now viewed as something altogether sinister.

They were convicted and punished without even a trial.

Making her way home that evening, Sorcha was more conscious than ever of the way people took great pains not to cross her path, how they whispered behind their hands as they watched her progress up the High Street, her creel upon her back, their words dispersing about their averted faces in a cloud of white. Mothers placed protective arms about their children, some raised their eyes to heaven, their lips moving in silent prayer. Faces appeared at windows, doors slammed, barking dogs were dragged away and muzzled. It was unnerving; chilling, even. If Sorcha hadn't felt anger build within her, the hot tears burning behind her eyes, she would have felt the cold cloak of doom descend.

She began to think of what she'd write to Nettie — how she'd warn her to remain in Anster with her husband. She'd also write to Aidan. She composed sentences in her head, trying to explain these new developments without expressing her fear, her need of him and the comfort his mere presence bestowed. How, with him by her side, she would know the world hadn't descended into complete madness.

It wasn't until she reached the Mercat Cross, vaguely aware of the crowd gathered outside the Tolbooth waiting for news of Isobel that, distracted, she almost collided with someone.

As she took a step back, the apology died in her throat. It was Peter Morton.

Since she'd been released, she'd barely seen the lad and then only from afar — on the street, in the kirk. Keeping her distance, she'd mostly ignored him. Much to her surprise she felt no bitterness towards him, despite what had happened. He was only a lad, after all. A lad in thrall to the reverend. Had he ever been sick? Sorcha wondered now, as she looked at him. Was it really only a few months ago that he'd collapsed at her feet and writhed and convulsed as if possessed? She'd seen how the fit had come upon him so suddenly; how sickly he subsequently became. What she couldn't reconcile was how he identified her and her friends as responsible. All she could think was how much he must hate them. Him, or someone else.

Despite what had befallen Peter, he looked hale. His shoulders had filled out, his face too; he'd regained any weight he'd lost. No more a lad, he was very much a man. A man who appeared cockier and more assured than he had a right to be.

Surprised to see her, he stopped and stared, then dropped his gaze.

'Peter,' said Sorcha. Afraid of what she might say to him, the blame she'd lay at his large feet, even if he wasn't the only one responsible, she went to pass him. Before she could, he blocked her passage.

'Mrs McIntyre, Sorcha, I —'

'Have nothing to say to me. Nothing I want to hear.' Sorcha regretted the words as soon as they were out of her mouth.

'Nae,' said Peter bitterly. 'I'm sure you save all your words for your fine incomer, don't you?'

Chin high, Sorcha took a few steps past him, slowed, then spun around. How strange that Peter should raise Aidan when he was so much in her thoughts as well. Unable to help herself, anger flared. Whereas Peter Morton had been the cause of so much misery, Aidan had tried to effect happiness and hope — to protect her and others. That Peter dare speak of him in such a way infuriated her, especially when she knew he must have also played a part in ensuring the captain was no longer in the Weem.

'Bit difficult to utter any words to Captain Ross when he's stationed in Bavaria. Not even a witch could shout that far.' Her eyes narrowed. 'But I'm sure you and your friend the reverend know all about that.'

The look of astonishment on Peter's face was a performance that almost outdid the one he had enacted daily for months in his bedroom. With a click of frustration, Sorcha began to walk away.

'Wait,' said Peter, running after her. He grabbed her arm. 'Wait, Sorcha, please. I didn't ken about Captain Ross. He's in Bavaria, you say? Why? When?'

Sorcha shook his hand off and looked him up and down. 'Why do you think? He was posted there weeks ago. I doubt I'll ever see him again and I know who I've to thank for that.' Once again, Peter couldn't hold her glare.

The sky was darkening as thick clouds gathered. A flock of birds cawed their way north. 'Now,' said Sorcha finally. 'I'm going home to write to the very same man. Someone needs to know what's happening around here before it gets out of hand. Again.'

This time Peter let her go. Sorcha was astounded by the level of relief she felt.

That might have changed if she'd seen the expression on the lad's face, how it altered or where he headed next, striding away with fuming purpose.

It wasn't until she was inside her cottage, a piece of paper and her quill and ink ready, a small dram beside her, and had begun to record the latest events in Pittenweem, that the tightness in her belly started to unfurl. Not that she relaxed completely. Every footfall, raised voice and even the crash of the waves and the rain as it drummed upon the roof set her nerves on edge.

As night fell and the room grew darker and the downpour became heavier, she finished her letter. When it grew lighter, she would take the missive to Mrs Fraser and ask her to ensure it was sent. Then she carefully washed, using a perfumed soap, dressed in her best clothes, combed her hair and tied a fresh scarf about her head. Shaking out her shawl, she wound it across her shoulders, pinning it with her mor's favourite brooch. 'Twas of a mermaid. Sitting with her legs stretched out before the fire, she soaked in the sights, sounds and smells of her cottage. The way the windows rattled with every gust; how the embers in the fireplace looked like living creatures huddled together for warmth. How the smell of dinners past melded with the briny scent of the ocean, the almost mint-fresh odour of the rain. How the wooden arms of the chair felt beneath her callused fingers, the fabric of the worn cushions almost silky through her skirts. How the plates in the dresser gleamed, the patterns swirling as if they too were alive in the shadows cast by the flickering light. With her hand atop the letter clearly addressed to the captain, she waited for dawn to herald what she knew would happen.

The guards would come for her. Just like Isobel, she'd be marched through the streets and to the Tolbooth. Only, unlike the last time she was there, she understood that on this occasion, despite what she'd written, despite the pleas they'd all make, there'd be no escape, not unless a miracle occurred or, worse, another tragedy.

THIRTY-NINE

*The minister having got account of this from Mr Cook, he sent for her
[and] he threatened her very severely and commanded the keeper to put
her into some prison by herself under the steeple least (as she said) she
should pervert those who had confessed.*

— A Letter from a Gentleman in Fife to
his Friend in Edinburgh, *1705*

Despite Sorcha's fears, the constables never came for her. Not that
night nor the ones after. Beatrix and Nicolas were not so fortunate.
Being in Anster ministering to her ailing husband didn't spare Nettie
either. She was dragged from his bedside and, along with the others,
thrown into the Tolbooth once more.

Not a day went past that Sorcha didn't linger outside their prison to
hear how the women inside fared. Racked with memories, trembling
as her mind took over her body, she forced herself to knock on the Tolbooth door, plead with Camron, if he answered, to pass on the food
she'd brought, the extra blankets and other comforts she knew all too
well the women would need. It didn't matter whether it rained, sleet
dashed or icy gusts howled, there was always a group of people loitering nearby. Some would spit and call her names, reminding Sorcha

that she too should be locked away. Others would turn their backs, pretend she wasn't even there. She tried not to let them see how much their venom, aroused by dread and uncertainty, affected her.

When she couldn't bear the hostility any more, she would walk down the High Street and stand in exactly the same place Aidan used to, willing Nettie to look out. It worked. Nettie would come to the window, push it open and wave. Sorcha would fix a smile upon her face and return the gesture, determined not to let her friend see the anguish eating away at her; grateful she couldn't see the tears streaming down her cheeks.

Guilt was a shawl she donned daily. She should be in there with them. Had not Mr Adam said she was named as one of the witches who tormented Mr McGregor? How she evaded arrest, she was yet to learn. From the looks cast in her direction, the shouts that followed her wherever she walked, there were many who felt she had escaped justice. God forgive her, every time she stood outside the Tolbooth, every night as her slumbering mind took her back to that cold, damp cell and the attentions of Mr Bollard, the reverend and the guards, she was grateful she wasn't. She despised herself for feeling that way.

As the days passed, she learned that Isobel's second confession, despite what they'd heard, was extracted after a series of beatings and pricking. A report on her arrest and that of her accomplices, along with Isobel's signed confession, had been sent to Edinburgh. Camron told Sorcha that as far as he knew, none of the other women had been hurt, though they had been questioned. Through Camron, Nettie passed thanks for the blankets and food and said that while they were warmer than they had been the last time they stayed (Sorcha had choked back a sob; as if the Tolbooth was an inn, their internment a holiday), they lacked the one thing they sorely needed.

Sorcha understood. What Nettie meant was hope. They were lacking hope. Truth be told, so was Sorcha, especially since the support they'd once had from the townsfolk had all but evaporated.

Word in Pittenweem was that Edinburgh had played them for fools by forcing the early release of the witches, putting everyone at risk of sorcery and malfeasance. If Edinburgh wouldn't look after them, they'd no choice but take matters into their own hands. Thank God for the reverend, people said.

Sorcha felt like screaming.

Look at us! she wanted to cry out. You've known us our whole lives. Comforted us when we skinned our knees as bairns, shared your bannocks, blessed our unions with your sons and brothers, passed us your wee ones to hold when they were born; cried with us at funerals, celebrated when the drave was fine and the ships came home. Why, Beatrix's husband had been the town treasurer, feted and admired. How many of those baying for blood had not only brought their ripped shirts for Isobel to mend, but fantasised about bedding her? Sought Nicolas's herbs and lotions when they were hurt? How many had benefited from the work of Nettie and Janet?

Sorcha was forced to face the truth. Reverend Cowper had found his witches. In doing so, he'd not only divided the town, he now had the majority on his side. Sorcha was heartsick. Children started throwing clods of mud at her whenever she appeared and, as early snows fell, clumps of ice were aimed at her head. Cow and dog shit were smeared on her front door one night and even, after she'd been fruitlessly trying to sell fish around the outlying farms, left inside the big pot in her kitchen. When she came home one evening to find some of her mor's plates smashed, and curdled milk spilled all over the chairs and bedding, she began to lock her door — unheard of in the Weem.

She may have been spared arrest this time, but in the villagers' eyes, she was as guilty as if she'd flown on a broom through the night skies raining curses on all and sundry. If it wasn't for Moira Fraser and a few of the others, she would have starved or frozen to death as winter descended upon them in a fury of storms, snow and gale-force winds.

It wasn't just Sorcha who was targeted by frightened and zealous folk. Fishwives, even those who'd never been accused, were being refused service in shops, hounded wherever they walked. Unable to sell their fish as no one would buy from them, they ate what the men caught. They may not have earned coin from the extra catch, but at least they didn't starve.

Along with Nicolas's and Beatrix's husbands, the other fishermen were denied ale and whisky at the tavern. Furious at first, the fishermen soon jumped back in their boats and rowed to Anster to drink at the Dreel Tavern. Although they were regarded with some suspicion, they weren't rebuffed; coin was coin, after all.

To the people of Pittenweem, it was as if by turning their backs on all those who associated with the accused witches, they were somehow convincing the reverend, the council, God and even themselves, of their innocence. Scorning the witches' families, friends and allies was a form of protection, a talisman against evil. With heads held high, they'd attend the kirk each Sunday and heed, with increasing fervour, Reverend Cowper's sermons. Sermons that Sorcha knew were thinly veiled calls to act against malfeasance — threats against the likes of her.

Listening to the reverend, Sorcha marvelled that this man of God, who should be alleviating people's fears, was exacerbating them. When he should be encouraging unity, he was fostering discord and suspicion. How was this helping the town? It wasn't. It was destroying it and giving Cowper the power he relished. She could see it in his face, hear it in his voice. It shone in his eyes every time they landed upon her. A self-satisfied gleam that some might read as godly fervour. Without words, he was telling her she was next. Part of her wanted to whisper to him to come and get her; the other part quailed in terror.

After another dismal day and another fish supper, instead of retiring to bed and the consolation of dreams (not that they'd offered much of that of late), she found some paper and writing implements and determined to write to Aidan again, keep him informed of events. When she first wrote to him, she'd explained what had happened to Nettie, Isobel, Beatrix, Nicolas and Janet, sparing him her more dismal thoughts. Gazing out the window, she wondered where he'd be when he read her words. What he was doing? Was he safe?

About to set down everything, she hesitated. It wasn't fair to subject him to her tribulations, her apprehension, not when there was nothing he could do. Picking up the quill, instead she wrote about winter's arrival, the way the clouds gathered over the mouth of the

Forth, billowing ever forwards towards the shore, emptying their load of rain upon the township, causing rivers of water to rush down the wynds to the harbour. How children and animals were to be found splashing in the puddles. She described how the masts of the clippers leaving Edinburgh with their mighty sails full would catch the early or late sunlight, appearing like a group of angels hovering above the water. She chronicled the small catch, what she was reading, and how often she prayed for his safety. What she didn't write was how much she yearned for him. It was an ache so deep, it was like missing a limb.

In a postscript, she asked if he'd heard anything of Robbie. She didn't expect that he would, but thought if nothing else, making enquiries about her brother might distract him from the danger he faced.

She sealed the letter and, once it had cooled, pressed the wax to her lips, closed her eyes and tried to conjure an image of Aidan. The jet-black hair and coal-dark eyes. The evening shadow that limned his chin and the angular cheeks that made him appear so very rakish. She thought of the warmth of his body, the feel of his lips against hers. Heat that had nothing to do with the fire and everything to do with her memories swamped her. She pressed her hand against her belly. She was so very lonely and not just for that, but for him and the pleasure his presence bestowed. All those she cared about in the world had been taken from her. *Please, God, let Aidan not be taken too, forever and ever. Amen.*

If it wasn't for the women in the Tolbooth, she would have left the Weem. But when she tried to imagine packing her burlap, locking the cottage door once and for all and setting out upon the road, she could not think where she would go. She couldn't go to her sister, that was evident. The city held no appeal whatsoever. All she really knew was this sea life — the fishwives' lot and the comfort of her daily tasks. But after one particularly rowdy sermon that had half the congregation on its feet chanting and punching the air, looking about for someone on whom to unleash, even that option was denied to her. Cornelia Gurr, the wife of one of the boat owners and someone Sorcha had always had an easy relationship with, came to see her and asked her not to come to work at the harbour any more.

'We've no need of you at present, Sorcha, what with the drave being so poor and no one buying.' Standing outside the cottage, declining the invitation to come in and sit by the fire, Cornelia refused to look Sorcha in the eye. Instead, she turned her head towards the spire of the Tolbooth, squinting into the fading light. 'Far better you remain at home and look to your own self. Look to your boat. Or, if you be inclined, do what some of the other lasses do nowadays, chase the herring up the coast. We'll manage without you.'

'Better for whom?' asked Sorcha softly.

This time, Cornelia faced her. 'For us all, lass. For us all.' She hesitated. 'If you don't mind a wee bit of advice, I'd steer clear of the Tolbooth. All you're doing lingering down there is reminding folk that you should be inside.'

First making sure there was no one to see her, Cornelia touched Sorcha's arm. 'This will be over soon. Then we can all get back to living.'

Her choice of words took Sorcha's breath away.

Cornelia scuttled off down the road as if the hounds of hell were baying at her heels. In her mind, perhaps they were, thought Sorcha, trying to be affronted but feeling forlorn. Cornelia was right, this wasn't living.

The next day, the men who'd been sent out to search for Margaret Jack and Lillie Wallace — who'd both been named in Isobel's deposition — returned. The women had disappeared completely, thank God. If only she could too. But Sorcha wouldn't leave while Nettie and the others were confined. Especially not now she knew it was because of Peter Morton that she was not.

Unable to withhold the information from her, perhaps hoping she'd look upon him with forgiveness, if not something more, the lad had followed her home after kirk last Sunday. Aware someone was behind her and assuming it was children up to mischief, Sorcha twisted around, fists raised.

Upon seeing Peter, she'd lowered her arms. 'Och. It's you.' She continued walking.

'Mrs McIntyre,' cried Peter and ran to catch up.

'I haven't changed my mind, Peter. I've still nothing to say to you,' said Sorcha glumly. The last thing she needed was this man trailing her. She could scarce look at him, let alone speak.

Peter grabbed her skirt and wrenched her around. 'You could at least show me a little gratitude.'

'Gratitude?' Sorcha stared at him in disbelief as she tugged her skirt out of his hand. There was a tearing sound.

'Aye. If not for me, you'd be up there with that lot,' said Peter, thumbing in the direction of the Tolbooth.

'What do you mean?' Sorcha examined her skirt with exasperation. The rip was wide. She wished she really was a witch and could not only repair her skirt with a spell, but cast one that would make Peter Morton vanish. The thought made her lips twitch.

Mistaking her smile, Peter stepped closer. 'I refused to corroborate what Mr McGregor said, to name you, that's what I mean.'

Sorcha frowned. 'I don't understand.'

Peter pulled an impatient face. 'When the reverend asked me to support Mr McGregor in front of the bailies and identify the witches, those he'd revealed had come to murder him, I said it couldn't possibly be you because I saw you in your cottage that night. I said you never left it. After that, Mr McGregor couldn't claim you were in his house. He withdrew your name.'

Biting back a sour laugh, Sorcha threw up her hands. 'Why would you ever have thought to name me in the first place? Why would *he*? Like the others, I wasn't there. Like the others, I *was* at home. That part at least is true. I'm no witch. Though, in case you've forgotten, you were ready to call me such once.'

'That's because he ma—' Peter bit his lip. His eyes darted left then right.

'*He?* Who do you mean, Peter?' Sorcha closed the distance between them. Further down the street, a group of small children were chasing a chicken.

Burying his hands in his pockets, Peter shrugged. 'I didn't mean nothing. All I meant was I could have said you were one of them, but I didn't.'

'Nae,' said Sorcha, her eyes flashing, her anger rising faster than a tide at full moon. 'But you named innocent women, Peter. Caused them to suffer terribly before and again now. You've ruined their lives.' *You almost ruined mine.* 'Why? Why did you do it?'

'Why? Why do you think?' He leaned towards her. Their noses almost touched. His chest was heaving, his cheeks flushed. 'Because they're not innocent. They are the devil's servants and they seek to recruit all of us into Satan's army. Steal our eternal souls. I see they tried to steal yours too. Don't you ken? In naming them, I've saved them. They'll be baptised now, or if they refuse, God will give them their dues. You should be thanking me, not blaming me.'

Taken aback by his vehemence, his ignorance, Sorcha studied his face, the earnestness in his gaze; earnestness and something else.

'If that's so, then why didn't you name me? If you think you're saving them, then why not save me too?'

Before she could say anything more, he grabbed her face and kissed her.

His lips were hard. His tongue, clumsy and rough, plunged so deep into her mouth she almost gagged. His whiskers grazed her chin, his fingers dug into her cheeks.

She wrenched herself away, drew back her hand and slapped him with such force her palm burned. 'You want-o-wut blaggard!' Fury made her slip into local dialect. 'You fasionless dowgit. How dare you!'

Peter lightly touched his cheek, which was fast becoming red, and staggered back from the heat of her rage.

'What'd you do that for? Don't you understand? Now your capt'n's gone, you can be mine, Sorcha McIntyre. *I* can protect you.'

Sorcha gaped in disbelief. 'You think I'd look at you whether the captain was here or not?' She spluttered, 'I'd rather be locked up in that Tolbooth and named a witch than have you ever touch me again, you hear? Protect me? You near killed me.'

Immediately, Sorcha regretted her words. God, she'd called the lad stupid and thoughtless, limp and downtrodden, as if he was an abused pup. His face changed like a summer sky before a storm as a welter of emotions came and went. She saw confusion, before hurt took its place followed by a hardening of his eyes and mouth. His hand rested against where his face flamed. Much to her horror, his eyes began to well. He dashed the tears away.

'You'll regret this, Sorcha McIntyre. You mark my words. You tell me you'd rather be locked up than kiss a man who gives you his love; who wishes you safe. Wait and see. What you said'll come true.' He tried to glare at her, but his swimming eyes relayed only sadness and pain. 'And that'll just prove the reverend right, won't it?'

'What do you mean?' asked Sorcha, wanting to hate the lad, but finding only pity.

'I'll recant and name you the witch that you are. A witch that steals men's hearts and then fucking well breaks them.'

With one last look of loathing and longing, he turned and stomped down the road, pushing through the group of children, one of whom fell in a puddle and began to howl.

Something Sorcha felt like doing herself.

Just as word of the discovery of another coven of witches spread about the countryside bringing those sightseers prepared to brave the cold and snow back to the Weem, gentlemen from Edinburgh also came. There were a number of lairds among them — Randerston, Lyon and Kellie. Once again the lawyers, Mr Ker of Kippilaw and Mr Robert Cooke, made an appearance.

Insisting on interviewing each of the accused witches without either the reverend or a member of the local council present, they also asked to see Peter Morton.

Sorcha could only imagine how the lad felt about that, especially after he'd been sent home from the city in disgrace. Whereas the townsfolk had been in two minds about his treatment then, this time most were sympathetic and ready to defend his claims. Including, Sorcha imagined, when he named her a witch.

Ignoring the disdainful looks of those gathered outside the Tolbooth, Sorcha had risen before dark and found a position as close to the studded door as she could get. This time, if she was to be identified, she didn't want to be hauled from her house or taken unawares. She wanted any announcements or news firsthand. No amount of pushing, whispered threats or loud insults were going to move her. Call her a witch, would they? Well, she'd bloody well act like one, she thought, glowering at the Crawford women.

By the time the sun rose, revealing a patchy sky of grey cloud washed with insipid blue, and the wind began to wail up the wynd, bringing with it the sounds of gulls crying, waves crashing and the shouts of the inshore fishermen from across the water, a sizeable mob was spilling into the High Street and milling around the Mercat Cross. The mood was dark. Many had already decided that it didn't matter what the city toffs declared, the women were guilty and they all knew it.

Sorcha's heart was a lead weight. In her bag she carried extra blankets, food and a large boat hook. If she had to use force and threats to clear the way for her friends, or defend herself, she would. She also needed to let Nettie know that Thom was bedridden. Unable to work on the foreshore, Sorcha had gone to visit him and Rebecca in Anster. It was evident Thom was not long for this world. Nettie would be crushed.

The town clock tolled midday before the first of the gentlemen emerged from the Tolbooth. Warmly dressed in fine suits and coats, with ruddy-coloured cheeks and fleshy paunches, they were a stark contrast to the dowdy Weem folk with their worn clothes and thin faces.

Talking among themselves, they were largely oblivious to the crowd who, despite bold assertions before the men appeared, parted without a murmur. It wasn't until a pale face flanked by two burly guards appeared that the crowd reacted.

It was Nettie. Behind her was Isobel, her sweet face bruised and bloodied, then Beatrix and, finally, Nicolas. Sorcha's throat grew thick. Her vision became blurry. They were there. They were alive. Thoughts battered her mind like waves against the braes. It was going to be all right. It was over.

Thank God. She was wrong. Cowper hadn't won.

Blinking like startled owls in the light, the women stood together in the doorway. The guards used pikes to keep the crowd, who were becoming restless, back.

'Nettie!' cried Sorcha. 'Beatrix, Nicolas, Isobel!' She waved her arm above her head to attract their attention. Nettie saw her and, with a wide grin, pushed past the guards and beckoned the others to follow.

From within the crowd, Mr Adam came forward, taking his daughter's hand, ensuring no one shoved or threatened her. Mr Brown also appeared, using his stick to create space, and Mr Lawson. When the women reached Sorcha, she hugged each of them tightly.

'Come, let's get away from here. We can talk later.' Sorcha couldn't help but look over her shoulder, wondering if there was a guard waiting to take her into custody. Best not linger. She had what she came for.

'Come to our house,' said Mr Brown. 'I'll have the lasses run hot baths and Mrs Gower has a stew in the pot. More than enough for all.'

Pulling Beatrix gently to his side, he set off down Cove Wynd. Linking her arm through Nettie's, Sorcha waited for Isobel and her father and Nicolas and her husband to go ahead, before taking up the rear.

They hadn't gone very far when they heard a clamour behind them. Spinning around, Sorcha saw two guards holding someone between them. Thinner than anyone had a right to be, with greyish flesh covered in sores, her hair looking more like a bird's nest than human, was Janet Cornfoot. Hacking and coughing, she stumbled along the cobbles, her dress tripping her up as her crooked toes caught in the ragged hem.

'Dear God.' Sorcha stopped. Unwinding her shawl, she pulled out the blankets she'd shoved in her bag and, leaving Nettie where she stood, ran to Janet. The guards tried to prevent her getting too close.

'Simon Wood and Gerard Stuart. Don't you dare,' she growled. Discounting them, she wrapped her shawl around Janet and thrust the blankets into her arms. Then, slowly, carefully, she embraced the

woman. She smelled of musty old caves, fear and hunger. Of nightmares and endless days of loneliness. She smelled of defiance.

Janet hugged her back, her grip weak but determined.

'You're here.' Sorcha pulled away from her and scanned her face,
took in the wrinkly neck, the missing teeth in the smile that Janet
gave, one that even after all this time, reached her eyes.

'Despite the bastards,' said Janet. 'And they'll ken I am too, Sorcha.
Mark my words.'

Before she could say any more, Simon and Gerard shoved her forward. 'Sorry, Sorcha. We've orders from on high. Back to the cave
with you, Mrs Cornfoot.'

'You're not free?' began Sorcha.

'Not yet. Not until the lairds and lawyers consider what I told them,
then I'll be released. But I be fine, Sorcha,' said Janet, resting a curled
hand on her arm. 'I be fine. Hello there, Nettie, looking good, hen,
looking good,' called Janet. 'You too, Isobel and Nicolas. But you,
Beatrix, you're still the same auld clash-bag you always were.'

Beatrix began to laugh. They all did. 'And you too, you silly auld
cow,' cried Beatrix, dissolving into tears as soon as Janet's back was
turned.

They watched as she was led down to St Fillan's Cave, the crowd at
the top of the wynd jeering and shouting.

'Why are they taking her back?' Sorcha asked Nettie. 'What's there
to consider?'

Leaning heavily on her, Nettie grinned in admiration. 'What I
understand, lass, is that Janet, the gennick auld bitch, recanted everything she *ever* confessed to the reverend. Better still, she told the men
from Edinburgh she only said what she did the first time because the
reverend beat confessions out of all of us. She warned them not to
count anything that was said or signed before or now. That they were
as false as the reverend's claims to be a holy man.'

Sorcha's mouth dropped open. 'She said *that*?'

'Aye. You can imagine Cowper's reaction. He told the Edinburgh
gents Janet was "a woman of very bad fame" and a liar. That's why,

when the lairds suggested Janet be kept in custody while they investigated *her* claims further but he was to release us, he didn't complain. A bird in the hand and all. He has his witch — for now — and while he has Janet, he still has a hold over us.'

'But surely they didn't mean for him to keep her in St Fillan's Cave?' Sorcha watched as the guards fumbled with the locks to the entrance.

'They're not here any more to see where he holds her, are they? The cave or the Tolbooth, he's obeying their instructions — keeping her under lock and key.'

Sorcha nodded slowly. 'While he has Janet, he can use her to ensure our co-operation — make sure we don't make things worse for him.'

'And no doubt try to make Janet retract what she said.'

They stared at each other in grim contemplation, then, arm in arm, continued towards Beatrix's house.

As they passed St Fillan's Cave, Nettie shook her head. 'If there's one thing Cowper won't tolerate, it's being made to look a fool again — not by anyone.'

'Especially not a woman,' said Sorcha.

They walked in silence a while.

'He won't hurt Janet further, though, will he? He wouldn't dare, would he?' asked Sorcha as they turned onto the shore road. Waves rolled up on the sand before retreating. Rows of kelp had been dumped on the beach, forming a miniature breakwater. Fishwives roamed among the slippery cordons, lifting smaller pieces into their creels. Some were kneeling over by the rocks, prying mussels away. Maybe now they could join them again.

'Nae, he wouldn't,' said Nettie, catching the direction of her gaze. 'Not now those city gents know what he's accused of doing. They'll want to question her further. Us too, no doubt.' Aware they'd been dawdling and the others were some way ahead, Sorcha and Nettie increased their pace. 'You wait,' added Nettie, satisfaction making her voice stronger. 'Janet will be free soon. Then no one can touch her.'

FORTY

Nor have we ever read or heard of any [witch] grown rich by Witchcraft.

— A True and Full Relation of
the Witches at Pittenweem, *1704*

The residents of Pittenweem were forced into an uneasy truce. The women accused of witchcraft for a second time were deemed not guilty by the city authorities and the Queen's law and therefore set at liberty.

All except Janet Cornfoot, who remained in solitary confinement in the damp darkness beneath the kirk.

As December drew to a close, Sorcha, Nettie and Nicolas returned to their trade once more, baiting lines, mending nets, sorting the fish, wielding their knives to scale and gut the catch before throwing it into their creels and padding the snow-covered lanes and wynds to sell them. They may not have been welcomed back to the harbour, but they weren't entirely rejected, either. Sorcha wondered if it was out of sympathy, for not long after Nettie was released, Thom White died.

Instead of crumbling under the weight of her grief, Nettie used her rage towards those who'd unjustly imprisoned her and taken her away from her husband when he needed her most to fuel her resolve not to kowtow to their desire to drive her away. She refused to have her husband buried in Pittenweem because she didn't want Reverend Cowper to preside over the service, so Sorcha, Beatrix, Isobel and Nicolas, along with a few of the other fishwives and their men, took the coastal path to Anster one sleet-driven day to pray as Thomas White, mariner and former bailie of Pittenweem, a man once held in high esteem who'd loved his wife so much he'd allowed her freedoms most women only dreamed of, was laid to rest.

After that, Nettie leased her house in Anster and Thom's in Pittenweem and came to live with Sorcha. It was as if by staying together they could ward off the ongoing hostility of the townsfolk and watch each other's backs as they made their way to the harbour before dawn each morning and tramped home through the snowdrifts and mizzle each freezing night. They took to roaming the countryside to sell fish together as well. Nicolas often joined them. When they did encounter trouble, usually groups of cupshotten men, they put on a bold face and laughed. It was the best way to silence the jeers and the threats, to make a mockery of those issuing them by reminding them of their mothers, sisters, daughters and their own flaws and foibles.

It didn't always work.

There were a few who refused to be muzzled or cease their efforts to instil fear. Fuelled by their own inner demons and the words of the minister each Sunday, these people, mostly men, would march up to the women and shake their fists, spit in their faces and try and intimidate them. When it became physical, the men were led away by their companions or wives. Only after they'd gone would Sorcha breathe a sigh of relief and still the trembling in her knees. Only then would her heart return to normal.

Sorcha was afraid it was only a matter of time before someone, bolstered by drink, friends, or a sense of godly duty, would do something that could not be undone. And if not His duty, then because of the thoughts Reverend Cowper continued to plant in each and every head at kirk.

Sickened by what the minister said, his ceaseless sermons about witches and the threat they posed to the community, the women nonetheless attended each week. Partly to show a brave front and remind people that they were innocent by law; that the likes of the reverend upon whose every word most hung, was wrong, partly to avoid the hefty fines the reverend threatened should they absent themselves, and partly to arm themselves in the event of more trouble.

Nettie believed the worst was over. 'Give it time,' she would say each night as they huddled before the fire. 'Give it time.' The men would soon forget about them, especially once winter passed and the drave improved and spring brought warmer weather. Sorcha prayed she was right and echoed Nettie's optimism in her letters to Aidan, though she still hadn't heard from him. Never did she reveal what was happening. Instead she imbued her words with hope and dreams of what might transpire if Aidan came home.

Not if... *when*... she would remind herself.

But as first Yuletide then Hogmanay came and went and there was still no word from Bavaria, and Janet wasn't released (though there was talk a move to the Tolbooth was imminent), and no directives came from Edinburgh, Sorcha began to doubt Nettie was right.

If there was to be no more trouble and they all really were free according to justice and the law, why was the reverend still preaching so vehemently against witches?

More importantly, why was he still holding Janet captive?

FORTY-ONE

They asked her how she came to say any thing that was not true; she cryed out, alas, alas, I behoved to say so, to please the minister and bailies…

— An Answer of a Letter From a Gentleman of Fife, *1705*

Compared to St Fillan's Cave, the room on the first floor of the Tolbooth was luxury. Not only was it filled with light, and the bed of straw more comfortable, but Janet had the blankets Sorcha had given her to keep warm. She also had the guards for company. Changing at least three times a day, she knew them all; had done since they were bairns suckling on their mothers' breasts. Not that it made a difference. With the exception of guileless Camron, the Stuart brothers and that Wood lad would act as if she were one of the incomers — welcome only while she spent coin. If only she could…

At least here, in the Tolbooth, she knew what time of day it was as daylight, rain, snowfall or moonbeams were visible through the window. Fresh air, no matter how frigid, streamed in. She was fed, and didn't want for water either. They even gave her a pail for washing some days. Best of all, she could look out and see the town, well, parts of it; it was almost like being amongst folk again. Almost. The High Street, a combination of brown sludge and pristine white depending on the time of day, was there to behold and, if she stuck her head out far enough, ignoring how the cold bit her paper-thin skin or the sleet behaved like the pricker's needles, she could see all the way to the Mercat Cross one way and even catch a glimpse of the sea if she looked the other.

Not a day went by that she didn't spend some time gazing out the window, inhaling the scent of the ocean, listening to its melancholy lullaby, relishing the feel of the wind, rain and whatever else the sky chose to unload. Since Hogmanay, she'd taken to trying to catch snowflakes on her tongue, just as she used to when she was a bairn running over the braes with her friends, plunging into snowdrifts, making angels with her arms and legs or scooping up chunks and casting them down upon the unsuspecting fishwives and men working in the shelter of the rocks at the base of the cliffs. She and her friends would erupt with merriment and scoot away into the wind-blasted heather followed by curses and shouts. Her favourite thing to do now she had the opportunity was watching people, people she'd known her whole life — and a few she'd never seen before — strolling up and down the street, or racing between shops and residences, clecking away, going about their business and trying to escape the weather. Unaware of her scrutiny, they'd argue betwixt themselves, or carry on lost in thought, despondent, enraged, day-dreaming, their lips moving even when there was no one to listen. From her vantage point, she could see who was at odds with whom, who was in favour, including one buxom young lass and a recently married fisherman who would appear upon the High Street around the same time. Chuckling, Janet recognised the looks they exchanged, the way their fingers would brush casually against each other, their shoulders bump.

Janet would try and imagine what the folk she spent hours viewing were thinking, saying, feeling. So many stories circled around in her head. Dogs would scamper past, some chasing rats or chickens. She even saw two piglets run squealing down the frosty cobbles, slipping and sliding, a young girl panting after them as if she were running the cutter. No doubt she'd get a beating for having let them escape. Seagulls would swoop upon unguarded creels, flapping towards the sky, their booty tight in their claws, cawing their triumph. Cats would slink into the shadows, chickens dance across the snow and corbies sit upon rooftops, their glossy black feathers stark against the white-blanketed tiles. Birds that saw her gazing out the window would eye her suspiciously, squawking a warning.

Aye, I'd be warning others too, thought Janet, if the likes of me was watching. If she was feeling generous, she'd break off bits of bannock and throw it to them. They never thanked her.

Rarely did a day pass that Sorcha, bless her, and Nettie along with Beatrix, and even Nicolas and Isobel would stand beneath the tavern shingle and wave to her. She'd heard about Thom White passing and thought Nettie looked rather peely-wally, not that you'd know it from the way she shouted.

Passers-by would swing wide of the women, their extreme efforts not to associate with them making her laugh. Sometimes she could hear her friends talking to Camron or the Stuart lads below. Janet knew that meant they'd delivered something for her to enjoy — fresh bannocks, a flask of whisky and even, one time, a fish pie. That had been a good day. But it wasn't only her friends who took it upon themselves to ensure she was fed. Other packages would arrive — slices of mutton, smoked fish, coddled eggs. The guards wouldn't say who delivered them, but Janet had a suspicion. It was the women folk — well, some of them. Others would spit as soon as look at her, as they did to Sorcha and Nettie. But there were those who, by disobeying their men, quietly, anonymously, demonstrated a support she'd thought had all but gone. It gave her a warm feeling right between her breasts.

Why, she thought, gazing around at the remnants of her last meal, if she kept eating like this, they'd have to widen the door to let her out. Holding the fabric of her waistband away from her, she grimaced. She hoped she wasn't going to be imprisoned that long. God, but she was like a speet. It wasn't only the way her skirts swam on her that made her pull a face, but the stains — blood, sweat, tears, gravy and grease. Her ma, one of the fussiest people she knew, would be rolling over in her grave if she saw her lass. Two of her could fit into the filthy skirt and there'd still be room for half of her again. She examined her hands. Scarred from the pricking, they were sprinkled with spots and marred by ropey veins — veins that looked bigger now her hands had begun to resemble birds' claws, even curling into her palm the way a jackdaw's might. At least all the loose flesh upon her arms and thighs remained to keep her warm. All in all, considering where she was and why, things weren't so bad.

Anyhow, she'd no one to blame but herself, not really. If only she hadn't given in to the bloody reverend and that fucking pricker the first time. If only she hadn't recanted her confessions. But then, if she hadn't told Mr Cooke and Mr Kippilaw what the reverend really did to her and the others, the threats that burbled out of that sliver of a mouth like water gushing into the burn, how he'd promised her that if she admitted to the things he said she did with the devil (och, she only elaborated to please him), he'd not only baptise her again, but she'd be set free, then she'd likely still be in the cave. As it was, she was akin to illicit goods brought back by a smuggler: too dangerous to touch.

She picked a flea out of her hair and broke it in half, smearing the blood between her fingers. Aye, she smiled, that was her, dangerous.

If only Reverend Cowper were a flea. He was as irritating as one.

Reflecting back on her time in the cave, for all it had been a miserable, cold way to pass the days and weeks as they all bent one into the other in the dark until they were a crushing weight, at least she hadn't been tortured any more. Dear God, but that was something she hoped never to go through again. The way that bastard Bollard took such pleasure from inserting his instruments into her auld flesh, her sagging lugs and even her cunt for Christ sakes... She shuddered. There was something not quite right about someone who could inflict that level of pain on another human being, divest a woman of her robes without blinking a cold eye nor show any emotion as he pawed her flesh, pulled and searched... Searched, my arse. It was as if his soul had been dislodged or evaporated altogether. And they called *her* a witch.

It was thoughts of how she would enact revenge on all the bastards who'd locked her away that kept Janet's spirit strong. If that cocksucking reverend wanted to call it malfeasance, so be it. She was filled with it, devil take his balls. When she was free, och, how she'd celebrate with the lasses who, just as they did when she was shut deep in the cave, would call out her name, tell her stories and cackle to lift her spirits.

A noise outside the door distracted her thoughts. Who had come this time? It had been too cold to remain by the window and it was too early for a change of the guards. Why, the clock had scarce struck one.

There was the rattle of keys.

The door screamed open and in stepped Reverend Cowper and a large man she'd seen once before. A grubby-looking lad who, Camron told her, had been a soldier. With fists like hammers and a way of wielding the stick he carried so it left bruises but rarely broke bones, he had a smile frostier than the ice-floes of the north. Janet's heart fell into her feet but she forced a grin nonetheless. They would not see her trepidation. Not if she could help it.

'Good afternoon, Mrs Cornfoot,' said the reverend.

Scrambling to her feet, Janet bobbed a curtsey. Wouldn't do to let manners slide. 'Afternoon, sirs.'

The reverend dragged a stool over and invited Janet to sit. The last thing she wanted to do was comply, but she did. She'd learned it made the punishment less brutal if she did what she was told.

Taking her seat as if she was a lady entertaining in a grand salon, folding her soiled skirts under her skinny rump, she raised her head. 'And to what do I owe the pleasure?'

The hefty soldier shut the door, but not before she'd seen Camron's pale, wide-eyed face. That unnerved her far more than having the reverend there. The soldier — what was his name? — tramped towards her, swinging his stick. Janet gulped, and gathered her hands in her lap to hide their quivering.

'Thing is, Janet,' said the reverend, squatting down beside her, as if she was a naughty bairn about to be delivered a lesson. 'You've gone out of your way to make a right slabber of me. Here I was with your confession written out, signed, sent off to Edinburgh, ready to baptise you again and admit you back into God's graces and our Christian family here in the Weem, and what do you do? You tell the city gents it's all a confeck. That it's all lies.'

Janet sighed. So, it wasn't over yet. Never mind that this whole business started because a lad supposedly fell victim to a sea-charm. Didn't matter that the woman accused of it — and all her accomplices — had been acquitted. He had to punish someone.

He had to make someone pay for being made to look a fool and that someone was going to be her.

Janet opened her hands and regarded them again. They were auld hands. Well used. They'd worked hard her entire life; held bairns, and not just her own. They'd touched the flesh of men, stroked cocks, dried tears, made bannocks and bread, scaled and gutted more fish and baited more lines than she cared to remember. If she screwed up her eyes, she could still make out the tiny cuts and deep grooves from her first clumsy attempts to learn the fishwives' craft. God, what was she then? Five? Six? And now? Seventy-two? Maybe. Maybe younger. Maybe older. It didn't matter. She'd lived a good full life, known the love of a few good men and, even better, the loving friendship of many a good woman. Good women who were also being asked to pay for this man's wounded pride and whatever else drove him. Pay for his devotion to a cruel and stupid God. Not her God. Not the one she knew and to whom she prayed.

Enough.

Enough.

She'd done all the reverend said and still he punished her. Repeated the words he drilled into her head until she could recite them in her sleep, and still he didn't let her go, didn't stop tormenting her or the others.

What did she really have to do for the reverend to say she was accepted back into God's good graces? She knew. In her heart, she knew. It wasn't what this man said, despite his religious garb, training and the smooth words he claimed were God's that tumbled out of his mouth. It didn't matter what she said.

No more. She would find her own way and, as far as she was concerned, the way to the Lord was by walking the path of truth.

Drawing on what remained of her courage, sending a silent prayer to the God she knew could see into her heart, she met his eyes.

'They weren't no lies,' said Janet. 'As you well ken. I merely said what I did the first time to please you, minister, and the bailies.'

'And this is what you told those lairds.'

'Aye. And if I had my time over, I would tell them the same again and any other gent who might listen. So do your worst.'

The reverend stood, his knees creaking. Staring at Janet and rubbing his neck, he sighed. 'If that's your final word.'

'Nae. But I'm hoping that you've said your last.' Janet raised her chin. 'I'm mighty sick of your blethering, let me tell you.'

The reverend stepped back and, with a flick of his hand, indicated that the soldier was to take his place.

'Private Smith. The witch is now yours.'

Och, Smith. That's right. That was his name.

With a toothless grin, Smith raised his stick. Janet shut her eyes and waited for the blow to fall.

FORTY-TWO

The keeper put her into a prison in which was a low window, out of
which it was obvious that any body could make an escape...

— A Letter From a Gentleman in Fife
to his Friend in Edinburgh, *1705*

'You heard me, Camron,' said Reverend Cowper, moving away from the window and giving the rest of the cell a cursory glance. 'Move her down here immediately.' He pushed his scented kerchief against his nose. Dear God, but the place smelled wretched. Even weeks after the women had been released and Brown had died, he could smell them — their distress, their leavings. He could see the rust-coloured stains upon the floor where they'd bled. Instead of rousing him to pity, it made him angry. If only the foolish women had confessed earlier; if only they'd admitted their ungodly, devilish practices, then they would have been freed — one way or another — long ago.

Denied the burning he'd been secretly hoping for, a cleansing the township needed now more than ever — arguments over whether or not the women were witches and concerns over the treasury erupted with alarming frequency — Janet Cornfoot had ruined everything. She and the other women whose very presence was an affront to any good Christian soul.

It wasn't enough that they were refused service in the town's shops, shunned wherever they went. There were still those who dared to buy the fish they tried to sell, secretly offered them succour and support. Just like the accused, these people sought to make dupes of him and all who believed the women were what he knew they were in his heart: witches, with malfeasance running through their veins. They were a blight on his authority.

Even so, God had found ways to punish them. Firstly, Sorcha's lover had been sent to Bavaria. (Even though he had had something to do with that, he still attributed it to God. Had not the Almighty planted the idea in his head? Allowed those he contacted to see the right of his suggestion?) Then Janet Horseburgh's husband had died. Two women, whores and witches by any other names, were answering to God for the sins of their souls. Forsaken by the men who supported them, who, bewitched as they must have been, bedded them, they were adrift without a male to anchor them, to hold their heads above the waters that even now were rising to sweep them away. Smiling, he thought of Nicolas Lawson. Aye, she still bore the scars of her internment and it was said her husband couldn't bear to touch her any more. No doubt he saw what Bollard and he too had seen — the marks upon her body where the devil had suckled; where, of her own admission, she'd taken him as a beast does its mate. Shuddering, though not with displeasure, Patrick forced an image of Nicolas's lithe body from his mind and thought instead of auld Beatrix Laing, that shrivelled prune and, finally, the wizened woman in the cell above — Janet Cornfoot.

'Leave the window, Camron,' barked the reverend as the keeper tried to close it. 'The woman likes fresh air, let her have some.'

'But, reverend, it's not s'posed to be ajar.'

The reverend smiled sympathetically at the young nyaff. 'Janet Cornfoot is an auld, auld woman and weak. Weak now we've wrangled the devil from her soul. An open window is the least of our worries or hers.'

If Camron thought differently, he didn't argue. 'I'll see she brings her belongings with her then, the blankets and such, shall I?'

Not wishing to stay any longer, unable to escape the memories that seemed to leach out of the stone, an irrational fear that the walls were crowding him, the reverend made to leave. 'Nae, Camron. She's to be brought here alone, without bedding or blankets, do you hear me?'

Camron appeared about to object. He was becoming too bold. The reverend frowned. 'You're not to give her any nourishment either, you hear?'

'Do you want me to leave her water so she can wash away the blood?'

The reverend pretended to give this suggestion some thought. 'Nae, Camron, I don't want you to do that either. What I *do* want is for you to escort her down here, lock the door and then leave her alone. It will do her good to reflect on what she's done; to whom she owes loyalty. God or the devil.'

Camron scuffed his boots along the floor.

The reverend paused at the door. 'Take the night off, Camron. Don't object. I'm ordering you. The guards have been given permission to go and enjoy themselves. You've been extraordinary in your duty, lad, a mighty fine keeper. It's only fair that you have a night free as well. Go to the tavern, see your friends. Or go home to your ma. Just take yourself away from here.' He looked around and gave a dramatic shudder.

Camron blinked and his thick-lipped mouth dropped open. The reverend almost laughed as a beaming smile lifted the lad's entire face before it fell back into its usual blank expression. 'But, reverend, if I do that who will watch the Tolbooth? Who will watch Mrs Cornfoot?'

'The Lord, Camron. That's who. God will watch over the witch.'

'Why do you think he moved her?' asked Nettie.

Sorcha looked up from where she was bent over the pot, stirring the soup and shrugged. The steam made her cheeks pink and her curls cling to her forehead. Ever since they'd left Beatrix's early that evening, having learned from Mr Brown, who heard it from Camron, who'd called into the tavern for an ale on his way home, that Janet had been shifted into the lower room of the Tolbooth, they'd been debating what it meant.

The two women had stopped by the Tolbooth on their way back to the cottage, and had managed to slip some more blankets, a clean shirt and some food to Janet. Camron had been worried Janet would not only freeze, but starve. The window wasn't as low as they remembered, but low enough that all Sorcha had to do was hoist herself onto Nettie's shoulders to pass the goods through the open window. They even managed a quick conversation as the wynd was empty. No wonder, the way gusts swept down from the north, pummelling them with ice and rain.

Calling out to Janet quietly, Sorcha was relieved when she came straight to the window, crying out in shock when she saw her balanced just below the sill.

'Hush,' said Sorcha. 'You'll alert the guards.'

'Nae, I won't, lass. They're off-duty.'

'What?' asked Sorcha. Surely Janet must be mistaken. There were usually four armed guards hovering about the building, outside the cell doors.

There was no time to waste. 'How are you keeping?' asked Sorcha quickly, pushing the blankets through the gaps in the grate. She was surprised how loose the bars were.

'Better now, thanks to you.' Janet tugged the blankets inside, then pressed her face to the iron, trying to see past Sorcha. 'How are you, Nettie love? Carrying some extra weight, I see.' She winked at Sorcha.

'Pity they haven't beaten that poor sense of humour out of you,' grumbled Nettie.

'Aye, well,' said Janet hesitantly when Sorcha relayed Nettie's words to her. 'Hasn't stopped them trying.'

Though it was dark, lights from the houses at the top of the High Street cast enough of a glow for Sorcha to see Janet had a swollen cheek and lip.

'What have they done?' she cried and grabbed Janet's wrist as she thrust the shirt and package of food into her hands.

'Nothing I couldn't cope with, lass. Don't worry. I might be auld, but they breed us tough here in the Weem. Fishwives tougher than most.'

Blinking back tears at the bold words, the courage it took for Janet to utter them, Sorcha could see the welts on Janet's arms now her sleeve had ridden up. She squeezed Janet's wrist gently, conveying with that slight pressure all the love and confidence that she could.

'You'll be out of there in no time. We're writing to the Privy Council and to Mr Kippilaw and Mr Cooke — the lawyers you spoke to. When they learn what Cowper's done, they'll order your release.'

Janet gave her a wistful smile. Sorcha wanted to caress her battered face, reassure her, but wasn't sure how. Not when her safety and her freedom were at the mercy of others.

'I wouldn't hold my breath, lassie,' said Janet finally. 'But thank you all the same. I don't ken what I'd do without you.' Releasing Sorcha, she flapped her hands. 'Now, you best be going before anyone catches you. Or you break Nettie's spine. You don't want to be giving the reverend an excuse to lock you up again, much as I'd appreciate your company.'

Sorcha slid off Nettie's back onto the ground. Nettie tried to reach Janet's hand, but failed to bridge the distance. 'There be anything else you need, Janet?'

'Cowper's head on a platter would be nice,' she replied.

Nettie chuckled and nudged Sorcha. 'Told you if anyone'd be all right, it would be this woman.' She cupped her mouth. 'And if we can't supply you with that, how about some whisky?'

'I wouldn't say nae.'

Voices drifted from the High Street.

'Be gone, quickly.' Janet began to withdraw into the darkness of the Tolbooth. 'Fare thee well and God look after you both and the others; you be as dear to me as if you were my own daughters.'

Sorcha looked at Nettie and frowned. Janet was speaking as if she'd never see them again. It wasn't like her to be so maudlin. The sooner she was set at liberty, the better. Nettie didn't appear to have heard; she was too busy looking out for whoever was approaching.

'Come away lest it be the guards,' hissed Nettie.

Hearts beating fast, the pair picked up their skirts and stayed close to the shadows of the kirk, then slipped into the graveyard before they were seen. Dodging the tombstones that loomed like soldiers in the night, they silently wove their way back to Marygate, coming out at the entrance not far from Sorcha's.

Only once they were inside the cottage with the candles lit, the fire stoked and a soup on the boil did they allow themselves to consider Janet's plight.

Why had she been moved to a lower cell? What were the reverend's intentions?

'I don't like that he's denied her *any* comforts,' said Nettie, accepting a bowl of soup gratefully. 'That's not been his way; not after he extracted confessions.'

'Aye, but don't forget, Janet retracted hers very publicly.'

'And he locked her away for that and, from what you saw, had her beaten again.'

'She suffers, though you won't catch her complaining.'

'Not to us, anyhow,' said Nettie. Janet was the kind of woman who made a career out of complaining about the small things just to get a rise out of people. When genuinely afflicted, she was as tough as a Highlander's fist.

'It's a puzzle. I cannot think what the reverend hopes to gain by allowing her nothing. Moving her to the lower cell makes no sense. And to leave the window unsealed and with the grate so worn and loose a bairn could shift it...' Sorcha stared at the burning peat, the soup forgotten.

Outside, the wind howled, the sea rumbled and groaned, throwing itself against the shore and the harbour wall. Tomorrow banks of kelp would lie upon the sand like ploughed fields, waiting for the fishwives to reap their harvest.

Grateful she wasn't the one confined to the Tolbooth any more, she recalled how it felt when she was emancipated. How she'd never really appreciated her freedom until it was taken from her. A thought struck her. She stopped the spoon halfway to her mouth.

'What is it?' asked Nettie.

Sorcha's eyes were wide. 'You don't suppose the reverend put Janet there, in that room, so she *would* escape, do you?'

Nettie's spoon dropped into her bowl. 'Dear God —'

'If Janet does, then the reverend can not only call in the constables to arrest her...'

'Worse, hen, he can send guards out to hunt not an auld woman, but an escaped witch...' Nettie glanced towards the window. Rain lashed the glass, rattling it fiercely.

'She said something that didn't make sense before, it was so... final. But now it does.' Sorcha repeated Janet's words of farewell.

'Och, the foolish auld woman...' Nettie began to stand.

Putting down her bowl, Sorcha leapt to her feet. 'Come on, Nettie. We have to go back to the Tolbooth and stop her.' Throwing her coat on, Sorcha reached the door first. 'That is, if we're not too late.'

FORTY-THREE

She made her escape that night...

— A Letter from a Gentleman in Fife to his
Friend in Edinburgh, *1705*

*W*hile Janet waited for the bloothered soldiers in the street to finish their conversation and head to the comfort of their lodgings, she donned the clean shirt over her filthy one, then wrapped the blankets Sorcha had provided about her body. One went over her head and around her shoulders, the other she tied about her waist, intending to also drape it over the frame as she levered herself out the window. As for the food, she thought about eating it, but knew she might need it once she found shelter. Not that she would seek that for a while. She wanted as much distance between herself and the reverend as possible before she even thought of stopping.

Leaning against the window ledge, she tried to regulate her breathing. By God, her heart was thumping like a soldier's drum and damn it if that gale wasn't more glacial than Beatrix's stare. Could she do this? Never had she felt her age as she did now. But thinking of Nettie and how she could silence a man with a mere look, gave her strength. So did Sorcha. How was it she and Nettie could defy the reverend and bring her supplies? Hearing Sorcha's voice and then leaning out to find her right there had almost stopped her heart. Just as well they'd been out of the Tolbooth a while and able to recover or she doubted Nettie would have been able to bear Sorcha's weight.

It was nice to see them. Better than nice. To get the chance to say goodbye. Escaping had been on her mind ever since the reverend first put her in St Fillan's Cave. There was no use trying to get out of that infernal dungeon. Janet knew she had to bide her time and, as soon as she learned she was being moved to the Tolbooth, let alone the lower cell, she knew it had come. Did they forget the weeks she'd already spent in this very same room last year? She knew every corner and crevice as well as those on her own body. Admittedly, the window was sealed last time she stayed, but they often used to talk about what they'd do if they could get it open and how it faced straight onto the wynd. They used to boast about how they'd sprint to the water and leap into the sea and swim as if the devil was on their heels — a dog-shaped devil and all.

She grinned and peered out the window again. The men had gone. Wrapping her fingers around the iron bars, she pulled. The metal barely resisted. Stone crumbled at the base and she shook the bars, loosening them further. In no time at all the entire grate had come away and she heaved it onto the floor, then dusted her hands and pushed the window out as wide as she could. Well, she'd no intention of making her way to the sea, not when she had a sister at St Andrew's who would take her in. There she could lie low until all this blew over. Still, she'd be sad to leave the Weem, her home; she'd worry about her neighbours, the fishwives and fishermen, never mind the lasses. She wouldn't put it past the reverend to punish them for her escape.

Somewhere an owl hooted and she could hear faint laughter. How had it come to this? Fleeing the place she was born like a common criminal, turning her back on all she was and had been and all because of a godforsaken minister who didn't know the difference between an angry auld woman who called a herring a herring and a cod a cod and a fucking witch. Or maybe he did and that was the point.

Casting one last look at the dark, empty cell, whispering a curse to the man who put her there and those who'd done nothing to stop him, she hoisted one leg over the sill and froze. Nae. 'Twas naught. Just cats fighting. There was no sign nor sound of anybody now. Only a mad person would brave this weather — a mad person in league with Satan.

Chuckling, she slowly lowered herself onto the ground, falling slightly at the bottom and twisting her ankle. Pain shot through her body and she braced herself against the wall, sucking air into her lungs and with it, determination. She undid the blanket from around her waist and flung it over her shoulders, grateful for the extra warmth, and wished she could ease the window shut. With one last curse at the Tolbooth and a healthy spit for good measure, she crept past the Mercat Cross and turned into Routine Row, slowing as she passed the house and smithy where all this cursed nonsense began.

The smith, Patrick Morton and his blasted lad, Peter, were sitting in the kitchen, the other bairns arranged around the table like a picture-perfect family. Sitting among them like another son was the guard, Simon Wood. So, this is where he chose to spend his night off. The mother, that scrawny excuse for a woman, was running around after them. They were blethering away as if they hadn't a care in the world, all of them enveloped in smoke and the umber light of candles and no doubt a fire in the hearth; she could almost feel its warmth as she stopped to drink in the sight. Did she envy them this togetherness? They looked almost holy.

Nae, not when it came at the cost of all those she called friends. Not when it meant she was exiled from her town, her home, for the foreseeable future. There was nothing holy about them, about Simon, or their eldest son. Peter was responsible for the damn mess they found themselves in, the lying widdie; and Simon, a lad she'd known since he was in his ma's belly, had shown where his sympathies lay, beating her and denying her food and water. Funny how, when given the chance to be cruel without consequence, even seemingly decent people would take it. Bowing her head against the rain that was falling steadily now, she turned aside as two men passed. Ignoring her, they continued on their way and she released the breath she'd been holding.

It wasn't until she reached the outskirts of town that she stopped again. Already her ankle was throbbing, her head swimming. Wet and uncomfortable, she was thirsty, hungry and the thrashings and sleepless nights were taking their toll. Even with Sorcha's blankets wrapped around her, it was bitterly cold — worse now she was drookit. Standing on the ridge, a hand against her breast as she fought for breath, she looked across the Forth. The rain had eased until it was just a spittering. Lights from ships' lanterns were dotted across the black expanse and the lighthouse on the Isle of May swung its huge beam across the waters like a road that, it was said, the spirits of drowned sailors walked along. She thought of her own bonnie lad, Clinton, taken too soon. She thought of Sorcha's dad, kind Charlie, and his sons, Erik and Robbie. Good God, but they'd all given so much. Had their hearts and souls wrung until there wasn't any more to squeeze from them. And what of Sorcha's husband Andy? A dull man, he'd never been right for one such as Sorcha McIntyre, but Janet well understood why the lass had married him. Was she secretly glad when he died? When she no longer had to pretend a contentment it was evident she'd never felt with him? If she had, the guilt that came when the bairn was born dead would have swept that away.

She thought of Sorcha now. She'd heard rumours she'd found happiness with that lad from Skye, bonnie Captain Ross. She prayed it was so. The lass deserved at least some of that in her life. But he was gone now, too, like the ever-changing tides. It would be hard — for her, for poor Nettie too. Women without men to speak for them — control them more like. It was a bleak day when Reverend Cowper arrived in the Weem and began to preach against women of her ilk. He was the kind who saw her and the other fishwives as Eves in a seaside paradise — temptations to lure men away from their wives, as if the men were fish and the lasses bait.

Hopefully, when Janet returned — and return she would — it would be to a different Pittenweem. One where witches were dismissed as the product of fevered imaginations or, more to the truth, the by-product of revenge. Revenge for what? For being a woman. A scold. Independent, headstrong and able to make her way. Well, she prayed to God that Sorcha, Nettie and the others made their way, with whomever and in whatever direction they pleased. For now, hers lay that way — towards St Andrew's.

Turning her back on the sea, she lowered her head as sleet began to whirl about her, the wind making her nose run and eyes water. Janet put one foot before the other and left behind all she'd ever known and all she'd ever been.

Not forever, she promised herself. Only for as long as it took for justice to be served.

FORTY-FOUR

She was a person of very bad fame, who for a long time was reputed a witch...

— A Just Reproof to the False Reports and Unjust
Calumnies in the Foregoing Letters, *1705*

$\mathcal{A}$s soon as they realised Janet had indeed escaped the Tolbooth, Sorcha and Nettie's first instinct was to find her and force her to return. Staring helplessly at the grateless open window as the rain hammered down and they whispered about where to look for her, it slowly dawned on them that searching the lanes and byways would draw attention to what she'd done. Without another word, they drew their coats over their heads and returned to the cottage. Far better they let the woman get a head start and pretend they knew nothing.

Only, that was harder than Sorcha thought. Unable to sleep, she moved between the chair and the window all night. A chill had crept into her bones, no doubt from the drenching she'd received, but she felt it was more than that. It was as if something dark and dire had lodged in her soul. She couldn't shake it. Nettie drowsed in the bed, waking occasionally to ask if Sorcha had heard or seen anything.

'Only the snow and wind,' whispered Sorcha. 'Go back to sleep.' And the sea, she thought. Always the sea.

Before dawn, the women tidied themselves, ate a small breakfast and then, retrieving their creels from where they'd stored them the day before, made their way to the harbour as if nothing was amiss. There were a few people abroad. Moira gave a wave as she released Crabby to run about the graveyard. The streets were wet. Deep puddles reflected the grey sky, giving the road a strange pitted feel, like a foreign landscape. Not that Crabby cared as he plodded through them. Birds wheeled in the heavens, so high their cries were muted, as if they were afraid to land. Underlying the ever-present brume of hearth-smoke was a salty, metallic smell, like hundreds of shucked oysters. Instead of ducking into Water Wynd as they usually did, Sorcha and Nettie chose to go down Cove Wynd and past the Tolbooth in the hope they'd learn something.

As they rounded the corner, they came upon Camron MacGille and the Stuart brothers talking animatedly to a group of soldiers. The men were tense in their frayed uniforms. Weapons were drawn, faces hard. Some were jabbing their fingers towards the water as they spoke, talking in hushed voices. Nearby, outside the baker's, a group of men and women watched on warily, arms folded, eyes flickering. The main door to the Tolbooth was open. The window of Janet's cell had been closed.

When Camron and the others caught sight of Sorcha and Nettie, one by one they ceased to chatter. The faint sounds of activity in the streets nearby, doors closing, folk being hailed, and the grind of cart wheels, could now be heard. The town was waking to the news.

Before Sorcha could approach and pose a question to the men, Gerard Stuart came running up the wynd from the direction of the manse.

'Right,' he called. 'Camron, Private Smith and Corporal Inglis, Sergeant Thatcher says you're to come with me. We're to search the witches' houses.'

Camron swung to look at Sorcha and Nettie, but no one else noticed.

'The rest of you are to work in pairs.' He began to allocate tasks. 'The reverend wants you to go to St Monan's, and you lot to Anster and Crail, see if anyone has seen sight or sound of the witch. She can't have gone far, not in the state she was in and in this cold —' Gerard suddenly spotted Sorcha and Nettie. Pushing aside the soldiers, he marched up to them. 'Where have you been?'

Sorcha glanced at Nettie in surprise. 'And a fine morning to you too, Gerard.'

Gerard snarled.

'Why, nowhere yet, lad,' said Sorcha with a smile. 'Why are you asking?'

'You haven't seen anything of that auld witch, Janet Cornfoot?'

'How could we?' said Nettie. 'She's locked in the Tolbooth, isn't she?' She nodded towards Janet's cell.

Gerard's eyes narrowed. 'You'll both learn about it soon enough. She's escaped. And if you've had anything to do with it, you'll take her place.' He pointed at the building. 'Care if we search your cottage, Sorcha?'

'Be my guest,' sad Sorcha, aware they'd find nothing to incriminate her or anyone else.

With a barely concealed look of disappointment, he swung away, but before he could rejoin the men, there were shouts and raised voices. The sound of boots, shoes, and the steady tramp of feet grew.

Marching up Cove Wynd was a large group. Some were waving pitchforks, others hammers, axes — two even wielded old swords. While their words were at first unclear, their intentions were not.

'Thou shalt not suffer a witch to live!'

'Raise your weapons for God!'

'Find her, find them all!'

There were cheers. Doors were wrenched open and figures darted out to join the mob. More stood on their stoops and watched the rabble pass. As the swelling crowd came into view, Sorcha saw who led them. It was none other than the reverend.

Within a few yards, the horde had grown to twice its size. Some remained at a distance, watching, waiting, whether to join or flee, Sorcha couldn't be certain. But she knew what she must do.

Clearly news of Janet's escape had spread. The people were looking for scapegoats; just as Gerard threatened, they wanted women to
replace the one they'd lost.

They wanted a witch.

There was only one place she and Nettie would be safe.

Ensuring their creels were fastened securely, Sorcha and Nettie darted into Routine Row and began to run up the incline. They
bolted past men running towards the High Street, ignoring them.
Some women stood in their doorways and cheered. They didn't dare
respond, or look. If they were quick, they should reach the harbour
and the safety of the other fishwives and fishermen before the mob
found them.

If they didn't, then God help them.

FORTY-FIVE

'As far as I'm concerned,' said Patrick Cowper, pacing the room,
'we're better off without her.' He swung around to face the other
councillors.

He'd insisted on bringing them into the cell where Janet Cornfoot had been held so they could see for themselves what her unnatural strength had done. How she'd pried the grating off with her own
two hands before leaping from the window. They weren't to know
a bairn could have breathed on the metal bars and they would have
fallen. He'd ordered Camron to remove the evidence and sweep the
floor. He'd also insisted clean straw be laid and her blankets brought

from upstairs. It had to look as if they'd at least attended to her basic needs. She was entitled to that, as the lairds from Edinburgh had been keen to remind him.

Outside, the crowd had increased. There were those baying for blood, for justice. Wild rumours were spreading that Janet had flown off in the night, that she'd cursed the town; that all the witches were planning to have a sabbat and recruit whoever remained to the devil's cause. Children were crying; some women were openly weeping. Others were white-faced. The men were furious. They wanted this to end, to put a stop to the terror and suspicion, only they didn't know how.

They didn't, but Patrick did.

Still, no one in the cell said anything. They shifted uneasily on their well-shod feet. Not even their coats and cloaks could keep out the bitter cold. The air was freezing; the walls damp and the place reeked of putrid water, rotting food, sweat and old stockings. Dried blood had seeped into the floor. The air was thick with that too, and silent screams. Patrick saw William Bell ploughing his hair with his fingers, as was his habit, staring and swallowing. He half-expected the man to lose his breakfast. Wouldn't be the first time.

Patrick longed to retreat to the comfort of his study, a fire and a dram, but he had to persuade these men that what he was about to propose was right; that he was right. That they all were.

By God, but they were weak men. Bailie Whyte was again conveniently out of town. Bailies William Bell and Robert Vernour wouldn't meet his eyes. Cleiland was making notes — about what, Patrick couldn't fathom — anything to avoid a decision. Only Robert Cook had the gumption not only to hold his gaze, but nod in consent.

'She won't last long out there at this time of year.' Cook gestured towards the window. 'More snow's due.' He picked at a scab on his large chin. 'You said she had nothing in here with her?'

A cheer erupted outside.

'Nothing,' said Patrick, forced to raise his voice to be heard. 'As Camron can confirm.'

The bailies turned to Camron who blushed to the roots of his thinning hair and gulped.

'Men are searching nearby towns as we speak. Others are checking the convicted witches' houses and combing the fields. We'll find her,' said Patrick. He waited for someone to challenge his use of the word 'convicted'. No-one did.

'And what of the rest of those McGregor named?' asked Bailie Cook when no one spoke. 'What are we going to do about them?'

'Nothing... yet,' said Patrick. 'Our priority has to be the Cornfoot woman. Once we have her back in custody, then we can discuss what to do with the others.'

'He's right,' said Bailie Bell finally. 'Only, the people might seek retribution — for Cornfoot's escape. They may well hold her friends, her fellow accused, responsible.'

'Perhaps they're right,' said Patrick.

'Maybe. But shouldn't we be keeping those women safe? After all, Edinburgh acquitted them.' Bailie Bell pointed to the window. 'Listen to the folk out there. They want blood. They want justice.'

'Let's be clear here: they want witches' blood.' Patrick folded his arms.

The men stared at each other.

'In order to distract them from doing anything... hasty,' said Bailie Cook, 'to guarantee their, let's say, co-operation in apprehending the main offender, I think we need to offer a reward for Mrs Cornfoot's return.'

'How much?' asked Patrick, worried the kirk might be asked to provide it.

The bailies exchanged a look. 'Ten pounds should suffice,' said Bailie Vernour. The others nodded.

'I take it the town council will raise the money?' asked Patrick.

Wincing, Vernour looked to Cleiland, who gave his agreement. The other men assented too.

'Very well,' said Patrick, suppressing a grin. 'Ten pounds it is then. Camron, ask the Stuart brothers and Sergeant Thatcher to meet me at the manse. I will organise for news of the reward to go not only to the people of the Weem, but to outlying parishes as well.'

'The sooner the better,' said Bailie Bell as another roar came from outside.

'Aye. The sooner we catch the witch Cornfoot, the sooner we can ensure that this time, the right judgement is delivered.'

Patrick gestured for the bailies to proceed him out of the cell, his mind racing. At last he had the freedom to bring at least one of the women to trial. While he might not have Sorcha McIntyre in his grasp yet, it wouldn't be long before all the witches would face the Lord's justice for their devilish crimes.

And this time, there'd be nothing Captain Ross or Edinburgh could do about it.

FORTY-SIX

God forgive the minister.

— The words of Janet Cornfoot to Mr Ker of Kippilaw and Mr
Robert Cooke the Advocate, 1704

*I*n all her three score and ten — or more — years, Janet couldn't remember being so cold. Or stiff. Or sore. Barely able to move as the frost that coated her clothing during the night seeped into her limbs and froze them, she rolled onto her side, crackling and groaning, and forced her eyes open.

Never again would she think kindly of woods or barns, even if they were attached to large farmhouses or filled with straw and the warm bodies, breath and farts of bovines and sheep. Not after the night she'd endured. At least there were water troughs nearby. Not too proud to drink from them, once she'd cracked the sheet of ice that coated the top, she'd drunk her fill. You'd think the bloody animals would be grateful she'd given them access to their water and let her sleep beside them. Not these dour mulls.

Unable to curl against the hawkit cattle or sheep because, as soon as they felt her trying to settle next to them, they started lowing, kicking and bleating, drawing the attention of the farmers, she'd been forced to move on. Back out into the wretched snow, tramping through drifts and along muddy roads. Shaking with fatigue as well as cold, her ankle aching, by the time she'd finally found an empty barn and some stinking straw to burrow in, the moon was in its descent.

She'd no idea where she was, but prayed she was still heading towards St Andrew's.

In the pale light piercing the planks of splintered wood that formed the walls of her sanctuary, she could see it for what it was. A broken-down sty. It still smelled of the pigs that had once rooted about within its tight confines. The trough was empty, the straw brittle and dry — thank the Lord. Barely protecting her from the hard ground and bitter night, it was better than nothing.

It took all her strength to sit up and slap some warmth back into her limbs. Each time her hand connected with her flesh, it was as if hot bolts had been driven into her palms, her fingers. God, but she was freezing. Her breath poured out of her mouth and nostrils in clouds. Peering through the opening where a door had once hung, she could see it had snowed again. It lay upon the ground, drifting into the sty like a wave, frozen solid before it touched her. Maybe she could find a vessel to gather some in and, maybe, if she was really fortunate, the means to start a fire and melt some. All her food had gone. How long ago had she eaten the bannocks and coney Sorcha had given her? Was it only one night? Felt like years.

What a numptie she was. She'd underestimated not only how long it would take her to get to St Andrew's, but her strength. She also hadn't considered how slow it would be travelling on foot this time of year, what with her ankle paining, snow to wade through, the occasional passers-by to hide from and the little bit of foraging she'd managed to do that had done naught but make her stomach cramp.

With the help of the sty walls, which creaked as she leaned against them, she hauled herself upright. Unsteady, she waited until the room stopped spinning, wiping the back of her hand across her mouth.

If she didn't get moving and soon, she never would again. Aye, well, as tempting as that was, she wasn't ready to give up. Not yet.

First taking a piss, she searched for something to put snow in. There was nothing but a rusty pail with a great broken seam.

Nae bother, she thought, throwing it against the wall. The noise was loud in the great silence. It was as if the world had gone quiet. There wasn't a sound. No birdsong, no animals, no voices. That at least was good. If she could just get going again, she'd be in St Andrew's and sitting in front of her sister's hearth being coddled with soup, bread and whisky by evening.

With those cheery notions swimming in her head, she set off across country, careful to avoid the farmhouse that appeared at the top of a rise a short time later, staying within the trees and praying that if the people did see her, they'd think she was a gypsy or a stray animal and pay her no heed.

As she trudged along, she wondered what was happening back in the Weem. Would they send a search party out? Or would the reverend think she was too much trouble? Either way, she didn't care, so long as Cowper didn't punish those she'd left behind for her sins. Her perceived sins. Anger made her forget her hunger, her weariness, her sore body. She began to move faster.

Uncertain how long she'd been walking, placing one worn boot in front of the other, her stockings sodden, her head pounding, her mind wandering, it took Janet a moment to understand that what she saw looming through the trees before her was not a figment of her fevered mind, but an actual kirk.

Staggering out of the woods, she noted how dark the day had become, how thickly the snow fell. For all she was an escaped witch, an emissary of the devil who had turned from God and denied her baptism, the huge grey stone building with its cross piercing the heavens was one of the most welcome sights she'd ever seen.

Dropping to her knees, she crawled the last few feet to its door and rested her back against it. Why, with its little graveyard, the falling curtain of snow and the black skeletons of the trees, it was quite pretty really. She sent a prayer to the God she thought had forsaken her, twisted slightly and, with her last remaining strength, banged on the wood.

The Reverend George Gordon was dozing in his office when he thought he heard something. He tried to ignore it, but the noise persisted, and a flare of annoyance at the intrusion dashed away his last chance of returning to sleep.

He pushed back his chair and, ensuring his robes were in place, left his office at the back of the kirk and marched up the aisle, imagining what he'd say to the men who, no doubt, had forgotten they'd stopped by earlier and were there to repeat the news he already knew: a witch had escaped Pittenweem and there was a ten-pound reward for whoever should find her.

What he could do with ten pounds! Who on God's good earth couldn't use such an amount these days? Unless, of course, they were the Queen with a royal treasury at her disposal. Or Laird Bairnscliff with his numerous houses. Or Mr Craigieburn, who owned more sheep and ships than a man had a right to yet couldn't find it within his tight-arsed heart to donate enough to repair the roof of the kirk.

'Come away with you,' he called out to whoever was knocking. It wasn't loud, just persistent, like a spoiled child demanding attention. Maybe it wasn't those rough-looking soldiers after all. Maybe it was a bairn seeking shelter from the elements.

He reached the door and unlatched it, offering a prayer of forgiveness as he did. He knew he shouldn't be locking the door, but after finding that family slumbering away inside over Hogmanay, and the fire they'd lit at the base of the pulpit, well, he didn't want to risk just anybody entering.

'Dear God!' exclaimed Reverend Gordon, as a body fell back against his feet. 'What have we here?'

Two grey-blue eyes in a weather-bitten face stared up at him. 'A wretch that seeks your help and that of the good Lord.' The voice quavered with misery.

Offering a hand, he helped the woman sit up. The poor thing was filthy and she smelled of the outdoors and something less palatable. She was nithered from being out in the weather, shaking like a half-drowned kitten. Her hands, which she'd wrapped with cloth she'd clearly torn from her skirt, were reddened and callused. Her lips and cheeks were cracked, her breath foul. Her boots were also held together with strips of fabric and he could see grey toes and torn, grubby nails where her stockings had worn away.

'Well, lass,' he called her, even though she looked old enough and thin enough to be his grandmother — and she dead these last ten years, God bless her. 'You've come to the right place. The Lord will protect you and so will I. Now, come away in and let's get some food and a drink into you. Then, if you can, I want you to tell me what it is that's brought you all the way out here to Leuchars on such a plashin' day.'

Janet could scarce believe her good fortune. Relatively clean, wrapped in warm blankets and placed by a roaring fire, she sat with a whisky in one hand and a freshly baked bannock in the other. It was like she'd died and gone to God's good heaven. Not that there was a bad one, she supposed.

When the minister first found her, she'd no intention of revealing who she was. He was a man of God, wasn't he? She knew what that meant. Someone who hid behind the name of the Lord and His teachings to excuse their own shortcomings. Shortcomings in Patrick Cowper's case being insecurity, greed, lust for power and a desire to have everyone conform to his way of thinking. The man was a beast; someone who feared what he didn't understand. What he didn't understand most of all, as far as she could discern, was women. Rather than seek common ground, he burned it so no one could tread there. She'd met a few ministers in her long life and was yet to meet one who'd prove her estimation wrong. It was just unfortunate that Cowper was the worst of those she'd encountered. She'd no doubt this ruddy-faced man who smelled of sleep, ale and mutton was no different.

And yet, he was.

Helping her into his office first, he swiftly decided she needed more comfort than the sparse room could offer and led her to the house that adjoined the kirk with encouraging words. He summoned his housekeeper to not only bring hot water so Janet might wash and find some clothes for her to change into, but extra blankets and, even better, food. The whisky he brought himself from another room, deeper in the house.

Worn down not merely by her terrible journey and lack of sustenance and the damn cold, but by his gentle manner, before long she found herself telling him everything.

As the room darkened and the housekeeper came in and out, bringing more food, stoking the fire, asking the minister if there was anything else they needed, casting suspicious but also sympathetic looks in her direction, Janet felt herself relaxing. At one stage, a man-servant entered and was instructed to prepare a bed for her. She almost squealed with delight. A bed. A real bed. When was the last time she'd slept in a bed? She could scarce remember. Her mind wandered, her tongue too. Was it the whisky? Aye, possibly. But it was also a compassionate, non-judgemental ear that loosened her lips.

When, after the clock struck seven, the minister asked her outright if she was one of the witches that had been pardoned by Edinburgh, making the Weem a bit of a laughing stock among the other parishes for advertising they'd caught witches and being so righteous about it when they were clearly just unfortunate women, Janet knew she'd found a like-minded soul and sent another prayer to God. So many this day already, the Lord must be suspicious.

Watching the way the reverend spoke to his housekeeper — so kindly; to his manservant — with respect — and to her, with such caring deference, gratitude overwhelmed her. Hot tears welled and, before she could prevent them, fell.

'There, there,' said the minister, producing a scented kerchief and passing it to her. 'You've been through so much already, Mrs Corn-foot. More than should be asked of anyone. How about you allow me to get Mrs Glaren to take you to your room?'

Nodding and snuffling, trying to thank the minister, but finding the words were banked up in her throat, she nevertheless managed to convey how very appreciative she was.

The Almighty hadn't abandoned her after all, but led her to a place of sanctuary and, she hoped, forgiveness for whatever sins He felt she'd committed and that had led to her being hounded by an earthly leader of His flock.

As she climbed into bed and pulled the soft sheets and blankets over her bruised and exhausted body, her last thoughts were of Sorcha, Nettie and the others, and how, when she was back among them, she'd tell them, not all men of God were bad. Some, like the Reverend George Gordon, were akin to angels here on His earth.

Sealing the letter, Reverend Gordon indicated for his manservant to come forward. First he made sure the door was shut, then leaned over the desk and lowered his voice.

'Listen carefully. As soon as day breaks, you're to ride to Pittenweem and find the Reverend Patrick Cowper. When you do, give him this letter then wait until he pays you. Do you understand? You're not to leave his side until that ten pounds is in your hand.'

'I understand, sir,' said the servant and, with a small bow, left the room.

George Gordon fell back in his chair and gazed at the fire. He refused to feel remorse. After all, was not the woman a witch? From her own mouth she convicted herself.

Anyway, ten pounds would go a long way to repairing the kirk roof. What was a witch's life and liberty compared to a house of God?

FORTY-SEVEN

Ye'll no draw a strae across my nose.
(You'll not provoke me into a fight.)

30th January 1705

*I*t was impossible to concentrate. Tipping a creel of fish onto the table, Sorcha stared at the silvery bodies slipping and sliding in a slick wash of brine across the wood and, for a moment, forgot what it was she was supposed to be doing.

Janet's escape had stirred everyone into a frenzy of fear and fury, led by Patrick Cowper. Yesterday, under the pretence of calming them, the reverend incited more anger by inviting that drunken sot Alexander McGregor, and even Peter Morton, to speak outside the Tolbooth. The townsfolk listened and demanded justice.

If she had any sense, she'd tell her friends to gather their things and run. Leave Pittenweem and never look back. Only, they couldn't. Not while Janet roamed the countryside. Sorcha was afraid not for what might be done to her — Sorcha knew her too well — but what might be done to those she cared about. She also couldn't leave now she'd heard from Aidan.

Was it a cruel irony or a blessing that just as she thought things couldn't get any worse, a bundle of letters arrived from Bavaria?

Brought by one of the ships that risked sailing the rivers that wove their way through the lands where war was being waged, they'd been written some time ago.

Just as she'd avoided relaying any bad news to Aidan, so too he had sought to protect her. His letters were full of stories about the countryside the battalions marched through, the witticisms and strange habits of the Duke of Marlborough, also known as General John Churchill, and the other commanders, Cutts and Orkney. He wrote about Bavaria, the wide flowing rivers, the peaked mountains and green grasses. How gun smoke would sit in the valleys for hours after a ceasefire until the northern winds swept down and blew it away. There were fat cows and sweet-faced sheep everywhere, so he never hungered. Rain fell often and the men had to wade through mud, the supply wagons and camp followers becoming drenched or bogged or both. Bread grew mouldy, feet too. But these were the only misfortunes he mentioned. If Sorcha didn't know better, she'd be persuaded he was one of the gentry embarking on a Grand Tour rather than marching to war. It was from the ship's captain, Reginald Foggerty, that Sorcha learned many bloody battles had been fought, with great loss of life. The French had been defeated and the allies were victorious, but still the enemy would not surrender.

When Foggerty had left the army to sail home, it was based in a place called Ilbesheim, near Landau where a treaty between Austria and Bavaria had been signed, allowing the Hapsburgs access to Bavarian goods and revenue, effectively marking the end of French dominance in the region. When Captain Foggerty last saw Aidan and agreed to take his letters, he seemed well, apart from a mild fever. The news wasn't much, but Sorcha drank in every word and tried not to press the tired captain more than necessary.

In every letter, Aidan wrote how he imagined her down by the harbour, close to the sea and, as he followed rivers towards battle and victory, or better still, peace, he knew that water connected them even though they were so far apart.

Gazing out over the ocean, Sorcha tried to imagine Aidan right in that very moment. In her mind she built a bridge that spanned the great distance between them.

A shout brought her back to the present. Another load of fish was tipped onto those waiting for her, some striking her quiescent hands. The bridge, like her daydreams, shattered.

Nettie threw her a look of concern. Sorcha returned a watery smile and began sorting. The catch was still poor, and that was unlikely to change soon. The women gathered around the table and baiting the lines could more than manage. Gone was the blether and laughter that had always accompanied their tasks. There was no song, no whistling, either. Even the men were dour-faced, the bairns too. Everyone was thinking about Janet.

Except for her: she was thinking about Janet *and* about Aidan.

Billows of seagulls and terns whirled above, cawing and crying, waiting for an opportunity to dive on a boat or an unsupervised table and grab a fish. They watched the fishwives as if they were the prey. Not unlike the men who lined up like regimental soldiers along the harbour wall. Dressed in thick coats, arms folded, some with pipes protruding from their mouths, they'd murmur to each other, their frowns deep, their thoughts dark. Wanting to ensure no other witch walked among them, they'd taken to observing the women at work — any work. The weavers reported being watched, the milkmaids, spinners, seamstresses and nursemaids too. But the one group that attracted the most attention and earned the closest vigilance was the fishwives. After all, Mr Bruce said, had not the reverend pointed out it was the occupation that produced the most witches?

Trying to ignore the men and their baleful stares, Sorcha finished sorting and helped Nettie scale and gut. She was keen to get away.

It wasn't until hours later, when she'd sold the last of her fish and bought some smoked herring from Mr Murdoch, that Sorcha was able to go home. Already the day was darkening, even though the bell hadn't long tolled three of the clock. A low bank of heavy clouds was rolling in from the east. Lightning split the grey heavens, great gashes of brilliance that presaged a mighty storm. With a shudder, Sorcha prayed it didn't signify anything else.

As she came up the High Street, she finally understood why the lanes were so quiet, why there'd been barely a soul about to sell fish to. At the top of the road a huge crowd had gathered outside the Tolbooth.

Sorcha broke into a run, uncaring that her creel slapped hard against her back. She dropped it at the corner and pushed herself into the throng, trying to find someone who'd tell her what was going on. Familiar faces were contorted into ugly, shouting shapes; people shook their fists; strangers' faces stared at her with disdain and curiosity as she jostled and thrust through the press of bodies, trying to find someone who would talk to her.

'Nettie,' she gasped, clutching her friend.

'Oh, Sorcha, thank God. I was about to come looking for you.'

'What? What is it?'

Bumped and shoved, it was hard for Sorcha to keep her footing. Maintaining hold of Nettie, she tried to pull her out of the melee. Around her one name was repeated over and over: Janet's.

'Have they found her?' asked Sorcha, dragging Nettie clear.

Panting, Nettie nodded. 'Aye. Moira told me a man rode into town this morning with a letter for the reverend. Seems our Janet made it as far as Leuchars before seeking refuge in the kirk there.'

Before Sorcha could ask any more, Isobel and Nicolas joined them, their faces pale, their brows furrowed.

Nettie quickly told them what she'd shared with Sorcha.

Sorcha glanced at the gathering. It was becoming louder. Steel glinted in the strange light that accompanied the gloaming. Knuckles punched the air, arms were brandished like weapons.

'If Janet sought refuge, why would the minister there inform the reverend?'

Nettie clasped her hands in hers. 'Because of the reward.'

'*What?*'

Isobel's hand flew to her mouth. Nicolas shook her head, eyes blazing.

'The ten pounds Reverend Cowper and the bailies offered for the return of Janet,' said Nettie, outrage making her words blunt. 'The bastard Leuchars minister is claiming it. The reverend sent the Stuart lads to collect her. They're bringing her back any moment.'

Sorcha glanced at the growing mob, horrified. This is why people had assembled. 'To this?'

'Aye. To this.' Nettie followed the direction of her gaze.

They looked helplessly at the mass of baying men and some women. The bairns were just imitating the adults, yelling, making angry noises, shaking their wee fists. The air was fizzing with anger, alarm and something else. Sorcha had felt it before, back at the farm on St Andrew's when she stayed with her sister. When a cow or sheep was killed for the table, the hunting dogs were tied up so they couldn't interfere. They would watch, their hackles raised, their snouts trembling, howling, their heads raised to the heavens. Their bodies shaking with longing. It was blood lust. That was what Sorcha sensed now.

Her heart seized. Taking Nettie's arm and gesturing for the others to follow, she walked down as far as the tavern and stood beneath the shingle.

'We have to do something.' Sorcha looked left, then right. There were others standing back, cautious, fearful, trying to gauge the mood and getting ready to respond. If only she could round them up, bring them together. There was strength in numbers, wasn't there? But what if the number was only small?

She had to try. They had to. If they could ensure Janet had a fair hearing, got a fair trial, it would guarantee any others did as well.

Turning to her friends, Sorcha spoke quickly, before she lost her courage. 'If they're coming from Leuchars, then they'll bring Janet from the west. I think we should go to the gate there and, at the very least, accompany her back, don't you?'

Nettie and Nicolas agreed. Nettie linked her arm through Sorcha's. Only Isobel hesitated, one eye straying to the fervent pack. Reluctantly, she nodded.

'Come away, then,' said Sorcha, putting iron in her voice, in her heart.

'What about your creel?' asked Isobel, looking for a reason to delay.

'It can stay. I'll fetch it when I go home.'

Home.

Looking at the furious mob, she wondered if the Weem even was that any more.

FORTY-EIGHT

... the rabble was up...

— The Annals of Pittenweem, Being Notes and Extracts from the
Ancient Records of that Burgh, *15th of February 1705*

*B*urning rage was all that kept Janet atop the horse, rage and an acute sense of betrayal and shame at how gullible she'd been. Taken in by a man of God when she should have known better; taken in by his whisky, warm fire, bed and fresh clothes more like. It would never happen again, she scolded herself. *Do You hear that, God? You have chosen poorly, sir, and need to rethink whom You allow to speak on Your behalf. They're lettin' You down, these men. They pretend a consideration they don't feel; they lie and cheat and call it Your will. Their hearts are filled with greed. They take Your name in vain.*

As she watched the swaying back of Gerard Stuart riding in front of her, aware of his brother Angus behind her, she swore a silent oath. Never again would she darken the door of a kirk except to spit on the threshold. Call her a witch, would they? Well, she'd show Cowper all right. If it was a witch he wanted, a witch he'd get. She muttered curses under her breath, taking pleasure from sending them out into the encroaching evening.

The brothers ignored her dire mumblings and said nothing. Janet eventually slumped into a seething silence. It was with some surprise that, just as the last beams of sunlight touched the glistening snow-covered hills, she saw they'd reached the edge of town. For the first time since she was dragged away from the comfort of that dirty betrumpin' minister's kitchen, she felt a flicker of fear. Fear and foreboding. It might have been the eerie light making the Forth glow like a devil's urn, the forked lightning that split the horizon, or the fact that, as she looked down upon the township, she saw something unexpected — the glimmer of many torches. Tiny fires that could erupt into an inferno.

Forced to dismount, she began to walk towards the dark walls, the men remaining on horseback either side of her, their pikes held high. The scent of the ocean washed over her. Inhaling deeply, she allowed the brackish air to fill her lungs, remind her of simpler times when all she worried about was getting the men to their boats dry, baiting lines, laughing, blethering and arguing with the fishwives as they waited for the catch to come to shore. The air was tinged with smoke, fetid water from puddles and the metallic smell that presaged snowfall; she relished it all and yet… The white rooftops and bleached walls of the cottages with their hollow windows like accusing eyes tormented her. Were people watching? What were they thinking? What was going to happen?

Unaware she'd stopped walking until Gerard prodded her hard in the back, causing her to cry out, she reluctantly put one foot in front of the other. For the first time since they left Leuchars, she became aware of how sore she still was. How much her whole body hurt. Ached from within. This was not physical; this pain rose from her soul and was devouring her breath by breath.

Determined not to let the lads see she was spooked, she lifted her chin and continued.

It was only as she entered the walls that she saw them: Sorcha, Nettie and Nicolas racing up the lane. Janet's eyes widened and her mouth broke into a grin.

'Janet!' cried Sorcha and, blithely ignoring Gerard's warning, flew into her arms, followed by Nettie and Nicolas.

Janet sank into their embrace, knowing she'd reached, if not a safe harbour, at least a friendly one.

'What are you doing here, lasses?' Janet shouldered the women away and drank in their faces. 'You should be at home by a fire keeping warm.'

'So should you, Janet,' said Sorcha, looking accusingly at the Stuart lads. They pretended not to notice. 'Why, you're freezing.' Sorcha removed her shawl and went to wrap it around Janet. Nettie and Nicolas started to do the same.

Janet shook her head. 'Nae, lasses. Save them for yourselves, I'll not take them.'

Instead of arguing, Sorcha quickly explained that Isobel had tried to be there too, but halfway to the gate, her father had appeared and forced her to go home. What she didn't say was how afeared he was for Isobel's safety.

Janet nodded approval at Mr Adam's decision. She turned to her guards. 'Where are you taking me, lads?'

'The Tolbooth,' said Gerard Stuart, swinging a leg over his horse and dropping to the ground.

'To the reverend,' said Angus simultaneously as he also dismounted.

Sorcha and Nettie exchanged a look.

'Och, then, lads,' said Janet. 'You can let an auld woman fetch a shawl to keep her warm, can't you? My house is just down there.' She pointed at the nearby wynd.

The Stuarts eyed each other and shrugged.

'Sure,' said Gerard. 'What harm can it do? We can leave the horses in Mr Murray's stables. But keep your distance, you hear?' he said to the women. 'Mrs Cornfoot is our prisoner and you can't frat her eyes.'

Angus regarded him strangely. 'Frat her eyes? You mean fraternise, you great dozie.'

'Aye. That's what I said.' Gerard poked him in the ribs with the butt of his musket.

Sorcha eyed the weapon with distaste. Why on earth were they carrying them? Janet wasn't dangerous. Her thoughts flew to the crowd outside the Tolbooth. Try convincing those in town that was the case.

She looked at the brothers, turned into custodians for the sake of the reverend's and bailies' fear of women. Some women. It didn't suit them. It never had. 'We won't fraternise, Gerard and Angus, but we will walk with our friend. I pray you to at least allow that. The poor woman is old and frail.'

Nettie bit back a laugh.

Sorcha mouthed 'Sorry' at Janet, who waved her apology away.

'She weren't so frail when she was resisting arrest,' muttered Angus.

'Resisting?' said Janet, turning towards him. 'I was trying to keep my balance while you dragged me across the minister's flagstones. Which I couldn't do with my hands tied.'

It was only then that Sorcha realised why Janet hadn't returned their hold. Her wrists were bound.

Angus glared at Janet and might have been ready to change his mind about allowing her to get some extra clothes, when Nettie, one hand gently upon Janet's back, encouraged her forward.

'At least untie her, Angus. How can she fetch anything like that?'

By the time Janet was unbound and with Angus breathing down her neck the entire time, had fetched a shawl, Sorcha, Nettie and Nicolas weren't the only ones accompanying her to the Tolbooth. Word flew around and more and more people ran up the hill from the tavern, the shops and the harbour, spilling out of their houses, lanterns raised, pikes, shovels and other instruments in their hands. Whether it was to defend or attack Janet, Sorcha couldn't be sure, but she liked it not.

Some ran back towards the centre of town and soon a cry went up that made Janet stop in her tracks.

'The witch has been found! The witch has been found.'

'Dear God,' whispered Janet, pulling closer to Sorcha and Nettie. 'Get away, lasses, while you still can. I don't want you tarred with the brush they're going to feather me with.'

Sorcha felt sickened as she glanced at the faces around them in the torchlight; some were sympathetic, but most possessed an open-mouthed zeal that the flames captured and cast into crazed shadows. From the looks on Nettie's and Nicolas's faces, they were too. Mr Adam had the right of it. 'We're not leaving you until we find the minister. Not even he can ignore the danger you're in.'

Janet's fingers gripped her so tightly, Sorcha knew they'd leave marks. She wanted to say something, offer Janet some solace, promise that it would be all right. But she could not.

When they arrived at the Tolbooth, at first Sorcha wondered where the mob they'd left only a short time before had gone — until she understood they were still there, surrounding her, Janet, Nettie and the guards. Not only had the crowd followed them, but they'd run along parallel lanes, baying and cat-calling, encouraging folk to join them, and were even now converging alongside the women outside the Tolbooth. There was not one friendly face. Nicolas was no longer with them, pushed aside before they reached the High Street. Sorcha prayed she was all right.

Spit rained on them with a savagery she'd never heard or felt the like of before.

As if Janet was possessed of a scythe, a path to the door of the Tolbooth opened. Folk grew quiet, staring at her as though she was an exotic creature washed up with the tide, instead of a woman they'd known their whole lives and whose family had lived in the Weem for generations. Janet may have escaped the town as the Cornfoot crone, but Sorcha knew that by returning in the company of guards, with a reward upon her head, she'd become the felon the reverend had tried to make her. He'd remade her to fit his purpose.

As a witch.

Gerard went to the door of the Tolbooth and banged on it. Janet, with Sorcha and Nettie either side, were immediately behind him.

The door opened a fraction. It was Camron.

'Summon the reverend, Camron.' Gerard's voice was loud enough to be heard. There were noises of approval.

'He's not here,' whimpered Camron. Clearing his throat, his words carried this time. 'The reverend's at Bailie Cook's house, having dinner.' Before Gerard could ask further questions, Camron slammed the door. There was the sound of a latch dropping.

'What do we do now?' asked Angus, standing behind Sorcha.

'Go to Bailie Cook's house,' said Gerard, scanning the crowd. For the first time, Sorcha saw concern flash in his eyes.

The mob, which had grown silent when the door opened, began to mutter again. Shoving people out of his way, using his musket and pike as extensions of his arms, Gerard cleared a passage. People stood aside, eyes fixed on Janet, sneers, leers and what Sorcha could only describe as hatred contorting their faces.

As they made their way towards the bailie's house, the horde fell in behind. A simmering, roiling mass that, like a great wave, threatened to break over them any minute.

Sorcha was afraid to let go of Janet's arm. She could feel the woman shaking; her bones like sticks about to snap. When Nettie took Janet's other arm, steering her away from a group that poured out of a house, their eyes met and Sorcha could see her own anxiety echoed in her friend's. Aware of the bodies moving around them, some creeping up as if to cut them off, Sorcha cast about for an escape route should such a thing become necessary.

When they arrived at Bailie Cook's house, the chatter lulled and folk grew orderly, shifting back from the door and making space. Sorcha wasn't sure whether to feel relieved or angry that they could quell their passions for the authorities.

Upon seeing who stood on his threshold, Bailie Robert Cook said nothing. He held a napkin in his hand and used it to wipe the glistening grease from his mouth, then signalled for them to wait and spun on his heel, going back inside.

Seconds later, the person everyone wanted to see appeared. Sorcha saw the flare of triumph that lit the reverend's eyes, even the beclouded one appeared to sparkle with victory before he rearranged his features into a semblance of regret. She willed Nettie to remain silent. Janet too.

'So, Janet Cornfoot,' he began, his eyes alighting upon Sorcha then Nettie. 'You've returned.'

'Not by choice,' said Janet.

There was a low growl.

Sorcha tugged at her clothing. It was time to stay mute.

'Now you'll finally answer for your crimes.'

The assembled crowd gave a cheer. Someone called out, 'Burn the witch!'

Nettie inhaled sharply.

Reverend Cowper raised a hand and shook his head. Waiting for the chatter to cease, he spoke, projecting his voice as if he was delivering a sermon. The light from the crowd's torches shone in his face, made the evening falling around them darker than pitch and impossible to penetrate. Yet Sorcha sensed movement beyond the circle of people around her, even if she couldn't see who or what was there.

'Nae, nae,' said the reverend, fondly, with such tolerance it was as if he was addressing an obstinate bairn. 'That's not the way we do things in Pittenweem, is it?' His brows drew together. 'Not that we have any say in how we do things here any more. Not since poor Peter was beset with his troubles.' There were more grumblings. 'Since then, it's Edinburgh that's seen fit to dictate to us Fifers. Telling us how we must treat those who seek to undermine our community. Those who sin against God and commit heresy, threatening our Christian souls.' He gave a smile that was all yellow teeth and chalky lips.

There were jeers at his words.

'What would they ken?'

'They canna tell us what to do!'

There were shouts of endorsement at this daring.

'Indeed, they cannot. Not any more.' Again, Cowper used his hands to pacify the assembly. 'Once this is over, I will be letting them know as much. Justice begins and ends here. With us. In the Weem.'

The crowd broke into defiant cheers. 'Bless you, reverend,' shouted a voice.

'What do you want us to do with the auld woman, reverend?' asked Gerard. The wind had picked up, bringing with it splinters of ice that plunged into exposed flesh, forcing breath out. The sky was a great glowering bruise above their heads. Flashes of lightning writhed within it, God's weapons primed.

Reverend Cowper lifted his face to the firmament. Throwing out his arms, he stood silhouetted against the doorway, his dark robes and pale hands picked out by the torchlight, casting giant shadows against neighbouring houses. His lips moved as, eyes closed, he prayed. He was larger than life. Larger than death.

The mob were awed into silence, as Sorcha had no doubt he knew they would be. After all, it wasn't every day you witnessed your minister communing with the Almighty.

When the reverend finished, he carefully surveyed all who waited before him. There were so many. Sorcha knew how much hinged on whatever he said next. What would this crowd do if his words didn't satisfy their need for justice? Justice, as he'd been reminding them every Sunday, that had been denied them before. Would they listen or turn on him? Sorcha's heart was beating so hard it hurt. What would the reverend tell them? He had the people of the Weem in the palm of his hand.

She felt Nettie's fingers searching for hers. Sorcha grasped them, bringing them together with Janet's. The three women huddled, hands bunched in a tight knot, mirroring the one in Sorcha's heart.

Finally the reverend released a great sigh, as if what he was about to say was not his will, his choice. 'Do whatever you please with her,' he said sharply. He locked eyes with Janet. 'I care not.'

'You can't! Nae!' shouted Sorcha, reaching for him, but her words bounced off his retreating back and were drowned by the roar of the exultant throng.

The door shut behind him.

Nettie strode to it and beat her fist hard upon the wood.

Gerard and Angus looked at each other.

The reverend's words were passed among the astonished crowd.

'Get her back to the Tolbooth,' yelled Sorcha to the Stuart brothers, trying to be heard as people surged forward. Nettie gave up on the door and flew to Janet's side.

Angus and Gerard began to clear the way. Sorcha and Nettie followed, keeping Janet between them and the lads' boots in sight, not daring to make eye contact with anyone. The noise around her grew louder and louder.

A stone struck Sorcha's shoulder. She cried out. Another struck Angus on the chest and he staggered into her. Someone darted forward and swung a stick at Janet's head. Blood sprayed across her face and she fell to one knee, her flailing arm hitting Sorcha, blinding her momentarily. Forced to let Janet go, Sorcha was bumped aside. There were shouts, a great tearing sound, followed by breaking glass. More stones were thrown, passing over Sorcha's head. Separated from Janet, Nettie was struck in the temple. Sorcha tried to reach her and to ensure Janet was in her sights as well. The milling bodies, the pushing and shoving, made it hard.

A gunshot rang out.

The mob scattered, exposing Gerard standing in their midst, his musket smoking.

'Get back, all of you!' The veins on his neck were ropes; his eyes started from his head. 'Go home. You've nae business being here.'

Horrified by what he'd done, firing his weapon, Gerard twisted one way then the other, the musket pointing into the crowd, causing folk to squeal and retreat. For the first time, the entrance to the wynd was free; there was a way out, a way to get to the Tolbooth.

Sorcha reached Nettie, who was dazed, and helped her to her feet, taking the kerchief someone shoved in her hand and pushing it against Nettie's temple to stop the bleeding. Out of the corner of her eye, she saw Janet. While everyone was distracted, unable to look away from Gerard and his gun, she'd managed to make her way to the edge of the pack. Small, bent and so very, very ancient, her eyes gleamed with possibility, her mouth cracked a smile.

Sorcha surveyed the fierce, frightened faces, the men and women twisted by prejudice, terror and so much more. They wanted, *needed*, to see what they believed to be retribution served. But what the reverend suggested was not justice. He could not wash his hands of Janet as if he was Pontius Pilate and leave her fate to the angry mob.

Nettie whispered to her. Sorcha nodded and, leaving Nettie where she was, tried to reach Janet and lead her to the relative safety of the Tolbooth before something terrible happened. Nettie was right. She had to do it now, while people were startled into co-operation by an anxious lad with a deadly weapon.

A few of the men decided Gerard needed to be taught a lesson. Sorcha recognised Clem Brady and Seumas Cowper. Another man moved stealthily towards Gerard. She'd never seen him before. Circling around Gerard, he lunged and snatched the musket out of his hands.

'Och!' exclaimed Gerard and went to wrest it back. Before he could, the stranger swung it and smacked Gerard on the side of the head. He fell to the ground. Immediately, Seumas began to kick him. Others ran forward and joined in.

Across the road, Janet locked eyes with Sorcha and gave a slight shake of her head, warning her not to interfere — either with Gerard's beating or her intentions. Through bloodied lips, she blew a kiss, then winked. Faster and more furtively than Sorcha could have imagined, Janet darted down a darkened wynd.

It was a mere second before the crowd realised the focus of their rage had vanished. When they did, the spell of the musket broke.

Seumas raised his head, Clem Brady and the stranger too. With an almighty bellow, they pointed to where Janet had been.

'Don't let her escape,' Seumas shouted.

In a crush of men, a few women and steel, led by the three who'd beaten Gerard bloody, the crowd took off after Janet Cornfoot, the witch who had got away once.

If they had any say in it this time, she would not again.

FORTY-NINE

What's done cannot be undone.

— Macbeth, *Act V scene i*

*I*t took Sorcha a moment to gain her bearings. When she did, she went to check on Gerard. Angus was trying to help him sit up. Gerard's lip was bleeding, there was a long gash on his forehead. One eye was already swelling. He groaned and spat a great glob of blood on the road.

'One of us must go to the bailie's house,' said Nettie, nodding in the direction of Bailie Cook's place. 'Tell them what's happened.'

'You're right,' conceded Sorcha, passing a kerchief to Gerard. She knew they had to separate to give Janet a chance. 'But we need to be careful.'

They were one whisky away from becoming the targets of this witch-frenzy.

'I'll go with Gerard,' said Nettie, indicating the constable who, daubing at his head, gave a reluctant nod. 'I'll be safe enough.'

'Then Angus and I will try and follow Janet.' Sorcha waited for agreement from Angus before looking towards the water.

Angus hoisted Gerard to his feet. Those who hadn't bolted down to the harbour approached cautiously.

Sorcha wiped a hand across her forehead. 'Once we find her, we'll take her to the Tolbooth.' She didn't add what she was thinking — if it wasn't too late.

Nettie folded her into a tight hug. Sorcha squeezed her one last time, then before she could change her mind or allow the terror batting at the edges of her mind to overcome her, signalled to Angus. Nettie and Gerard left at the same time.

The closer Sorcha and Angus came to the waterfront, the louder the clamour became. There were shouts, taunts and mocking laughter. Dogs barked frenetically; somewhere, a horse whinnied. A scream rang out before it was abruptly cut off. Rounding a corner, Sorcha almost collided with the rear of the crowd. Leaping up and down, she saw what had slowed them.

Seumas Cowper and a couple of other men she didn't know appeared to have taken charge and had not only caught up with Janet, but herded her towards the seawall, the crowd forming a tight circle around her. One of them darted forward and punched her in the head, knocking her down. A great cheer resounded. Two men grabbed her by the ankles and began to drag her over the wall and down towards the water.

'Nae!' screamed Sorcha, but her cry was lost in the melee.

'Lynch her!' the crowd began to chant.

'Throw her in the sea.'

'Cuck the witch!'

Trying to lever her way through the press of people, blocking her ears to their bellowing, Sorcha forgot all about Angus as she tried to squeeze her way between the furious, excited men, but it was impossible. Unable to reach Janet, she could hear her terror-stricken howls as she was dragged over the seawall and dropped onto the sand.

Much to Sorcha's relief, a contingent of soldiers appeared, led by none other than Sergeant Thatcher. With weapons drawn, they tried to prevent the rabble joining the men on the beach. But it was as if they weren't there. Townsfolk simply barged past, pushing them aside like brushwood. Weapons were wrenched from hands. A thickset man snatched a gun from a soldier and levelled it at him.

'This doesn't concern you,' he yelled. 'Keep your distance, or else.' He wasn't even a local, but English.

'Do as he says, lads,' barked Sergeant Thatcher, palms outstretched in a gesture of peace. His features were twisted in fury, but with so many against them, he had no choice. He had to protect his men.

Throwing their hands up in surrender, the soldiers backed away. Sorcha's heart deflated. If the soldiers couldn't do anything, who could? Skirting past, she heard Sergeant Thatcher issuing instructions to two of his men who, waiting until the bearded Englishman left, bolted up another wynd. Where were they going? Surely they were needed here, even if it was only to protect the other villagers?

She hoped Nettie and Gerard had reached the bailie's house and alerted the council. It was their only hope to stop what the reverend had started.

When she finally reached the harbour wall, the crowd lined its edges, facing the beach and pier. Men leapt onto the dusky sands, charging towards a large group closer to the sea. Somewhere, in the midst of all those people, was Janet. Sorcha could see shadows between the bursts of light from torches as others dared to run along the ruined pier, eager to witness what was unfolding. Men jumped onto the wreck of the *Sophia* and rushed to the prow of the ship to shout encouragement to those dragging Janet forward, beckoning them closer.

Didn't they know how dangerous it was up there? The wood was rotting, the deck slick with barnacles and seaweed. Walking upon it was to invite doom. As Sorcha watched in disbelief, three men clambered up the tallest mast, one of them carrying a coil of rope over his shoulder. It was then, with a sinking heart, she understood they knew damn well what they were risking and why.

The storm that had threatened to break all afternoon passed. The cloud filled with lightning, God's blazing swords, had moved inland, leaving the scene drenched in silver moonlight. The tide was almost full, waves breaking against the creaking hull of the *Sophia*, showering everyone with spray. An irradiated pathway crossed the Forth, shimmering and inviting.

Unable to get onto the pier as the way was blocked, Sorcha joined those along the harbour wall and stared helplessly as Janet was pulled closer and closer to the water's edge. Her hair was matted with a dark, wet substance. The shawl she'd fetched from her house had disappeared and her shirt and skirt had ridden up to expose torn and bloody arms and legs.

As Sorcha looked around in despair, she caught sight of Peter Morton. He stood back, away from others, observing the scene, a frown of disbelief on his features. His hair was dishevelled, his clothes as well. Blood spattered one cheek. Was it his? Or Janet's? Did he understand he was responsible for this? He and the reverend. Unable to look at him any longer lest the anger roiling inside her burst forth, Sorcha turned away.

She shut herself off to the noise around her, the excited cries and shouts of encouragement, and watched.

One end of a rope was affixed to the top of the *Sophia*'s mast, the other was flung over the derelict rails, towards the shoreline. The men standing over Janet caught hold of it. Uncaring that she barely moved, they tied it around her waist. Sorcha could see she was clearly dazed, but still alive. Picking Janet up as if she were a sack of grain, the men signalled to those on board, who began to heave on the rope. Sea-spray rained upon them as they stood knee-deep in the shallows, waiting for the rope to grow taut. One of the men slipped, almost dropping her.

Sorcha became completely still, utterly calm. Someone had to be. Someone had to bear witness. Apprehension tramped inside her chest, making it difficult to breathe.

A great shout exploded as Janet was released, hauled through the water and towards the side of the ship. The men raised her into the air until she was level with the deck, then paused and, with a great shout, released the rope. Like a rag doll, Janet struck the side of the ship before the swirling sea swallowed her.

The folk lining the harbour erupted, slapping each other's backs, roaring approval, their eyes wild, their mouths wide in ecstasy.

Once more men began to heave on the rope tied to the *Sophia*'s mast and, in moments, the ocean spat Janet back out. Yanked from the water, Janet coughed, spluttered and then opened her mouth in a pitiful scream. Laughing, the men tugged and pulled until she was suspended above the waves, then let her go again.

With a cry that echoed in Sorcha's ears, Janet plummeted back into the water. Her scream cut off when she smacked the surface and sank.

'Witch! Witch!' The incantation was taken up. Folk shouted at the top of their lungs, raising fists, pitchforks, knives, bottles of half-drunk whisky. Words punctuated the night, dark stars that echoed along the street. Sorcha turned to look at Peter, hold him to account. There was no sign of him. Not near the houses, not on the wall or the shore. He was gone.

Some of the men jumped from the harbour wall onto the sands, running towards the edge of the sea with sticks and picking up pebbles and rocks. Seeing what they were doing, others bolted to the cottages along the foreshore and searched among the fishermen's gear, snatching hooks, nets, weights, anything they might use. It was like a wicked spell had been cast, transforming ordinary people into something evil. Sorcha couldn't credit what it was she was seeing. What she could feel all around her.

When Janet was pulled out of the sea again, they were ready. Running as close to the water as they dared, the men flung whatever they'd found at her. Some missiles struck their target, hitting with sharp cracks, causing Janet to wail and those watching to crow in delight. Others struck with dull thuds, tearing brittle skin, causing fresh blood to flow.

Bile rose in Sorcha's throat. She looked in disbelief at the faces around her, lit by the combination of the moon's radiance and the torches. Who were these people? They were demonic strangers, twisted, hardened, possessed.

Janet was dragged out of the water again and again, the men tugging on the rope handing the chore to others when they grew weary. Those willing to take their place lined up along the pier, climbed onto the ship. With each ducking there were calls to keep her submerged longer.

Sorcha had seen enough. Despondent and heart-weary, she withdrew and waited. When this... brutality stopped, when this wickedness had run its course, she would go to Janet, no matter what.

One by one, others turned away and joined her. Silent, with tears streaming down their faces, they prayed, shaking their heads in disbelief at the cruelty they were observing. There were friends of Janet's, a cousin, a nephew, a brother-in-law as well. But there were also those who bore no relation. Sorcha was relieved to see many felt as she did. It was then she caught sight of Beatrix.

'Dear God, Sorcha, what has happened to us?' asked Beatrix, her eyes swollen from weeping. 'When Sergeant Thatcher came to the door, I couldn't believe what he was telling me.'

Sorcha wasn't sure how to reply until, as she gazed at those beside her, she saw past them to a familiar form standing alone at the end of the harbour wall. Reverend Cowper. His eyes were fixed on what was happening aboard the *Sophia*. A scene he'd orchestrated as if he'd cast the actors and given them their lines.

Do whatever you please with her. I care not.

'Him, that's what happened,' whispered Sorcha, but Beatrix didn't hear.

A short time later, Nettie appeared.

'What did the bailies say?' asked Sorcha.

Nettie pressed her lips together. 'I don't know. Angus and Gerard convinced me they'd speak to them; that it was better I wasn't seen.'

Casting a wary glance at the *Sophia*, Sorcha knew the lads were right.

'They promised they'd make sure the bailies acted. I want to believe them; they were as shocked by the crowd's reaction as we were. But then, they didn't see this.' Nettie's eyes glimmered with unshed tears.

Together, Sorcha and Nettie stood and beheld Janet's torment, unable to speak, just holding hands.

For two hours, Janet endured. Sorcha didn't move. Nettie, Beatrix, Therese Larnach, Jean Durkie and Nicolas, who'd eventually found them, kept a silent vigil to their friend's suffering. When it was evident the men were in no hurry to stop, Nicolas eased herself into a position beside Sorcha and whispered in her ear. Sorcha started then gave a nod of understanding. Leaning over, she shared what Nicolas had told her with Nettie, her eyes never once leaving the scene upon the water.

When the men finally tired, they heaved Janet out of the dark seas one last time and, while she was still attached to the mast by the rope, flung her onto the sands. She was barely conscious. That didn't stop those lingering on the shoreline attacking her with sticks and more rocks.

Sorcha was crying openly now. Nettie too. Uncaring of the hands that tried to prevent them, the whispers of warning that urged caution even as folk, afraid of where the men might turn their attention next, fled back to their homes, they made their way down to the shore, standing where the rough wall met the water.

There, on the edge, they shouted at the men prodding Janet, trying to goad her to rise. Dear God.

'Haven't you done enough? What's wrong with you?' Sorcha screamed.

'She be an auld woman, you bastards. Leave her alone!' screeched Nettie.

The men, some mere lads and a few incomers with no right to dispense so-called justice, let alone be free with a Weem woman, ignored them and continued, spurred on by their challenge. This time, they used their boots as well.

Uncaring of the danger, Sorcha clambered onto the sands. Lifting her skirts, she ran across the pebbles and along the shore, over the exposed rocks and through the incoming tide, stopping just short of the mob. This time, others joined her — Nettie, Nicolas and her husband, Beatrix and Mr Brown, Isobel Adam's father and a few more. Much to Sorcha's relief, Sergeant Thatcher appeared. He was carrying a fresh musket.

'Allow me, Mrs McIntyre,' he said, stepping forward. 'This should never have started in the first place.' Levelling his weapon, Sergeant Thatcher stood with his feet apart. The soldiers with him also aimed their guns at the gang. 'Didn't you hear the lasses? Enough!' he boomed.

The men attacking Janet froze and turned to see who was interrupting their sport. What they saw was the sergeant, his dark eyes like steel. They slowly lowered their fists and sticks. Their chests heaved. Blood spattered their faces, ran in rivulets down their necks, streaked their clothes. Janet's blood.

'Get to your homes,' snarled Sergeant Thatcher, 'before I arrest you all.'

Much to Sorcha's astonishment, the bunch of sodden rags in the sand stirred. Janet lifted her head and groaned. She looked about, coughing wetly. Blood ran into her eyes, down her cheeks. When she saw Sorcha and Nettie, she gave a defiant grin.

'Take more than a wee dunkin' to finish me off.' Her mouth was red, her gums seeping.

Before anyone could act, before Sergeant Thatcher could render aid, and with what must have been the last of her strength, Janet lumbered to her feet, loosening the rope that, like an umbilicus, attached her to the ship. She stood swaying, her hands out to her sides to keep her balance. Then, with a great moan, slapping away Sorcha's arm, she stepped free of the rope's coils and staggered through her attackers and towards the town.

FIFTY

That the officer went to the other two bailies... but they concerned themselves no further...

— The Annals of Pittenweem, Being Notes and Extracts from the Ancient Records of that Burgh, *1526–1793*

Sorcha, Nettie and Sergeant Thatcher watched with open mouths as Janet disappeared up the wynd. Sorcha's heart sang then, as she looked at the shocked and furious faces around her, she registered what Janet's audacious survival meant to those trying to kill her.

There was a beat before the attackers streamed after Janet with cries of outrage tinged with dreadful anticipation.

'The witch has escaped! Get her! Kill her!'

Not even Sergeant Thatcher's threats or the primed weapons of the soldiers gave them pause.

'You've got to help, sergeant,' gasped Sorcha, clutching the man's sleeve. 'They'll tear her apart given half a chance.'

'Aye. They will at that.' Sergeant Thatcher barked orders at his men. Knowing he was defying strict instructions by interfering, risking punishment for himself and his men or worse, Sorcha couldn't have been more grateful.

The soldiers dashed back across the sand, leaping onto the road and running towards the centre of town.

'I've told them to try and cut them off,' explained the sergeant as his men veered in a different direction to Janet's pursuers. Mr Adam, Mr Brown, Mr Lawson and some brave others trailed after them. The sergeant looked towards where the rope still swung from the mast. 'I ken we're not supposed to meddle in Weem business. Arresting an escaped woman's one thing, but this, this continued barbarism can't be ignored.'

There were a series of shrill screams accompanied by yells.

'Nae. It cannot,' agreed Nettie.

'Not by anyone,' said Sorcha. 'And that includes us.' Taking a deep breath, she faced her friends. 'Go to the Tolbooth and see if Janet's there. Either way, convince Camron to let you in.'

'Let *us* in?' asked Nicolas.

'Aye,' said Sorcha. 'If they can't find Janet, the mob will look for someone else to satisfy their thirst for blood, for vengeance. And that means *you*.' She eyed each of them in turn, trying to convey how serious she was. 'You'll be safer in the Tolbooth than anywhere else.'

'What about you, lass?' asked Beatrix, confused by the exchange.

'I'm not in any danger. McGregor retracted my name, remember?' As she uttered the words, she thought of Peter Morton.

'If you think for a moment I'm not coming with you, hen —' began Nettie with a look and a tone Sorcha recognised.

She curled grateful fingers around Nettie's. 'Nettie and I will try and find Janet then join you. At least until this —' she lifted her chin towards the town, 'dies down.'

Before she could put her plan into action, Sergeant Thatcher grabbed her by the elbow. 'Nae, lass. Your involvement ends now. Here. I promised the captain I'd look after you. Both of you.' He silenced their objections with a sharp wave of his hand. 'My men and I will do what we can to try and restore order, but as we've seen, it won't be easy. The mob is of one mind and not even soldiers carrying weapons are a deterrent, let alone pleas from the likes of you lasses.' His eyes were compassionate, despite his words. 'I ken you're brave and

Mrs Cornfoot is your friend. But you're not to go near that unhinged lot. Take the advice you gave these lasses. Go to the Tolbooth, to your cottage, theirs —' He indicated the older men loitering by the wall. 'Just don't go anywhere near Janet Cornfoot be she at the Tolbooth or not.'

Sorcha knew better than to contradict the sergeant. She pinched Nettie's inner arm to prevent her from saying anything.

Assuming he'd be obeyed, Sergeant Thatcher released her into Beatrix's care. With a thin attempt at a confident expression and a touch of his cap, he strode off, his remaining men falling into step behind him, weapons drawn. It was as if the town had gone to war.

Once the sergeant was out of sight, the fishwives and Beatrix wasted no time. With pointed looks and guarded smiles, they quietly parted ways. They'd a friend to help and no incomer, certainly no man, well-meaning as he might be, was going to stop them.

Praying Nicolas was right about where she thought Janet would go, Sorcha and Nettie ran up a nearby wynd. It was dark, the cobbles slick and oily in the patches of moonlight. A cat yowled; a dog growled and a baby coughed piteously. There were raised voices in one cottage, the sound of glass breaking in another; even while madness possessed the Weem, life continued. Rising above it all were the distant shouts of the mob. The women pressed on, chests tight, legs tremulous as they forced themselves to keep moving.

Sorcha was the first to round the next bend. As she did, she saw a figure darting from shadow to shadow. Patrick Cowper.

With a finger to her lips, she pointed towards him. Nettie snarled as they held back, only resuming their pace once he had scarpered around the corner. They were just in time to see him go back into Bailie Cook's house. What was he up to now?

Not wanting to stop, but understanding they had to if they were to learn what was going on and be of any help to Janet, the women squeezed themselves into the porch of a shop, eyes fixed on the Cooks' front door. They didn't have to wait long. Soon the councillors, along with Peter Morton and his father poured out, flinging on coats and hats.

'Listen to them,' said Bailie Cook grimly. 'You realise if they find her, they'll likely kill her. There'll be consequences.'

'Why do you think I came and fetched you, Robert?' grunted Cowper. 'Not even that sergeant and his men could contain them. This has got out of control. If we're to salvage anything, we need to make it appear as if we expended every effort to stop the townsfolk taking matters into their own hands. The Mortons here will bear witness to our response, won't you, lads?'

So, thought Sorcha, that's where Peter Morton disappeared to — reporting to his allies in this madness.

Peter and his father nodded.

'What about those who aren't so obliging and who heard what you said, reverend?' asked Bailie Bell. 'There were hundreds outside Robert's house earlier. No wonder they tried to drown the woman. You gave them the permission they sought.'

With a swiftness that belied his age, the reverend grabbed the man's collar. Thrusting his face into Bailie Bell's, he hissed, 'I only said what you all knew I would. What you endorsed while we were dining, in case you've forgotten.' He pushed the bailie away in disgust. 'You fucking coocher. You're all piss and wind, prepared to have others make the hard decisions.' He looked at the men with righteous fury, daring them to disagree. 'Well, I did what was needed. Or would you rather the mob turned on *us*?'

'We don't have time for this,' said Bailie Cook with revulsion. 'The reverend's right. We have to be seen to be doing something. And now.' Turning towards the house, he called out. The Stuart brothers appeared, looking worse for their earlier encounter.

It was all Sorcha could do to stop Nettie flying at them.

There was a low conversation and then they all left, heading towards the Tolbooth. Once they were out of sight, Sorcha and Nettie emerged from the darkness.

'I was right to doubt those Stuart lads,' snarled Nettie.

'Save your anger for the reverend,' said Sorcha. 'And the bailies, the fucking cowards. The Stuart lads do what they're told — they've no choice. Remember, the crowd didn't hesitate to attack them either when they thought the lads were protecting Janet. They'll be worried for their own safety and standing with the bailies as much to protect themselves as to try and quell this... this madness.' She drew in her breath and, not caring if Mrs Cook or the other wives who remained inside the house saw her, stepped back onto the lane. 'At least none of them have worked out where she went yet.'

Nettie managed to find a smile. 'Aye, there's that at least.'

With one last withering look in the men's direction, they strode down a nearby street towards Nicolas Lawson's house.

After all, they didn't need to hurry. Not any more. Listening to the reverend and the councillors cover their spineless tracks, she knew with certainty Janet was in the last place they'd look. A place where there'd be medick, poultices for her wounds; a place where, Nicolas had whispered, Janet would go in her hour of need.

FIFTY-ONE

Peine forte et dure.
(Strong and hard punishment.)

*W*hen Sorcha found Janet at Nicolas's house, she was being washed gently by Nicolas's sister, Jenny. Nettie rushed to assist. Standing by the window, arms wrapped tightly about each other, their faces pale, were Nicolas's mother, aunt, a cousin and some of the neighbours. As soon as Sorcha explained that Nicolas knew Janet would come here, but rather than arouse suspicion by coming herself, had gone to the Tolbooth, potentially facing another kind of danger, the men left to see what they could do. Only as they sealed the door again did Sorcha worry about what they might encounter out there. What would happen to those who tried to restore order when there was only chaos?

With her cheeks washed and the worst of the wounds on her face and head patched, Janet still looked terrible. Her breathing was raspy, loud. One eye was swollen closed, the other redder than a robin's breast.

'They've broken my ribs,' she wheezed, flinching as she tried to move in the chair.

'Hush. Don't speak,' said Sorcha, kneeling at Janet's feet. She and Nettie dabbed some warm water infused with fennel and lavender on Janet's ruined hands. The barnacles on the hull of the *Sophia* had ripped her aged skin, torn strips from her arms and legs. Sorcha could barely look at her face. It was distended with bruises, lumps where rocks and sticks had struck. Her front teeth were missing, her nose had been badly broken and even as she sat there, bubbles of blood and snot leaked from her nostrils.

Sorcha reached up and softly wiped it away. 'Och, Janet, I'm so, so sorry.'

'Why are you sorry, lass?' mumbled Janet, her head heavy. 'This isn't your doing. This all rests with one person and those too weak to stop him.'

Sorcha met Janet's good eye and they both nodded. They weren't going to say his name, lest by uttering it he be made manifest.

'God will make him pay,' said Jenny.

'Rather the devil does that,' wheezed Janet.

'Sooner the better,' added Nettie, wiping Janet's nose again.

Distant shouts and the tramp of boots made Sorcha look up. Nearby doors were hammered upon; dogs barked and whined, bairns wailed.

'They're coming closer,' whimpered Jenny.

'Go. Go,' said Janet weakly. 'All of you. I don't want you here when they come lest they turn on you as well.'

'Where will we go?' asked Mimi Foster, a cousin of Nicolas and Jenny.

'Now's not the time to run away,' said Nettie, rising to her feet. She rested her fingers lightly upon Janet's shoulder.

Sorcha stood as well. 'Only by standing up to this, saying it can't go on, will it stop.' She took in the frightened faces, the looks of uncertainty that were exchanged. 'But Janet's right, *you* don't have to do this. This isn't your fight. You've not been accused. Those men out there, they've lost all reason. I will stay. I will remain with Janet —'

'Me too,' said Nettie.

'Nae —' gasped Janet.

Sorcha reached for her hand and nursed it. 'You're in no condition to argue.'

'Sorcha's correct.' Jenny returned to Janet's side. 'This isn't your fight,' she said to the other women. 'But it's my sister there at the Tolbooth, this is her house, and it's my friends those bastards have hurt.'

'I'm not going anywhere,' said Mimi, swinging away from the window, fists on hips. 'You're my family and friends too. The Weem is my home. I'll not be turned from it by a frothing tumult. You're wrong, Sorcha McIntyre. This *is* our fight.'

The women looked at each other with shining eyes and grim smiles.

Sorcha wanted to cheer. How proud of them Nicolas and Beatrix would be. How proud was she? Was Nettie?

'Very well,' she said, praying they couldn't hear her racing heart. 'Then we'll face the mob together and, like the men who are seeking to defuse this, we'll try and appeal to common sense.'

'They have none,' whispered Janet.

'Then we'll appeal to their purses instead,' said Nettie and continued bandaging Janet. 'If Edinburgh finds out about this, how folk sought to take the law into their own hands, punish someone without a trial, then not only will the authorities seek to bring the perpetrators to account, but the entire town will be fined and it will be hefty. Who's going to want to pay that?'

The women gazed at her in admiration.

'If there's one thing Nettie, Beatrix, you, Janet, and even Captain Ross taught me,' said Sorcha, 'it's that loss of money is a pain everyone feels.'

'Depends how much pain a person can tolerate,' muttered Janet.

They didn't have to wait long to find out. Minutes later, there was hammering at the door.

Sorcha tensed and the words she'd spoken so bravely before dissolved into a puddle of dread. Memories of anger, blood, the glee of the men and the way they had treated Janet crowded her head. She could smell her fear. It wouldn't do to let the others sense it.

'Open in the name of the Queen!' bellowed a deep voice.

One of the women squealed before pressing a hand over her mouth.

The relief that flooded Sorcha made her knees weak. ''Tis all right,' she said. 'It's a friend.'

Gesturing for Jenny and Mimi to help her, Sorcha pushed the chest they'd used to barricade the door out of the way. In stepped Sergeant Thatcher, followed by four of his men. Still more stood guard outside, their dirks drawn, guns aimed down the street.

Upon seeing Janet, Sergeant Thatcher blanched. 'Mrs Cornfoot,' he gulped. 'Glad to see you... alive.' He glanced at Sorcha and Nettie. 'I thought I told you two to go home.'

'You did,' said Sorcha.

Nettie bit back a laugh at his expression.

Sergeant Thatcher shook his head. 'Captain Ross did warn me...' he sighed. 'The mob aren't far behind us, I'm afraid, and now that my men are stationed about the cottage, it's like we've hung a shingle over the door. They'll know exactly where you are, Mrs Cornfoot.'

'They would have found out eventually,' said Janet.

The women clustered together by the window again, casting anxious looks outside, but not one of them left.

'The good news is,' continued the sergeant, 'the council have assembled some men to help us. They're making their way here. Once they arrive, we'll make sure you are safe and comfortable, Mrs Cornfoot, then we'll see to getting you back home.'

Janet shook her head, grimacing at the effort. 'I'll not be safe there nor comfortable. Not on my own.' She held her ribs and winced. 'I want you to take me to the Tolbooth.'

Sergeant Thatcher raised his brows. 'You're sure?'

'It's fortified,' explained Sorcha. 'And her friends are there.' Mine too, she wanted to add. Hopefully, Mr Laing, Mr Lawson and Mr Adam and their companions had reached there safely.

They began to prepare Janet to be moved. Taking a shawl Jenny offered, Nettie draped it over Janet's shaking shoulders. Mimi came forward with a hot beverage. 'Here,' she said. 'Drink this. It has valerian and some feverfew. It will help ease your pain.'

Taking it in her hands, the fingers brutally twisted and torn, with Sorcha's help, Janet swallowed some. A great deal dribbled down her grazed chin. Sorcha blotted it away, trying not to let Janet see how deeply her injuries affected her. Rancour and nausea bubbled inside her.

Sensing how she was feeling, Nettie rested a hand briefly upon her. Sorcha drew succour from her touch.

Outside, the sound of people assembling grew. Angry people. Sergeant Thatcher went to the window and pulled back the curtain. 'The councillors' men have arrived.' He grunted. 'There's fewer than I'd hoped.'

Sorcha looked out. Why, half the Weem were milling about the street, unafraid of the soldiers, their guns or the men the council had sent, men who only hours before had been throwing missiles at Janet. Sorcha's stomach began doing somersaults.

'What do we do?'

Sergeant Thatcher gazed at her. His eyes were a brilliant hazel in the firelight, but even she could see the uncertainty in them. 'Wait. Hopefully, they'll grow weary of this and leave.'

An argument rose above the general din, muffled but fierce.

'What are they saying?' croaked Janet. Nettie tried, unsuccessfully, to divert her.

Sorcha couldn't make the words out, but whatever was being said was fraught. There were shouts, then a screech followed by a long, low roar. Steel clashed and clattered, there was a grunt followed by a loud groan. Something slammed against a wall. The women jumped; the windows shook.

The door was flung open and in burst a group of men. Behind them were the guards, subdued now their firearms and daggers had been forcibly taken. Armed with what they'd snatched from the soldiers and a range of makeshift weapons, the intruders took one look at Janet and, pushing first Nettie then Sorcha to one side, fell upon her.

'She's here! The witch is here!'

'Nae!' screamed Sorcha. 'Leave her alone. Haven't you done enough?' Someone kicked out, but she managed to dodge the boot, wrapping her arms around Janet who clung to her, trembling. Nettie landed a blow upon a soldier, earning a fist to the cheek for her efforts. It didn't stop her crawling back towards Janet and shielding her.

'I'll not let them take you,' whispered Sorcha.

'Me neither,' said Nettie.

'I won't let them hurt either of you,' said Janet and tried to stand.

Slapping aside those who tried to grasp a hold of Janet, Sorcha and Nettie used nails, teeth, feet, whatever they could. Shirts were torn, skirts became caught in someone's pike, pinned by a knife, ripped.

Sergeant Thatcher lunged at the men as he tried to pull Sorcha and Nettie to safety. The butt of a rifle connected with his skull and he tumbled to the floor, out cold. More pushed their way through the door, throwing their fists about, waving their weapons, uncaring now the soldiers had been disarmed. A gun discharged. The women screamed. The round went into the ceiling, sending a shower of plaster and straw upon everyone below.

The fire was kicked, peat and smouldering lumps rolling out of the hearth. Smoke belched and billowed. It was difficult to see; to breathe.

Torn from Janet's side, Sorcha fell hard against the window, almost shattering it. There was another scream. Nettie was hurled against a wall and fell to the floor unmoving. Janet was lifted into a pair of burly arms. It was the bearded man who'd tied her up on the beach, the incomer. He was helped by two others Sorcha didn't recognise and a few others she did.

Bodies pressed against her, pushing, crying, shrieking, whimpering. Unarmed soldiers barged into the room fists hooked. One was stabbed, another toppled unconscious, too close to the fire. Jenny tried to stamp out the flames before they took, shoving the burning peat back into the hearth.

Carried out of the house, Janet was flung onto the road. Sorcha clawed at the window, trying to open it, but it was jammed. Pinned against the glass by the press of bodies, she was unable to move; forced to watch as a wide circle formed around Janet.

The bearded man began shouting instructions, his voice unclear to those inside the house. A couple of men disappeared briefly. There was the splintering shriek of tearing wood. It was the signal the crowd had been waiting for. Their approval was deafening.

Janet lay bleeding and crying on the road, curled on one side, her knees against her chest, unaware that two men were marching up the road carrying a great wooden door. They halted next to Janet, their eyes fixed on the Englishman.

The crowd grew quiet. Janet rolled painfully onto her back to see why. When she saw the men, the door held high above their heads, a terrible prescience dawned. She craned her neck as far as she could.

Sorcha locked eyes with Janet, willing her to focus on her and her alone. The old fishwife lay there, still as could be. As they stared at each other, Sorcha poured all the love and memories of their years together into her gaze: as fishwives, as friends, labouring by the ocean, helping the men. She recalled their shared history, the bonds that linked them in ways others could not comprehend. Slowly fear and uncertainty drained from Janet's face. A smile curved her lips as she mouthed something.

As if she stood beside her, Sorcha heard the words clearly. 'Live for me.'

They were like a punch to the stomach.

The bearded man made a chopping motion with his hand and, in one movement, the men holding the door threw it down on Janet. There was no hesitation. It slammed into her, the force making her legs and arms fly upwards. Before it had even settled, the men leapt onto it, jumping up and down, beckoning those watching to join. Pulling volunteers up beside them, they stomped upon the wood, drinking from flasks, bottles, crying out in celebration, as if a woman wasn't being crushed to death beneath their boots.

Janet's head lolled to one side. Her mouth fell open and her tongue escaped. Where her blood flowed, steam rose into the chilly night air, weaving the murderers with their sweaty bodies and hot whisky breath, in an insubstantial mist. All the while the moon shone its lambent glow upon them, making Janet appear ephemeral, ghoulish, and those killing her evil spectres who'd been granted grey flesh for the night.

Sorcha saw the moment life left Janet. Her eyes, bright with pain and disbelief, widened, grew glazed, then empty.

Janet Cornfoot was gone.

Sorcha stayed at the window, unable to look away. She prayed for Janet's soul and that those who committed such a foul act, including the man who was really responsible, would pay. Eternal damnation was not enough. What was this if not damnation made manifest? She would never forget what she was witnessing. None of them would. She felt scraped, hollow, as if all the light in the world had been extinguished and a great darkness had taken up residence. A darkness thicker than pitch and just as evil smelling and evil tasting.

Around her, the women wept. Some of the men too.

Nettie stirred, crawled her way to the window and held Sorcha in her arms. They neither cried nor spoke, simply stared.

At some point Sergeant Thatcher regained consciousness and, learning what was happening, clambered to his feet and said something to Sorcha. She gave the barest of nods and he left, taking some of the soldiers with him. They could do no more for Janet Cornfoot, and he was certain she and Nettie were safe for the time being. But they could try and help protect those who'd gone to the Tolbooth. Sorcha hoped with all her wrung-out heart that this time, the soldiers' presence would be a deterrent.

Those dancing atop Janet didn't notice them leaving the house; they were too busy.

Minutes or hours later, Sorcha no longer knew, a cart was dragged up the lane by a man in a large floppy hat, who invited people to jump in the back. When four people obliged, he wheeled it back and forth across the door. Across Janet. When it became stuck on the edges, the men were quick to free it, holding it by the sides to make sure it didn't roll off.

A quiet figure among the revelry finally drew Sorcha's eye. Nudging Nettie, she jerked her chin towards it. He may have his head covered and be draped in a black cloak, but they knew him for what and who he was. Once more, the reverend gazed upon his handiwork. Was he horrified to see what he'd incited? What he'd given birth to?

'God, don't forgive them,' whispered Sorcha, 'for they know exactly what they do.'

'Amen,' said Nettie softly.

It wasn't until the cart was wheeled away and the door finally removed from Janet, allowing the crowd to see she was indeed dead, that people, mostly subdued, started to disperse. Even then, there were those who prised her off the road and held her broken, bloody body up for Sorcha and Nettie to see.

It's not Janet. It's not Janet. Sorcha kept the mantra going. She had to, she had to believe it. This bent, malleable form was not human. It was a scarecrow divested of its stuffing, a skin without contents. Janet was with God now. Her God.

Annoyed that Sorcha, Nettie and the others appeared unmoved, the men shouted they would be next. Sorcha simply stared through the glass. When the remaining guards hefted weapons in their direction, the men's bold pronouncements faded.

'To the Tolbooth!' shouted one of them. 'There be more witches there!' The cry was taken up.

Scooping Janet's body up, as if she were a great catch brought to land, they swiftly departed, taking her corpse with them. As dawn broke across the Weem, sending the winking, blinking stars to bed and shedding a pale mauve light over the town, the horde marched through the streets, singing, drinking, celebrating, torches raised high.

Sorcha could hear them. For ages, their voices continued to ring. Finally, after all this time, they had their justice. They'd protected the Weem, each other, their homes, their families — and from what?

An old fishwife whose greatest sin was to speak the truth.

FIFTY-TWO

Dummy wunnae lee.
(Here is visible evidence, so you need not argue.)

'You said they wouldn't harm her further, that they'd bring her to the Tolbooth,' blared Bailie Cook, shoving his face into the reverend's before beginning to pace again. 'Well, fuck that. What are we supposed to do now?' The question was directed at Bailie Vernour.

Having returned from the Tolbooth, where they'd ordered a group of soldiers guarding the door to find Janet Cornfoot, the Pittenweem council were reconvened in Cook's dining room. The remnants of their earlier meal as well as the odours of whisky and tobacco mingled with the men's sweat and trepidation at what they'd just learned — their concern not so much what had happened to Janet Cornfoot, but what her demise portended for them. Their faces were red, their words clipped and angry.

Patrick Cowper clapped his hands together. He needed to take control of the situation before these weak men capitulated to Bailie Bell's suggestion and sent to Edinburgh for troops to subdue the townsfolk.

When he was certain he had their attention, he turned towards Gerard Stuart. 'Tell us again what happened after they —' Cowper swallowed, 'after they placed the door on her.' Gerard might be injured, but he was the only one to adopt a semblance of calm amidst the turmoil.

Gerard cleared his throat. 'They hardly placed it, reverend — they slammed the fuc—'

'I said,' Patrick stared at him firmly, 'after.' The last thing they needed was a recount of the bloody goings on outside the Lawson house. He could only pray the soldiers and guards they'd mobilised managed to control the rampaging men.

'As I said before,' sighed Gerard, swiping a dirty fist across his forehead. 'They carried the body of Mrs Cornf— I mean, the witch, about the streets. My guess, they were in search of any others they might —' he hesitated.

The reverend waved impatient hands at him. 'Then what?'

'They returned to Nicolas Lawson's house.' He glanced at his brother. 'It's our belief that they intended to either frighten or even capture Sorcha McIntyre and Nettie Horseburgh and inflict the same punishment upon them. They were… unhappy they tried to interfere earlier, you ken. Prevent them from finishing Mrs Cornf— the witch — when they had her by the shore.'

The bailies murmured. William Bell was shaking his head. Robert Cook poured himself another dram and drained it.

'But they weren't there,' said Patrick blankly.

'Nae, reverend. There was no sign of them. All that remained were the family of Nicolas Lawson and some friends of Janet Cornfoot.'

'Did the men try and find Mrs McIntyre?'

'Mrs McIntyre?' snapped Bailie Bell. 'Why are you so concerned about her?' He swung to Gerard. 'It's Janet Cornfoot we need to think about, not the blasted McIntyre woman or Nettie Horseburgh or any of the other accused. Where's the body now?'

Gerard Stuart shifted his feet uncomfortably. 'Far as I know, it's where the mob left it, sir. Back on the cobbles where she died. Me and Angus, we thought about moving her, but didn't ken where we should take her.' His eyes sidled to his brother's. 'She's not in a good way.'

'An' she be a witch,' added Angus.

'Indeed,' said Patrick quickly, clamping a hand on Gerard's forearm to shut him up. He faced the bailies. 'Would you they brought the body here?'

There was a swift response. 'Nae. Nae.'

'Where then?'

'The Tolbooth or the cave,' answered William Bell. He lowered his head. 'They shouldn't have left her on the street. Not where anyone can see her — the bairns, the women. It's not right.'

'Not right?' Patrick spoke through clenched teeth. 'What's not right is that a witch lives.' Understanding he had to alter the mood and fast, Patrick stood with his back to the fire and waited until they all looked to him again. 'We've done no wrong here, lads. Understand this. The townsfolk could no longer abide having a witch in their midst and sought to take justice into their own hands. The justice they were denied by Edinburgh.'

Angus nodded vigorously. Patrick gave a cold smile.

'That might be,' said William Bell. 'But Edinburgh are hardly going to be happy that two accused witches have now died in Pittenweem and under our watch. They'll blame *us*.'

'They cannot. We'd naught to do with what happened tonight. Naught.' When the men turned away from him, Patrick adopted a different tone. 'Think about it. The woman escaped from prison. We tasked men to find her. In the process of returning her to her cell, she escaped again and the townsfolk, terrified a witch was on the loose, acted. Where were we when they snatched the woman? Where were we when they decided to lynch her? Hmmm? We were in your house, Robert.' He thrust his finger towards Bailie Cook. '*Your house*. Eating a meal, being served by your patient wife and lovely daughters. We had no idea what was happening.'

'That's not entirely true. Why you left and —' began Robert Cook.

'True?' snapped the reverend. 'What's true is that we were deserted by the authorities in our hour of need. When we pleaded with them for our safety, demanded they protect us from malfeasance, what did they do? I'll remind you: they released those who were tormenting us, threatening our way of life, our very souls, back into the community.'

Silence.

'Did you tie a rope around Janet Cornfoot and throw her into the sea?' Patrick asked William Bell softly.

'Nae,' said William swiftly, shaking his head.

'And what about you, Robert Cleiland? Did you beat her and kick her and drag her about the streets?'

'Not me.'

'And you, Robert Cook. Did you call for a door to be thrown upon her and for your neighbours to leap upon it?'

'You ken well I didn't, reverend.'

'Aye,' said Patrick, his voice rising. 'There you have it. When Edinburgh questions us, we'll tell them the truth. That we had naught to do with tonight's events. We were ignorant of what was happening until such time as the guards alerted us. When they did, we sent for soldiers to break up the swarm and see to the witch's safety. Is that not so?'

It was some time before the men answered. 'Agreed,' they said, one by one, unable to meet each other's eyes.

'Good. Now,' said Patrick, slapping his thigh and indicating Gerard and Angus. 'I want you to take me to see the witch's body. Are the horde still about?'

'Nae, reverend,' said Gerard. 'They grew tired and, being unable to find any other witches, drifted back to their homes.'

Patrick frowned. 'I see. Well, Robert, if you could kindly ask for my coat to be fetched, I'll take it upon myself to confirm the death of Mrs Cornfoot and decide what to do with the body. Does that meet with your approval, gentlemen?' Knowing they'd be keen to wipe their hands of the situation, Patrick wasn't surprised when they assented.

Without another word, he took his coat from the shy maid, who bobbed a curtsey then fled from the room as if it were a devil's sabbath and not a meeting of the finest men in town.

With a nod and thanks to Bailie Cook for a delicious meal, Patrick put on his coat and, for the third time that night, left the house, Gerard and Angus behind him.

Patrick braced himself upright with one hand against the wall, bent over and stared at the oleaginous muddle on the ground. He couldn't remember the last time he'd vomited so violently. At first he thought the lads were playing a joke bringing him to see that... that... It wasn't until he recognised the Lawson cottage and the other houses around it, that he realised what he was seeing. Watching Janet Cornfoot's death unfold from a distance earlier, he'd been able to persuade himself her demise was no more than she deserved. But now... Unable to shut out the sight of the shattered cheekbones, the twisted limbs, the crushed ribs; all the blood, bones and other matter spilled over the cobbles congealing in shining lumps in the grey dawn light, he heaved again.

With some distaste he looked at the toes of his boots, the hem of his long coat. They were splattered with his repulsion.

Wiping his mouth, he kept his back turned to the street. He waited for his stomach to stop spasming, his throat to still, and breathed deeply, screwing up his nose at the stench of his own horror — a horror mixed with the smell of blood and the stink of shit and other bodily fluids.

'How many have seen her?' he asked Gerard hoarsely.

Uncertain whether to offer sympathy or pretend he hadn't just witnessed the reverend throw his guts and more upon the street and walls, Gerard didn't appear to hear, he stood so far away.

Only when Patrick repeated the question did the lad shuffle closer.

'I'm not sure, reverend. All those who witnessed her death plus anyone in the houses about here, I imagine.'

Not trusting himself to speak further, Patrick nodded, thrusting his fist against his lips as a sour belch budded in his mouth.

Angus glanced at his brother and raised a brow.

'What do you wish us to do about her?' asked Gerard after a while. 'I mean, the sun be rising and folk will be setting out for kirk soon.'

Dear God, thought Patrick. He would have to address the townsfolk — those responsible for the obscenity behind him. Had God really willed such a punishment? Patrick finally stood upright. 'Aye... we have to do something.' He raised his head to the sky. *What would You do, my Lord, in this situation? The witch recanted her baptism and so couldn't in all fairness be given a Christian burial. 'Twould make a mockery of all we've stood for, make a mockery of me. Of You too, God.*

'Reverend?' Gerard's voice broke into his thoughts.

It was getting lighter. Birds had taken wing, their cries welcoming the day. He could hear noises coming from inside the cottages. Smoke began to cough from chimneys. Somewhere in the distance, a rooster crowed. They must do something, remove Janet's remains before anyone else saw her, before those who were there last night saw what they'd done in the broad light of day and held him to account.

The reverend almost sickened again.

'Gather her up.'

'Us?'

He saw the shocked look on Angus and Gerard's faces.

'Who else?' he hissed. 'Get some auld sails from outside the fishermen's cottages, some linen, I care not. Wrap her up and throw her on the braes. It's what we did with Thomas Brown. It's the best we can do for this witch.'

The men studied him in dismay. For just a brief moment, he saw himself as others must: a man of God who disappointed. Who coolly pushed aside love and clemency in favour of power and punishment. Well, they were the Lord's weapons as well.

'Come away with you,' he demanded, shooing the lads with his long fingers. 'Get it done now. I've a sermon to deliver and can't be dealing with this.' He began to walk down the wynd, towards the sea he could hear but needed to feel and see as well. He passed by a cottage without a door, the hinges hanging, the door frame splintered and torn. A dark unblinking eye, it accused him, condemned him. Let it. God knew he was guiltless in this; that right from the beginning, his only concern had been for the good Christian souls of the townsfolk. 'On second thoughts,' he said, taking only a couple of extra steps before stopping and talking over his shoulder. 'Dig a shallow grave. After all, once Edinburgh reads her confession and recognises her for the witch she was, they'll pardon her death and demand a burning. We don't want to waste time and money digging her up again, do we?'

The men simply stared.

'Come to the manse when you're finished. I want to ken how you went. Then we'll go to kirk and pray. Together. After all, it's Sunday. The Lord's day.'

'Reverend,' said the Stuart brothers in chorus. Half-expecting them to fall into step beside him as they too had to venture to the harbourfront for material to wrap the corpse in, the reverend was strangely disconcerted when they didn't.

It was as if he, the saviour of the Weem, the man who brought stability back to the town, was now a pariah.

PART FOUR
February to May 1705

It is much easier to believe that the crowd, satisfied in their own minds of the reality of Cornfoot's compact with Satan, dreading the fearful consequences of her malice, and indignant at the Privy Council for refusing to prosecute... took the law into their own hands.

— Privy Council Minute, Murder of a Pittenweem Witch, 15th February, 1705, *Annals of Pittenweem, Being Notes and Extracts from the Ancient Records of that Burgh, 1526–1793*

... it's very well known, that either of them (the magistrates [bailies] or minister of Pittenweem) could have quashed the rabble, and prevented that murder, if they had appeared zealous against it. I am sorry I have no better news to tell you, God deliver us from those principles that tend to such practices.

— *A Letter From a Gentleman in Fife to his Friend in Edinburgh*, 1705

FIFTY-THREE

'Tis certain that Mr Cowper, preaching the Lord's day immediately after in Pittenweem, took no notice of the murder, which at least makes him guilty of sinful silence.

— A Letter From a Gentleman of Fife to his Friend in Edinburgh, *1705*

Looking at the pious faces of the congregation, the warm, shared smiles, the exchanged nods of peace and understanding, Sorcha wanted to scream. She wanted to rage at them, ask how they could sit there as if there wasn't blood on their hands, in their hearts. How could they act as if nothing had happened? Was it really just a fortnight ago that many of these same people had taken part in the most brutal and bloody of murders?

She didn't have to close her eyes to see Janet's body. To recall the great weeping gashes, her broken limbs, shattered jaw, and her blood. So much blood. To remember the cart being driven back and forth over the door, crushing her even further. At least she'd been dead by then and couldn't feel anything.

But Sorcha did. A mixture of impotent wrath and futile sorrow that bruised her very soul.

Ever since Janet died, sleep had evaded her as she tossed and turned, reliving that night, wondering what she could have done to prevent what happened. What any of them could have done. The rational part of her knew there was nothing. The townsfolk had behaved as if possessed, driven by an unnatural hunger. Like ravening beasts, they'd stalked their prey, wounding her over and over until she could defend herself no more. And yet, when that Sunday dawned, they'd shaken off their weariness, washed their clothes and hands and presented themselves at kirk as if naught had occurred. According to those who'd attended, the reverend made no mention of what had transpired, but delivered his sermon for all the world as if it was just another Sunday, not one that would be marked forever in their consciousness.

Sorcha hadn't gone to the kirk that day nor the following Sunday. Neither had Nettie. But they'd been told to show their faces today lest rumours start. God forbid that should happen, thought Sorcha.

Sitting beside her, Nettie bunched her hands in her lap, her eyes staring straight ahead while people prayed, listened and responded with beatific smiles on their faces.

Sorcha was irrevocably changed. She'd gone to bed one person and woken up another. All her friends felt likewise. The billeted soldiers, who had not only borne witness to events but been physically hurt by them, described similar feelings. One of Sergeant Thatcher's men had to have his shattered leg set by the Anster doctor; the following day he was carried to Edinburgh in a cart, along with a couple of other men who also had serious injuries, one a terrible knife wound. The sergeant said he doubted he'd see them again.

'One can't fight with a broken body or a broken spirit.'

Sorcha knew he was also thinking of Janet.

The sergeant's words made her determined not to let that bloody night and the days that followed break her. Someone had to ensure justice was served; that Patrick Cowper and the bailies answered for what they'd done. As she discussed with Nettie, Beatrix, Nicolas, Sergeant Thatcher and Janet's grieving relatives and friends in the aftermath, they'd done the worst thing they could have: nothing. Just as they'd done naught to staunch the growing rage towards Janet and passively endorsed whatever action the townsfolk chose to take.

Forgoing all promises only to write to Aidan about general goings-on and not alarm him, with Nettie's help she set down everything that happened while it was still fresh in her mind. Not satisfied with that — after all, what could Aidan do from Bavaria? — she wrote to his former commanding officer as well, a Colonel Johns in Edinburgh. Knowing the disturbing contents might be dismissed if she signed it as a woman, she signed this one exactly as Aidan had those he'd written about events in Pittenweem: 'A Gentleman of Fife'.

She entrusted the missive to the injured soldiers, knowing it would be delivered. In the meantime, she thought constantly about that dreadful night, equally appalled and saddened that the people of Pittenweem continued with their lives as if nothing had happened. With few exceptions, Janet's name wasn't mentioned. It was as if she never existed.

That Sunday after Janet was murdered, she and Nettie had waited until people had flocked to the kirk as usual and then walked down to the harbour, passing the Lawson house and the exact spot where the murder had taken place. The body was gone, the cobbles scrubbed. It was only when they arrived at the waterfront and saw the other fish-wives, who'd also declined to go to kirk, that they learned from Jean Durkie that Janet's corpse had been placed in a shallow grave on the western braes.

'Just like Thomas's,' said Jean.

'Not quite,' corrected Sorcha. 'Thomas was never buried.'

The next day, Monday, shops opened as usual. People bought goods, ordered milk and eggs from the farms, purchased fish from her and Nettie when they tramped through the lanes, blethered and gossiped. As the days went by, they fell sick, gave birth, laughed and wept. No one raised the matter of Janet Cornfoot: not with Sorcha, Nettie, Beatrix, Nicolas, Isobel, the Cornfoot family, nor with any of the fishwives. Sorcha didn't know whether to be grateful or furious.

As it was, she just felt hollow. The town was a place she no longer knew.

A few days after Janet's death, Nettie, Beatrix, Nicolas and Isobel gathered around the fireplace in Sorcha's cottage, untouched quaichs of whisky in their hands. While it wasn't the fishwives' way to revisit tragedy, Nettie had determined this was different. Only Sorcha had borne witness to Janet's final moments. In order to survive whatever lay ahead, whatever monster Janet's death had unleashed, they needed to know the details. For Sorcha's sake, for all their sakes, they had to speak of this.

'Tell us, hen,' said Nettie, reaching across and laying a reassuring hand on her leg. 'Tell them what you saw.'

Sorcha had been prepared to share everything with her friends, longing for the release of speaking the truth and the comfort of their understanding. Looking at the four anxious faces she loved, she knew she could not. It would not be fair. She was strong. She could bear this. What choice did she have?

Instead, she chose a different tack.

She recounted Janet's last moments. How brave she was, how defiant. How even when she knew the intentions of those who hunted her, that they would stop at nothing until she was dead, she refused to bow to fear, to the terror and chaos they tried to create.

'You know what her last words were?'

As she spoke, the women wept. Great tears streaked their cheeks. Beatrix had her arm around Isobel. Nicolas clung to Nettie.

'Keep going, hen,' said Nettie huskily when Sorcha hesitated. She too was finding it difficult to speak.

'She said, "Live for me".'

Nettie sucked in her breath. The weeping stilled. There was silence.

'Then that's what we must do,' said Nettie finally, reaching first for Sorcha's hand, then Beatrix's, Isobel's and Nicolas's, bringing them together in the centre of their tight circle. One by one, the women nodded.

After that, they never raised the matter again. When they saw each other over the following days, and when Sorcha and Nettie would stumble home exhausted each night after working at the harbour and selling fish upon the streets, they would ask about each other's families. They'd discuss the catch, the cold, which ships had returned and where the rest were. The condition of the boats and the harbour. Every time, the women would ask after Aidan. Sorcha had told them she'd written to him. She also admitted to writing to his colonel in Edinburgh about Janet's death, but thus far she'd had no response.

By tacit agreement, what no one shared was how hard it was becoming for them; how they were terrified that what happened to Janet might yet befall them; that the lunacy that had infected the Weem that night would reignite. More and more shopkeepers were refusing to serve them, more and more townsfolk turned their backs when they arrived on their stoops with fish, or simply strolled past on the streets. Dark mutterings followed them once more, dark mutterings and a sprinkling of abuse.

With each passing hour, it was getting worse.

Every night, Sorcha would lie under the covers and stare at the ceiling, uncaring of the shapes above. They no longer had the ability to transport her to other places and times. Instead, she'd wait for dawn to arrive.

Looking around the kirk now, two weeks since Janet's passing, Sorcha wondered if the people here slept at night. Or did they, like her, find shutting their eyes meant reliving what had happened? How did the women feel, knowing their husbands, brothers and sons had lynched, beaten and stomped on an old woman? Dragged her through the streets, kicked, punched and brutalised her? She shuddered at the thought of any one of them lying beside her, sharing a pillow, touching her.

How could they behave as if they were as pious and deserving of the Lord's grace as a saint? Perhaps that was the only way they could deal with it — by pretending it never happened. That way, the stain of remembrance didn't have to be cleansed; that way, they could retreat into the solace of sleep.

Barely able to look at the man delivering the sermon, she wondered how he could stand before them, speaking of justice on the one hand but also warning what happened when malfeasance was allowed to flourish on the other, and how it took the strongest of souls, the most just and brave of men and their women to resist the devil. Sorcha marvelled that he didn't collapse under the weight of his hypocrisy.

Strangers were seated among the congregation — incomers from the north and the borderlands; some from the city. They'd come to view the witches, watch events unfold. What did they make of what happened? She glanced at them now, in their different clothes, with their odd manners, some with accents so thick they were hard to understand. Why were they still here? Was it because they hoped for more entertainment? She knew the reverend and bailies prayed they'd stay, encouraged them to linger and spend their coin. Already, work had recommenced on the pier and even the harbour wall. The town couldn't afford to have these people leave. But why did they not speak out against what they saw? In her mind, by their silence they were as complicit as the bailies.

Yet, was she any better? Were any of Janet's friends or family? They sat there among them, mute. Too scared to challenge the reverend lest they were named witches. That was all it took. The bestowing of a label and all the connotations that came with it. Fishwife, people could accept, albeit begrudgingly. But witch, that was the name for an outsider in every way, an un-woman not worthy of God's protection or grace. A witch brought ill with her and infected a community. It was a name to be feared. By the bestower and those branded with it. That's what Janet's death had taught her — taught them all. To be called a witch was to be reborn. Anything done in the past was obscured by the new identity. Forget the fact the witch was a mother, daughter, sister, neighbour, lover, grandmother, healer, fishwife... A witch was a canker on the body of the community that must be excised.

The name turned a person from a child of God into a devil-made creature, fair game for hunters like the reverend and those who took pleasure from such sport.

Sorcha had no desire to play their deadly game.

'Live for me.' Those were Janet's last words, her final wish. 'Live for me.'

Sorcha made up her mind there and then that she would do what-ever that took. Even if it meant singing and praying alongside murder-ers who used God as a shield to protect their crimes and justify their cruelty.

As she was thinking that, she caught the eye of first Nettie, then, seated two rows over, Beatrix, Mr Brown, Nicolas, Isobel and Isobel's father. It was important she remember there were also those who saw through the mask of righteousness, saw the town and the reverend for what and who they were — people caught in a spell that, if she had any influence, would soon be broken. She would cleave to those she trusted and keep working to ensure Janet's memory — and that of Thomas Brown — lived on.

Someone had to.

Live for me. If that meant pretending to be aligned with the rever-end and his supporters for now, so be it.

During the last hymn, Sorcha, Nettie and a few brave others left before the reverend had a chance to step down from the pulpit. They might attend for the sermon, show themselves to be members of the kirk, but be damned if they would shake the murdering bastard's hand.

FIFTY-FOUR

... the Lords do hereby recommend to Sir James Steuart, Her Majestie's Advocat, to raise a process and lybell at this instance... against the magistrats of Pittenweem, for their not keeping the peace of the place, and suffering such tumults and rables and other such outrages to be committed within their burgh... also recommends to... raise a process... against (Here follows the names of five persons), or any other persons who have had any hand in, and been accessory to, the murder committed upon Janet Cornfoot at Pittenweem...

— The Annals of Pittenweem, Being Notes and Extracts from the Ancient Records of that Burgh, 1526–1793

'Who told them?' shouted Patrick Cowper, staring down the bailies as they sat before him in his study. 'Who among you lily-livered blaggards informed the authorities? Hmm? Which one of you was it?'

As he spoke, a face appeared in his mind. A lovely face with sea-coloured eyes and full lips. Of course... who else would it be?

The reverend could scarce see the men as rage stole his sight, turned them into a morass of dark lights and shifting shadows. What else did he expect? The lass had to interfere; she couldn't leave well enough alone. Didn't ken when to respect the wishes of her betters. She had to stick her nose into lads' business.

With startling clarity he recalled the time she caught him with her mother. If he'd had but a few minutes more, there would have been nothing for her to see, no guilt to attribute. But she'd caught him at the worst moment, just as he was about to have his way. Her mother's gown torn and bunched around her waist, her hands captured by his, her quiet weeping, his damp, hot face; his breeks bunched around his knees. He forced the memory away.

He took a deep breath and his vision returned to normal, even if his heart did not. Unwilling to share his suspicions yet about who had alerted Edinburgh — the most literate of the fishwives, the one who brazenly turned her back on his suggestion she remarry, rejecting the fine offer of his son, and yet boldly sinned with that meddlesome Captain Ross — he would wait until he was certain, and once he knew, act.

Heat suffused his cheeks and his throat grew dry. What a damn nuisance. The last thing he needed was a contingent from Edinburgh descending upon Pittenweem again, not now when everything was under control. Half the town were in his hands and the other half too afraid to challenge him lest they suffer a similar fate to Cornfoot.

All except one brazen besom.

What happened to the Cornfoot carline would be nothing to what he'd do to Sorcha McIntyre and her friends. Or, better still, what the townsfolk could…

The clock ticking on the mantelpiece crawled into his head, bringing him back to the present, the warm room and the disgruntled, anxious men arrayed before him.

'None of us are responsible, reverend,' said Bailie Bell finally, starting to rise to his feet, then thinking better of it and sitting back down. 'None of us informed Edinburgh.'

'It would not be in the interests of anyone here,' added Bailie Cook. William Bell cast a grateful look towards him.

The reverend kept his anger in check and pretended to be placated. He knew it wasn't the bailies' fault. 'Nevertheless, they're sending lairds here to pass judgement upon us. Again. Upon events that occurred more than two weeks ago.' The reverend flicked the letter in his hand. The sound was like an arquebus shot.

The bailies flinched. All except Bailie Vernour.

'Calm down, man,' he said, folding his arms and huffing.

The reverend's eyes widened; words tangled in his throat.

Bailie Vernour continued quickly, 'At least you're not named, unlike Robert here.' He gestured with his thumb to Bailie Cook, who nodded and swallowed miserably. He was all but being blamed for Janet's murder. Why? Because the council happened to be dining at his house the night it occurred.

'They're accusing me of doing naught,' said Cook, wringing his hands. 'But they weren't *here*. They didn't see the mob, feel their rage, their determination. There was nothing we could have done. By God, not even the soldiers could control them. As it was, we're lucky there was only one body to deal with.'

Patrick bit his tongue, swallowing the recriminations that crowded his mouth. He knew it was only a matter of time before they were held accountable for failing to send the rabble home and, worse, inviting them to do what they wanted with Janet.

Before *he* was.

Much to his surprise, although a few guarded looks passed between the men, nothing was said.

'Well,' he said eventually. 'There's no use fighting among ourselves, not when, according to this, they'll be upon us tomorrow, asking questions, and we must have answers.'

'What will we tell them?' asked William Bell.

Patrick had given the notion much consideration and was waiting for the right time to apportion blame. It hadn't suited his purpose to identify the culprits too soon, not while so many incomers remained in town, hoping something more was going to be done about the witches who, as he reminded anyone who'd listen, were still at large. The incomers' coin had been very useful. Maybe, just maybe, it was time to speed them on their way, but not before they served one last useful purpose.

He took his time regaining his seat, then placed his forearms on his desk, leaned forwards and lowered his voice. The fire crackled in the hearth, the flames reflecting on the walls behind the bailies, making it appear as if they were trapped in a furnace.

'What we'll tell Laird Anstruther and his Edinburgh cronies is that no one *from Pittenweem* was responsible. That it was the incomers who were out of control and who sought to put an end to the woman they believed to be a witch.'

The bailies stared at him, then each other as the idea slowly took hold. He could almost hear their thoughts whirring.

Patrick continued, 'We've heard from the Stuart brothers about what happened down at the harbour —' Patrick found his notes, as if he hadn't seen for himself exactly what had occurred. 'The lynching. It's clearly an English custom. We'll remind them of that. The idea to dunk Mrs Cornfoot didn't originate from anyone here. We'll say it was the Englishman who roused the folk.'

There were nods of approval.

'It wasn't just him,' objected Bailie Cook. 'They'll never believe one person was responsible. We'll have to provide other names.'

'We should add a local one as well, so as not to appear biased,' said Bailie Bell.

'Och, I have just the one,' said Patrick, snapping his fingers. 'Rob Dalzell.'

Robert Vernour frowned. 'His da's the skipper on the *George*, isn't he?'

'Aye,' said Patrick. 'And you ken what that means, don't you, lads?'

Slow, sly grins broke out.

'What he'll pay to have his son kept from trial, let alone gaol,' added Bailie Cleiland, rubbing his hands together.

'What he'll pay to *us*,' corrected Patrick. 'Unfortunately, we could probably get a great deal more if we kept his name out of it altogether. But too many people saw him. Saw what he did to the witch.' A vision of stomping boots, of a fist slamming into Janet's head arose.

The men mumbled among themselves.

'Who else?' asked Robert Vernour.

Patrick returned to his notes. 'There's a Walter Watson from Burntisland been identified, and a watchman from the Orkneys. He's staying at the Cod and Sole up in Backgate.'

'What about the four who dragged her onto the *Sophia*?' asked Cook.

'Aye, I've their names here — and the Englishman among them. We'll have to provide the lairds with their names as well,' said Patrick, putting the page down. That his own son had been omitted from the list, he did not mention. 'Eight will suffice. Especially if we emphasise the role of England and the Orkneys in this.'

Relaxing, the men looked to their drinks, which had remained largely untouched.

A thought suddenly occurred to Patrick. 'What we'll also highlight to the lairds is that it all could have been much worse. If not for mobilising the soldiers when we did and our own guards, more women might have met the same fate.'

The men exchanged cautious looks that, as the reverend's words sank in, transformed into wide smiles.

'If anything,' continued Patrick, warming to his idea, 'Edinburgh should be congratulating us that the toll wasn't higher.'

'That might be going too far —' cautioned Cook, tugging at his waistcoat.

'I don't think so,' said Patrick, taking a healthy slug of whisky. 'You weren't among them. You didn't gauge the mood.'

'Speaking of mood,' said Bell, 'it's still volatile. Do you think we should offer the remaining accused some protection? I mean, we don't want a repeat of what happened to auld Janet, do we? There's no doubt, having those four women roaming about is making the townsfolk nervous...' He looked to his peers for support. One by one, their eyes slid from his. 'What if they decide to remove the lingering threat?'

'I don't think protection is necessary, William,' said Patrick smoothly. 'If we offer it to them, then we appear weak, as if we made a mistake locking them up in the first place. It's not like they're ordinary women.' With the exception of Bell, the men chuckled and Patrick glanced at the picture of Jesus on the cross, noting the way shadows wavered across the painting, as if dark forces were trying to consume it. 'Far better we let them fend for themselves. Lest you forget, they are witches, handmaids of the devil, indicted by their own mouths. If they can't protect themselves, then what can we mere mortals hope to do for them?'

The spectre of Janet Cornfoot hung between them. No one dared to mention her this time.

'Then we must at least move to arrest the men on that list immediately,' said Cook, gesturing towards the page.

Patrick repressed a smirk. Imprisoning these men would take some heat off Cook. It would also make it appear as if the Weem council was dealing with matters.

'Not only will having them in custody look good when the Edinburgh lairds arrive,' agreed Patrick, 'we can claim that by locking up the culprits we *are* protecting the remaining witches. Even you have to be satisfied with that, William.'

William Bell grunted while the other bailies beamed.

'Can you see to that?' asked Patrick of no one in particular.

'You can leave it with us, reverend,' said Bell after a beat.

It took some effort for Patrick not to make a sarcastic retort. It would be the first time he could leave anything to the council. An ineffectual, lily-livered bunch they'd turned out to be. Just as well he wasn't afraid to take matters in hand. But then, unlike these men, he had God on his side.

It wasn't until after the councillors left that Patrick took his dram to the window and gazed out into the mist-wreathed night. He was pleased with the decisions they'd reached. At least they had a sound reason for what happened, the names of the villains to give the authorities — it meant they would be regarded favourably.

He would make sure that his next sermon roused the town to watchfulness but not anger. If the witches were to continue to live among them for the time being, then let it be on terms he set, terms that made the women's lives as uncomfortable and wretched as any who sold their souls to Satan deserved to be. Just as long as there wasn't a repeat of what happened to the Cornfoot woman.

A horse rode up the wynd, startling him, and he wondered for a moment if the captain had returned. As far as he was aware the lad was still in Bavaria. Dead, if his prayers had been answered.

Thinking of the captain turned his thoughts once more to Sorcha. He knew instinctively she was responsible for this mess they found themselves in, yet again having to justify their actions — or inaction — to Edinburgh. Being held to account made him appear foolish, ineffectual.

Finishing his drink, he wandered back to his desk and put his glass down. Well, Mrs McIntyre was going to be disappointed when her plan failed.

Och, what he wouldn't give to see that disappointment writ all over her beautiful face.

FIFTY-FIVE

Like snaw off a dyke.
(Disappearing suddenly.)

𝒯he touch was so light, it wouldn't have woken Sorcha had she been deeply asleep. Rather, she was drifting in a nether world where dreams merged with reality. She was racing down a lane in pursuit of those dragging Janet. She could hear the woman's screams, her moans as she struck a sharp stone or someone ran forward to kick her. No matter how fast Sorcha moved, she couldn't gain on them. It was as if she was running on the spot. Twisting around to see what was holding her back, she saw Patrick Cowper clasping her skirt, laughing silently at her antics as she sought to free herself from him...

'Sorcha, wake up, hen.'

Sitting up suddenly with a cry, Sorcha threw out her hands, narrowly avoiding hitting Nettie.

Nettie patted Sorcha's cheek. 'That was some dream you were having. Get up and come sit by the fire. I've something to tell you.'

Shaking off the effects of sleep and with it her dream, Sorcha scrambled from the bed, searching for a shawl to put about her shoulders. She could hear Nettie fiddling with the fire in the outer room. What was going on? Why had Nettie woken her in the middle of the night? Wasn't she supposed to be in Anster with her daughter?

Sorcha pulled up a chair and sat down while Nettie threw more peat on the smouldering embers, found two quaichs and a bottle of whisky, poured a generous splash for each of them and settled herself opposite her friend.

'Sorry I almost hit you,' said Sorcha as they knocked their cups together, drained the spirit and then dispensed another. 'I thought you weren't due back until the morrow.'

'I wasn't,' said Nettie, staring into the fire's glow. 'But my Rebecca had some mending she asked me to bring over for Isobel, help her out now folk aren't so keen to have her fixing their clothes. Thought I may as well do it right away.'

Sorcha's heart swelled. Nettie's daughter was a good sort. There were plenty could do such work in Anster, never mind Rebecca herself; that she would seek out Isobel's services was beyond kind. If only there were others who would do the same...

'Anyhow,' continued Nettie after taking a drink and smacking her lips. 'I was coming up Cove Wynd when I heard the tramp of boots. I ducked into the graveyard and waited to see who it was from behind the wall.'

'And?'

''Twas the Stuart brothers, along with four soldiers. They were escorting some men. One was that big bearded Englishman who roused the mob the night Janet died. I only ken that because, as they drew closer, I heard his cussing. He was livid. There were two other men I recognised as well. They added their insults to the Sassenach's. They were incomers. But then I also saw the Dalzell lad and young Grayson Fleet.' She paused. 'I wondered what was happening until I saw them being taken into the Tolbooth. Looks like they've been arrested.'

Sorcha frowned. 'The Englishman *was* one of the ringleaders the night Janet... Janet was killed. The others were involved. But they were by no means the only ones.' She rubbed her chin.

'Do you think it's possible the council are finally seeking justice for our Janet?' asked Nettie.

Sorcha shrugged. 'I don't know. Either that, or they're being forced to. But if they're arresting even some of the culprits, it means something's afoot.'

'Aye,' said Nettie, sipping her whisky, staring at the fire. 'But what?'

Sorcha didn't say anything. She didn't want to spoil the mood by sharing her suspicions that the men had only been arrested because Edinburgh had got involved. Her letter must have borne fruit and now the bailies were doing whatever they could to cover their cowardly backs.

'It doesn't matter,' said Sorcha. 'What does matter is that the reverend and the bailies have no reason to ever lock any of us up again.'

Nettie raised her glass. 'Amen to that.'

Aware something was amiss, it wasn't until Beatrix appeared at the harbour wall around midday the following day and called the fishwives over that Sorcha and Nettie learned what had happened.

'Five lairds rode into town at first light and went straight to Bailie Cook's house,' said Beatrix breathlessly. 'My William saw them with his own eyes.' She was clearly bursting with news. 'After that, they went to the Tolbooth.'

The arrests of the previous night had been on everyone's tongues when Sorcha and Nettie walked down to the shore that morning. Some soldiers had been happy to share what they'd heard, as were the fishermen and their wives. Not much escaped those who lived in the Weem, especially with tensions still running high and folk minding what everyone was doing and saying. But the arrival of the lairds was fresh news.

'Were they there long?' asked Nettie.

Beatrix shook her head. 'Not long at all, according to Mr Brown. A few hours and then they left.' She waited until some of the other fishermen and folk from the nearby cottages drifted closer. Beatrix always did love an audience.

'What did they have to say for themselves?' asked Mr Porter, the cordwainer.

Beatrix's eyes narrowed and she drew herself up. The lines on her face were so deep, they were like the skerries jutting into the Forth. 'What Mr Brown heard is that they came to say they're initiating legal proceedings against the burgh magistrates — against the bailies — and, you're not going to believe this — against the reverend as well.'

There was a collective gasp. Sorcha felt Nettie's hand seek her own.

Raising her voice so that it carried across the harbourfront, Beatrix continued, 'They said the reason the bailies were being charged was for "Suffering such tumults and rabbles and other such outrages to be committed within their burgh".' Beatrix folded her arms beneath her breasts, a smug look upon her weathered face.

'They used the word "outrages"?' asked Sorcha in disbelief. Around her everyone broke into discussion.

'Aye, lass, they did. Better than that, they've ordered the five men who're currently in the Tolbooth be sent to Edinburgh for trial as soon as possible. Them, and any others who had a hand in Janet's murder.' Beatrix scanned the crowd. No one looked away. There was not one among them who'd participated.

Sorcha's knees felt weak. She sat down fast on an upturned creel, pulling Nettie beside her. 'Can this be true?' she whispered. This was better than she hoped. Not only were the men who murdered Janet going to face justice, but the entire Pittenweem council, including the reverend, would be forced to account for their role in her death.

Nettie pinched her hard on the arm. Sorcha squealed. 'Aye, hen, you're not dreaming this time. It be true,' said Nettie then hugged her tightly. 'At last,' she murmured. 'At last.'

Nicolas and Therese swooped on Sorcha, engulfing her in a warm embrace.

'But, you ken why this has happened, don't you?' Beatrix hadn't quite finished. The crowd around her grew quiet. Nicolas and Therese released Sorcha and turned to Beatrix. 'I have it on good authority,' she smiled at her words, drawing a few chuckles, 'that it was because of a letter sent to a military man in Edinburgh, which he then forwarded to the Privy Council, that justice for Thomas Brown and Janet

Cornfoot and all of us who have been wrongly accused will finally be rendered.'

The men and women looked at each other in astonishment. They didn't know about a letter. There were only a few among them who could put pen to paper. Nettie nudged Sorcha, who prayed Beatrix wouldn't reveal the author. She didn't write it so she might be praised, but so it would serve the purpose it had. That was all that mattered.

'The Laird of Anstruther said it was an excellent if somewhat disturbing missive that warranted all their attention be turned to the events here in the Weem and that the writer was to be commended for his bravery in seeking to shed light on such terrible doings.'

Attracted by the raised voices and evident excitement, the crowd around Beatrix grew.

'I wonder who wrote it?' asked someone. The question was repeated.

'Happens I ken who did.'

'Tell us, Beatrix,' demanded a voice. The cry was taken up.

Sorcha wished the sand would part and swallow her. Consternation began in her toes, rising like a tide to drown her, and enveloped her entire body. White spots appeared before her eyes. The call of the gulls became screams, the weak sunshine blazing heat. The raised voices cries for her head.

Before she could stoop below the harbour wall and disappear into the shelter of one of the boats, Beatrix pointed at her. All eyes fixed on Sorcha. Nettie stood, leaving her friend alone upon the creel.

'They say the dispatch was signed "A Gentleman of Fife". And I happen to ken who that *gentleman* is. 'Tis a lass. 'Tis our very own Sorcha McIntyre.'

There were more gasps. Whispers. Some dark murmurs that were smothered by loud cheers.

'And I, and all those who believe in justice and Almighty God, thank her from the bottom of my heart.'

Two of the fishermen stepped forward and, before Sorcha could object, lifted up the creel she was perched on, turning it into a throne. Hoisting it onto their shoulders, they paraded about the sands to the claps and whoops of those present.

Children emerged cautiously out of houses, mothers with bairns on their hips or suckling at their breasts appeared in doorways, drawn by the laughter and merry-making, something they hadn't heard for so long.

Throwing caution to the wind, pushing aside her feelings of foreboding, Sorcha became caught up in the impromptu celebration, catching a wreath of seaweed one of the fishwives hastily assembled, wearing it like a crown.

'Sorcha! Sorcha!' chanted the crowd. 'Long live justice! Long live the Weem!'

The men twirled her about, forcing her to grab the creel so she didn't slide off. She began to laugh too. It was once the men stopped spinning her about and the sea, sky and land became still again that she spied him.

The laughter died in her throat as she saw Reverend Cowper standing at the far end of the harbour wall, his hands hanging by his sides, his face stern but unreadable. Behind him a large crowd had gathered, looking equally foreboding as they crossed their arms and regarded what was happening upon the shore with silent disapproval.

Sorcha leapt off the creel, landing on her knees in the sand. As she was helped to her feet, calls rang out to head to the tavern once work was finished, but she couldn't help but feel that somehow what had just happened was an omen.

The triumph her friends felt, the quiet sense that proper legal processes had been set in motion, was temporary, a mirage that would dissolve faster than frost beneath the sun. Sorcha and her deed may have risen, but the heights were short-lived as she was flung onto her knees.

Onto her knees before a man who, she knew in her heart, wouldn't forgive her.

It wasn't that she'd brought the lairds to the Weem or that they'd ordered a trial for the murder of Janet Cornfoot and forced the council to answer for their part in it that would earn his wrath. It was because in doing that, she'd not only undermined his authority, but worse, made a right galoot of him and all he stood for.

FIFTY-SIX

We are perswaded [sic] the government will examine this affair to the bottom, and lay little stress upon what the magistrates or the minister of Pittenweem will say to smooth over the matter...

— A Letter From a Gentleman of Fife to his Friend in
Edinburgh, *1705*

'Now,' said Bailie William Bell, drawing together the documents spread out on the table in the council room on the top floor of the Tolbooth, 'we need to discuss how we're going to afford *this*.' He shook the paper he plucked from the pile. 'This latest directive from the lairds in Edinburgh demands that the men we arrested be taken to the city for trial as soon as possible.'

Bailie Robert Cook's head slumped into his hands and he clutched what remained of his hair. 'Just when we've some funds to continue repairs to the pier.' He raised his chin and, reaching for the letter, took it from William and scanned it quickly. 'It's not just the cost of transporting the prisoners. They expect us to pay for their upkeep while they await trial in the city as well. The cheek!'

'Knowing how slowly the wheels of law grind in Edinburgh, that could be weeks. Months even,' said Bailie Robert Vernour, scraping back his chair and rising to his feet. He locked his fingers behind his back and began to wear a track in the floor.

Below them, within the cell on the first floor of the Tolbooth, the most recent captives could be heard. The low grumble of voices, a wet cough and clearing of the throat, the steady thump of a boot or fist striking a wall.

'Bad enough we've to keep them here. But to finance their stay in an Edinburgh gaol —' Bailie Bell shook his head. 'That's another expense we can ill afford.' He wearily smoothed the material of his coat and stared at the pile of papers in front of him without really seeing them.

For all he gave the appearance of being focussed on the latest orders from Edinburgh, Patrick Cowper was thinking about Sorcha McIntyre, Nettie Horseburgh and Beatrix Laing. Would nothing quell those women? They needed to learn their place; to be schooled in it, and by him. Congratulating Sorcha McIntyre the way Beatrix did down by the harbour that morning — making a spectacle of the woman who'd not only been arrested once herself, but ever since had done nothing but actively undermine the authorities, *his* authority, and turned them into laughing stocks — it would not do. He would punish Beatrix first. After all, was she not the cause of all this? If she hadn't put that charm outside the smithy last year, none of this would be happening. And she still bore the stain of the McGregor affair, having been named leader of the damned coven. It would be easy to justify disciplining her again. Shut that wicked mouth once and for all. After that, he'd turn all of his energy to Sorcha. He looked forward to that moment.

In the meantime, as Bell noted, there was the problem of the prisoners — specifically, the cost of transporting them, then maintaining them at inflated city prices. And that was before he even began to consider the fate awaiting himself and the Weem council once Edinburgh initiated proceedings against them. What was the old saying? There was more than one way to skin a seal? Or was it a cat? Time to sort this out.

'Gentlemen,' Patrick began, stretching his arms out on the table in front of him, waiting until the blether ceased. 'I've an idea to put to you that may save us all time and money, may even restore our good name in the eyes of the city officials.' Vernour paused mid-stride. All eyes were upon the reverend. 'What if, instead of sending the lairds the prisoners as they demand, *you* ride to Edinburgh and present our case to them in person?'

The men looked at each other, their interest piqued.

'How do you propose we do that?' asked Cook. 'The lairds read all the witches' confessions, the retractions, even the council minutes and still concluded we were to blame for the events a few weeks ago.'

'Say it, Robert,' grumbled Bailie Bell. 'That we were to blame for the *death* of Janet Cornfoot.'

The wind rattled the windows. A lamp briefly guttered before flaring to life again.

'Aye, the lairds held you liable.' Patrick waited for a protest that he excluded himself from responsibility, but none came. He lifted the letter from the table and slid it towards Bell. 'But did you not also read that it won't be *those* lairds, the ones who came here before, who will hear the case, but a different group. Some other magistrates according to this.' His finger stabbed the page. 'One presumes they'll bring fresh eyes and ears to our sorry tale. A new perspective.'

Cook left his seat and he and Bell bent over the document; as he did, a look of optimism altered his expression. Vernour snatched up the paper and read quickly. 'By God, you're right.' His eyes lit up with something that had been in short supply of late: hope.

Patrick worked quickly to keep it there. 'If you leave at first light tomorrow, present our case to *these* magistrates along with all our supporting documentation —' he gestured at the stack in front of Bell, 'there's no reason to send the prisoners.' He paused. 'Even if you're forced to remain a few days, the costs will be a fraction of what we'd incur should those men below be sent to languish at Her Majesty's pleasure. If we do this — if you do —' he corrected himself, 'then we take care of two problems at once.'

Vernour didn't waste a moment, but strode over and clapped the reverend on the back. 'It's a brilliant notion, Patrick. You've outdone yourself.'

'Aye,' agreed Bell and Cook, exchanging a look of blessed relief.

Cook rubbed his face and gazed around. 'I for one will be grateful to escape the Weem for a day or two. This… this matter has consumed the town. I'm heartily sick of it.'

'It's consumed us all,' said Patrick. 'And when we've done naught wrong but obeyed the word of the Lord, and for that matter the law, in all things.'

'Aye,' agreed Cook. 'It's time to go to Edinburgh and lay it to rest once and for all.'

'Put the lairds and the Edinburgh magistrates straight,' said Vernour.

'And in their place,' muttered Patrick as seats were resumed and plans swiftly made. A budget was agreed upon.

As the councillors, with the help of their notary, organised which documents they'd take and which they'd leave safe in the Pittenweem council rooms, and debated what points they would emphasise and those they'd try and deal with swiftly, Patrick made his own plans.

FIFTY-SEVEN

... he [Reverend Patrick Cowper] exercised more of the civil authority than any of the other bailies...

— An Answer of a Letter From a Gentleman
of Fife, *1705*

*C*louds scudded across the moon, turning the path that ran along the seashore between Anster and Pittenweem into a nether world of shadows followed by bursts of silver. Not even her thick woollen shawl protected Sorcha from the barbs of icy-cold sea-spray that showered her. Blasts of wind drove the watery arrows deep.

Sorcha thought about Beatrix, safe now, staying with Nettie's daughter Rebecca and her husband in Anster until the fuss died down. Until either the reverend's temper — and thus that of the kirk — was restored, or Edinburgh brought the threatened legal proceedings against the council. What a brave lass Nettie's daughter was, welcoming Beatrix, giving her a comfortable bed in the attic and a small space where she could read, or sew or otherwise occupy herself. It was worth the risk to visit her and ensure she was settled — well, as settled as one could be when they were all but hounded from hearth and home. At least, with a few exceptions, no one knew Beatrix's whereabouts.

Between them, Sorcha and Nettie spread a rumour that Beatrix was wandering outside the Weem walls, awaiting the reverend's pardon, and seriously considering moving to St Andrew's once that occurred. It was gossip Mr Brown, who remained in Pittenweem for his wife's sake, and the Lawsons, also fuelled.

As Sorcha walked, she lifted her head occasionally to gaze across the shifting waters of the Forth, catching sight of the lighthouse on the Isle of May and the dark silhouettes of ships anchored in the wide expanse. Soon, she prayed, one of those ships would bring Aidan home. Thinking of Aidan brought to mind Sergeant Thatcher, and how less than a week ago he'd come to the cottage door to bid her farewell.

After the murder of Janet Cornfoot, he had accepted a posting to join his captain in Bavaria. A number of the billeted soldiers would also be leaving and would be replaced, and a new officer appointed.

'I never thought I'd say this, Mrs McIntyre, Sorcha,' he'd said quickly as she started to correct him. He smiled. They'd been through too much together to rest on formalities. 'But I think it be, if not safer, then more honourable fighting the bloody French for Queen and country in a foreign land than fighting auld women and an enemy I cannot see here in Fife; even if it's in God's name.'

Stepping forward, uncaring who might see, Sorcha had thrown her arms around him. 'Be safe, Stephen. And please, bring Aidan home with you.'

When she planted a kiss on his cheek, she was astonished to see it redden. Squeezing her tightly, delighted by her affection, he'd released her reluctantly. 'I'll do my best, lass. Now, do you have a letter for him?'

Sorcha did and gave it to the sergeant, who'd tucked it beneath his plaid, bowed and left.

Though he'd only been gone a short time, she missed him terribly. The town wasn't the same without the sergeant and his men, even though a few of Aidan's soldiers still remained, awaiting the arrival of the new troops. Truth was, the town wasn't the same without Aidan.

Keeping her head down as the wind grew worse and the salty water stung her eyes, Sorcha thought of all that happened since he left. Believing Janet's death and the arrest of the men responsible would mark the end of their torment, she'd been wrong.

Furious that, once again, Edinburgh had undermined his authority, Patrick Cowper renewed his efforts to rouse the fears of those in the parish still worried about the so-called witches being free. If he couldn't punish the women himself, then he'd make sure the townsfolk did it for him, only this time, within the bounds of the law.

As a consequence, Beatrix especially, but Nicolas as well, were having a miserable time. To an extent, Isobel was protected by her father. Sorcha, by the families of the fishermen contracted to her boat, while both she and Nettie were shielded by Janet's relatives and friends, who never forgot what they did that night or the letter Sorcha had written to Edinburgh. If only the protection she had could be extended to Beatrix and Nicolas. But people were afraid. Neighbours still turned on neighbours and the reverend did nothing to stop it. On the contrary, he encouraged it.

Shopkeepers refused Beatrix and Mr Brown service. The windows to Beatrix's house were broken. It wasn't rational or fair that Beatrix became the object of folk's anger, but nothing about this was.

When Beatrix was told that if she was ever discovered alone, she'd be treated the way Janet was, she could stand it no longer. With her husband's blessing, she wasted no time, and before the bailies had even left to go to the city, had appealed to Edinburgh to demand the Pittenweem council provide her with protection so she might go about her daily business.

When the reverend found out, he ordered her brought to the Tolbooth — the place where Janet's murderers were confined — so they might discuss the matter further. Warned of his intention to seize her once more, with Nettie's help, Beatrix disappeared.

In the meantime, acting on the advice of the reverend (and Sorcha knew what that meant), the remaining council members ignored Edinburgh's directive to help Beatrix. They replied declaring that they couldn't provide a bond to protect Beatrix Laing against any rabble that might assault her, because 'she may be murthered in the night without their knowledge'.

The hypocrisy infuriated Sorcha. They refused to offer surety for Beatrix because anyone might kill her at any time and they'd know naught about it.

Visiting Beatrix in Anster that afternoon, bringing her much-needed news and messages of support, Sorcha was content that her friend at least was safe. Happy was too much to expect when she was torn from her home, worried about her husband, and in danger.

Reaching the outskirts of Pittenweem, Sorcha adjusted her creel and decided to continue along the foreshore. It might be cold, but at least here, closer to the wall, the spray wasn't so bad or the wind so wild. Directly in front of her were the rounded shapes of the western braes, where Thomas Brown's body had been so carelessly thrown before it disappeared. Janet had suffered the ignominy of a shallow grave. Three days after she'd been consigned to the dirt, her sister, cousins and neighbours, with help from Mr Adam and Nicolas's husband, had crept up one night and dug up her body for burial elsewhere. Sorcha had donated coin to help pay for a service, but that was all. The family wouldn't allow her to do more. They didn't want anyone to know where Janet was laid to rest, lest they also be punished should they be caught.

The reverend and council had been furious but, in this instance, they'd also been impotent. A situation Sorcha knew the reverend would find intolerable; if he could, he would make someone pay. The notion filled her with disquiet.

She wondered if it was thoughts of the reverend that made her finally turn away from the sea and wander up Cove Wynd. Walking past the houses, she could see the glow of lanterns and candles, smell the peat burning in hearths and see the flicker of shadows as folk moved by the curtained windows. There was conversation, some laughter. In one house an argument raged and a cheeky bairn demanded attention. Passing St Fillan's Cave, she thought of those who'd wasted months in there, first Beatrix, then Janet. Only one had survived — and was currently in exile. All because of superstition, fear, spite, and something so deep and dark Sorcha was too afraid to prod it.

In her heart she knew that whatever started this whole series of tragic events, it was still there. Waiting, biding its time. Whether it would bring everything to a conclusion or envelop them in more misery, she was uncertain. All she knew was that she could feel it, a great black mass with gnashing teeth that threatened to blot out the light, to burrow into her soul.

There were lights on in the manse, too, as she walked past. Through the window she spotted a fire blazing. It was the reverend's study. The flames cast a lambent glow, revealing an unoccupied desk stacked with neat piles of paper and a glass decanter half-filled with umber liquid. Where was the reverend, she wondered. She'd feel safer if she knew. Perhaps he was watching her even now.

She picked up her pace, lifted her chin, and searched the darkness more thoroughly. The bell tolled the hour, making her leap in her skin and flatten herself against a wall. Eleven of the clock. It was that instinctive reaction to a loud noise that not only covered her approach, but meant she saw him first.

Propped against the door of the Tolbooth, the reverend was in a huddle with five wretched figures.

On the other side of the road, Sorcha stayed as still as she could. Who was the reverend talking to at this time of night? And outside the Tolbooth?

The clouds parted, and the moon's luminescence shone upon the scene. Sorcha sucked in her breath. Reverend Patrick Cowper was not only in hushed conversation with the men who'd been arrested for Janet's murder, but he was cutting their bonds. As they rubbed their wrists, she watched him place a coin in each fist. Then he pointed first towards Routine Row, then the High Street and, finally, Cove Wynd.

With terse nods and a few grunts, the men bowed and left one by one. Two headed towards her and Sorcha prayed they wouldn't sense her. Adrift in their own thoughts, they passed swiftly, their stench lingering long after they'd gone.

Only after the men had well and truly departed did Sorcha breathe again. Now it was her turn to bring a tale home for Nettie. For if she wasn't mistaken, Reverend Cowper had just set free the prisoners.

Prisoners, if she understood correctly, the Privy Council in Edinburgh had demanded be sent to the city for trial. Patrick Cowper was breaking the law by letting the felons go. Or had he found others to blame for Janet's death? The thought made her feel sick. She wanted to be home, safe in her cottage; she wanted to share what she'd just witnessed, try to unravel what it meant.

About to continue on, something held her back. Sure enough, the reverend remained, staring in her direction. Had he heard her? Seen her? Her heart was thumping loud enough to accompany pipes. Forcing herself to keep utterly still, she tried to fix on him. Praying he wasn't heading home just yet, that he wouldn't pass her hiding place, she stayed where she was, growing colder even while sweat slipped between her breasts.

Finally, with a shake of his head, he turned and re-entered the Tolbooth, closing the door behind him.

Sorcha waited a few minutes longer, then finally peeled herself away from the wall and retraced her steps back towards the harbour. She would walk the long way home tonight, back along the seashore and past the old priory, and think about what she'd just seen.

She didn't doubt that it boded no good for the Weem. No good for her and the other fishwives.

Upon reaching the harbourfront, she wasted no more time but adjusted her creel, picked up her skirts and, throwing caution aside, ran.

FIFTY-EIGHT

That's the end o' an auld sang.
(Something familiar has gone forever.)

*O*nly once she reached the safety of her cottage did Sorcha relax. She closed the door, leaned against it, and expelled the air from her lungs.

'I was about to come looking for you,' said Nettie, peeling her arms out of the coat she'd been in the middle of donning. 'What took you so long, hen? Is everything all right in Anster?'

They'd agreed it would arouse suspicion if both of them had gone to Anster to sell fish, let alone visited Rebecca, so Nettie had remained in the Weem.

Unwrapping her shawl and draping it near the fire to dry, Sorcha shook her head as if to clear it. 'You're not going to believe what I just witnessed.'

'Before you tell me that,' said Nettie, patting the chair opposite, 'sit and tell me how Beatrix fares. How's my daughter?'

As Sorcha swiftly explained Beatrix was safe, there was no sign of her having been followed, and how welcome she'd been made to feel, Nettie smiled.

'We were right to send her away. You ken the council are still looking for her?'

Taking the cup of tea Nettie proffered, Sorcha looked at her quizzically. 'How do you know that?'

'Because guards came here.'

Sorcha put down her cup slowly. 'Again? They didn't hurt you?'

Nettie waved a hand in the air as she sat down, taking off her boots. 'Nae, hen. Threatened, aye, but it was from them I learned that on the morrow they're going further afield. Seems the reverend's determined to find Beatrix. Claims he's concerned for her welfare.'

Sorcha snorted, then drained her tea and put the cup down carefully. 'He can be as determined as he likes, soon it won't matter.'

'How so?'

A mysterious smile hovered on Sorcha's lips. 'Because I've the means to end this persecution once and for all. To ensure we're left alone and that the reverend will never threaten us or our loved ones again.'

She had Nettie's full attention now. 'What? You saw him making a pact with the devil?'

'Just as good.' Sorcha laughed at the expression on Nettie's face. 'You asked what took me so long to get home? Well, I decided to go via the harbour and, as you're wont to do, turn up Cove Wynd. Happens I saw Reverend Cowper. Guess what he was up to?'

Nettie shrugged. 'Running naked among the tombstones?'

'Nae,' chuckled Sorcha then grew serious. 'He was releasing the prisoners from the Tolbooth.'

Nettie's eyes widened and her jaw dropped. 'Get away with you. He was not.'

'Och, he was. I also saw him give them money and tell them to get away from Pittenweem as fast as they could.'

Nettie flung herself back in the chair and stared, a smile slowly forming. 'So, the bastard's finally shown his true colours.' At once, her features altered. 'But why would anyone believe *you* over him? After all, you be a woman; a witch too, remember?'

'Cowper might call me a witch, but even I can't magic prisoners out of the Tolbooth. God knows, if I could, I would have made us vanish all those months ago. Nae,' said Sorcha as Nettie's mischievous grin reappeared, 'this time the evidence speaks for itself. Forget Beatrix, if the guards should go in search of one of *these* prisoners, I'm sure it wouldn't take much for them to confess who it was released them, let alone why. The reverend's afeared of what they'll tell Edinburgh... what their stories about what happened the night Janet died will reveal about *him*.'

Nettie gave a whoop and jumped out of her chair. She began to pace. 'You ken what this means? If word of what he did reaches the city, the reverend'll be for the stocks.'

'Or worse,' nodded Sorcha. 'Breaking the law, releasing felons the officials ordered the council arrest, and when a delegation from the Weem was in the city as well. He'll lose the kirk.'

Nettie spun around. 'He could lose his life.' She mimicked being hung.

They both nodded gravely as Nettie lowered her fingers.

The possibilities stretched between them.

'Does he ken you saw him?'

Sorcha shuddered, remembering her fear of being discovered, how close he was to her. 'I don't think so. But he'll know once I confront him.'

Nettie frowned. 'Confront him? Are you sure that's wise? I mean, I understand we have to use this information, but shouldn't you wait? Inform Edinburgh first?'

'Why? What good has that done so far?' asked Sorcha. Then she saw the expression on Nettie's face and gave a long sigh. 'Nae, you're right.' Rising, she searched the shelves for a bottle of whisky. Finding one, she grabbed two quaichs and poured. Passing one over to Nettie, she tapped the lip of hers against her friend's. 'Confronting him will only warn him. He'll come up with a story to explain the escape, one that likely condemns us further.' She sank back into her seat. 'It's just that he's determined to tear Fife apart to find Beatrix and, once he does, he'll have her tortured again, no matter what he states. Don't forget, like you, she's still an accused witch — one that's fled. He can arrest and question her. This could stop that.'

'But if we wait and allow the reverend to weave his web of lies, apportion blame and excuses as to why the prisoners escaped, *then* the truth comes out, it will be even worse for him.'

Sorcha's eyes sparkled. 'That's true. You be a wicked woman, Nettie Horseburgh.'

'Nae, hen,' said Nettie smiling. 'Like you, I be a wicked witch. A sea-witch.'

They both snickered.

Suddenly serious, Sorcha sat up. 'Very well. I'll write to Edinburgh and give them a chance to act. While we're waiting, I think we should let Beatrix and the others know what's happening. It will not only forewarn them, but offer them some reassurance as well.'

'Aye, it will,' said Nettie.

'Do you think Rebecca can hide Beatrix for a couple more days?'

'I'm certain she can.' Nettie drank slowly then stared at the window, not really seeing it. 'I'll go to Anster first thing, let the lasses know what's going on.'

Sorcha nodded approvingly. 'That's a grand idea. I'll tell the others.'

Nettie narrowed her eyes. 'You're not thinking of doing anything rash while I'm gone, are you, hen? Like accosting the reverend yourself?'

'Me?' asked Sorcha, trying to look innocent and failing. She threw up her hands. 'I promise. I won't even think about confronting him until we hear from Edinburgh and you're back. How's that?'

Trying to look satisfied, Nettie eventually agreed. 'Very well.' She settled into the chair and crossed her ankles. 'It'll be good to see Rebecca and Billy, that fine man of hers, Beatrix too. We can hide her in the cellar if we have to.'

Sorcha grinned. 'So long as there's whisky for her, there'll be no complaints.'

They chuckled softly.

'If we leave before dawn breaks,' continued Sorcha, 'I can be back home before the sun rises. And if you stay away for a day or two, if anyone asks where you are, I can say you left for Anster this afternoon. That's long before the reverend released the murdering bastards.'

'If that doesn't allay any suspicions...'

'Aye,' said Sorcha.

They clinked cups and drank. Sorcha sank deeper into the seat, curling her legs under her. They sat quietly, their thoughts busy. Outside, the wind wailed and flurries of snow struck the windows. The fire crackled and spat and the clock ticked ponderously, offering a comforting contrast.

'If nothing else,' said Sorcha eventually, unfurling, leaning towards the flames, 'Janet's murder and what's happened since has made me realise this is never going to end. Not until the reverend's destroyed us, Nettie. You, me, Beatrix, Nicolas, Isobel, our families and friends too. What's left of them. Margaret and Lillie were lucky they fled when they did. Cowper's desperate. He's been made to look a right gowk with Edinburgh, and with the Weem. He needs to show he's right, to prove we're *all* witches. He'll use God, guards, torture, fear, lies and whatever else he can to do that. If we're condemned by our own words, even better. This is about more than simply exposing us as witches, or the righteous might of God, this is about saving his reputation.'

Nettie took a generous swig of her whisky. 'And that makes him more dangerous than ever before.'

Cradling her drink, Sorcha went to the window, her thoughts in turmoil. She could hardly credit that she finally had the means to bring Patrick Cowper to heel, perhaps more. The man who'd hurt her mor, her family, her friends, who'd threatened and harmed her as well. Enough. It was time to put an end to the unnatural control he had over too many of the townsfolk once and for all. She had to remind herself he wasn't an emissary of God, no matter what he said. No one God sent to do His work would behave as Cowper had, with such disregard for the truth, clemency and justice. He was a mere mortal, and an evil one at that.

Outside, the wind began to really howl, shaking the windows and driving heavy rain against the cottage. The roar of the ocean could be heard, a mighty surge that presaged a storm. She pressed a hand against the glass.

'It be a wild night out there,' said Nettie, joining her.

'A wild night for a wild reckoning,' said Sorcha softly. Her thoughts turned once more to Aidan. Aidan and Robbie. 'Hopefully it will blow over before we're ready to leave.'

Wherever Aidan and Robbie were, whatever they were doing, at least when they came home — and she had to believe they would —

the reverend wouldn't be able to touch them or threaten them ever again. Not once she used the information she had to bring him down once and for all.

Sorcha leaned her head against Nettie's shoulder. 'After I tell the others what we know, I'll head down to the shore and start work as usual. That way, no one will suspect anything.'

Nettie kissed the top of Sorcha's head. 'Shall we compose this letter to the high and mighty lairds, then?'

'Aye. And pray that this time, at least, God is on *our* side.'

They knocked their cups together again and finished the contents, sharing a secret and, for the first time in months, a triumphant smile.

FIFTY-NINE

Mackerel skies an' mare's tails,
Man' suckle ships take' little sails.
(Dark blue-grey skies or long wispy clouds foretell wind.)

𝒯he storm abated slightly as the night went on, introducing in its stead a heavy fall of snow. Dressing in the dark a few hours later, Sorcha made sure she wore plenty of layers. She donned her coat, wrapped a neepyin tightly around her head, and waited as Nettie threw on her coat and mittens.

Whirls of snowflakes spiralled in the air. Through the window, Sorcha could see how the moon shone upon the white-covered ground, creating an almost ethereal light. With a last glance at Nettie, she gave a nod and opened the door. The air was glacial, striking her face and ploughing her lungs. Shutting the door quietly behind them, the women held hands and trudged through the snow.

Out of the corner of her eye Sorcha saw a shadow keeping pace on the other side of the road. Her heart leapt into her throat until she realised it was Mrs Lentrow's moggie Bait, probably out hunting mice. She silently wished her happy hunting as they passed the Mercat Cross and the junction.

Uncertain what it was that made them turn down Cove Wynd, a reckless streak perhaps, they glanced up at the silent Tolbooth, its closed windows like hollow eyes peering down at them. The kirk was silent, too. Only the manse had a pale glow from somewhere deep inside, and Sorcha wondered whether the reverend was up, praying to be forgiven for his many sins. More likely it was his put-upon house-keeper, rising early to have a chance of completing her chores.

Down by the waterfront, the women whispered farewells and shared a swift embrace. Tucked inside Nettie's coat was their letter, which she promised to mail from Anster that very day. Sorcha remained where she was until Nettie was all but swallowed by the darkness, then turned and headed towards Beatrix's house. She thought it only fair Mr Brown learn what they knew first.

Awake even though it was still dark, Mr Brown listened with wide eyes and exclamations of first disgust, then glee, as the meaning of what Sorcha had seen became clear. He tried to persuade her to stay until at least the wind abated, but Sorcha was determined to deliver her message before the sun rose and declined. When she arrived Mr Brown had been pallid and drawn, but now as she waved goodbye he had colour in his cheeks and a sparkle in his eyes. She continued on to the Adams's cottage.

The blanketed roads shimmered in the moonlight. It wouldn't be long before the white covering was trampled to sludge by numerous boots, hooves and carts. It was market day, so the farmers and their wives would be coming to town to sell produce; tinkers too. As far as Sorcha was concerned, the more people in Pittenweem today, the bet-ter. More witnesses if the reverend reacted badly, not only once news about the escaped prisoners spread, but in case he should turn on those who remained when he discovered Beatrix really had slipped his grasp.

A few rats scurried down the wynd, ducking into holes in walls, finding a pile of rubbish to burrow into as they sensed they were no longer alone. There was a flash of lightning over the Forth followed by a long, low rumble of thunder. The storm hadn't blown itself out at all, but was preparing to return with renewed force. The idea invigorated Sorcha and she inhaled the acrid smells of nature, tasted the twirling wet snowflakes on her tongue and blinked them out of her eyes as she made her way to the Adams's cottage on the eastern side of town, before heading to the Lawsons and then on to the shore.

Nicolas and her husband took Sorcha's news to heart. Seeing their hollow eyes fill with purpose and their shoulders straighten, Sorcha knew her decision to share what she'd seen was the right one.

Having informed her friends, she continued towards the harbour, approaching the pier from the west. Lost in thought, hoping that now, with this new knowledge, their torment would be over, she only slowly became aware that the air was closer, colder, and the copper tang that presaged a mighty storm had grown. The sense of something off-kilter began to grow in Sorcha, as if a giant hand had wrapped itself around her and was pressing upon her lungs. It was hard to breathe. She kept glancing at the tenebrous sky, noting how swiftly the stars were being extinguished. It was as if the world was being swallowed.

She hadn't gone very far when the rain began. It was no light spittering either, but dropped from the sky, a pounding like none Sorcha could remember. Chin tucked into chest, she forged ahead as it lashed her body, and gusts of sleet-driven wind tried to knock her feet out from under her. Down by the western shores, the road was little more than filthy snowdrifts interspersed with mud-filled holes. Wrapping her coat more tightly about her, she pushed on.

The journey was taking much longer than she intended. Around her, the familiar landscape of the fishermen's cottages and their piles of disused creels, nets and lines, that had been nothing but a black labyrinth when she left her house, slowly began to take shape. To her right, the sea had become a seething wash of crashing waves and sea-spray that boomed against the distant pier, smashed against the rocks and showered her with frigid lances. Fighting against nature's forces, refusing to seek shelter, her only chance of slipping home unnoticed was to hope that the fishing had been delayed. What would folk think if they saw her out in this tempest? Not even the foolhardiest of men would launch their boats in this weather, let alone take a stroll. The market would be cancelled and people would keep to their homes until the storm passed.

Wouldn't they?

As the rain continued and the wind grew stronger and wilder and the sea groaned and growled, Sorcha couldn't help but worry about what state Pittenweem would be in when this blew over. It had been a long time since they'd endured such a battering and then it had taken out half the pier and ruined the harbour wall and many livelihoods in the process. If this continued, the few repairs the council had paid for with incomer funds would be undone, and her boat and the rest would be forced to anchor in other ports, meaning a loss of revenue for the town.

Screwing up her eyes, she tried to see the pier ahead. For a moment, she thought she spied a lone figure moving along the eastern road. Instead of heading up the nearest wynd so the houses might offer some protection, she decided to continue lest whoever she thought she saw was some daft fishwife or fisherman appearing for work. After all, she couldn't get much wetter and, despite the impossible swirls of snow, she knew where she was heading. She wondered where the escaped prisoners were and how they'd travelled. They would have had to seek shelter, surely.

Dear God, but she was cold. Her face was a mask of ice. Her hands, even in their thick mittens, refused to co-operate, they were so stiff and wet. Yet she felt somehow lighter, freer than she had in eons. Stopping where the pier began, a ruinous path into the Forth, she squinted. There was no sign of anyone. As she suspected, it had been a figment of her imagination.

Opening her mouth, her breath was snatched away. Her lungs burned. The roar of the ocean was an untamed beast, shouting in her ears, deafening. Even so, there was something mesmerising, liberating, about the swirling snow, the blasts of rain and desolate wind, the tossing seas and the great thunderous chorus they formed that held her there. So often when a storm broke they were too busy working to secure the boats, the creels and other equipment to appreciate its beauty, its raw song.

The sky continued to brighten, the air to grow colder. Squalls of rain came and went. The rolling grey-green of the sea was like a living field. If it hadn't been for the explosion of white each time the water struck the walls, it would be easy to believe you could step onto its surface, ride it to another destination. She began to think of the sirens who lured sailors to their deaths, their beauty and that of their natural element an irresistible lure for those who felt bonded to the ocean.

Stepping closer to the edge of the damaged pier, aware of fishermen's houses behind her, the small boats cracking and moaning as they were pummelled at their moorings along the harbourfront, she inhaled the tangy scent, the purity of brine and the sharp, acerbic scent of snow. The canting wreck of the *Sophia*, the site of Janet's trials, listed beneath the mighty swells, grousing and whining as the hull rocked back and forth, its rotting timbers forming a chorus to the ocean's choir; a dirge for her friend.

Instead of being afraid, Sorcha felt surprisingly calm. Bitterly cold, but assured in a way she hadn't been for such a long time. She was on her own. The sea, the town, were hers briefly. Stepping carefully onto the pier, minding her footing so she favoured the mended parts, she began to make her way along its treacherous length, towards the raging might of the Forth.

Her thoughts travelled to Aidan and Robbie. The more time passed, the harder it became to recall with clarity what her mind and heart needed to sustain hope, especially for Robbie. Refusing to allow her recollections of either of the men to melt away, she worked to rebuild them again and again, asking herself questions and finding answers, no matter how foolish, to aid the process. She did it now. The way Robbie's eyes would crinkle when he smiled. How, when he thought no one was looking, he would use his finger to clean not only his bowl, but hers as well. Even the way he used to say her name in a sing-song manner that was akin to a purr. She recalled the way Aidan would gently tug at his hair when he was thinking, or how, when he poured a dram, he would tip a wee bit extra into the quaich — especially hers. Then there was the magic of his dimples... Were they somewhere out there, her lads? Lost in this wet wildness? Wreathed in the thick heaviness of storm-soaked clouds unable to find their bearings?

Afraid? Or resigned? Bold? Or missing her too? So close and yet so far away.

A wave washed along the top of the pier, saturating her boots. Jumping sideways, she laughed. She could hardly get wetter; what did it hurt anyway? A shower of salty water drenched her and she threw her head back, tugging her hair free of the neepyin, shaking out her wet curls, surrendering herself to the storm, to the mighty Forth. She pulled off her sodden, useless mittens and threw them into the heaving waters, making an offering of them along with her scarf. The sea had taken so many of her loved ones, but she still felt such an attachment to it. Somehow, she knew, deep in her heart, in her sea-charmed soul, it would not take her. Not even while she walked like a wuidwoman, teetering along the pier with its missing planks and gaping holes, its barnacles, slippery moss and seaweed-strewn surface. She didn't falter, she didn't misstep, she simply moved forwards.

As she walked, she prayed. For Beatrix, Nicolas, Isobel and Nettie. She prayed for all those Cowper accused, for the fishwives and fishermen and for her town. She prayed for Thomas Brown and Janet Cornfoot, for Lillie Wallace and Margaret Jack, wherever they were. Most of all, she prayed for Aidan and Robbie and asked the sea-gods to bring them safely back to her.

Toss them onto land if you must, only, she whispered, *please spare them the finality of your watery embrace.*

Like all the fishwives, she respected the ocean's raw power; that it gave as much as what it took away. And here it was, on display, just for her. Uncaring of the dousing she was getting, Sorcha stopped a few feet from the end of the pier and raised her arms, bracing herself against the howling wind and churning water, the creaking and swaying, the shifting timbers beneath her, and laughed with the glorious fury before her.

The sea serenaded her, a combination of deep notes and whistles, throaty grumbles and whispers. And so, she returned the favour — she began to sing to it. It was a song her mor had taught her, a traditional Norwegian song called '*Eg rodde meg ut*'. Rising from the depths of her soul, it poured out of her in her mother's tongue.

I rowed out to my fishing place.
It was early in the morning.
Then came Olav from Karelunnen
And placed his boat beside me.
So I hit him with my fishing rod
So that he fell unconscious in the bottom of his boat.
I was so happy that I started singing.
I had the place all for myself
Sudell-dudeli-dudeli-dei-ho
Sud—

The blow fell hard. Sorcha staggered and would have toppled into the water, only she grabbed hold of an old, coiled anchor chain. Another blow struck her shoulder, narrowly missing her head. She fell across the rusty chains, slicing open her hands, the hot gush of blood a shock across her freezing palm. Before she could turn to see who was attacking her or raise her arms to save herself, another blow struck.

There was a bright flash of light before darkness descended and Sorcha knew no more.

SIXTY

I never said eechy or ochy.
(I refuse to take sides.)

There was a hoarse roaring in Sorcha's ears, as relentless as it was loud. Silently, she pleaded for it to cease so she might return to her slumber. Only, her bed seemed to be most uncomfortable and there were no blankets. She couldn't move her hands. Worse, she was saturated.

She tried to open her eyes and was met with stinging resistance. A combination of ocean spray and driving sleet slapped her cheeks and eyelids. She tried to twist away from it, but couldn't.

'It's no use struggling,' shouted a familiar voice. 'You'll not escape justice this time, no matter what you do.'

Wide awake now, she stared in astonishment. At her feet knelt Reverend Cowper. He must have come upon her on the pier and felled her. Why?

There he was, tying her ankles together. Beside him lay a length of rope. He was drookit. His robes were plastered to his body as he fiddled with knots. He wore no gloves and his red fingers weren't co-operating. Seawater swirled about his knees, making him slide sideways before he propped his boots against a folded sail.

'Reverend Cowper,' she gasped. 'What are you doing?'

He tilted his head to look up at her, a tic in his cheek working furiously. 'Och, I knew a blow wouldn't kill you, witch. And for that, I'm glad. There's yet time to save your black soul.'

Sorcha shut her eyes and leaned back against the mast. The reverend had lost all reason. Madness twisted his features, his one good eye was as cold and hard as iron as he continued to bind her ankles together.

Blinking, she raised her chin. The storm was at its peak. Gusts of wind battered the harbour. Kelp had been flung against the seawall and lay strewn along the sands. From where she was, she could see the town's lanes and wynds awash with sea and rainwater. Gushing back down to the shore, the foaming wash carried a catch of baskets, buckets, pieces of wood, a broken wheel and the dead bodies of birds.

A wall of water rose and broke against the stone wall that edged the pier, sending a fresh curtain of spray over her. Coughing and spluttering, she shook her head, fighting as her body tried to pull her back into the ease of unconsciousness. She had to resist, she had to. But where exactly was she? Why was the pier over there?

'Please, reverend,' she shouted as realisation struck. 'You must release me. We have to get off this ship. It's not safe.'

'Safe!' The reverend finished what he was doing and stood, grasping the mast above her head to stop himself falling as the deck lurched. 'Nowhere you are is safe. That's why I have to finish this once and for all. Cast Satan out of you, out of all you witches, and return the Weem to the godly haven it used to be.'

His face was so close to her, she could smell his stale breath, the whisky he'd drunk, the wine and ale as well. Stumbling, he fell against her but made no effort to pull away. Their noses touched.

'I see you for what you are, Sorcha McIntyre.' His breath was hot against her cheek. 'What your mother was as well. A temptress, sent by the devil himself to test me. To test all good Christian men.'

With his free hand, he pressed against her breast, squeezing hard.

Sorcha refused to cry out, even as he stared at her and twisted her nipple. She gritted her teeth. 'Aye,' she shouted. 'I knew you were tempted, reverend. Did I not see what you tried to do to my mother with my own eyes? I saw how when she turned to you for comfort after the death of her husband, her son, you leapt upon her, ripping the clothes from her body so you could fuck her.'

The reverend pulled away, his eyes narrowing. ''Twas not me, but the devil in her that made me do it.'

Sorcha threw back her head and laughed. It was more like a scream. ''Twas not the devil in her, but the demon in you!'

With a yowl of rage, he stepped forward and slapped her hard. Sorcha's head rebounded against the wood and blood filled her mouth.

'Liar! Bitch! 'Twas your filthy incomer mother who tempted me, with hair like silver and those blue eyes. She came to me in my dreams and whispered in her strange tongue and told me to take her. Who was I to resist? I'm a mere man and she, she was a witch. A witch in league with the devil, just like her daughter. A witch who, from the moment I arrived in the Weem, cast her spell upon me.' The ship tilted and he fell against her again. His mouth was so close, his nose bent against her cheek. 'Just like you.'

Sorcha felt his sour desire in his every panting breath. Just as she feared he was about to kiss her, he pushed himself away with a cry of rage.

'But God has spoken to me. He has shown me what I must do to save myself; to save us all.' As he spoke, half his words were whipped out to sea. He picked up the remainder of the rope and wrapped it tightly around her waist, restraining her arms by her sides. 'Janet Cornfoot shouldn't have died,' he yelled as he worked. 'Not the way she did.' For a fleeting moment Sorcha thought he was expressing regret.

'She should have been lynched good and proper, like the witch she was.'

With a sinking heart, Sorcha understood what was about to happen. Through the heavy rain, she tried to see the harbourfront, the shore. There was not a soul about. No one to witness what this deranged man intended to do. No one to stop him.

He untied her from the mast, casting aside the bindings. The rope around her waist had been flung over the crosstree of the main mast and hung loosely until the reverend grabbed it and twined it around his forearm. Sorcha eyed it warily as it tightened as he dragged her towards the middle of the deck. She tried to free her arms, her wrists, but it was no use. Helpless, shaking uncontrollably, she stood looking from the deck to the freezing roiling waters, aware of the binding about her middle growing increasingly taut. She knew she didn't have much time.

'Reverend,' she shouted, facing him. 'Listen to me. Edinburgh will not tolerate another death. Not without a trial. You have me now, arrest me, lock me up and await their judgement. Prove to them I'm the witch you believe me to be. But don't do this.'

The reverend began to laugh. It was a sound to make the hair on Sorcha's neck rise. 'Prove it? To them? I ken what you are. I heard you chanting your spells down on the pier, calling up a storm fit to wreck everything we've worked to repair. That's what you witches do. Destroy, wreak havoc and mayhem.'

Sorcha stared at him. Was he referring to the song she sang? The song from her mother's homeland?

'That was no spell, you fool!' She worked at her wrists, twisting them first one way then the other, trying to loosen the ropes that bound her. 'That was a song my mother taught me when I was a bairn. A song about the sea, about fishing.'

'Nae,' said the reverend, unwrapping the rope that connected Sorcha to the mast from his arms and twining it around his midriff. He dropped to his knees before her and began to heave upon it. 'It was about death.'

Without warning, Sorcha was lifted off her feet. The air was dragged from her lungs as the rope drew tight around her waist. She rose into the air, swinging as if she was already upon the gallows.

'Forget Edinburgh. Forget the Privy Council,' the reverend hollered into the rain and wind, as if they were his congregation and this his sermon. 'They know not what they do. You have bewitched them, you and all your damnable coven. This —' he pulled down hard on the rope, 'this is justice. This is what the town wants. This is what God wants.'

Sorcha made one last attempt to appeal to him. 'This is not God's will, this is yours and you will be punished for it; just as you will be for releasing the prisoners from the Tolbooth.'

The reverend froze. 'How do you ken that?' He half-rose and she plummeted towards the deck before being drawn up short. 'There's no natural way you could. If I'd any doubts you be a witch, there be naught now.'

He struggled to his feet, leaning back, holding the rope firm and panting heavily. 'And you ken what I'll tell the authorities, don't you? I'll tell them it was you, Sorcha McIntyre. You who freed those men who killed Janet Cornfoot. Everyone knows there be no loyalty betwixt witches. You'll betray and cheat each other if the devil tells you to. Unless the likes of me punishes you, you'll keep on doing it, too.' A spray of water doused him and he laughed. The sound was shrill, loud. 'You released them and, seeing what you are, they turned on you and put you to death the way they tried to kill Janet Cornfoot.' He laughed at the expression on her face. 'Aye, you be right, witch. This is what I want. I want to silence you forever. You'll take your secrets, my secrets, to your grave. No one will ken my part. The sea might have given you a life, but now it'll be the death of you.' Shoving her hard with one arm, he swung her off the deck and over the side of the ship. He braced himself and released the rope.

With a scream, Sorcha plunged into the water. She hit hard, the freezing ocean closing over her head, streaming into her mouth, her nose. It was dark. She had no control. She sank deeper and deeper, the water folding around her, icy cold, bitter. The faint light from the surface vanished. She was in total darkness.

Twisting and turning, she tried to free herself, to kick her way upwards, wherever that might be. She tried not to panic, praying the reverend would do what the men had done to Janet, just dunk her a number of times; she forced herself to be still as she sank, peering desperately through the murky depths. It wasn't as dark as she first thought. There were shadows. She could just make out the hull of the ship. Barnacles and weed clung to its rotting wood like a disease. Her lungs began to ache as they willed her to release what was trapped in there, the air she knew was fast running out. Her wrists stung. Her ankles. Her eyes were burning, she wanted so badly to breathe, to feel the air in her throat, the cold, sweet air, the sharp shard-like spray of the waves upon her face.

Although she forced her mouth to stay closed, bubbles still escaped. She watched as they spiralled away, above her head.

Just as her feet touched the soft, silty bottom, she was hauled upwards. Her head broke the surface and she gulped great mouthfuls of air. Coughing and retching, she was lifted above the water, above the thundering waves until she was level with the deck once more. Level with the reverend.

'Make your peace with the Lord, Sorcha McIntyre. Deny Satan and accept that God is your saviour before it's too late.'

Sorcha stared at him as she swung, doubled over now, the rope squeezing her and making words difficult.

'God has always been my saviour, reverend,' she spat. 'But who is yours?'

With a shout, he let her go again.

It was much the same as before, only this time, he left her under longer. When he finally hoisted her out again, higher than the last time, she could barely breathe.

'Deny the devil, witch. Deny him,' he screamed.

Uncaring that her wrists were rubbed so raw they were bleeding, she began to work at her bonds, trying to wriggle free, loosen the rope about her waist and ankles.

'Very well,' she panted back. 'I deny you, Patrick Cowper, for you are the devil incarnate.'

He released the rope.

This time, when he brought her out, she spun around and around, first facing the Forth, then the ship and the reverend, then the shore. Though dawn was breaking, nobody appeared. In her head, she cried out for Aidan, for Nettie, for Beatrix, Nicolas, anyone — even Dagny. She shouted to God, to her mother, her father, her dead brothers, Andy, her wee dead bairn. But no one came.

Down she went. Breaching the surface, she sank fast. Spinning like a piece of bait. This time, she was ready. She kicked hard, coming close to the hull, bumping against it, cutting her arm, her thigh. Keeping her mouth sealed, even though every instinct was to cry out, blood streamed into the water. She wriggled like a fish in a net. The rope was getting looser, greasier.

Before she could do any more, she was dragged out.

Again and again she was dropped, but each time she managed to steer herself towards the hull, directing her bound wrists and ankles towards the sharp shells clustered there. Missing and striking, slowly, the rope began to fray. When it finally snapped on her seventh dunking, she made sure she kept her hands together when the reverend raised her.

Leaving her suspended, he wound one end of the rope around an exposed stanchion and came to the railing. Panting, he shook his head in sorrow. 'I knew I was right. You are a witch, Sorcha McIntyre. The sea-witch I always thought you were. No Christian soul would have survived this. And so, witch, say your farewells and ask your dark master to prepare himself to welcome you, for I cannot do this any longer. Have you any last words?'

Their eyes met. Sorcha opened her mouth to curse him, to send his soul to hell, then shut it. She was not a witch. Just a woman. He would not remake her in his image.

'Very well then, witch,' he said and, with a flip of his hand, unlooped the rope from the stanchion, keeping it about his waist before letting the length go.

Taking a deep breath, as soon as Sorcha hit the water she shrugged her arms loose and untied her ankles, peeling off the rope from around her middle. It was harder than she thought and the push and pull of the tide meant she was swept past the ship. Other dark hulls bobbed above her. She knew as soon as she was unbound, the reverend would feel the slack. She had to act fast.

Her head began to ring with want of air, bright bursts of colour flashed in front of her eyes before she finally freed herself. Pushing off from another boat, cutting her feet in the process, she swam towards the surface, all the while thanking her da that he had taught her to swim. Taught all his bairns. He could never understand how the folk of Pittenweem could put their trust in the sea and then fail to learn how to move within it. Not that it helped him or Erik. But it would help her.

The reverend was right about one thing, she thought as, pushing aside her pain, she used even strokes to make her way to the surface. She was a fishwife, a woman who understood the ocean and respected it.

Drawing in air, she floated, getting her bearings, grateful now for the wailing wind, the timpani of rain that hid the sound of her movements. Above her loomed the other side of the *Sophia*. It was too high and too damaged for her to climb, but the boat next to it wasn't.

Using the last of her strength, she pulled herself into it and sprawled on her back on the deck, panting, allowing the rain to fall upon her. As much as she wanted to lie there, she knew she didn't have long. Scrambling to her feet, she used the rope attached to the boat to drag it closer to the pier. From there, she climbed onto the stones, some crumbling back into the water. She looked over her shoulder, but couldn't see the reverend. Surely he wouldn't have left? Assumed she was dead? He'd want evidence, if not for the council, then for himself.

She crept towards the bow of the *Sophia*. It was bent and broken, half-embedded in the pier that held it and the remains of the bowsprit within its stony grasp. Quietly she leapt across, her bare feet making no noise that could be heard above the constant rain, booming waves and whistling wind.

Around the side of the forecastle, behind the first mast and past the old coils of rope, collapsed sails and other equipment, she found an iron bar and hefted it in her hand.

The reverend was bent over the railing, searching the surging water.

She came closer and closer.

'Lost something, reverend?' she yelled.

The reverend jumped and spun around. When he saw her, he gasped, then his eyes narrowed. 'I was right. You're a black-souled witch, Sorcha McIntyre.' He tried to run at her, his clawed hands ready to latch onto her neck. 'The devil's handmaiden sent to torment us. Well, not while I still have breath in my body and the Lord to give me strength.'

Sorcha swung the bar to protect herself. It missed his head and struck his arm, causing him to sway and trip, one foot landing neatly in the curl of rope on the deck, part of which was still looped around his waist. Refusing to be cowed, Sorcha lunged at him, determined this time to hit her mark. He backed away, hands raised. 'You can't hurt me, I am a man of God.'

'You are a wicked man who uses God as a weapon,' said Sorcha. 'Now, feel mine.' She brought the bar down.

The reverend twisted hard to one side, the bar narrowly missing him, but as he did, he overbalanced and fell back against the railing. There was a great crack. Wood splintered and broke, tumbling into the sea below. The reverend wheeled his arms in a desperate bid to regain his balance. For a second, he was splayed like a crucifixion against the space. Behind him was the town, below him the dark sea, above the weeping sky.

Then, with a great blood-curdling cry, he fell.

The rope slithered after him, a serpent trying to escape. If Sorcha hadn't leapt out of its way, it would have wrapped its sinewy coils around her and taken her over the side too.

Bounding to the rail still in place, Sorcha looked down. There was the reverend, struggling and splashing in the heaving water.

'Help!' he cried. His head went under and bobbed back up again. He swallowed water, coughing, choking. 'Help me, I can't swim.'

For a fraction of a second Sorcha was tempted to turn away and never look back. Only, she could not. Had not her da taught her to help those in need? Especially when it came to the sea. Even a misguided reverend deserved a fishwife's help. A fishwife's, not a witch's.

'Use your arms,' shouted Sorcha, demonstrating quickly what he should do, before searching for something to throw him. The man was beginning to panic. His arms were flailing, the waves were going over the top of his head. He was swallowing more seawater. 'Head for the boat,' she cried between cupped hands, pointing at the same boat she'd managed to climb onto. The reverend ignored her and went under again.

In the distance, she could hear shouts. There. At the end of the pier figures were running towards her. Relief flooded her body, relief followed by dread. What if they thought she was responsible for the reverend's plight? What if he convinced them to finish what he'd started? She should escape. But where would she go?

All of this occurred to her in a matter of seconds. Looking down at the water, there was no sign of the reverend. Then he surfaced again. Around his neck, across his arms, was the rope. Somehow, he'd managed to get himself tangled in it. Before she could cry a warning, he went under again.

There was no time to think, no time to argue or prevent what happened next. The pro tempore bailies, Mr Borthwick and Mr Carter, appointed to cover the duties of those still in Edinburgh, as well as Jon Durkie and Mr Adam and three soldiers, leapt aboard the *Sophia* and slipped and slid their way to her. First making sure Sorcha was all right, the men began to heave on the rope still attached to the mast and looped over the crosstree.

Under instructions from Jon Durkie, the soldiers pulled and pulled, using all their strength. At some point, Mr Brown, Beatrix's husband, came aboard and made his way across the deck. He took off his coat and placed it over Sorcha's shoulders. 'Dear God,' he said in her ear. 'What happened to you?'

Sorcha didn't hear, she was too busy watching what the men were doing. Shrugging off the coat and pushing Mr Brown aside, she leapt into action.

'You have to pull faster,' she snapped at the soldiers. 'He'll drown if we don't get him out of the water now.' She added her weight to the rope, bending and straightening, pulling with a strength she didn't know she still had in her. Her heart was pounding, her body ached, but still she kept going.

The rain had begun to lessen, the wind to drop. Still they worked the rope. Almost the entire length had sunk beneath the waves. More and more people emerged from their houses and lined up along the harbour. Ignoring the dangers of the decaying pier, many ran along its length to see what was happening aboard the *Sophia*.

Thus it was that most of Pittenweem bore witness to the moment
the reverend was hoisted from the murky depths of the sea he never
trusted by the woman he tried to kill.

When he broke the surface, there were those who swore he was still
alive as his legs jerked and danced. Others said it was just his body in
its final death throes, that his soul had already departed.

But Sorcha knew he wasn't quite dead when they hauled him out.
The rope that had twined itself around his neck hadn't yet squeezed
the life from him. He kicked a few more times, unable to raise his
hands as they were bound to his sides in the welter of rope and weed.

Their eyes met — the sea-witch and the reverend. Hatred filled his
gaze, hatred and a terror that came with the knowledge his end had
come. There was nothing anyone could do. He opened his mouth to
say something, to shout out in protest at such a dishonourable death.

The words never came. Instead, his swollen tongue lolled from his
lips and his scorching eyes dimmed. Even though the men backed
away in horror at the sight their reverend presented, releasing the rope
and sending him back to the water, Sorcha saw the moment life left
the reverend. The darkness he swore was within her had taken him
instead.

SIXTY-ONE

Fair is foul, and foul is fair.

— Macbeth, *Act I scene i*

*B*y the time the reverend's body had been recovered and taken to St Fillan's Cave, Sorcha was sitting in Katherine Marshal's cottage being tended to by Jean, Therese, Katherine herself, Mr Brown and Isobel's father. Her cuts and scrapes had been bathed and bandaged, she'd downed more drams than she likely should have, and was just beginning to feel the benefits of the warm fire, clean dry clothes and the reassuring voices of those around her.

Of all those voices, it was Mr Brown's she'd most heeded in the immediate aftermath of the reverend's death. He'd pulled his coat back over her and sat her down on a gunwale out of the way as the bailies ordered the soldiers to fetch hooks and a stretcher so they could retrieve the reverend's body, and get all the onlookers off the pier before more tragedy struck.

Insisting she keep the coat on, despite it being too large and becoming wet and heavy, he'd whispered she should hide the rope burns and wounds on her wrists, legs and other parts of her body. Her skirts were shredded, she'd lost her boots, how would she explain that?

Dazed and filled with crazed wonder at what had happened to her as well as disbelief at the reverend's final moments, it took Sorcha a beat to understand what Mr Brown was saying. When she did, she nodded grimly, eyeing the bailies, who stood near the shattered railing, examining it closely, turning to regard her with what she could only surmise was suspicion. She no longer cared. She was too weary.

Nevertheless, she wasn't so weary that she didn't repeat Mr Brown's version of events when the bailies finally crossed the deck and spoke with her.

'I'd come to the harbour to see if anyone was working, then I saw the reverend on the *Sophia*. Before I could reach him and ask what he was doing, he fell overboard. The rest you ken,' she said quietly, gesturing to the rope they'd all hauled upon together that had finally hanged the man.

The bailies shuddered with the memory.

If they wondered why she was so bruised and bloodied — and then only the parts of her they could see — they never said. After all, if they accused Sorcha McIntyre of killing the reverend then they were just as culpable. Had they not also heaved upon the rope that had lynched him?

When Sorcha began to cry, dropping her head into her hands and murmuring that she'd only tried to save him, they insisted Mr Brown take her away.

'The lawyers from Edinburgh will no doubt want to investigate this too,' Mr Borthwick said, his expression revealing he was already imagining what the officials would make of it and cursing the absence of the regular bailies who were in Edinburgh, elevating him into sudden officialdom.

Sorcha could tell from the glance he cast in Mr Carter's direction that the last thing either of them wanted was to be indicted for a crime they didn't commit or to be seen in any way as responsible. If they accused Sorcha McIntyre, then they, old Mr Brown, Mr Adam, and Jon Durkie as well, would have more than a bit of explaining to do.

'I wouldn't think there'll be much to investigate, would you?' asked Mr Carter. 'It's clearly a terrible accident.'

'A tragedy,' added Mr Borthwick.

The men nodded gravely.

Mr Brown squeezed Sorcha's arm to keep her silent. He needn't have worried. She had no intention of speaking more than she had to.

'Off you go, Mrs McIntyre. Just be sure to make yourself available when the authorities want to question you.'

As they walked carefully along the slippery pier, it was evident the storm had wreaked even more damage. The sun, which had been trying to make an appearance, was a radiant glow in the grey heavens, squeezing the clouds in an effort to shine. Gulls pirouetted above, crying out in protest that the fishermen weren't bringing in a catch.

Before she'd reached land, Nicolas and Isobel joined her, marvelling at what had happened, relieved she was, if not entirely unharmed, then at least safe.

'Let Nettie and Beatrix know what's happened,' whispered Sorcha. Isobel, after a quick word to her father, took off down the road to Anster.

Fishwives and fishermen had commenced work along the harbourfront. The men checking the state of their boats, the women baiting lines and preparing nets. The storm likely meant the fish would be biting and, though the seas were far from calm, it was too good an opportunity to miss.

Expecting the townsfolk to avoid her or shout insults and curses, Sorcha was astonished when more than one came up to her and clapped her on the back, or thanked her for what she did.

'We saw you, Sorcha,' said Hetty Collins, wee Mary in tow. 'You were mighty brave to try and save the reverend.'

'Aye,' agreed Rachel Mowbray, a long-time friend of the Cowpers inclined to regard Sorcha and the fishwives with loathing. 'It was a Christian act.' She said it as if it was the last thing she expected.

Perhaps it was, thought Sorcha. After all, in Rachel's mind and so many others, she was a witch. Thanks to the reverend.

After that, many others came forward. Mr Donaldson the brewer offered to bring her a gallon of his finest, while Michael Bruce promised her a few drams when next she stopped in at the tavern.

Overwhelmed and wanting to simply get back home and if not sleep, then think on what had happened, Sorcha wasn't to be let off the hook.

She found herself with Nicolas in Katherine's cottage, her wounds tended, a meal and some whisky forced upon her while endless visitors dropped by.

From harlot and harridan to hero; from wanton witch to worthy woman — thanks to the reverend. The man would be turning in his grave. That is, thought Sorcha wickedly, once he was put in it.

Sorcha stared at the hearth and released a silent moan as the cold that had leached into her bones slowly and painfully receded. She couldn't help but be glad the man was dead given all the pain, strife and sorrow his zealotry and obsession with witches had brought to the Weem. Not only would he get the burial he'd denied Janet Cornfoot and Thomas Brown, but likely he would get a funeral service filled with honours and prayers.

Unable to help herself, Sorcha cursed his soul. Remembering what he was prepared to do to her, the blame he was set to lay upon her shoulders for his own acts, the lengths he would go to maintain control, she was glad he was dead.

In thwarting his plans, surviving his calculated torture and his attempt to kill her, she was doing what she promised Janet she would: living.

It was almost evening by the time she was able to head home. All day folk had come in and out of Katherine's cottage, wanting to hear exactly what had happened from Sorcha, from Mr Brown and any other witnesses. After midday, Nettie and Isobel burst in and Sorcha had to tell her tale all over again. Many brought food, even those who'd denied service to her and the other accused witches and shouted at them in the street, their offerings by way of apology. Part of Sorcha wanted to throw their largesse back at them, but she had to live among these people and she no more wanted the schism Cowper had created to continue than she did to say a prayer for him. So she smiled and thanked them prettily, listened as they contributed gossip they'd heard, putting the past behind her as best she could. Her da had taught her well and would have been pleased.

Nonetheless, she was grateful that not one person who had been involved directly in Janet's death sought her company. Those she wasn't ready to forgive or forget.

Early afternoon, the fishwives and some of the fishermen arrived, bringing with them the finest fish from the catch. Others brought fresh news from St Fillan's Cave, where the coroner from Edinburgh, who happened to be visiting Laird Anstruther's place in Anster Easter, had been summoned to examine the reverend's body.

'They say his lungs were full of water,' reported Mr Adam, arriving as if he'd run the entire way from St Fillan's. Sorcha supposed he had. 'But he also had some very deep cuts on his legs and arms.' He slashed his own limbs with his finger to show where he meant. 'They reckon some were so deep, he'd lost a great deal of blood.'

Sorcha resisted the urge to touch the bandages beneath her sleeves and skirts. Some of hers were deep as well.

'But it was the hanging what killed him in the end,' said Mr Adam. The crowded room fell silent then and Sorcha wondered, if like her, they were thinking of poor Janet Cornfoot. Nettie gripped her hand and she knew where her thoughts lay. Her other hand crept up to touch her own neck and she sent a prayer to God that she'd been spared. It wasn't the first time she'd had a word with the Lord that day, and it wouldn't be the last.

As she approached her cottage, Nettie beside her, the gloaming unusually bright as it oft was after a storm, the air still fresh and clean, there was the remnant of a rainbow glimmering above the Isle of May. She saw her street, her town, with new eyes. Returning the friendly waves and coy greetings that issued from each shop, business and home on the High Street, she was astounded to note that, whereas

Thomas's and Janet's deaths had brought such sorrow and suspicion in their wakes, the reverend's seemed to have drawn a line, or at the very least, written the last in a sorry story. A story that everyone seemed keen to rewrite. Maybe now they could close the book.

Mr Brown and Mr Adam insisted on accompanying the women home, along with two of the soldiers. As they ambled towards the kirk, passing the Tolbooth, Sorcha tried not to think of the reverend's cold lifeless body lying in St Fillan's Cave, the place where he'd once kept Beatrix and Janet. What would Beatrix have to say about that, a reversal of fortune that meant she could now come home for good? Would she want to, considering all the reverend and council had put her through? Would folk allow her and Mr Brown to live in peace? Would they allow Nicolas and the rest of the women?

Glancing at Beatrix's husband, she wondered if he was thinking the same thing. She refused to look at the Tolbooth, but couldn't help considering how long it would be before she could pass the building and not be reminded of what had happened to her and her friends inside it. Or if any of her friends would be able to, for that matter. Would time heal them or would it take a miracle?

As they entered Marygate, her footsteps slowed. The cuts on the soles of her feet were very tender. She waved to Moira Fraser and Crabby, standing on their stoop. The golden hound barked with joy when he saw her and raced from his mistress's side to bump his wet nose into her thigh. She winced and laughed and ruffled his coat. 'Good evening to you, Crabby, Mrs Fraser.'

'And to you, brave lass,' cried Moira, whistling to Crabby who, after enjoying a bit more attention, bounded away, tail wagging. Other neighbours waved from their stoops or windows. Sorcha couldn't remember being so popular.

As they reached her cottage, she was surprised to see smoke rising out of the chimney and light glowing behind the windows.

Just as she reached the door, it swung open. Standing on the threshold was the man who'd occupied her thoughts and dreams from the moment she met him.

The world stilled.

It was Aidan. His hair was longer, his face thinner, older. But his smile was the same. The truth of his presence dawned on her slowly, achingly, like a dream fulfilled. The love that flowed within her bubbled to the surface, making all her actions heavy, as if someone else altogether had taken control of her body. She tried to speak, to utter the words caught in her throat, but before she could, much to her astonishment, instead of gathering her in his arms, he stepped out of the way.

Another man took his place.

Nettie gasped.

A tall, gaunt man with a golden beard and dazzling sea-green eyes filled the doorway, staring at Sorcha, willing her to know him. A deep scar cleft his right cheek, and she noticed he had three fingers missing from one hand. Leaning on a stick, he tilted towards her, his smile at once sad and terrible, kind and wise.

Sorcha released Nettie's hand. Her heart was beating so loudly, she could scarce hear what Nettie or the others were saying. Dimly aware that the neighbours were whispering, making sounds of delight and disbelief as they poured out of their houses and gathered behind her, she couldn't really comprehend why. This man, this familiar yet strange man could not be...

Nae. It was impossible, wasn't it? He wore a clerical collar about his neck...

'Robbie?' she whispered, taking a tentative step. 'Is that you?'

The man propped his stick against the doorway and held out his arms, his smile deepening. 'Come here, lass, give me a hug and find out for yourself.'

With a great sob, Sorcha forgot all her aches and sorrow and, hesitantly at first and then with an energy that came from her heart before it burst into every other part of her body, ran and threw herself into his arms.

'Robbie!' she squealed, laughing and crying all at once.

He spun her around and around as she buried her head in his neck to the sound of cheers and shouts. As she wept the tears she'd denied herself from the day he'd left, he whispered his love for her and his everlasting joy that he was returned and they were a family once again.

A family that, as he turned and opened his arms to Aidan and Nettie, included the others she loved with all her boundless, hurting heart as well.

EPILOGUE

Ye've tae spill afore ye spin.
(You can't be perfect right from the beginning.)

Autumn 1706

*I*t was still hard for Sorcha to get used to seeing her brother standing in the pulpit. The first time it happened, she thought she'd have to leave before he started the sermon as she kept overlaying his frame with that of his predecessor's. But once Robbie commenced talking and his rich, melodic voice explained the word of God, calling for kindness, understanding and compassion instead of whipping up suspicion and fear, she was spellbound — as was the rest of the congregation.

When that word flew into her mind, she spluttered, covering her mouth before she released a volley of coughs. Beside her, Nettie shot her a concerned look, and touched her gently on the arm. Shaking her head, she reassured her with a smile that was starting to appear more frequently. She would explain later how, here she was sitting in the kirk, along with all her friends, absolved of witchcraft or any wrong-doing in the death of the reverend, and the word that jumped into her head to describe her brother's preaching was 'spellbound'. Really, it was almost funny.

It was eighteen months now since the death of Patrick Cowper, and there'd been a few objections when Robbie McIntyre was first put forward as his replacement — mainly from the older Cowper children, bailies Cook and Vernour, Peter Morton's family and other staunch supporters of the reverend. But they'd quickly been overridden by the rest of the town. Not only had Robbie acquitted himself well in the wars in Bavaria and survived time in a French prison, but he was a Weem lad who understood the ways of the fisherfolk and the sea better than Cowper ever did. You wouldn't catch him hovering by the harbour when the fishermen were casting out to sea, threatening ill-fortune just by his watchful presence. The last thing they needed was another incomer when they had their own reverend, born and bred.

Peter Morton himself could make no objections. In the immediate aftermath of the reverend's death, his father awoke one morning to find his son gone. In the following months, rumours circulated that he'd gone to the city, fled north, even boarded a ship bound for the colonies in the New World. None were ever confirmed. Sorcha wondered if, once his mentor and friend the reverend was dead, Peter was unable to live with his part in it all, in the deaths of Thomas and Janet, in the persecution of innocent people. She wanted to believe he wasn't a bad lad, but she could never reconcile why he manufactured his affliction and maintained it for so long, pretending to be affected by witchcraft. She could never forgive him for that either. In her soul, she felt God would understand.

In the days after Robbie's return, it had been strange for Sorcha to wake and find him rummaging about the cottage. Not only was he back in his old bedroom, but he had a way of filling the space that she'd so missed. Leaving his books, robes, paper and inkhorns lying about, empty quaichs, and his boots, she loved the reminders of his presence, even if she knew it was to be short-lived.

The reasons for him leaving the cottage were a cause for celebration, not commiseration. Four months after he returned, he moved into the roomy manse beside the kirk. Reluctant to shift the large Cowper family out before the orphaned children could find relatives who'd care for them, Robbie insisted they wait until summer and the roads were in better condition. Most of the children were off to Dundee and a distant cousin. The older two had decided to try and make their way in Glasgow. For them, Edinburgh was too close. Sorcha understood their need to get away, far from where the names Pittenweem and Cowper carried the connotations, curiosity and dread that they did. And for Seumas Cowper, the guilt.

With the arrival of spring, more incomers had travelled to the town to see for themselves the place where witches had been found and where death had haunted the streets and docks. It had been tempting to try and extract coin from these visitors. But whereas that had once been the goal of the reverend and the council, reminders of witchcraft and what had happened were now an embarrassment. The incomers were given no truck, their questions answered bluntly or not at all. Angered by the lack of information, their anticipated excitement thwarted, they never remained long and soon ceased to come.

Still, the thought of leaving Pittenweem for good had preoccupied Sorcha for weeks. Even Dagny, who came for a brief visit once she heard Robbie was back, bringing her two youngest bairns with her, had suggested Sorcha leave. She hadn't offered her home, not that Sorcha expected or wanted it. But the temptation to turn her back on Pittenweem once and for all and start afresh had been very real. If Robbie hadn't returned, she might have accepted Aidan's invitation to go to Skye with him and begin a new life there. With Robbie home, and the witch craze all but over, and Nettie, Beatrix, Nicolas, Isobel and the others all returned to their homes and livelihoods, she could no more leave than throw a fine fish back into the ocean.

Thank the good Lord that Aidan understood her need to remain. It had been one of the hardest things she'd ever done, telling him she couldn't go to Skye. She owed him that — her honesty, her heart as it really was, not as he wished it might be. It was what she had never had the courage to give to Andy and she wouldn't make that mistake again.

Likewise, he'd told her true as well — everything, from what had happened in Bavaria, how he'd found Robbie, to his need to return to Skye.

It hadn't been easy to track down Robbie in France. Taken prisoner during the first year of fighting, he'd been moved about the country-side. French records were poorly kept and trading prisoners was virtu-ally unheard of. So many died in the squalid conditions of the gaols. Robbie believed if he remained, he would meet the same fate, either dying from dysentery or some other disease, or being killed to quell potential riots among the prisoners and stoke fear and obedience. So he and three other prisoners had escaped.

They fled into the countryside. Two of the soldiers were killed, the third recaptured. Only Robbie found freedom. He sought shelter in a monastery and remained there for over three years, virtually becom-ing one of the monks.

'I knew I couldn't worship God their way, but I discovered, much to my surprise, I did want to devote my life to Him. He saved me and so many others, and I felt I owed it to Him to dedicate myself to His service. I'd had enough of killing, I wanted to think about living instead. Living a good and worthy life, helping others to do the same.'

While Sorcha didn't feel the devotion to God her brother did, she understood the sentiment. How different he was to his predecessor.

'I left the monastery and rejoined the duke's forces in Moselle as their minister. It was there I met Aidan.'

Aidan had taken the story up after that. Falling ill after the cap-ture of Landau, Aidan, along with the other sick and wounded, were moved to a field hospital in Trier. Asked to administer last rites, Rob-bie had found a group of men who, far from dying, were healing well. He discovered not only that Aidan was Scottish but that his last post-ing had been Pittenweem.

'Imagine that,' said Robbie smiling at Aidan. If there was another joy Sorcha had derived from Robbie's return, it was the close friend-ship that had developed between her brother and the man she loved. 'Not only did he know Pittenweem, but my little sister as well.'

Sorcha had the grace to blush. Robbie might not have meant 'know' in the biblical sense, but the smirk on Aidan's face didn't help.

He'd intended to be home a great deal sooner, but after another victory the Duke of Marlborough and his men — including Aidan —

had at Trarbach in late December, the Queen commanded that the captured colours of the enemy cavalry and infantry be paraded through Westminster, so all of London could celebrate the duke's achievement. Newly promoted Major Aidan Ross was elected for the task and asked if Sergeant Thatcher, who'd recently joined them, and Robbie could accompany him.

'By that stage, I'd already written and told you I'd found Robbie.' He looked at her apologetically. 'I did write again as soon as I found out we were coming home as well, albeit via a stay in London, but the ship carrying the mail was lost and —' His words petered out.

Sorcha had risen from her chair and kissed him on the mouth. 'I don't care. I'm so happy you're here to deliver the news in person. Both of you.' She reached for Robbie's hand. 'That's better than a letter any day.'

Thinking back on the day they'd appeared so unexpectedly, as if conjured by some blessed magic, and how they'd spoken well into the night, she smiled forlornly. God, she missed Robbie's presence in the house — but even more, she missed Aidan. Letters were all she had now he'd gone. A veritable pile of them, delivered regularly once a week from Skye.

Aidan was a fine writer and from his missives she learned the farm was doing well, his family too. His ma and da had been so pleased to see him home safe and his brothers were happy to have him and the newly retired Stephen Thatcher helping with the ploughing, planting and shearing; his sisters did little but pester him about Sorcha. He wrote about the fish in the two lochs, the mists that tumbled down the mountains and covered the farm, the harsh winds that blew in from the sea, scattering them. He described the veils of rain that would fall most days, parting to reveal resplendent rainbows that always made him think of the day he came back to Pittenweem. Afeared he'd find her interned or worse as a witch, he'd arrived to see her hailed a hero, the reverend dead and the town he'd grown so fond of, despite its tendency to superstition, on the mend.

Rereading his letters, Sorcha oft wondered if she'd made the right decision. Skye sounded so beautiful. Och, she'd see it one day, she'd no doubt. But she knew deep in her heart, much as she might fall in love with it, as she had its son, she could never call it home. That title belonged to Pittenweem, the defiant little town that beat the odds, that was filled with people who were curious, hard-working, hard-fighting and inclined to doubt and gossip. But it also had folk who were passionate and, as she knew well, mostly kind and loyal.

At least here she knew who to call friend and who foe. Nae, that wasn't right. There were no enemies here, not any more. The people were, at least, neighbours and at best, a makeshift family filled to the brim with all the muddling love and conflict that entailed. That suited her fine.

It was an odd consequence of those awful months that the death of the reverend bonded the townsfolk in ways the witch hunt and the deaths of Thomas and Janet never had. If that was to be the reverend's legacy, so be it. It was more than he deserved.

Beatrix returned permanently to the Weem the day after Patrick Cowper died. No one objected. Mr Brown's business was recovering and Beatrix was slowly learning to guard her tongue. Isobel's services had become even more popular since Cowper's death, and when Alexander McGregor died two months after the reverend, she could scarce keep up with orders.

McGregor had wandered over to St Monan's one night to drink in the tavern there, and had foolishly decided to walk back along the braes, only to take a tumble down the cliffs. His body was found the next day by one of the fishing boats and brought back to the Weem. Without him to cast aspersions on Isobel and with her father ready to challenge anyone who dared, Isobel was mending clothes faster than they could be made and was even stepping out with a fine lad from a nearby farm.

Therese Larnarch, Jean Durkie and the others continued to work beside Sorcha, Nettie and Nicolas each day and, as the weeks went by and the weather grew warmer, the events of the last year seemed like a dream. Only they weren't, as the acute absences reminded them.

Before the matter of the Weem witches could be laid to rest, Nettie set about suing bailies William Bell and Robert Vernour for wrongful imprisonment. She asked Sorcha and the others to join her in the suit. Sorcha was the only one to agree and they awaited the decision of Edinburgh. In the meantime, the bailies and, indeed, the entire council had gone out of their way to accommodate them in every regard. It would have been amusing had their co-operation not been born of such pain.

When Nettie declared she was moving into the manse with Robbie, tongues wagged, especially with Nettie being a widow. But there was no romance or wrongdoing in what she intended. She was like a big sister to Robbie. Sorcha was glad. Nettie would manage the household, ensure he remembered to eat, and bring the best of the drave from the harbour for his table. 'Put some fish on those scrawny bones,' as she promised. Knowing it was really her role and feeling a little guilty she wasn't taking up Robbie's offer to shift in with him, Sorcha knew her brother understood the decision and forgave her.

After all, how could she leave her cottage now?

Finishing the last of the mopping, the hearth gleaming in its newly blacked state, the pots and pans shining and the curtains smelling sweet, Sorcha put her hands upon her hips and looked around one last time. Bright flowers stood in a quaich of water. She'd baked some fine bannocks and fresh fish were ready to cook. Mr Durkie had managed to acquire some Rhenish wine from associates, and there was even some delicious cheese to accompany it. She'd purchased eggs and butter at the market and some jam. The sheets on the bed were clean, the bedroom furniture polished to a high sheen. All that was left to do was tend to her own toilet.

This was what one should be doing in spring, not autumn. Not that anyone would object. It was a ritual that wiped away the old, shed any dark, unpleasant memories and made way for the new, regardless of the time of year. While there were memories she'd never forsake, and did not want to, there were some that were becoming easier to bear as each day passed and fresh experiences overlayed the more painful ones, softening them, dampening them down, burying them beneath layers of sweeter recollections.

Washing quickly, enjoying the rose petals and other herbs she'd infused in the water, Sorcha studied her reflection in the mirror. Her hair had grown quickly once she had a decent diet again, it fell well past her shoulders now. Her cheeks had filled out and so had her breasts and body. The Weem was still poor, with most crops failing again this year and meat scarce, but at least the fish were biting again. More coal had been discovered nearby, promising work for those prepared to mine it, and there was talk of doing something with the saltpans. Maybe, just maybe, things were looking up. That's what Robbie reminded folk each week — to count their blessings, not tally their losses.

Heeding her brother's advice, that was what she was doing.

Sorcha put on her best shift, and then tied her finest skirt over it. Tucking in the embroidered shirt her mor had made, she was about to tie a neepyin about her head, then changed her mind. Instead, she brushed out her hair, leaving it loose. She pinched her cheeks to infuse colour in them, and wished she had something to put on her mouth to redden it like other women sometimes did. The thought made her blush, and she ceased to pluck at her cheeks, laughing with embarrassment and something more.

It was then she heard them. The clop of hooves, the whinny of welcome that Liath always gave when she came near the cottage. How the horse knew, Sorcha could not divine. The voices grew louder as they came closer.

Her heart beat furiously. She wanted to run to the door, but forced herself to walk sedately, a laugh purling in her throat. Wrenching the door open, she watched her friends approach.

There was Nettie, resplendent in green, leading Liath. Next to her was Isobel, her fair hair woven with flowers, a wide smile upon her lovely face. Beatrix walked the other side of Liath, looking fine in a gold skirt and bronze shirt, her limp lending her dignity. Around them were the other fishwives, their usual skirts, neepyins, boots and cloots discarded for this very special day. Twelve in total, they looked grand, womanly and proud, bestowing smiles on the neighbours who'd all gathered to watch and fall behind as Sorcha was escorted to the kirk.

Embraced by all her friends, her sisters of the sea, it was Nettie who helped her onto Liath's back, the horse turning her noble head to whicker. Patting her withers, Sorcha leaned over and kissed the velvet space between her ears. 'Take me to your master,' she whispered.

As they rode along Marygate, the sun shone brightly and the Forth sparkled and sighed below it, a blanket of shimmering diamonds. Across its surface were a fleet of boats and some tall ships, their flags and sails billowing gently in the breeze. The scent of the women's flowers blended with that of brine into a heady brew. Sorcha inhaled, looking around, smiling as if she'd only just learned how and relishing the way it made her feel, as if the sunshine itself had taken up residence in her soul.

And so she was delivered atop a beautiful silver mare onto the steps of the kirk where her brother waited. Taking her hand to the smiles and quiet approval of nearly all the townsfolk, Robbie passed it to the man to whom she'd plighted her troth, the man who, though he could not persuade his bride to reside with him on Skye, had been prevailed upon to join her in Pittenweem.

Together, they would manage the *Mistral*, help breathe life back into the Weem, a good life; one not governed by suspicion, fear of God and what others might say or do, but guided by hard work, honesty, kindness and, as they looked into each other's eyes, love.

As Aidan Ross took Sorcha McIntyre's hand, assisting her as she mounted the steps, she thought of all the other support he'd given her. The letters he'd written to Edinburgh before he really knew her, demanding justice, informing the authorities about the travesties being committed by the minister and a group of councillors in a small town in Fife. Knowing that, as an officer in the Queen's army, he was forbidden to involve himself in such matters, he'd simply signed his letters as 'A Gentleman of Fife', a moniker Sorcha had borrowed to good effect. In doing so, between them, they'd not only kept an account of what had really happened, but ensured that, in the end, a kind of justice was served.

It may not have been the outcome she'd sought — after all, Thomas and Janet had died — but it was what she'd been given and, by God, she'd take it.

Just as she'd take this brave, loving man as her husband.

When Robbie joined them before the fishwives and their families, former soldier Stephen Thatcher and the townsfolk of the Weem, according to the laws of God and man, she sent a silent prayer to her da, her mor, her brother Erik and her baby son. To Andy who, though he'd not been the husband she'd wanted, had been a good man. He'd be happy for her, she thought.

He'd also be pleased about the new life growing within her, the one that belonged to her and this man beside her, her husband, who had given her the fresh start she once desired, blessed hope and a child to share with him.

Cheers rose for the newly-wedded couple and they exchanged a long and not-so-chaste kiss. Sorcha closed her eyes and melted into Aidan's embrace, tasting his warm lips, feeling the beat of his heart as he held her against him.

It was then she also heard the sea.

Breathing in and out, pulsing like Aidan's heart, giving the town life, it was singing softly. Just for her. Listening intently as she stood in Aidan's arms, she heard in its dulcet notes its promise to her, and to this man, both of whom had chosen to stay in this wee town wrapped along wild and wonderful shores.

It promised her that from this day forward she and Aidan, and their burgeoning family, could put all that led to this moment, the death, doubt and dread, in the past and look to the future.

A future in which a fishwife, sometime witch and her sea-sisters could love and, above all, live.

THE END

AUTHOR'S NOTE

Fishing villages, in general, seem also to have contributed more than their fair share of witches.

— Lizanne Henderson, Witchcraft and Folk Belief in the Age of Enlightenment: Scotland, 1670–1740

$\mathcal{T}$his is the part where I get to reveal to you, dear reader, what led to this novel's creation and how and where history and fiction meet and where they go their separate ways. As it says on the cover of this book, *The Darkest Shore* is based on a true story. But like many true stories, the truth is not only stranger than fiction, but much crueller as well. When I first read about the Pittenweem witches, I thought I had to tell their tale as it happened. But then, in a stroke of good fortune, I read something the wonderful historical novelist Susanna Kearsley wrote regarding her book *A Desperate Fortune*. She noted:

> *Writers can't truly change history, but we can decide… where a story should end. Not being fond of the beginning of Mary's tale [the heroine of A Desperate Fortune], I wrote a different one. A better one.*

I not only wrote a new beginning for the Pittenweem witches by introducing the fictional character of Sorcha McIntyre and her family, but also gave many of the real women the role of fishwives and placed them at the heart of the story in every way. I also altered the real ending. In doing that, I gave these women and, indeed, Pittenweem of that era, the conclusion I felt they and it deserved.

But to really honour all the actual people involved in this story, in particular the accused women and Thomas Brown, I feel I have to tell you how their story actually concluded according to documented history.

But before I do that, let me explain how and why I wrote about fishwives.

The idea was first touted by my very good friend Mark Nicholson. When Mark discovered I was travelling to Scotland for the wedding of two beloved friends (as he was as well), he told me about the Herring Lasses who used to roam the coasts of Scotland during the height of the fishing season, sorting, gutting and selling the catch, repairing nets and lines and so much more. As Mark spoke, my skin goosed and my mind was transported. At one point, I could no longer hear what he was saying, I was already lost in a story. When Mark's great mate (and mine too) Bill Lark also started telling me I had to look into these lasses, I was hooked (forgive the pun). But when Mark whispered, 'You know some of the fishwives were associated with witchcraft as well?' that was it.

I began to do some research from Hobart, but in no way was I equipped for what I would discover when I finally reached, not just Scotland, but more specifically, East Neuk and the Fife coast.

Travelling with my husband, Stephen, and our best mates, Kerry Doyle and Peter Goddard, we stayed in the port town of Anstruther (called Anster by locals), in The Boathouse right on the harbour. Looked after by our lovely host, Blane, we stayed for four days and explored the coast, travelled to the Isle of May (where we experienced one of the remarkable and rapid changes of extreme weather upon the Firth of Forth), the beautiful St Andrew's, and walked the coastal paths between Anster, Pittenweem, Cellardyke (called by its original name of Silverdyke in the novel), Crail, St Monan's etc. and generally did intense on the ground research. But it wasn't until we went to the Fisheries Museum in Anster and I spoke to someone in authority there that I began to learn not only about the Herring Lasses (who were predominant in the 1800s and early 1900s), but about how the stain and shame of witchcraft and what had happened in Pittenweem (and other areas around Fife) back in the seventeenth and eighteenth centuries still affects people today. When I asked about witches and witchcraft, this person I interviewed immediately went into a vehement denial, becoming incredibly defensive and telling me it was all rubbish! There were no witches. Ever. I said to him, 'Well, if that's the case, how come you're selling this book?' and held up Leonard Low's marvellous *The Weem Witch*. I was so taken aback by the (until then very nice) gentleman's hostility, I don't really recall the specifics of his answer, but that he mumbled something about it being written by a local so he had no choice.

As you can imagine, part of me was a bit despondent to think maybe there was no story involving witches (but hey, I consoled myself, you write fiction, make it up), the other part of me was determined to get to the bottom of why my question had provoked such a reaction.

Along with Stephen, Kerry and Peter, we then walked to Pittenweem and hunted and asked questions. Not only did we find the loveliest of towns — the only one in the area still committed to fishing — and people, but we found witches.

When I finally read Leonard Low's book, I was horrified, mesmerised and enthralled in equal measure. I also became a little obsessed. What followed was intensive research. I read history books, archives, a great deal of academic research on witches, about the Bargarran case mentioned in the novel — which was real — and many others that occurred in Pittenweem and the surrounding areas throughout the period. I also read contemporary sources of the era (including letters and local council records) and so much more. I knew I simply had to bring the women involved in this terrible tale (who are often just names and dates in the various sources, which tend to provide conflicting information) as well as their families and friends, to life, to flesh them out, give them words, emotions, loves, friends, enemies and occupations and in doing so, somehow explain or at least try to understand what motivated such a dreadful series of events.

After I returned to Australia, I discovered that for a number of years Leonard Low has been trying to get a monument or plaque erected to Janet Cornfoot and Thomas Brown. In fact, a few years ago, Mr Low began a petition. While thousands signed, it was ultimately defeated. There were more in the Fife area who did not want to be reminded of the shameful events of yesteryear. So to this day, there is still nothing to commemorate the victims of the terrible witch hunt of 1704–1705. In 2019 it was announced that the BBC were about to start filming a documentary about witches and witchcraft in Scotland, including the Pittenweem witches, which may yet change people's views on a memorial. Let's hope so.

In some ways I understand the locals' reaction, but I'm also of the conviction that you cannot embrace growth and change and a promising future without acknowledging every aspect of the past, including the horrific and dishonourable — that goes for individuals, nations and towns. If we don't acknowledge our mistakes, the tragedies, how can we learn from them let alone be certain we won't repeat them?

Despite this, it's due to the diligence and wisdom of many writers — from historians both amateur and professional, journalists, hobbyists, fiction writers and others — that my novel was given some good bones, including from those who still call the Weem home.

I was able to utilise not only some fabulous academic work (which I will mention shortly), but also the *Annals of Pittenweem 1526–1793*, and the *Annals of Anstruther*, which cover the council minutes of these towns, including the events I write about. I also managed to purchase copies of the letters from the anonymous *Gentleman of Fife*, which record a version of what happened in Pittenweem over that time, and the rebuff to those two letters, *A Just Reproof*, which offers a vehement and, frankly rather hollow defence of the reverend and the bailies. The quotes at the beginning of various chapters are often taken from these documents as are some direct quotes, which I place in characters' mouths.

Apart from Sorcha McIntyre and her family, Aidan Ross and Sergeant Thatcher and various shopkeepers, neighbours and merchants, everyone mentioned in the novel existed and mostly — with some tweaking and artistic licence including imagined conversations, motivation and thoughts — acted as described. Sorcha and Aidan became my vehicles for exploring the people and events and, as you now know, I attributed the letters from *A Gentleman of Fife* mainly to Aidan (one to Sorcha), imagining that many might have been written, but only two have survived intact. These letters gave me the basis for Aidan's character, just as learning about the tenacity of the fishwives gave me the basis for not only Sorcha's character, but also for many of the other women in the book.

Fishwives were both loved and loathed. Independent, strong, in control of their lives and, when married, of their husband's lives and the family finances, they were robust, capable women who didn't suffer fools and broke with the traditional idea of a woman's role. They were often regarded as a necessary threat to social order. You can see how the term 'fishwife', used in a derogatory sense, comes down to us now. I like to think of these women as life-affirming and bold; the courage it took to do what they did, particularly in the early 1700s (and before and since), labouring in a man's world, given the losses they would have experienced is remarkable. They worked long hours at a range of tasks, many raising families, and from what I can gather, took pride in their work. I wanted to examine the women before fishing became an 'industry' (for want of a better word) and they became known as 'Herring Lasses', and instead look at the lives of fishwives during a time when Scotland was at war and Pittenweem itself was reeling from the loss of many men in earlier conflicts as well as a poor harvest and drave and was, indeed, in grave financial straits.

The historical context in the novel for the events in Pittenweem is accurate, including the fact soldiers were billeted in the town and that rapes happened. A woman named Isobel Courie did fall pregnant to an already married soldier and the reverend was angry that some of his parishioners chose to drink with the soldiers rather than attend kirk. Likewise, the other witch cases mentioned and the names attached to these (e.g. Maggie Moran et al) are real.

Now, here's where I get to the difficult part. Where I separate out the fiction from the fact and tell you what really happened in Pittenweem between 1704 and 1705.

In terms of the book, Janet Cornfoot (also called Corphat and other variations of the spelling), Beatrix Laing, Janet Horseburgh (who I call Nettie to avoid any confusion), Isobel Adam, Lillie Wallace, Margaret Jack, Thomas Brown and their families existed. Everything that happened to them, from the accusations, their incarceration and terrible torture in the Tolbooth and St Fillan's Cave, and the duration of these and the manner of their deaths, occurred. Using historical records of torture (not in the Weem per se), I recreated/imagined the scenes in the Tolbooth and later the horrific ones with Janet Cornfoot. I should add that Janet did indeed survive her two hours or more of dunking and beating, managing to escape briefly to a house before she was dragged from it and met her horrible death. She was crushed by a door and then a cart was rolled over it. Incomers were later blamed for her murder, and yes, Patrick Cowper did unlawfully release them despite Edinburgh demanding they be sent to the city for trial. He was never held to account for this.

Lizanne Henderson, in her fascinating book *Witchcraft and Folk Beliefs in the Age of Enlightenment, Scotland 1670–1740*, believes that posterity should remember Janet Cornfoot not as a scapegoat for a fear-driven community seeking 'cleansing', but as a martyr. This notion really struck me.

Brian P Levack acknowledges that what happened in Pittenweem over this time generally, and to Janet Cornfoot specifically, led to a change in the laws in Scotland some years later and put an end to witch-hunting in general (but not the beliefs).

While I don't know the real name of the pricker hired by the council, I have given him one — Mr Bollard. The pricker did exist and according to the history of torture and what was involved in the barbaric act of pricking, what I describe is correct. If anything, I likely understate what the women endured — the lack of food, sleep, sanitation, etc. I know, isn't that awful to consider!

Reverend Patrick Cowper was a real person. Sometimes his name was spelled Couper or another variation. He was a widower with eleven children. He appears to have had a hold over the people of Pittenweem that was extraordinary, even for a preacher of the time.

Leonard Low believes the man was evil incarnate and I'm inclined to agree. In relation to the first release of the women from the Tolbooth, after the death of Thomas Brown and upon orders from Edinburgh, Low believes that Cowper felt cheated and was determined that the 'witches' should have been brought to trial and burned. Low further writes, 'he [Patrick Cowper] was in complete control and would revel in his popularity and importance. He would destroy the women with God on his side.'

Rather than present Cowper as one-dimensionally Machiavellian (which would have been easy), I have tried to understand his psychology, emotional state and motivation, approaching it from the point of view of his religious beliefs, but without minimising the dreadful impact he had or the deeds to which he was party. Furthermore, he really did preach the morning following Janet's gruesome death without making one reference to her or the brutality that had unfolded.

Not only did Peter Morton — also known as Patrick Morton, but in one account from the times I read, he was called Peter, so again, to avoid confusion and having three Patricks (Morton's father was also Patrick), I opted to use that name — collapse and become ill after a water/sea-charm was left outside his door by Beatrix Laing, but his 'affliction' went on for months. He also manifested the symptoms described in the book and the reverend did indeed sit with him daily. The accused women were also paraded before Peter in his bedroom while his face was covered, and were subsequently imprisoned. I have, to a degree, imagined the influence of the reverend (there's no doubt in my mind he coached the boy) on the young man and why.

The Bargarran witch trial involving young Christian Shaw near Paisley really happened and was not only known to Fifers and those in Pittenweem due to the spread of news and pamphlets but, according to contemporary sources, Cowper read and talked about the young girl's symptoms to Peter. In some accounts, he read the story over and over again, in others (*A Just Reproof*) he only mentioned it one or two times and then barely. Folk would also have known about Salem and the witch-hunt there. As Brain P Levack notes in his book *Witch Hunting in Scotland: Law, politics and religion*, there was a narrative

of demonic possession circulating at the time that those affected followed. He notes that Cowper read Shaw's account to Morton, and
writes: 'Demoniacs (those possessed) in all societies act the way in
which their religious culture tells them they should act.' Peter Morton
was no exception. Internalising his beliefs and his fears, he likely col-
lapsed/fitted, became caught up in a kind of 'hysteria' and then was
coached to maintain a level of behaviour/symptoms that resembled
possession as it was understood back then. As Levack adds, 'Christian
Shaw's possession provided a script for yet another Scottish possession
(Morton's).'

Alexander McGregor is also a real character, a fisherman, and the
events he was involved in also happened. The incident with Isobel
Adam at Hogmanay really occurred, as did his remembrance of it
almost a year later as an act of malfeasance that involved more than
one woman, with terrible consequences. I tried to imagine the circumstances and conversations around all this and the role of the reverend
(who was involved). His death, however, is a fiction.

In terms of the imprisoned women, the reverend was integral to
their torment. He often ordered the torture, the restrictions imposed
upon them, and washed his hands of them as described in the book.
Whether or not he knew the guards were eating the food provided
for Thomas Brown and his cellmates, I'm uncertain, but the family
— and the Gentleman of Fife and the Edinburgh magistrates and
lawyers — certainly believe Brown's death shouldn't have occurred.

Where Reverend Patrick Cowper is most guilty, however, is in his
behaviour in the lead up to, and during, the horrific murder of Janet
Cornfoot. He was behind her incarceration in St Fillan's Cave, and in
having her put in the lower cell of the Tolbooth. One can only assume
he knew it wouldn't be hard for her to escape (the grating was loose).
He did dine with the bailies that night, and told the townsfolk, upon
her arrest and return, to do what they wanted with her.

Now, we come to parts I simply couldn't accept (keeping in mind
I was already devastated by what had happened to these women,
Thomas Brown and their families and the impact this had on their
relatives and the entire town): not only did no one *ever* get punished

for Janet's shocking murder (or Thomas's), but Patrick Cowper lived for years afterwards, remaining in charge of Pittenweem parish and conducting services in the kirk every Sunday. While there's evidence to suggest his popularity declined (years after the events, the parish tried to fine him for allowing his cow to graze in the graveyard), he never, to use the parlance of the period, paid for his sins. In fact, he continued to instil fear and division in the community and hunt those who'd evaded his earlier attempts to have them seized and tried.

According to Lizanne Henderson:

1708, Rev. Cowper and fellow minister William Wadroper from Anstruther East once again brought charges of witchcraft against [Beatrix] Laing and Nicolas Lawson. Though the case was promptly dropped and the women released by a circuit court judge, the men would not let it rest and issued another warrant in 1709. The women were tried in Perth and found innocent.

The man never gave up!

It is this bit of information that also contradicts an account of what happened to Beatrix Laing as given by Mr Low. According to Low, she wandered outside the town walls and was, weeks later, found dead outside St Andrew's. But, as we can see from contemporary accounts above, she faced charges of witchcraft again more than three years after the events at Pittenweem. Like Sorcha, Nettie, Isobel, Nicolas and the rest, I gave Beatrix the ending I felt she deserved — peace with her husband and friends in the town she'd lived in all her life.

The names of most of the Pittenweem bailies and their basic actions are according to history. The state of the harbour and pier was real as was the need for funds to repair them. Likewise, the *Sophia* really was a floating wreck that listed against the pier, a reminder of the town's failing fortunes. Sightseers did flock to Pittenweem when Peter Morton first fell ill and witchcraft was believed to be the reason. Janet (Nettie) Horseburgh did seek to fine the bailies for their torment of her and in fact, in 1710, Bailie William Bell admitted not only to his part in her torment, but alluded to the fact that, in many ways, the case against the women was completely fraudulent. There's little doubt guilt at his role ate at him and he felt he needed to cleanse his conscience.

I think it's also important I remind myself and you, dear reader, that it wasn't only Scotland that tried and punished witches. Witch-hunting and persecution were rife across Europe and the United Kingdom, resulting in dreadful penalties and horrific deaths for far too many.

I read so many books on Scottish history, witchcraft in Scotland, England and throughout Europe, as well as about fishing and Pittenweem and East Neuk/Fife and the sea-life to write this book and I am indebted and inspired by the writings of these authors and wish to pay tribute to as many as I can:

There was Neil Oliver's *A History of Scotland*, Alistair Moffat's *Scotland: A History from Earliest Times*, Chris Bambery's *A People's History of Scotland*, Hugh Trevor-Roper's *The Invention of Scotland: Myth and history*, and David R Ross's *Women of Scotland*.

The Makers of Scotland: Picts, Romans, Gaels and Vikings by Tim Clarkson, *Curious Scotland: Tales from a hidden history* by George Rosie, *Walking Through Scotland's History, Two thousand years on foot* by Ian R Mitchell and *The Landscape of Scotland* by ER Wickham-Jones. Also excellent were *The Domestic Life of Scotland in the Eighteenth Century by* Marjorie Plant, and *A History of Everyday Life in Scotland 1600–1800* edited by Elizabeth Foyster and Christopher A Whatley. *A Handbook of Scotland's Coasts* edited by Fi Martynoga was a delightful read and took me back to Scotland and the many, many walks I did while there. I also used some books with a very local flavour that I purchased while in Pittenweem and Anstruther, and these were so useful. *In My Ain Words: An East Neuk Vocabulary* by Mary Murray — what a rich and marvellous way of expressing themselves the people of this region have! *Auld Anster* by Alison Thirkell — a wonderful little resource. I also used a photographic record of old Pittenweem simply called that by Eric Munson, which not only supplemented the many photos I took, but transported me back to another time and place.

In terms of books on witchcraft, apart from those mentioned above, I also used *Witchcraft and Trials for Witchcraft in Fife* by Johan Ewart Simpkins, *The Scottish Witch-hunt in Context* edited by Julian Goodare, *The Witches of Fife: Witch-hunting in a Scottish shire 1560–1710* by Stuart Macdonald, *A True and Full Relation of The Witches At Pittenweem [&c.]* — Primary Source Edition, 1704 (various authors), *A Collection of Rare and Curious Tracts on Witchcraft and the Second Sight with an original essay on Witchcraft by David Webster* (1820), and, of course, the wonderful and deeply disturbing *The Weem Witch* by Leonard Low.

I also utilised many websites and newspaper articles about Pittenweem and the witches.

I bought a fabulous resource, *The Scots Thesaurus* edited by Iseabail Macleod with Pauline Cairns, Caroline Macafee and Ruth Martin, as well as other books that helped immerse me in the language and culture — that is, apart from my own wonderful memories of my Ross grandmother, Margaret, and relatives and Fraser step-grandfather, Charles, and my friend Robbie Gilligan with his beautiful, musical way of saying things.

Books on fishing and actually going fishing also helped. *The Real Price of Fish: The story of Scotland's fishing industry and communities* by Linda Fitzpatrick, purchased at the Fisheries Museum in Anstruther, was so useful. Other books and many videos also helped set a context.

I burrowed into contemporary accounts of what happened — as I said above, mainly from the parish records, letters and pamphlets of the period. It shows that the conflict caused by the accusations of witchcraft against these women and Thomas Brown, the notion of possession and malfeasance, caused huge schisms in communities, even though they were very religious. Add to this the other political divisions between those who supported English rule and the Jacobites (who wanted a Scottish king and the return of the Stuart line), as well as famine and poverty, and the setting was ripe for fear, intimidation and scapegoating. Once again, the more I write about the past, the more I see frightening parallels in today's society.

Of course, I also read some magnificent fiction, including Susanna Kearsley's fabulous *The Winter Sea* and Susan Fraser King's *Lady Macbeth*, the thrilling works of Diana Gabaldon and Dorothy Dunnett, and a raft of crime fiction from my favourites, Stuart MacBride and Anne Cleeves' *Shetland* series, to Ian Rankin, Pete Brassett, MC Beaton and Keith Moray, among many others.

As I wrote, I listened to a range of fabulous Scottish and Celtic music, but have to give a special shout out to Emily Barker's 'The Witch of Pittenweem' (which my husband discovered as I was in the middle of editing — it's about what happened to Janet Cornfoot and is just amazing and I had to force myself to stop replaying it over and over) as well as the rousing Bareknuckle Pipes and Drums of the Albannach band.

Likewise, the beautiful, moving art of Davy Macdonald — I am fortunate to have two prints of the fishwives hanging on my walls (a beautiful gift from hubby) — inspired and deeply affected me.

I hope that this book, while dark and harrowing in parts, is understood as I intend it — not only to showcase female friendship, the great bonds and love that can exist between good and decent men and women, even when all about them is unravelling, but also to honour the community of Pittenweem and especially those who fell during these bleak and terrible times. I love Scotland, from whence my father's family and thus part of my bloodline came. It's a magnificent country with a rich and enthralling history and present, made all the more remarkable by its wonderful, resilient people.

Above all, *The Darkest Shore* is a love-letter to the fishwives and all the other 'wicked women' out here; a tribute to strong, resourceful women whose boldness and courage, and that of their families and the men who stand by them, is cause for wonder, celebration and commemoration.

Any mistakes are my own and any accuracies are because of the marvellous works and research of the clever and talented people mentioned above. Thank you.

Slàinte.

GLOSSARY

Bannocks: a round, flat cake made on a griddle
Braes: hillside; slopes
Betrump: deceive
Bloothered: noisy fools
Brazen besom: a local expression for a shameless woman
Brooks: heavy cotton over-pants worn by fishermen
Clash-bag: gossip; a tell-tale
Clecking: chatting; gossiping
Cleckin' o' women: a group of women gossiping
Contermashus: argumentative
Coocher: coward
Cowking: vomiting
Creel: woven basket the fishwives owned and which, when they walked
about the countryside, were held to their bodies with a strap around
the shoulders or even across the forehead
Drackie: damp, wet and misty
Drave: the name once given to the herring season; also used here to
signify the potential for a good haul of fish or to exaggerate
Drookin': drenching; drookit: drenched
Dwamish: dreamy
Eldren: older (as in an old person)

Fakin' the nets: folding them properly so they will run cleanly from the boats

Gairnsey: a fisherman's hand-knitted jumper created on four needles with no seams; the pattern denoted the wearer (often a way of identifying a body when washed ashore); sometimes called a *gansey* in other parts of Scotland

Gennick: genuine

Gowk: fool; simpleton

G'nirl't: half-frozen

Grauvit: scarf

Haar: cold mist or fog

Hawkit: stupid

Hirple: limp

Hizzie: disparaging term for a woman

Knabbie: having means or position

Maucht: physical strength; mightiness

Muckle sumph: fool, idiot

Neeps: turnips

Neepyin: scarf a fishwife would tie over her hair

Nithered: pinched or stunted with cold

Nyaff: someone of no account

Peely-wally: drawn

Pintle: slang term for penis

Plout (o' rain): very heavy shower

Quaich: bowl-shaped drinking cup

Quhillylillie: slang term for a penis

Ragabash: riff-raff; a motley crew

Shieled (mussels or oysters): local word for 'shelled'

Skerries: rocky ridges that jut out to the south-west of the town into the Firth of Forth like skeletal hands

Souff: a lazy person, a drunk

Speet: very thin (local expression)

Splewing: local word for vomiting

Sprauchle: feeble, weak

Sprouse: to exaggerate or brag
Tawpie: foolish
Tirl: kiss
Tossel: slang for penis
Whillywha: a flatterer
Widdie: a wicked person
Wuidwoman: mad woman

LIST OF CHARACTERS

*Denotes a real person

Sorcha McIntyre: widow and fishwife

*Reverend Patrick Cowper: in charge of the Presbyterian kirk in Pittenweem and member of town council

*Nettie Horseburgh (Janet Horseburgh/White): fishwife and friend of Sorcha's. Wife of Thomas White

*Janet Cornfoot: fishwife

*Nicolas Lawson: fishwife and healer

*Beatrix Laing: married to Thomas Brown; friend of the fishwives

*Mr Thomas Brown: fisherman and accused witch

Captain Aidan Ross: officer in Queen's army, in charge of troops in Pittenweem, originally from Skye

Sergeant Stephen Thatcher: Captain Ross's second-in-command in Pittenweem

Jamie Dyson: young soldier from Anster

Private Burne: soldier

*Isobel Adam: young seamstress and accused witch; friend to the fishwives

*Alexander McGregor: fisherman, known for his love of whisky and ale

Laird Nicholson: owns the estate outside St Andrew's that Dagny's husband Kennocht manages

Dagny McIntyre: Sorcha's sister

Erik McIntyre: Sorcha's brother (deceased)

Charlie McIntyre: Sorcha's father (deceased)

Astrid Grimmsdatter: Sorcha's mother/mor. Originally from Bergen, Norway (deceased)

Robbie McIntyre: Sorcha's brother; prisoner of war, presumed dead

Andrew Watson: fisherman; Sorcha's husband (deceased)

Davan Watson: Sorcha's stillborn son

James Crawford: local fisherman; drowned at sea

Mrs Porter: local gossip

Moira Fraser: neighbour of Sorcha's and owner of the Labrador, Crabby

*Bailie Robert Cook: member of Pittenweem town council

*Bailie William Bell: member of Pittenweem town council

*Bailie Robert Vernour: member of Pittenweem town council

*Jean Durkie: fishwife

*Lillie Wallace: fishwife

Mrs Oliver: Pittenweem local

Mr Browning: Pittenweem local

Cameron McDougall: Pittenweem local

Malcolm Moray: owns the local colliery

*Margie Strang: Pittenweem local raped by stationed soldiers

*Isobel Courie: fell pregnant to Corporal Robert Varner

*Corporal Robert Varner: disreputable soldier who impregnated Isobel Courie

Widow Adams: Pittenweem local

*William Brown/Laing: Beatrix's husband

*Peter Morton: apprentice blacksmith and son of Patrick Morton. Grossly afflicted by a curse laid by Beatrix Laing

*Patrick Morton: Peter's father and town blacksmith

McKenzie family: local Pittenweem family

Bailie Thomas Whyte: member of Pittenweem town council

Seumas Cowper: eldest son of Patrick Cowper

Mr Roberts: Pittenweem local

*Bailie Robert Cleiland: member of Pittenweem town council

Mr Baker: Pittenweem local

Hetty Collins: butcher's wife

Mary Collins: her daughter

Rachel Johnson: Pittenweem local

*Mrs Dore: an accused witch from St Monan's

*Christian Shaw: accused a group of her family's servants of witchcraft in 1697. Eight of them were subsequently sentenced to death

*Margaret (Lillie) Wallace: fishwife

*Katherine Marshal: fishwife

Benjamin Brown: Pittenweem local

Therese Larnarch: fishwife

Mrs Robertson: Cooper's second wife

Graham Donaldson: brewer

Michael Bruce: tavern owner

Widow Agnes: Pittenweem local

Mark Smith: constable of Pittenweem

Simon Wood: constable of Pittenweem

Gerard Stuart: constable of Pittenweem

Angus Stuart: constable of Pittenweem

Mr Frost: Pittenweem local

Alick Brigstowe: former fisherman who lost a hand and was given job of Tolbooth keeper

Mr Bollard: Bailie pro tempore

Mr Chifley: Pittenweem local

Burn: dog

Crabby: Moira Fraser's dog

Bait: moggie

*Richard Dugdale: Fife man, accused of being a witch and put to death

*Margaret Jack: fishwife and accused witch

Camron MacGille: replacement Tolbooth keeper

Rab Burne: Pittenweem local and ne'er do well

Dr Duncan McLeod: Pittenweem doctor — only completed a year of training in Edinburgh, so uses the title under sufferance

Jen Hazell: fishwife

Angus Riding: local who fell asleep on a gravestone

*Mr Ker of Kippilaw: Advocate

*Mr Robert Cook(e): Advocate from Edinburgh (I added the 'e' to his name to distinguish him from Bailie Robert Cook)

*Earl of Rothes: Edinburgh aristocracy

*Laird Anstruther: local laird

Mrs Tyler: Pittenweem local

Mr Butterworth: Pittenweem local who drank Irish spirit and almost drowned

McDonald lads: Pittenweem locals

Ellie Brown: Pittenweem local

Colonel Leslie Johns: Captain Ross's commanding officer and cousin to Earl of Rothes

*Duke of Marlborough: also a general and in charge of the Queen's army in Europe

*General Overkirk: high-ranking officer in the Queen's army

*Queen Ann: English monarch at time

Mr Donaldson: Pittenweem local

*Cotton Mather: New England minister and author of many books, including about the Salem witch trials

Callum Gregson: former councilman and mercer

Caitlin Gregson: Callum's daughter

Brown family: Pittenweem locals

Thom Jack: Margaret's husband, fisherman and owner of valuable longlines

Gavan Wright: lives near Alexander McGregor

Joanna Browning: Gavin's wife

*Mr Iain Adam: Isobel's father (Mr Adam existed, but I have given him a fictional first name)

*Rebecca White: Janet Horseburgh's daughter with a fictional first name

Billy: Rebecca White's husband

Cornelia Gurr: fishwife

*Laird Randerston: one of the officials who came from Edinburgh to speak to the accused witches

*Laird Lyon: one of the officials who came from Edinburgh to speak to the accused witches

*Laird Kellie: one of the officials who came from Edinburgh to speak to the accused witches

Mrs Gower: Pittenweem local

Private Smith: soldier

Corporal Inglis: soldier

*Reverend George Gordon: reverend in charge of Leuchar's parish

Laird Barinscliff: Edinburgh aristocrat with land near Leuchars

Mr Craigieburn: wealthy landowner near Leuchars

Mrs Glaren: George Gordon's housekeeper

*General Cutts: officer in Queen's army, stationed in Europe

*General Orkney: officer in Queen's army, stationed in Europe

*General Churchill: also known as the Duke of Marlborough

Reginald Foggerty: English captain of ship that brings letters from the front

Mr Murray: owns stables near Janet Cornfoot's house

Clem Brady: Pittenweem local

Jenny Lawson: Nicolas's sister and friend to Janet Cornfoot

Mimi Foster: cousin to Nicolas and friend to Janet Cornfoot

*Rob Dalzell: one of the locals accused of rousing the town and implicated in death of Janet Cornfoot

*Walter Watson: man from Burntisland implicated in death of Janet Cornfoot

Grayson Fleet: Pittenweem local, implicated in death of Janet Cornfoot

Mr Porter: Pittenweem local

Mrs Lentrow: Pittenweem local

*Mr Borthwick: bailie of Pittenweem

Mr Carter: a bailie of Pittenweem

Jon Durkie: Jean Durkie's husband

Rachel Mowbray: local lass

*Andrew Bruce: minister Patrick Cowper replaced

*Alexander Griege: former bailie who called Nettie a witch against whom she brought charges of slander

ACKNOWLEDGEMENTS

*T*his book has been one of the hardest and yet also, in a strange and inexplicable way, one of the most fulfilling I have yet written. Being based on a true story, dealing with actual people and the shocking events that unfolded, the cruelty meted out and the impact this had on the lives of those in and around Pittenweem at the time became all-consuming — in a fraught but also good way. It was so important that I represented the women and men involved as well as I could, gave them three dimensions and took them from the sometimes cold, dry pages of history or academic discourse, or even from exploitative media tales, and gave them heart, soul, courage, loves, dislikes, flaws, friendships, work, and thus, I hope purpose beyond what we know. It also became absolutely crucial, the more I wrote, researched and learned, to reclaim the word 'fishwife'. For so long a derogatory and reductive term, used to remind women of their 'place' by silencing and discrediting them mainly by using the word as an insult, I hope this book goes some way to revealing what an amazing, hard-working, stoic and pragmatic bunch of women they were. I couldn't think of anyone I would want to call friend more — so aren't I lucky I have my own 'school' of fishwives who support me?

Like all my other books, this one wasn't written without the support, kindness, generosity and love of so many women and men, many of whom were not aware of how much their encouragement, patience, occasional query about progress, invitation to dinner and/or drinks, and ability to help me shed my self-doubt that I could do this tale justice meant. I now have the chance to publicly thank them. Before I start, I also want to pre-empt anyone I may inadvertently leave out — please know, it's only from these pages, not from my heart.

Firstly, I want to thank my wonderful agent and dearest of friends, Selwa Anthony. From the moment I told her about this idea for a novel about fishwives and witchcraft that had me hooked, she was too and encouraged me to pursue it. Giving me advice on where to modify a little or strengthen a theme, she was an advocate for the fishwives and their story from the get-go and I owe so much to this beautiful woman. Thank you, Selwa.

I also want to thank Jo Mackay from MIRA Harlequin and HC. From the outset, Jo was such a terrific champion of this story. She understood what I was trying to do and was determined it would get the title, cover and coverage it deserved. I am so grateful to you, Jo, for your understanding and support. I also want to thank my wonderful editor, Annabel Blay — a rock and a steady hand who guides the story ship safely into port. She also ensured I was once more working with the capable and marvellous Linda Funnell. Linda and I have worked together on all my historical fiction and I'm just so damn grateful for her insights, corrections, sharp observations, suggestions and the rest. Thank you. Thank you. A huge shout out to my eagle-eyed proofreader Annabel Adair as well. Thanks so much. I also want to thank the rest of the incredible team at MIRA Harlequin and HC — from the gorgeous Natika Palka and Sarana Behan, to James Kellow, Adam Van Rooijen, and the sensational Sue Brockhoff and to all those in marketing, sales, and the entire shebang. I so appreciate you.

A huge thanks as well to my US agents, Jim Frenkel, and Associates, in particular, Catherine Pfeifer. Jim and Catherine are such staunch advocates of this tale and my work in general — as well as being lovely to work with — and I am very grateful to be part of their literary family.

Then there's my darling Kerry Doyle. Kerry, her husband Peter Goddard, my husband Stephen and I all travelled to the UK together in 2017, in particular to tour Scotland, though we also took in parts of Britain and fabulous Wales as well. Stephen and I dragged them in and out of breweries, distilleries and bookshops (yeah, we're really crap friends) and occasionally I would peel away to do my own research. More often than not, they all accompanied me and became, particularly when we went to Fife, as transfixed and enchanted by the area and as captivated by the tale of witches in Pittenweem as I was. We spent hours together in the fantastic Fisheries Museum in Anstruther, walked miles along the coastal paths, explored the wynds of Pittenweem, the harbour, drank hot chocolate, ate seafood, were horrified by St Fillan's Cave, quietly contemplated the Tolbooth and kirk (and back then I didn't know a fraction of what had happened) and wandered through the graveyard. Everywhere we went in Fife and, indeed, throughout Scotland, we were greeted so warmly and with absolute generosity. It was a magic time that I hope to repeat very soon as more stories have taken root. But I digress... Kerry is one of my beta-readers and it takes a very special person to be willing to undertake such a task. They have to read a work-in-progress and feed back honestly to the writer what they think. Kerry is an experienced reader and a discerning one. I trust her both to be brutally frank yet kind when she reads — not an easy task — and she is all that and so much more. Thank you, Kerry, my lovely, my soul-sister.

Thanks to you, too, Peter, for your love, friendship and support and for being so much a part of this tale and its creation as well.

Then there are the marvellous friends who gave me the idea for this story in the first place: Mark Nicholson and Bill Lark. Both are fabulous people and great raconteurs and it didn't take much for them to convince me to search out this story. I hope I have justified your faith in my ability to do it justice. Bill also happens to be married to another of my friends — the kind you call on for a hug, a laugh and a shoulder and to share a few drams with — the superbly talented Lyn Lark. I also want to thank Bill and Lyn for insisting I stay in their 'shack' in Orford, Tasmania, for as long as I wanted to finish the book. I had a week by the cold, wild sea, with my dogs, imagination, research and words, and it was simply magic. Thank you so much for your incredible generosity. I did complete the book there.

Thanks as well to Mark's gorgeous wife, Robin. Also, to Simon Thomson, Lucy Wilkins, Clinton and Rosie Steele — all part of the Single Malt Motorcycle Club. Also, Mike Crew, the lovely Robbie (the Glaswegian Taswegian) and his beautiful wife and my friend, Emma Gilligan, and wee Harvey as well.

To one of my closest friends, the marvellous Stephen Bender — you are an inspiration in so many ways. Kiarna, Chris, Jake and Samuel Brown — thank you. To my most special friends, with whom I share political diatribes, joy in images, poems, films and books as well as celebrating each other's triumphs and mourning the setbacks, Professor Jim McKay, Dr Helen Johnston, Dr Liz Ferrier, Professor David Rowe, Professor Malcolm McLean, Professor Mike Emmison, Dr Janine Mikosa and Linda Martello, thank you.

I also wish to thank (though they might not know it directly, they have been a great support and presence), Dr Frances Thiele, Dr Lisa Hill, Sheryl Gwyther, Mark Woodland, Mimi McIntyre, Gav Jaeger and Jason Greatbatch, Margaret Wenham, Natalie Gregg, Geoffrey Shearer, Fiona Inch, Mick and Katri DuBois, Christina Schultness (How), Trevor Dale and Jeff Francombe, Donna Williams and Kerrie Ashwood, Rebecca and Terry Moles and Wendy Moles, and my lovely step-mum Moira Adams and her fabulous but now deceased Scottish parents. They, along with my nanna, Margaret Ross, had such a passion for Scotland, its myths and history, and I like to think they began to instil it in me as well a long time ago.

I also want to thank the IASH at University of Queensland where I am an honorary senior research consultant and the University of the Sunshine Coast, where I am an Honorary Senior Fellow.

Thanks also to the talented Tony Mak and Sharn Hitchins for their wonderful music and friendship.

I also really want to thank my readers. Where would I be without you? Or the booksellers and librarians, the custodians of stories — the matchmakers of the imagination — thank you to each and every one of you for being the guardians at the gate.

Thank you as well to my gorgeous Facebook friends on my author page and on Goodreads, Twitter and Instagram — you are simply terrific.

Also, a huge thanks to the friends of Captain Bligh's Brewery and Distillery. Every time I see you, you cheer me on and support what it is Stephen and I do — whether it be with beer, spirits or books. Thank you so much.

I also want to thank my much-missed inspiration and cherished friend, Sara Douglass.

Now it's time for my last thanks — my family. Starting with my remarkable sister, Jenny Farrell, whose unshakeable belief in what I do astonishes me always. Thank you.

Grant Searle — thank you for being one my (and Stephen's) best friends and a true support in so many ways — and when life has not been as kind as it could be to you. Here's to that changing and soon. Love you dearly.

To my furbies — my canine muses and beloved companions, Tallow, Dante and Bounty — I am so blessed you chose me as one of your humans.

To my beautiful very adult children, Adam and Caragh — both amazing creators in their own unique ways. They make me laugh, cry, remind me that real life can be both challenging and as crazily astonishing as the fictional ones I write. I love you both very much.

Finally, I have to thank my beloved husband, my partner in all that is wondrous and wondrously wicked. Together we've weathered some tumultuous, very frightening, sorrowful and damn tough times. But, like everything, we did it together. Able to bring me back to shore when I drift away, he's there to shine a light in the darkness and laugh with and even sometimes at me. As I wrote this book, he also listened to and held me as I wept for the women of Pittenweem and what they endured — the men too. Then he cheered me on when I determined to alter, where appropriate, the outcome. Stephen is always there, my anchor, my rock. I may not be his fishwife (though I don't think he'd mind), but I hope I'll always be his wicked writing woman.

Turn over for a sneak peek.

THE
GOOD WIFE
OF
BATH

by
KAREN BROOKS

Available July 2021

PROLOGUE

WHO PAINTED THE LION?

The Swanne, Southwark
The Year of Our Lord 1406
In the seventh year of the reign of Henry IV

$\mathcal{M}$y father would oft remark that the day I was born, the heavens erupted in protest. Great clods of ice rained upon poor unsuspecting folk, and the winds were so bitter and cold, those who could remained indoors. Any sod who couldn't, risked death in the fields along with the shivering, miserable beasts. He didn't tell me to arouse my guilt, but to remind me to hold up my head and stand proud. I may have been born the daughter of a peasant, but it wasn't every day a lass could say she made her mark upon the world.

I came into being on the 21st of April 1352, a day henceforth known as 'Black Saturday' and not because the woman who'd carried me the last nine months died moments before I arrived, casting a ghastly pall over what should have been a celebration.

The story I grew up with was that my mother's fate was very nearly my own as, even in death, her womb refused to expel me. It wasn't until the midwife, seeing the rippling of her stomach as if some devil-sent spawn was writhing within, understood the Grim Reaper had not yet departed the room. He was awaiting another soul to carry forth. Wishing him gone, she snatched his sacred scythe from his gnarly hand and ripped open my mother's body and, amidst blood and swollen entrails, pulled me forth like a sacrificial offering of old.

My father, hearing the screams of dismay and fear, forwent the sacred rules of the birthing chamber and burst through the door. Determining that the shade of blue colouring my flesh, whilst it looked fine upon a noblewoman's mantle, was no colour for a babe to be wearing, hoisted me off the bloodied rushes where the midwife had dropped me and, ordering her to cut the umbilicus, swung me by my ankles, slapping my flesh until it turned a much happier puce.

Only then did I bawl – loud, long and lusty.

The midwife promptly fainted; my father gathered me to his chest, laughing and crying while I hollered noisily, competing with the raging storms outside.

It was decided then and there (or maybe this is something I invented later) that though I was born under the sign of Taurus, I was a child of Mars – a fighter who stared death in the face and scared him witless. Papa declared, and the midwife – who came to at my screams – concurred: the moment I burst into life, the Reaper picked up his robes and fled the room. He even forgot his scythe.

But Mars was not alone when he blessed me with the blood and spirit of a warrior. Oh no. For while Papa, unaware Mama had died as he tried to soften my cries and sought for something in which to swaddle me, Venus, Mars' wanton bride, peered over his shoulder. Because she liked what she saw, she leaned forward and placed the sweetest of kisses upon my puckered brow. Not finished, she turned me over and pressed one each upon my peach-like buttocks as well. In doing this, the goddess of love and ruler over all Taureans thrice blessed me with her own deep desires. Desires that lay dormant for many years until they gushed forth, destroying all in their path.

God was preoccupied tending to my mother's swiftly departed soul and Papa's grief. His distraction allowed the pagan gods to claim me – Mars and Venus, Ares and Aphrodite – Roman or Greek, I'm partial to both.

Christened Eleanor, it was the name I wore for many years before fate forced me to change it. But I'm getting ahead of myself, something I'm inclined to do and pray you'll forgive me.

The years went by and the wheel of fortune turned until it forced God – who I swear until then barely acknowledged my presence, for He never heard my prayers – to notice me.

Before my monthly courses began to flow, my father passed from this earthly realm leaving me in the care of the woman who had elevated him beyond his wildest dreams. The Lady Clarice, a formerly wealthy landowner whose entire family and many servants died during the Botch, hired my father, by then an itinerant brogger who brokered wool for a living, as steward of her neglected sheep and fallow lands. Papa proved worthy of my lady's faith, increasing her holdings and the quality of her flock. Eternally grateful, or so she said, she made my father promises that, upon his death, she failed to keep. Foremost was that she would care for me if he died – unless you count being taken into service at the manor as caring. I was ten years of age.

Before handing me over to the housekeeper, Mistress Bertha, my lady imparted some words of wisdom. She told me I'd but one gift, the most valuable thing a woman could own. Misunderstanding her meaning, I waited eagerly for what she was about to bestow. Turns out, I was already in possession of it. My lady was referring to my queynte – my cunt. But, she made sure to emphasise, it was only of worth if it was untouched, pure and virginal. Then, it was an opportunity – something to be used to one day better my situation by marrying well. I was ordered to protect my maidenhead as the Crusaders did the walls of Jerusalem (though, one presumes, with more success).

From here on, said Lady Clarice, my body would be under siege – from the attentions of men and, much worse, the naturally lascivious thoughts a woman possessed and which I admit were already beginning to take up a great deal of space in my head. According to Father Roman, the village priest, women were the gateway of the devil, insatiable beasts who devoured hapless men with their longings. I recall looking at May, my rather plain and plump friend and fellow-maid, thinking the only kind of man she'd devour would be the cooked kind. Regardless, we women were all cast in the same lustful role, high born, low born and anywhere in the middle. Even me, only recently thrust from childhood.

Rather than God, it was the man I thought of as The Poet who saved me from falling victim to my naturally lewd nature. At least, that's how others tell it – especially The Poet. In fact, he's always taken credit for my story.

I call him The Poet because that was how he was first introduced to me. Later, I came to know him as someone possessed of many guises: a wondrous spinner of tales, a wine-merchant's son, a Londoner, John of Gaunt's lackey, a diplomat, a watcher, a cuckold, even an accused rapist. Eventually, I would come to know him in a very different way.

Regardless, he was the man who took my tale from me and became its custodian. I want to believe he meant well in committing me to verse, that he sought to rewrite my history in a way that gave me mastery over it. Mayhap, he did that. He also protected me from my sins – not the lustful kind. Despite what you may think, bodily desire doesn't make the angels cower. Rather, in writing my tale, The Poet sought to shield me from the consequences of my darker deeds by distracting those who would call me to account. For, while folk are titillated and shocked by his portrait, they don't see *me*. In retrospect, it was a clever manoeuvre. I never thanked him properly. Perhaps this is what this is – a delayed thank-you as well as a setting to rights of sorts. I confess, there are some versions of me he crafted I quite like and may yet keep. We'll see.

Alas, he's gone, and I'll never really know exactly why he portrayed me the way he did, with boundless avarice, unchecked lust, vulgarity, overweening pride and more besides.

The Poet equipped me with every sin.

Betraying my trust in him, using my secret fears and desires, he exposed my weaknesses – my strengths, too – and turned them into something for others' amusement. Oh, amused they were – and still are, for I hear them discussing the wanton Alyson, the Wife of Bath and her many flaws. Mind you, they're a little afeared as well, and I don't mind that so much. Either way, he's dead (may God assoil him), and it's time for me to wrest my tale back and tell it in my own way. As it really happened. And, when my story is complete, you can judge for yourself whose version you prefer: the loud, much-married, lusty woman dressed in scarlet who travelled the world in order to pray at all the important shrines yet learned nothing of humility, questioned divinity, boasted of her conquests and deceits, and demanded mastery over men. Or the imperfect child who grew into an imperfect woman – experienced, foolish and clever too – oft at the same time. Thrice broken, twice betrayed, once murdered and once a murderer, who mended herself time after time and rose to live again in stories and in truth – mostly.

All this despite five bloody husbands.

All this, despite the damn Poet.

PART ONE
The Marriage Debt

1364 to 1386
No sooner than one husband's dead and gone
Some other Christian man shall take me on.

— The Wife of Bath's Prologue, *The Canterbury Tales* by
Geoffrey Chaucer, translated by Neville Coghill

The man is not under the lordship of the woman, but
the woman is under the lordship of the man.
[Another writer has added in the margins: 'Not always'.]

— From the thirteenth-century regulations of the poulterers of
Paris, edited by GB Depping, *Réglemens sur les arts et métiers de
Paris rédigés au 13e siécle et connus sous le nom du Livre des métiers
d'Étienne Boileau*, 1837

The Tale of Husband the First Fulk Bigod

1364 to 1369
Wedding's no sin, so far as I can learn
Better it is to marry than to burn.

— The Wife of Bath's Prologue, *The Canterbury Tales* by
Geoffrey Chaucer, translated by Neville Coghill

ONE

Noke Manor, Bath-atte-Mere
The Year of Our Lord 1364
In the thirty-eighth year of the reign of Edward III

I stared in dismay at the old man standing in the middle of the room who, as the steward announced me in the coldest of tones, looked as out of place as a whore in a priory. On second thoughts, knowing some of the local sisters, mayhap not. What on God's good earth was that pariah, Master Fulk Bigod, doing here at Noke Manor, let alone in her ladyship's solar? His reputation as a peculiar loner who grunted rather than spoke followed him like the stench of his person. A farmer and wool grower, he lived on the outskirts of the village. With four wives already in the grave, it was said he bullied folk until they sold him their daughters or their sheep. Papa never had time for him – not that he was alone in that respect. The man was despised and mostly avoided. By everyone. By me.

Until now.

Dear Lord, was this was to be my punishment? Was this how I was to pay for my sin? I was going to be sent away and made to work for this man. It was said no servant he hired remained long. They fled the coop once they saw what roosted there. God help me. Though what was I doing requesting aid from the Almighty? It was a priest who got me into this mess in the first place. A mess that saw me locked away in my bedroom and now, days later, dragged before my betters.

I worried my lip as I regarded those who filled the room. There was my good lady mistress, her friend The Poet, the new steward Master Merriman, a number of servants – friends – who could scarce meet my eyes, and bloody, stinking Fulk Bigod.

Papa in heaven, help me.

Ever since *it* happened, I'd been kept in solitude and ordered to contemplate the shame my actions had brought upon my lady and my dead father. I was told to pray for forgiveness and my everlasting soul. Shocked by how swiftly my fortunes had undergone a change, as if the fates had suddenly given Fortuna's wheel a random spin, I didn't comply. Not straight away.

When I was first confined to my room and Master Merriman latched the door, warning me I'd remain there until the lady decided how to salvage the situation, I banged on the wood and shouted myself hoarse. When no-one appeared to release or console me, and the celebrations outside continued as if nothing momentous had occurred, I did indeed drop to my knees and pray to the Heavenly Father – for a few minutes, then I grew bored. It's hard to stay focused when there's no reply. May as well talk to oneself. I crossed myself, leapt up and pushed open the shutters to see what I was missing out on.

Beyond the manor house, the sun cast a mellow glow over the May Day celebrations that were in full swing. The Queen of the May, Mariot Breaksper, the baker's daughter, had been crowned. She looked mighty fine in her green kirtle, her golden hair unbound and a garland of flowers planted upon her head. Twirling around the maypole, holding the brightly coloured ribbons I'd helped attach, were my friends, their heads adorned with the greenery we'd woken early to cut from the nearby woods. There was clapping, stomping and much laughter, all accompanied by flutes, viols, pipes and drums. Fires were lit and, as the afternoon wore on and the smell of roasting meat carried into the attic to taunt me, I wished I was among it all. With a great sigh, I rested my elbows on the sill, my chin on my palms.

Movement in the courtyard below caught my attention. There was a gathering of horses and men and, in their midst, my lady herself. She looked regal in her blue gown, with a particularly lovely circlet of blooms atop her wimple. As I watched, she turned to converse with one of the riders. More soberly dressed than the others, having divested himself of his costume, was The Poet. He'd become a regular visitor over the last few years, and though I'd never really caught his name I always welcomed his presence. A relative of Lady Clarice's – a distant cousin or such – he was employed as a lawyer's clerk at Gray's Inn in London while studying for the bar, or so I'd heard. Thought to be clever, it wasn't his learning I anticipated – it was the stories he brought whenever he came, stories that transported all who heard them with their vivid descriptions of maidens in distress, knights on quests, lascivious friars, righteous monks, foolish millers, vain prioresses, gods, goddesses and mortals misbehaving or enacting deeds of marvellous courage. Whatever the tale, The Poet knew how to hold an audience captive.

Only the night before, on May Day Eve, The Poet had delighted us with the story of Cupid and Psyche. The beautiful young woman, Psyche, was to be married to a monster in order to protect the city. But when her wedding night came, the monster, who insisted they remain in the dark so his bride could not see him, was gentle and passionate. Asked to trust him and to never, ever attempt to look at him, the silly chit listened to her jealous sisters who, beset with envy at how their sister lived and how she described her lusty husband, persuaded her to break the vow. One night, Psyche held up a lantern so she could see who was sarding her. It was no monster. Taken aback by her husband's beauty, she tipped the lamp and spilled some wax, which burned the beautiful winged god to whom she was really married. He fled, and she then spent years atoning in an effort to find him again. Everyone clapped and cheered when it was finished and called for more. All I could think was how the stupid girl almost lost a grand opportunity. Imagine, being married to a god! Who cares what he looked like? I would have happily remained in the dark if I was given endless coin to spend, a beautiful house in which to dwell, lavish clothes and food aplenty. Never mind a deity to swive me.

The Poet was talking earnestly to Lady Clarice from atop his horse. I'd been looking forward to hearing more of his tales that evening. Now, as a witness to my shame, I was glad it appeared he was departing. I leaned as far out of the casement as I was able, but couldn't hear what was being said. The Poet nodded and touched his chest as if taking an oath. Lady Clarice passed him a purse, which he tucked into his tunic. I began to wonder if he would ever weave a story about me and what I'd done. It would be a good 'un. I forced a chuckle when all I really wanted to do was weep.

The Poet kicked his horse and, as he signalled for his squire to follow, looked straight to where I was watching and saluted me.

I leapt away from the window lest I incur more of my lady's anger. She'd been in a white-hot rage when she ordered Master Merriman to lock me away. With a deep sigh I sank onto the bed and thought about the reason I was banned from the celebrations.

Father Layamon.

He'd arrived at the manor a few weeks earlier and caused quite the stir among the household. Father Layamon had come to assist our priest, Father Roman. Rumour had it that Father Layamon was the Bishop's bastard son. Not only was having him at Noke Manor a huge honour for my lady and Father Roman, but his presence brought great prestige to the village. Not that I or the other maids cared about any of that.

Young, tall and ridiculously handsome with his jet-black hair, long lashes, twinkling dark eyes and soft pillow lips, Father Layamon was like the heroes of The Poet's tales. I could have admired him all day – and listened to him. Alas, Father Layamon of the honey pipes was rendered mute during mass, doomed to assist boring old Father Roman, who delivered Latin like a series of insults. In less time than it took to say two Pater Nosters, that windbag of a priest had warned the young Father to keep his distance from all the maids, especially me.

'Twas my hair that made me the target of Father Roman's injunction. Red was the colour of passion, blood and whoredom. According to our priest, I'd been conceived when my mother should have abstained, and was therefore doomed. 'As St Jerome wrote,' the priest would thunder, 'flame-haired women are hell-bound.'

Anyone with half a mind knew the worst thing to say to a young man – or woman for that matter, especially one with Venus as her ruler – was to forbid them to keep company. Cook should have known better when she urged me to keep my eyes off the young priest and eat my pottage. But how could I fasten my eyes upon grey gruel when there was a delicious alternative to feast on at the high table? And what about Father Roman? Why, he was drooling over the lad as if he was the goose Cook fattened for the Epiphany feast.

Cook's words – and the bloated Father's – fell on the deafest of ears. Ever since my courses began a few months back, I'd taken a particular interest in men. Actually, it would be more accurate to say I was interested in the effect I had on them. Previously ignored as a rude girl with too much to say for herself, suddenly men of all ages and ranks sought to catch my attention, exchange words, and, mostly, to fumble and steal kisses. Washing my face and neck carefully each morning, brushing my clothes and tying my apron so it accentuated my newly acquired waist, I would spend more time than ever ensuring my cap lay just so upon my locks, and my laces were undone enough to hint at growing bosoms. My face was nothing extraordinary, I was practical enough to admit that. I was in possession of big eyes, an even bigger mouth (so Father Roman kept telling me) with full lips and large teeth that had a generous gap between the front ones. Angry freckles scattered across the bridge of my nose and in other places besides. I did possess a set of dimples that were the envy of the stablehand's little sister and I made good use of those.

When I first came into Lady Clarice's service, there were those among the servants and villeins who remembered my mother and would say they saw little of her in me. They would remark what a beauty she was, breaking off mid-sentence when they realised they were talking about Melisine de Compton. With pinking cheeks, they'd drift away or change the subject. Not because they feared they'd offended my sensibilities. Nay. It was because, coming from a good home with a good name, it was felt my mother had lowered herself when she married my father, Wace Cornfed, a brogger. That was before the pestilence struck. I oft wondered if people would think differently about her choice now, since the world had transformed so. Well, because of that and other things, mostly Papa's hard work, luck, and the benefice of Lady Clarice and the fact there were no more de Comptons around – except me, I guess – Wace Cornfed had risen in the world. Not much, but, as Papa said, you took what opportunities you could and made them better.

Unless your name was Eleanor Cornfed, in which case you trampled all over them until they were nothing but a pile of shitty dirt.

You've probably guessed by now what happened. I lay with Layamon. It would be funny if it wasn't so serious.

For weeks, Layamon had been meeting me in the shadowy depths of the church, darkened hallways and even the stables. The fact he singled me out from all the other, much lovelier options about the manor fair turned my head. It gave me boasting rights I'd never owned before and a shipload of envious glances. We'd kissed, oh, aye, we'd done that many a time and I'd been delirious, flooded with hot, liquid sensations that burned my loins. I'd never felt that way before, even when that grizzled but handsome knight, Sir Roland, hoisted me off my feet and kissed me deeply. After I'd overcome the shock of his tongue slipping into my mouth, I'd been more amazed that he could lift me when he only had one arm, as if I were made of straw. Mind you, he'd dropped me right quick when his wife found us, walloping him so hard across the face I thought his neck would break. Then she'd kicked me in the arse, ruddy cow. I'd a bruised rump for days. But Layamon, his kisses were different – *he* was different. I melted into his arms – both of them – and he pulled me against him as if he would solder us together the way the blacksmith did iron.

He was forbidden fruit and, when I was with him, it was Paradise.

Over the days, I managed to resist his increasing demands to plough my field, to storm my heavenly gates. Even I, the brogger's lass, a servant, knew not to surrender my maidenhead to just anyone. Lady Clarice's words were lodged in my mind.

But Father Layamon wasn't just anyone, was he?

When he appeared from under the heavy boughs of a willow as I was picking gillyflowers to make myself a garland on May Day morning, I felt giddy. He dropped to his knees, calling me his princess. Overcome as he pressed his face into my tunic, his breath hot against my queynte, which was, I confess, becoming rapidly heated as well, it wasn't until he drew me down on the soft grass and lay atop me, pressing kisses against my mouth, my neck and my breasts, which he rapidly freed from my shift, that I began to feel uneasy. Why, anyone could come upon us. I asked him to stop. When he didn't, I asked again. When he began to lift my skirts and his robe at the same time, exposing his fleshy prod, my quiet asking became loud demands.

Instead of heeding me, he threw my skirts over my head, using his arm to press them into my mouth so my voice was muffled. I could feel his engorged prick poking my thigh. Kneeling upon my legs and slapping them hard to keep them open, he was about to batter down my postern gate when we were discovered. Lady Clarice, The Poet, Father Roman, monks from the nearby abbey, some more respectable of the villagers, such as the reeve, the ale-conner and the sheriff, heard my cries and, diverting their walk, came upon us.

There were gasps, much laughter and then shouting. Father Roman pulled Layamon away, taking care to cover his cock, leaving me to fight my way from underneath my linens. I sat up to see people gathered in a semi-circle staring, pointing, smirking and chattering. Layamon was being struck about the shoulders and head. I landed one swift kick to his exposed skin-plums, enjoying the cry he expelled. Sadly, I'd no time to fully enjoy his pain as I was wrenched away by Master Merriman. Immediately, my lady began to strike *me* across the neck and cheek using the rod she oft carried when she walked. Leaving Layamon aside, Father Roman also began to add blows, using words instead of birch.

'Filthy whore, temptress, how dare you! Try and force a son of God into sin? The devil take your soul, you corrupter of innocence, you foul weed in God's garden; you traitor of the tree.'

Cue the chorus.

'You dirty little slut! You foolish wench. What would your mother say? What would your father?' cried other voices.

I learned a harsh lesson that day. Didn't matter that Layamon was primed and caught in prize position, it was all my fault.

I tried to defend myself, protest, but Layamon added accusations, stabbing a trembling finger in my direction and forcing tears, the spawn-cursed coward. Calling me a doxy, a meretrix, he began to describe how I lifted my skirts and begged him to take me. Unable to resist, he was simply doing what his weak flesh demanded. All the time he was blathering, Lady Clarice wouldn't stop hitting me. My attempts to offer the truth were reduced to squeals and, very soon, weeping. It was only when The Poet stepped forward and said something that my lady ceased to wield her rod. Layamon and Father Roman both fell silent.

Amidst tears and loud sniffles, I tried to fix my clothes. I remember little more beyond asking God to curse Layamon so his balls shrivelled and his maypole shrank and dropped off.

Then I was shut away. It wasn't the first time I'd been punished in that manner. God's teeth, trouble was my middle name, or that's what Mistress Bertha always said, whether it was stealing kisses, bread, eggs, skiving off for an afternoon or making up stories about my past. If I hadn't been so good at spinning and weaving, she'd threaten, the twinkle never really leaving her eye, I'd be out on my plump arse. But I hadn't done anything wrong this time, not really – well, apart from lying half-naked with a man. His pike hadn't breached my defences, though not from want of trying. Why would no one listen? I was innocent – ish – in all this. God's boils, Layamon better be suffering. If his hairy nuggins weren't being roasted over hot coals right this moment, I wanted to know why.

But as the days went by, and no-one came (except the other maids, Joyce and May, to bring me bread and water, and they knew nothing), I wondered if it was because I was caught with a man of God that was the problem. Even so, priests lay with women (and men) all the time, and while they couldn't exactly marry them, everyone knew many kept wives in all but name. Layamon was the bishop's son and it was said Father Harold from St Michael's Within the Walls in Bath had a veritable herd of children with Goody Miriam.

I found the answers to some of my questions the day I was led into the solar.

I've already described who was present. The Poet was behind a large desk, a huge piece of parchment in front of him and writing implements all lined up like soldiers about to go into battle. He regarded me with something akin to wariness on his face. Was he afraid I was going to pounce and seek out his spindle? Not likely. For a start, he was old. Why, he'd be twenty-five if he was a day and, apart from his soft brown eyes and voice like burnt butter, he was ugly.

Then I saw Fulk Bigod. The fact he was there caught me by surprise. While everyone knew who he was, including me, we'd never exchanged a word. I often saw him standing on the edge of the Green on market days, or waiting by his horse. Drinking ale over near the well, or loitering near the manor gates, he'd watch as we maids did our daily chores. He'd been on the edge of the Green when we first danced around the maypole and played games on May Day morning. We'd nudge each other, laughing and nodding towards him, the man with no friends, knowing his mission to find servants, another wife, would fail. Ever since his last wife died a few years ago, the story was he'd been desperate to remarry. But the villagers kept their daughters away and refused his increasing offers in exchange for another bride. Silly old fool. I'd dismissed him from my mind then, just as I always did, but the tiny teeth gnawing away at my peace told me this time was different. My heart began to quicken. Nausea gathered in the pit of my stomach, rising to catch in my breast. I touched my tunic. It was cleaner than it had been only an hour earlier. My gown had been brushed and I'd been brought washing water and a fresh shift. A new scarf was found for my hair. My hand stroked it.

'Master Bigod,' said Lady Clarice, rising to her feet and addressing the farmer. 'It's been a long time since you graced these halls. I believe you know everyone, with one exception.' Fulk Bigod did what he always did. Grunted.

Lady Clarice turned in my direction. 'Allow me to introduce you to Mistress Eleanor Cornfed.'

Never before had she called me 'Mistress'. I liked it not.

Master Bigod gave a small bow. I wish he hadn't. It fanned the flames of his odour. I took a step back and screwed up my nose.

'Eleanor,' said Lady Clarice, stepping wide of Master Bigod and coming to my side. 'Allow me to introduce Master Fulk Bigod.' I lowered my head as I'd been taught. 'Now,' continued my lady. 'Do you have anything to say before we proceed?'

'My lady?' My voice was small, dry. I cleared my throat. 'I don't understand. Proceed with what?'

'Today, all things considered, is your lucky day, Eleanor.' Lady Clarice gave me a small push in the back, sending me closer to Master Bigod.

'Lucky, how?' I resisted the urge to press my nose into my arm.

'Today, my dear, you plight your troth to a husband.'

'A husband?' My ears began to ring. 'Me?'

'In less than an hour, we'll meet at the church door and there, before Father Roman and Father Layamon, you will marry.'

'Who?' I asked, my voice a whisper. I already knew the answer.

'Master Fulk Bigod.'

Cold enfolded my body, colour drained from my face and with a sharp scream I tumbled dramatically to the floor.

Made not a whit of difference.

Before the bells rang for sext that day, the plans Lady Clarice, The Poet and Fulk Bigod had made while I'd been locked away in the manor tower like a princess in a fairytale, came to pass.

I, the wanton Eleanor Cornfed, became Mistress Eleanor Bigod – wife to the most despised and dirty man in Bath. I married the monster.

Fulk was three score years and one.

I was twelve.

talk about it

Let's talk about books.

Join the conversation:

 facebook.com/harlequinaustralia

 @harlequinaus

 @harlequinaus

harpercollins.com.au/hq

If you love reading and want to know about our
authors and titles, then let's talk about it.